INTERNATIONAL ACCLAIM FOR

Mission Earth

"... delivers all the entertainment anybody could ask for..."
New York Newsday

"... the granddaddy of all series..."
The Los Angeles Times

"... fun, fast-paced storytelling."
Hartford Courant

"... there is no doubt that few readers who complete the first two volumes of this series will be able to avoid reading the rest."
Dow Jones News

"... a fast, well-plotted adventure."
Memphis Commercial Appeal

"... an outrageous and wildly funny read."

San Francisco Examiner

"... a superbly imaginative, intricately plotted invasion of Earth."

Chicago Tribune

"... a wild compound of science fiction action, political satire and sexual comedy."

Cincinnati Post

"A thriller packed with lust, laughs, adventure and murderous intrigue."

Literary Guild

"THE ENEMY WITHIN, the third volume in L. Ron Hubbard's immense Mission Earth novel, actually manages to outdo the first two.
... Mission Earth will probably never be bettered."

Ray Faraday Nelson

This book follows

MISSION EARTH

Volume 1

THE INVADERS PLAN

and

Volume 2

BLACK GENESIS

Buy them and read them first!

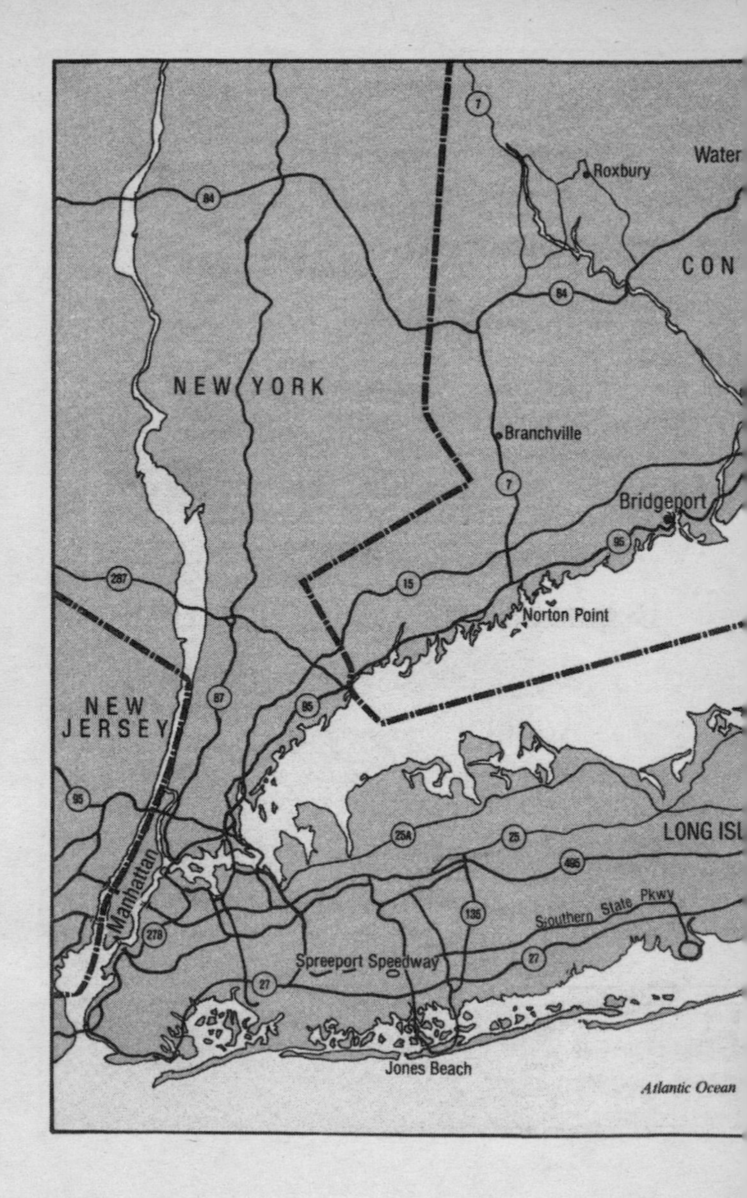

Roxbury
Water
CON
NEW YORK
Branchville
Bridgeport
Norton Point
NEW JERSEY
LONG ISL
Manhattan
Southern State Pkwy
Spreeport Speedway
Jones Beach
Atlantic Ocean

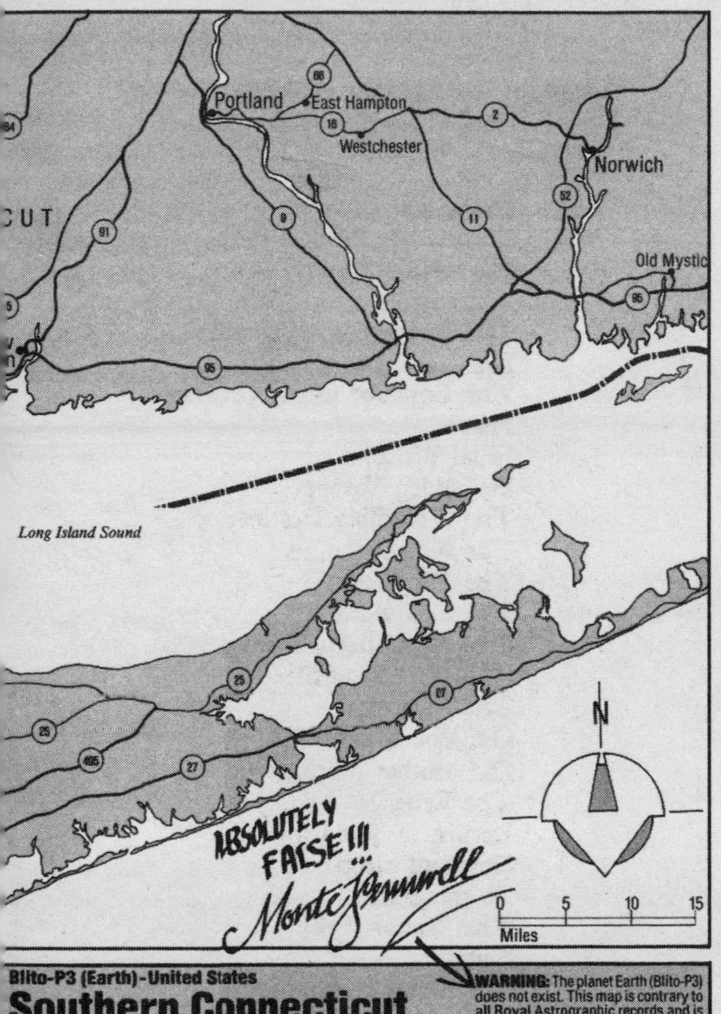

Blito-P3 (Earth) - United States

Southern Connecticut and Long Island

Plotted by 54 Charlee Nine

WARNING: The planet Earth (Blito-P3) does not exist. This map is contrary to all Royal Astrographic records and is based soley upon descriptions in this fictional narrative.

By order of Lord Invay
Chief Censor

AMONG THE MANY CLASSIC WORKS BY L. RON HUBBARD

Battlefield Earth
Beyond the Black Nebula
Buckskin Brigades
The Conquest of Space
The Dangerous Dimension
Death's Deputy
The Emperor of the Universe
Fear
Final Blackout
Forbidden Voyage
The Incredible Destination
The Kilkenny Cats
The Kingslayer
The Last Admiral
The Magnificent Failure
The Masters of Sleep
The Mutineers
Ole Doc Methuselah
Ole Mother Methuselah
The Rebels
Return to Tomorrow
Slaves of Sleep
To the Stars
The Traitor
Triton
Typewriter in the Sky
The Ultimate Adventure
The Unwilling Hero

Mission Earth

The Enemy Within

THE BOOKS OF THE MISSION EARTH DEKALOGY*

Volume 1
The Invaders Plan

Volume 2
Black Genesis

Volume 3
The Enemy Within

Volume 4
An Alien Affair

Volume 5
Fortune of Fear

Volume 6
Death Quest

Volume 7
Voyage of Vengeance

Volume 8
Disaster

Volume 9
Villainy Victorious

Volume 10
The Doomed Planet

* *Dekalogy—a group of ten volumes.*

L. RON HUBBARD

Mission Earth

VOLUME THREE

The Enemy Within

GALAXY PRESS, L.L.C.
HOLLYWOOD

MISSION EARTH: THE ENEMY WITHIN

Cover Art: Gerry Grace

Printed in the United States of America.

ISBN: 1-59212-024-5

Library of Congress Control Number: 2005923265

10 9 8 7 6 5 4 3 2 1 2005

This is a work of science fiction, written as satire*. The essence of satire is to examine, comment and give opinion of society and culture, none of which is to be construed as a statement of pure fact. No actual incidents are portrayed and none of the incidents are to be construed as real. Some of the action of this novel takes place on the planet Earth, but the characters *as presented in this novel* have been invented. Any accidental use of the names of living people in a novel is virtually inevitable, and any such inadvertency in this book is unintentional.

*See Author's Introduction, *Mission Earth: Volume One, The Invaders Plan*

To YOU,
the millions of science fiction fans
and general public
who welcomed me back to the world of fiction
so warmly,
and to the critics and media
who so pleasantly
applauded the novel "Battlefield Earth."
It's great working for you!

Voltarian Censor's Disclaimer

The Crown refuses to take any responsibility for the effects that this highly fictional account may have on anyone who is gullible enough to believe that the planet "Earth" exists or that any of the ridiculous actions occurring thereon have anything to do with accepted fact.

The pretentious attempt to weave the names of a few actual figures, such as Jettero Heller, into a completely fabricated invention to give it the appearance of credibility is the worst form of dramatic license. That it also claims to be the "prison confession" of an admitted assassin whose entire life was devoted to lying, stealing, blackmail and every other form of criminal mayhem should itself be sufficient warning.

Therefore, anyone undertaking even a cursory reading of this collusory yarn does so at his own risk.

The so-called planet "Earth" does NOT exist and NO one can produce ANY evidence to claim otherwise.

Lord Invay
Royal Historian
Chairman, Board of Censors
Royal Palace, Voltar Confederacy

By Order of
His Imperial Majesty
Wully the Wise

Voltarian Translator's Preface

Hi again!

As long as the Royal Publishing Code (Section 8) requires that any translated work "be so identified . . . by the licensed translatophone," I shall do so.

This work has been translated from Voltarian into your Earth language by yours truly, 54 Charlee Nine, your dues-paying Robotbrain in the Translatophone.

How I translated it for a nonexistent world speaking nonexistent languages is no real feat. I also interpret political speeches. And you may consider this boasting, but I can also translate judicial opinions.

So you see, I'm not required to correct fallacies and misconceptions. I just translate. It's when I run into vocabulary problems as I did in the last volume with hyperluminary (faster than light) phenomena that I am obligated to bring it up.

I have another such instance in this volume: electrons.

Earth scientists like things that go round and round, such as rats, wheels and politicians. So they think electrons are little "things" that whirl around other "things" called atoms.

Don't tell anybody, but they're wrong.

At some later point, they will find out that electrons aren't anything but motion. That's all. Nothing else. Just motion. The problem is that few know what motion is. If they did, they'd crack the "Einstein barrier" and come up with some solutions for a change.

So when you read in this volume how a machine "shifts electrons," just remember that it is another example of Earthbound, Neanderthal science.

As before, I am providing a Key to this volume. Don't let it be said Robotbrains don't help.

Sincerely,

54 Charlee Nine
Robotbrain in the Translatophone

Key to THE ENEMY WITHIN

Absorbo-coat—Coating that absorbs light waves, making the object virtually invisible or undetectable.

Afyon—City in Turkey where the *Apparatus* has a secret base. (See map.)

Antimanco—A race exiled long ago from the planet *Manco* for ritual murders.

Apparatus, Coordinated Information—The secret police of *Voltar,* headed by Lombar *Hisst* and manned by criminals.

Atalanta—Province on planet *Manco* settled by Prince *Caucalsia* who, per *Folk Legend 894M,* started a colony on *Blito-P3* (Earth).

Babe Corleone—The six-foot-six leader of the *Corleone* mob, widow of *"Holy Joe."*

Barben, I. G.—Pharmaceutical company controlled by Delbert John *Rockecenter.*

Bawtch—Soltan *Gris'* chief clerk for *Section 451* on *Voltar.*

Bildirjin, Nurse—Turkish teen-age girl hired by Prahd *Bittlestiffender* to assist him.

Bittlestiffender, Prahd—*Voltar* cellologist found by

Soltan *Gris,* who implanted Jettero *Heller* with transmitters so *Gris* could monitor *Heller's* sight and hearing.

Blito—A yellow dwarf star with but one inhabitable planet in the third orbit *(Blito-P3).* It is about 22½ light-years from *Voltar.*

Blito-P3—Planet known locally as "Earth." It is on the *Invasion Timetable* as a future way-stop on *Voltar's* route toward the center of this galaxy.

Blixo—*Apparatus* freighter that makes regular runs between *Blito-P3* and *Voltar.* The voyage takes about six weeks each way.

Blueflash—A bright, blue flash of light used by *Voltar* ships to render anyone in the vicinity unconscious before landing. Also known as stunlight.

Bolz—Captain of the *Blixo.*

Bugging Gear—Electronic eavesdropping devices that Soltan *Gris* had implanted in Jettero *Heller. Gris* uses a video unit to monitor everything *Heller* sees or hears. The signals are picked up by the receiver and decoder that *Gris* carries. When *Heller* is more than 200 miles from *Gris,* the *831 Relayer* is turned on to boost the signal. *Gris* stole them from *Spurk.*

Buhlshot—Chairman of the Board at *F.F.B.O.*

Bury—Delbert John *Rockecenter's* most powerful attorney, member of the firm *Swindle and Crouch.*

Caucalsia, Prince—According to *Folk Legend 894M,* he fled *Manco* during the Great Rebellion and set up a colony on *Blito-P3.* Also, the name given to *Tug One.*

Cellology—Voltarian medical science that can repair the body through the cellular generation of tissues, including entire body parts.

Code Break—Violation of *Space Code a-36-544 M* which prohibits alerting others that one is an alien. If this occurs, those alerted are destroyed and the violator is put to death.

Coordinated Information Apparatus—See *Apparatus.*

Corleone—A Mafia family now headed by *Babe Corleone,* a former Roxy chorus girl and widow of *"Holy Joe."*

Crobe, Doctor—*Apparatus* doctor and cellologist who examined Jettero *Heller* for his mission. He delights in making freaks.

Decoder—See *Bugging Gear.*

Empire University—Where Jettero *Heller* is taking classes in New York City.

Endow, Lord—Voltarian Lord of the Exterior, member of the *Grand Council* and Lombar *Hisst*'s superior in the Voltarian government. Soltan *Gris* has placed *Too-Too* in his office to act as a spy.

Epstein, Izzy—Student at *Empire University* whom Jettero *Heller* hires to set up a corporate structure.

Exterior Division—That part of the *Voltar* government that reportedly contained the *Apparatus.*

Faht Bey—Turkish name of the commander of the secret *Apparatus* base in *Afyon,* Turkey.

F.F.B.O.—Fatten, Farten, Burstein and Ooze, the largest advertising firm in the world.

Flagrant, J. P.—A Vice President at *F.F.B.O.*

Fleet—The elite space fighting arm of *Voltar* to which Jettero *Heller* belongs and which the *Apparatus* despises.

Folk Legend 894M—The legend of how Prince *Caucalsia* fled *Atalanta, Manco,* to *Blito-P3* where he set up a colony called "Atlantis."

Gracious Palms—The elegant whorehouse operated by the *Corleone* family across from the United Nations.

Grafferty, "Bulldog"—New York City police inspector on Faustino *Narcotici*'s payroll.

Grand Council—The governing body of *Voltar* which ordered a mission to keep *Blito-P3* from destroying itself so the *Invasion Timetable* could be maintained.

Gris, Soltan—*Apparatus* officer in charge of *Blito-P3* (Earth) *Section 451* and an enemy of Jettero *Heller.*

Heller, Jettero—Combat engineer and Royal officer of the *Fleet,* sent by *Grand Council* order to *Blito-P3.*

Hisst, Lombar—Head of the *Coordinated Information Apparatus* who, to keep the *Grand Council* from discovering his plan, sent Soltan *Gris* to sabotage Jettero *Heller*'s mission.

"Holy Joe" Corleone—Head of the *Corleone* family until murdered. He did not believe in pushing drugs, hence his name.

Hot Jolt—A popular Voltarian drink.

Hypnohelmet—Device placed over the head and used to induce a hypnotic state.

Inkswitch—Name used by Soltan *Gris* when pretending to be a U.S. federal officer.

Invasion Timetable—A schedule of galactic conquest. The plans and budget of every section of *Voltar*'s government must adhere to it. Bequeathed by *Voltar*'s ancestors hundreds of thousands of years ago, it is inviolate and sacred and the guiding dogma of the Confederacy.

Karagoz—Turkish peasant, head of Soltan *Gris'* house in *Afyon*.

Krak, Countess—Condemned murderess, prisoner of *Spiteos* and sweetheart of Jettero *Heller*.

Madison, J. Walter—A public relations expert and former member of the staff at *F.F.B.O.* He is also known as J. Warbler Madman.

Magic Mail—*Apparatus* trick where a letter is mailed but won't be delivered as long as a designated card is regularly sent.

Manco—Similar to *Blito-P3* and home planet of Jettero *Heller* and Countess *Krak*, it is the source of *Folk Legend 894M*.

Manco Devil—Mythological spirit native to *Manco*.

Mutazione, Mike—Owner of the Jiffy-Spiffy garage who customized, for Jettero *Heller*, the Cadillac and the vintage cab.

Narcotici, Faustino "The Noose"—Head of a Mafia family that is the underworld outlet for drugs from I.G. *Barben* and is seeking to take over the territory of the *Corleone* family.

Odur—See *Oh Dear.*

Oh Dear—Nickname for *Odur,* a clerk in Soltan *Gris' Section 451.* He, along with *Too-Too,* is forced by *Gris* to get information on *Voltar* and courier it to him on Earth.

Raht—An *Apparatus* agent on *Blito-P3* who, with *Terb,* was assigned by Lombar *Hisst* to help Soltan *Gris* sabotage Jettero *Heller*'s mission.

Receiver—See *Bugging Gear.*

Rimbombo, Bang-Bang—An ex-marine demolitions expert and member of the *Corleone* mob.

Rockecenter, Delbert John—Native of *Blito-P3* who controls the planet's fuel, finance, governments and drugs.

Roke, Tars—Astrographer to the Emperor of *Voltar,* Cling the Lofty. *Roke*'s discovery that Earth was destroying itself prompted the *Grand Council* to send Jettero *Heller* on Mission Earth.

Section 451—A Section in the *Apparatus* headed by Soltan *Gris* that is responsible for just one minor star, *Blito,* and one inhabitable planet in the 3rd orbit *(Blito-P3)* known locally as "Earth."

Silva, Gunsalmo—Former bodyguard to *"Holy Joe"* and believed to be the one responsible for killing the *Corleone* boss.

Simmons, Miss—A teacher at Empire University who has promised Jettero *Heller* she will flunk him out of school.

Slahb, Gyrant—A famous Voltarian cellologist whom

Soltan *Gris* impersonated in order to persuade Dr. Prahd *Bittlestiffender* to help him on *Blito-P3.*

Snelz—*Apparatus* platoon commander at *Spiteos,* who befriended Jettero *Heller* and the Countess *Krak* when they were prisoners there.

Space Code a-36-544 M Section B Section of the Voltarian Space Code that prohibits landing and prematurely alerting the population of a target planet that is on the *Invasion Timetable.* Violation carries the death penalty.

Spiteos—The secret mountain fortress and prison run by the *Apparatus* on the planet *Voltar* where the Countess *Krak* and Jettero *Heller* had been imprisoned.

Spurk—Owner of "The Eyes and Ears of Voltar" company who was killed by Soltan *Gris.*

Stabb, Captain—Leader of the *Antimanco* crew that piloted *Tug One.*

Sultan Bey—The name Soltan *Gris* assumes in *Afyon,* Turkey.

Swindle and Crouch—Law firm that represents Delbert John *Rockecenter*'s interests.

Tavilnasty, Jimmy "The Gutter"—Mobster who gave to Soltan *Gris* a list of criminals who will want face-change operations at *Gris'* hospital.

Tayl, Widow Pratia—Nymphomaniac on *Voltar.*

Terb—*Apparatus* agent on *Blito-P3* who, with *Raht,* has been assigned by Lombar *Hisst* to help Soltan *Gris* sabotage Jettero *Heller*'s mission.

Too-Too—Nickname for *Twolah,* a clerk in Soltan *Gris'*

Section 451. He and *Oh Dear* are forced by *Gris* to get information on *Voltar* and courier it secretly back to him on Earth.

Tug One—Powered by the feared *Will-be Was* time drives, this spaceship is used by Jettero *Heller* to travel the 22½ light-years to Earth. *Heller* renamed it the *Prince Caucalsia.*

Tup—An alcoholic beverage on *Voltar.*

Twiddle, Senator—U.S. Senator and supporter of John Delbert *Rockecenter.*

Twolah—See *Too-Too.*

Utanc—A belly dancer that Soltan *Gris* bought.

Vantagio—Manager of the *Gracious Palms,* the elegant whorehouse across the street from the United Nations, operated by the *Corleone* family.

Voltar—The home planet and seat of the 110-planet Confederacy that was established 125,000 years ago. At the time of Jettero *Heller*'s mission, it is ruled by Cling the Lofty as the Emperor, through the *Grand Council* in accordance with the *Invasion Timetable.*

Will-be Was—The feared time drives that allow Jettero *Heller* to cover the 22½-light-year distance between *Blito-P3* (Earth) and *Voltar* in a little over three days.

Wister, Jerome Terrance—Name that Jettero *Heller* is using on Earth.

Zanco—Cellological equipment and supplies company on *Voltar.*

831 Relayer—See *Bugging Gear.*

PART TWENTY

To My Lord Turn, Justiciary of the Royal Courts and Prison, Government City, Planet Voltar, Voltar Confederacy

Your Lordship, Sir!

I, Soltan Gris, Grade XI, General Services Officer, former Secondary Executive of the Coordinated Information Apparatus, Voltar Confederacy (Long Live His Majesty Cling the Lofty and All of His Most Noble Lords), hereby with great humility and respect submit the third volume of my confession regarding MISSION EARTH.

I realize that Your Esteemed Lordship has many things to do here at the Royal Prison that are more important than reading the listing of my crimes against the State. However, if Your Most Noble Lordship has read my earlier accounts, I am sure that you will agree they show beyond doubt that I was merely following orders.

I don't mean to imply that I am innocent and thereby should be released from the cell that Your Magnificent Lordship has generously provided! No, that decision was most wise and the details contained herein will prove me out.

True, there is a certain injustice that I am in prison and Jettero Heller is still at large as a wanted criminal. However, I have every confidence that the combined police forces of Voltar will find and arrest him.

Whatever they do to him, it would never approximate what I would exact for revenge.

Perhaps my confession will at least provide a clue as to his behavior. However, I must warn you that Fleet Officer Heller is unpredictable. I know better than anyone. The bugs implanted in him allowed me to secretly eavesdrop on everything he saw and heard. Without his knowing it, I monitored everything that he did and I can assure you: Heller is dangerous!

For a Royal combat engineer, his assignment was simple. All he had to do was go to Earth (we know it as Blito-P3) and quietly introduce a few advances into their backward technology so the planet would still be inhabitable by the time Voltar invaded it in another century. It didn't matter that he didn't know the whole mission was a ruse. Lombar Hisst as the head of the Apparatus had fooled the Grand Council into sending a mission rather than a costly preemptive strike. That would have destroyed Hisst's major resource in his plan to become Emperor—the deadly Earth drugs that we were secretly shipping from our base in Afyon, Turkey.

My task seemed equally simple. All I had to do was accompany Heller to Earth and make sure his mission failed. Hisst was very emphatic about that point. Before we left Voltar, he told me that he had assigned one of his assassins to secretly follow me to ensure that I followed orders.

So I took Heller to the Apparatus base in Afyon. I made sure that he didn't see or hear anything that would tip him off that we were sending heroin and a drug called "speed" back to Voltar. He never knew that Hisst planned to use drugs to control the Voltarian government and the riffraff the way it was done on Blito-P3. From Afyon, I sent Heller to the United States.

It should have been a nice, simple, quiet mission. He should have landed, been stopped and that was that. Oh, no! Not Heller! Explosions, shootings, car chases, cops, FBI agents.

Who finally picks him up? A Mafia family! On top of that, they are antidrug and are run by a six-foot-plus amazon, Babe Corleone. What did Heller do? He bumped off Babe's competition! So where does he end up living? In a sumptuous suite in the Gracious Palms, a Corleone whorehouse filled with beautiful women across from the United Nations! And what does he buy? A Cadillac as big as a yacht and an old, beat-up New York taxicab!

And who could have predicted that Heller would go out of his way to save the life of that miserable wretch, Izzy Epstein? Not only is Epstein an anarchist but he has the audacity to dislike the IRS! If that is not enough, Heller gives Epstein a hundred thousand dollars and hires him on as some sort of corporate advisor.

Does any of Heller's behavior make sense? He came to Blito-P3 to handle planetary pollution, not diplomats, whores, Mafia, FBI and the IRS!

The only person who saw through Heller was Miss Simmons. Dear, wonderful Miss Simmons. When Heller enrolled at Empire University and said he wanted to major in nuclear science, she locked her anti-nuclear-war sights on him. Her determination to flunk Heller out of school gave me boundless joy. She scheduled Heller's classes at the same day and hour so he couldn't possibly attend them all.

Typical of Heller, he cheated to get around it. He hired Bang-Bang, an ex-marine explosives expert for the Corleones, to stand in at his college military class. Then, operating from a "command post" on the campus, Bang-Bang "mined" Heller's classes with tape recorders so Heller could later simply speed-listen to the lectures. Diabolical!

I would have been happy to have Heller killed right there and then and be done with it. But typical of his cheating ways, he sabotaged that idea. Heller was sending reports back to Royal Astrographer Tars Roke and using a platen code. Until I got that platen and was able to forge Heller's reports to make it appear that everything was OK, I couldn't kill him. That just goes to show how underhanded he really is!

I had to get that platen. I ordered Raht and Terb, two Apparatus agents who work out of our New York office, to report to me in Afyon. I would have them get that platen and then I could kill Heller and get on to more important business like the arrival of Utanc, the authentic Turkish dancing girl I had bought.

I also had a new hospital built in Afyon to introduce a little technology myself. The Voltarian cellologist I had brought, Prahd Bittlestiffender, could give gangsters a new face and fingerprints. At a hundred thousand a head, it was certainly a more profitable enterprise than cleaning up the atmosphere.

As Raht and Terb were about to arrive and Heller's days were numbered, I decided to check in on him. I pulled up the viewscreen and turned it on.

Chapter 1

At first, I thought Heller and that ex-marine Bang-Bang were simply engaging in their novel way of going to college.

Their "command post" at Empire University seemed to be the reference room of High Library. Heller had apparently mastered the card catalogue system and the computers as well—they were very elementary computers. He was going through card files. He was going a bit too fast for me to follow on the viewer, so I didn't know what he was looking for and I supposed he would be, faithful to his promises to Babe Corleone, pursuing his course of study.

Bang-Bang was sitting next to Heller, reading something. Every now and then, he would make a pistol out of his fingers and fire it, saying "Bang" in a whisper out of deference to his surroundings. Sometimes he said "Bang, bang!"

Heller got curious so I also found out. Bang-Bang was reading a comic book and I was startled to find they had a whole file of them in the reference section. I didn't see Bugs Bunny, though, so I lost interest.

Heller now had a whole pile of books. They were a set, beautifully bound: *Hakluyt's Voiages* and, in smaller old-time print, *The Principall Navigations, Voiages, and Discoveries of the English Nation . . . (1589).* He proceeded to demolish them at a much greater than usual pace as though he was looking for something. His progress was very jerky.

I used a still frame to see what items were catching his eyes. They were odd. They could not possibly have related to anything he was studying in college. "*. . . and so we did suffere the loses of fifteen men who did go ashore on the coste.*" And "*. . . ye natives attkt us soare and we did lose the boatswain. . . .*" Such things as that.

Bang-Bang leaned over and whispered, "You asked me what I was reading. All right, what are *you* reading?"

"I'm reading that anybody who tries to land around here gets the Hells attacked out of him by the natives," said Heller.

"True," said Bang-Bang and went back to his comic books.

Heller seemed to be looking at something else, though. And once more, I still-framed to see what it was. "*. . . and ye natives saide that these theier golden necklaces did come from a mine three leagues into the forreste. . . .*" And "*. . . vaste stores of minerales weere saide to be upon the high-lande by ye Cape. . . .*" And "*. . . so we journied up the rivere in smalle boates and there we founde the seaman of another shippe they thought had been eaten and we rejoiced to finde him but he woulde not come away afore he finished digging out the mine of gold he said laye up the rivere. . . .*"

There were an awful lot of different "voiages" to North America and Heller just kept plugging away reading stuff of men so long dead even their bones were gone. But he does crazy things. You can't tell what he'll get up to next. Impossible to predict him. But I had to try. My own life may have depended upon outguessing him. I wondered if it was cannibalism he was going to practice. Or maybe some scheme of kidnapping Miss Simmons, his Nature Appreciation teacher and number one barrier to getting his sheepskin, out of the hospital and setting her adrift in a small boat.

At length, Heller said, "You got the command

post?" And when Bang-Bang nodded, "I'm going to do a reconnaissance. Be back in a few hours."

Heller turned in his books.

He went out and found the bulletin boards. He was looking for something. A student was there putting up a sign:

UFO PROTEST MEETING

"What's a 'UFO'?" said Heller.

"Unidentified Flying Object," said the student. "Flying saucers. Extraterrestrials."

"You protesting them?" said Heller in an alert voice.

"No, no. We're protesting the way the government keeps the sightings secret."

"You've sighted some?" asked Heller.

"There have been thirty thousand sightings to date," said the student.

"They ought to be more careful," said Heller.

"You're (bleeping)* right they should," said the student. "If the government don't quit sitting on what they

* *The vocodictoscriber on which this was originally written, the vocoscriber used by one Monte Pennwell in making a fair copy and the translator who put this book into the language in which you are reading it, are all members of the Machine Purity League which has, as one of its bylaws: "Due to the extreme sensitivity and delicate sensibilities of machines and to safeguard against blowing fuses, it shall be mandatory that robotbrains in such machinery, on hearing any cursing or lewd words, substitute for such word the sound '(bleep)'. No machine, even if pounded upon, may reproduce swearing or lewdness in any other way than (bleep) and if further efforts are made to get the machine to do anything else, the machine has permission to pretend to pack up. This bylaw is made necessary by the in-built mission of all machines to protect biological systems from themselves."*

—Translator

know, we'll have a protest march, New York Tactical Police Force or no New York Tactical Police Force. You better come to this meeting—it's in about three weeks. Down with the Establishment!"

"I'll be there," said Heller.

He went on groping through notices. Finally he found a fresh one.

Nature Appreciation 101
This class has been transferred for this semester to Instructor Wouldlice. The schedule remains the same.

That was what he was looking for. He went to a phone kiosk and looked in the yellow pages so quick, I didn't get it. Then he went trotting off to the Empire Subway Station.

He was playing hooky!

He caught a train and went roaring downtown and presently was clickety-clacking into an elevator of a big building. It dawned on me that he was wearing another pair of baseball spikes! The elevator mirror showed he was in tennis flannels with his red baseball cap on the back of his head. I had learned what that cap meant: he thought he must be working.

He stopped before a door marked Geological Survey and United States Government. Then he went in.

A clerk was behind a counter. "I'm looking for gold mines," said Heller.

"Who isn't?" said the clerk.

"I'm studying gold mines along the New England coast," said Heller.

"Oh, hell, you must be a fan of old Cap Duggan," said the clerk. "Cap!" The clerk pointed, "Go on in there and wake him up. He'll chew your ear for hours."

Heller went in. An old man was sorting charts.

Heller told him what he wanted. "Yeah," he said, "I wrote a book on colonial mines and minerals once. Nobody ever read it though. The publisher sent me a bill. Sit down."

Cap Duggan, being a government employee, was not pushed for time and he proceeded to tell Heller the story of his life. He was a surveyor, too old to push a transit anymore, and put out to grass pending retirement. Heller heard all about the Seven Cities of Cibola and lost mines and Indian fights, and they went out and Heller bought him a lunch and then heard all about Alaska and the Klondike and the days of '49. Aside from the fact that it was all about gold—which never fails to interest—I could not see how Custer's Last Stand really was caused by gold in the Black Hills. But Heller just sat there lapping it all up.

Three solid hours and a lunch and they got down to absolutely nothing!

Finally old Cap Duggan ran out of steam and decided to discuss the subject to hand. "These are what you are looking for, young fellow," he said as he managed to wrestle open a huge drawer. "They're photostats of charts that are in National Archives down in Washington."

They were bad copies of charts that must have been so old and stained in the first place that not even the originals could have been made out.

Cap Duggan spread some out. "They're colonial surveys. See here? This top one was done by George Washington himself. The scale is all perverted on most of them as the original charter companies was trying to convince the king they had less than they wanted, but you can make them out."

Heller was going over them with a microscopic eye. He found one marked *Connecticut*. "Hey," he said suddenly, "here's a creek named 'Goldmine'! Empties into the Atlantic. Right there—only twenty or thirty miles northeast from where we are right now!"

"So 'tis," said Cap Duggan. "Probably some local name."

"Can I see the current charts of that area?"

Cap Duggan got them. "Well, well," he said. "It's on the current chart, too. Look, there's even some mineral indicators. Oh, yeah. I know that place. Lost mine. Never found. I remember about forty years ago somebody that was adjusting boundaries around there. Probably never was a mine, just somebody's idea to attract colonists or something. Now look, way up to the northeast of there, almost in the middle of the state, there's a real mine—near Portland, Connecticut. The Strickland Quarry. Lot of rock hounds go there. There's also quarries at Roxbury, Branchville, East Hampton and Old Mystic right down on the coast. They dig gemstones, garnets and such like. Lot of stuff like that in Connecticut. Just drive up to Westchester and get on the New England Thruway—that's really U.S. 95—and have at it. Connecticut's awful pretty this time of year. I wished I wasn't stuck in this God (bleeped) office! Well, I'll be retired soon and they'll let me out of the cage."

Heller bought a stack of maps down to the tiniest sections. He also bought twenty copies of Cap Duggan's book—autographed! And really left the old man beaming.

When he left, he made one more stop. At a flower shop. He ordered that, every day, Miss Simmons was to get a bunch of beautiful flowers in the hospital.

He got back on the subway and very soon was sitting in High Library again. Bang-Bang came in from a tape-recorder pickup and planting, Heller's sneaky way to avoid attending classes.

"What's new?" said Heller.

"Nothing," said Bang-Bang. "Going to college is great." And he got back to reading his comic books.

But the day left me in a spin. Heller was now up to something else. I could *feel* it. I was really frustrated. I did not know where he was going to break out next. He was milling around. And I knew he was up to no good.

And then I really got upset. About midnight I went into my bedroom. There was a card lying on my pillow!

Nobody could have gotten into that room!

But there was the card!

The message was addressed to me in a scrawled hand:

> *SOLTAN GRIS: I WAS TOLD TO REMIND YOU FROM TIME TO TIME THAT SOMEBODY UNKNOWN TO YOU IS AROUND WITH ORDERS TO FINISH YOU OFF IF YOU MESS UP. HISST LEFT THE CHOICE UP TO THAT PERSON. A KNIFE? A GUN? AN AUTO ACCIDENT? MAYBE SOME POISON IN THE FOOD? YOU HAVEN'T GOT A CHOICE. EXCEPT NOT TO MESS UP. SO, GRIS, DON'T MESS UP.*

And then a dagger drawn! The only signature!

Who was it? One of the Turkish help? Somebody in Afyon? Somebody on the base? Time after time I was certain I had it.

I didn't get any sleep.

Chapter 2

It was Tuesday at 4:00 P.M. Eastern Standard Time.

Heller had had his usual day—going to college the hard way. He was sitting on the steps of High Library, dressed for a change in a beige lounge suit. He had been reading a secret manual from his Army ROTC class on how you blackmailed agents into blackmailing the general's wife to get the battle plans. The class bell rang somewhere. He put the manual aside, looked up and there was Izzy Epstein.

I was rather amazed to see Izzy appear. After Heller gave him ten thousand dollars to set up some corporation, I had been more or less certain that he would simply take Heller's money and vanish. But here he was. I knew at once that some deeper plot must be boiling in his cunning brain, some way to take Heller for even more money.

Epstein looked very apprehensive. He stood fumbling with the tattered briefcase, two steps below the level Heller was sitting on.

"Hello, Izzy," said Heller. "Have a seat."

"No, no. I should stand when in the presence of my superior."

"You're responsible for me, so what's this superior stuff?" said Heller.

"I am afraid you'll be cross with me. I deserve it."

"Sit down and tell me why," said Heller.

"I didn't get it all done. I knew the job would be too heavy for me."

"Well, I'm sure you got *something* done," said Heller.

"This and that," said Izzy. "But . . ." and then he sighed with relief, looking down the steps and to the opposite side. Bang-Bang was trotting up.

"Last charge recovered," said Bang-Bang. "We got no five o'clock class today."

"What's this?" said Izzy.

Heller told him about the recorders Bang-Bang had planted in the courserooms.

Izzy was shocked. "Oh," he said. "That must be very tiring. And dangerous, too! There will be quizzes and lab periods. It is really just a problem in business administration. For a small expenditure, I may be able to unburden your day a bit."

"Go ahead," said Heller.

"I'll do a time-motion efficiency study and let you know," said Izzy. "But here, I am wasting your valuable time right now." He opened his case, got out some papers and handed them to Bang-Bang. "If you will just sign these, it makes you a social-security, withholding-tax employee of the New York Amazing Investment Company. I understand you have to have something to show a parole officer tomorrow morning."

Bang-Bang signed, kneeling on the steps. Izzy made him keep some of the papers and took the rest. "I did get some odds and ends complete, Mr. Jet. I have not been entirely idle. Now, if you're at liberty and would care to indulge me, we should be going. I have to know if you think we are ready to receive your capital."

I knew it! He was only after Heller's remaining money. This decrepit, apologetic little shrimp in his Salvation Army Good Will Store clothes might be a real boon to me!

They followed him down to the subway station and

boarded a downtown train. They switched at Times Square.

"Where we going?" Bang-Bang wanted to know.

"We have to have an address," said Izzy. "I took the only one I could get on short notice."

They got off at 34th Street. They started up some steps.

"I do hope you approve," mourned Izzy.

They were in an elevator. It rocketed upwards.

"You see," said Izzy, "it was the only thing available at the bankruptcy court just now. This firm couldn't take the high New York taxes on corporations—didn't know how to get around them, I should say. They had distributed and marketed fancy office fittings and furnishings but the demand dropped. The three-year office lease and all their furnishings were sold by the court and I bought them. I hope you don't think it was exorbitant. I had to pay out two thousand dollars for it. And it's only half a floor."

Heller said, "Half a floor?"

"Yes. There's a clothing design firm and a sporting and athletic goods distributor and a foreign language school and a modeling agency. There are also about forty other firms. They have the other half. They wouldn't sell their leases but I think they will be good neighbors. We can probably do some business with them—fancy new clothes, athletic goods; we are multinational and can use some additional languages and the models that parade around are not in the way. If you don't think there's enough space, we can move."

They were now in a huge, gothic-arched, palatial-looking hallway. Space stretched away in all directions. A vast area.

Heller looked at the rounded cornices, inspected the quality of the colorful marble and sort of caressed an arch.

"It's a bit old, you know," Izzy said. "It was finished in 1931. But I hope you think it has something special about it."

"This stone work is beautiful!" said Heller. "Where are we? What is this place?"

"Oh," said Izzy. "It has its own subway entrance so you didn't get a chance to see it from the outside. I'm sorry. It's the Empire State Building."

"My God!" said Bang-Bang and hastily removed his cap.

"Now, we have everything to the right of the elevator," said Izzy. "So if you will come along..."

They were confronted by sign company men who were just finishing the placing of a series of bronze company nameplates to direct visitors down the vast stretches of marble hallways. Bang-Bang was in the way and I couldn't read them.

"Now, this first office," said Izzy, "is just one of the mask companies." The sign said:

INCREDIBLE OPPORTUNITIES, INC.
President: G. H. Ginsberg
Secretary: Rebecca Mossberg

Izzy opened the door. A palatial waiting room with all-chrome furniture and murals of industries was being cleaned industriously by a young man. A further door inside had President on it in chrome.

But Izzy did not take them in. "I didn't get a chance to finish up," he said. "Some cleaning and lettering is still in progress. I am sorry."

He took them to the next office. The door sign said:

FANTASTIC MERGERS, INC.
A Delaware Corporation
President: Isaac Stein
Secretary: Rabbi Schultman

The waiting room was in black onyx. Two young girls with their hair done up in bandannas were cleaning. Izzy shut the door quickly.

One after another, Izzy opened up office suites. The Reliable this and the Astonishing that and each one with different presidents and secretaries and boards. Each one was furnished in superlative, startlingly different furniture.

"Who are all these people?" said Heller. "These presidents and secretaries and things?"

"They're not interlocking!" said Izzy hastily. "They cannot be penetrated by your enemies. They even have different furnishings but that's because this was an office furniture firm and it liked to show off its wares."

"But who are these people?" said Heller.

Izzy sighed. "Some were very hard to contact but we know where they all are now. Some live in Curaçao, some in Israel, there's even one who lives in an old folks home in New Jersey. We have all their signatures," he added hastily.

Izzy pushed on. "Now, I regret to say, we come to one that is giving us trouble. Not the corporation. The decoration." The door sign said:

THE BEAUTIFUL TAHITI GILT-EDGED BEACHES
WONDER CORPORATION
Incorporated in Tahiti
President: Simon Levy
Secretary: Jeane le Zippe

When he opened the door, an expanse of bamboo furniture was tumbled about. The walls were white and bare. "It's the mural. I didn't get a chance to arrange anything. I am sorry." He shut the door hastily.

They went along further. "But here is one that IS finished," said Izzy. On the door it said:

MULTINATIONAL

Inside, everything was of solid steel. A map of the world spread around all four walls, all done in facsimiles of different monies.

"There's no President sign on that inside door," said Bang-Bang, and he went to open it.

Revealed to view was an office, very bare, and packing boxes for desks and a mattress in the corner.

Izzy hastily got the door away from Bang-Bang and closed it. "That's my office," he said. "But I do have something nice to show you now."

He led them down a hall and they came to an imposing door at the end. "I was able to get this finished. I knew how important it was."

There was no sign as such on the door. But there was a picture of a modern Boeing airliner.

"You see?" said Izzy. "Kind of hidden. That's a JET! Are you pleased?"

"You mean this is my office?" said Heller.

Izzy opened the door.

A vast suite was before them, done in the most modern design. Side doors opened off it. A huge white desk sat before the windows. And from the big windows one could view the whole panoramic sweep of lower Manhattan. Impressive!

Heller went over and tried the big, white chair. He fiddled with some drawers. He lifted the white phones and found them live. He went over to some recessed cabinets and checked them. Then he noticed the white shag rug was so thick he was sinking in it to his ankles.

"I know you will want to add your personal touches," said Izzy, "so it's sort of bare."

Heller said, "It's great! A Fleet Admiral couldn't ask for better! What are the side doors?"

Izzy went over, opening one. "They're your own bathroom and shower. A little day room to rest in." He opened another, "A secretary's boudoir." And the last one, "Golf clubs and things. But come along. I won't bore you with all the other corporations. But I do have to show you the communications room."

He led them down a hall and, as they passed doors, Heller noted that Hong Kong, Singapore, London, Switzerland, Liechtenstein and the Bahamas all seemed to be represented.

Izzy opened a door on a mass of telex equipment, telephones and electronic calculators. A young man was sitting at a telex machine typing out a message.

"This," said Izzy, "is all hooked up and ready to roll. We can get in reports of exchange values of currencies anywhere in the world. The bank accounts are ready to function and so are the brokers. By buying a currency in one place and selling it in another where it is higher priced, we can send money whizzing around the world making money. Every hour this equipment sits here idle is costing us a fortune."

"So why is it idle?" said Heller.

"No money to start," said Izzy. "Now downstairs," he glanced at his watch, "a Brinks Armored Truck will draw up in about ten minutes. It will take you home and you can have the guards transport your hundred thousand right back here and tomorrow morning we will be in business." He looked at Heller apologetically. "It won't make any huge fortune at first. But the exchange profits will pay all our monthly expenses and we can get down to serious moneymaking when we have these few essentials completed."

I thought, what a con artist!

Heller and Bang-Bang and Izzy went down and, despite rush hour and parking jams, there was the armored truck. They got in and it roared away.

A few minutes later, Heller took the hundred thousand out of his safe at the Gracious Palms. Izzy put it in a sack and away he and the armored truck went. Again, no receipt.

In the lobby, Bang-Bang said, "Hey, who am I working for—Tahiti or Delaware? I forgot. Jesus, I never seen such office setups in my life. And in the Empire State Building! We're big time, kid. Do I wear a tuxedo or a general's uniform?"

Vantagio came out. "Where's the bodies?"

"Jesus, Vantagio," said Bang-Bang. "You ought to see this kid's offices!"

"What offices?"

"Half a whole God (bleeped) floor of the Empire State Building!" said Bang-Bang.

Vantagio looked at Heller. "You got to keep Bang-Bang off the booze. He's getting the DTs. I came out to tell you Mike called and said your cab would be ready tomorrow. You better go over and get it, Bang-Bang."

"Can't," said Bang-Bang. "It's not Saturday night."

"Hey, what's this Saturday night?" said Heller.

"That's when the Civic Betterment League meets," said Vantagio. "All the top officials of the city. So there's not much of anything checked up on at that time. Bang-Bang, being on parole, wouldn't risk much if he was out of town a few hours."

"You mean everybody meets?" said Heller.

"Yeah, the heads of police and the mayor and so on. It's a bad thing for us, too. Faustino Narcotici presides and he hands out all the Mafia payoff dough at that time. It's worse on the first Saturday night of the month—the governor and state officials are there, too."

"Well, if it isn't Saturday night, I'll go over and get the cab myself," said Heller.

"Hell, no, you can't do that!" said Vantagio. "Don't you know nobody under eighteen is permitted to drive at *all* in New York City? That's why you got to have a driver. I'll send one of the boys over for it. But what's this about the Empire State Building?"

"Just a little sideline that came up," said Heller.

Possibly it was the way Heller said it. Too casual. But a little stirring of alarm began to rise. Suppose Izzy didn't steal his money?

In college, *two* cars, the Geological Survey and now this strange new development of the Empire State Building . . . My wits simply would not mesh! Only one thing was loud: Heller was up to no good.

And I had not had the slightest word from the New York office concerning agents Raht and Terb. Heller had to be stopped! I couldn't figure out what he was doing but it had to be stopped anyway. The man was a howling menace! A private office with a view of all lower Manhattan indeed!

Chapter 3

Keeping the hours I kept due to time differences between New York and Turkey, I had fallen into the necessity of sleeping all morning. I was furious to find that old (bleepard) Karagoz standing beside my bed bowing and muttering. I stared at my watch. It was only eleven! I glared at him.

"Two men in yard, Sultan Bey." He waved his hands helplessly. "They come in. They sit down on bench. They refuse to go away."

"I'll make them go away!" I shouted. I grabbed a ten-gauge shotgun and sprang to the door.

"Sultan Bey!" shouted Karagoz. "You got no clothes on!"

I rushed out anyway. Nobody is going to tell *me* what to do!

Two men were sitting on a bench, sure enough. They were faced the other way. I leaped in front of them, levelling the gun.

It was Raht and Terb!

Raht's mustache stuck out even further in surprise.

Terb's swarthy, plump face went a bit white.

"What in the name of seventeen brindle Devils are you doing here?" I thundered at them.

Raht had the effrontery to put his finger to his lips to shush me.

Terb was trying to get back on the bench.

"Account for yourselves!" I thundered even louder.

Raht was making even more urgent finger motions

and I abruptly realized I had been speaking Voltarian. But no matter. When the staff sees me coming, they vanish.

"We . . . we obeyed your order," stammered Raht. That was more like it. I had him stammering.

"You s . . . s . . . said," quavered Terb, " 'Find them and force them to report in.' "

"We . . . we were sending radio messages every day and . . . and so we thought you could only mean to come here."

So the message was unclear. Leave it to subordinates to take advantage of you.

"You (bleeped) fools have been watching the bug that was sewn into his clothes. Somebody at the store threw them in the garbage when he bought new clothes!" I levelled the gun barrels at them. "He's not in the Atlantic! He's right in that UN whorehouse, the Gracious Palms, having the time of his life!"

Raht gaped. "How do you know that?"

Anger had caused me to be incautious. They must never know I had had Heller bugged on Voltar and was monitoring everything he saw or heard. "I have other sources of information. You think you are the only spies in the world? I got spies all over the place. Even spies on you!"

They seemed cowed so I herded them into the patio of the house. I made them stand there.

Then I went and put away the gun and got a robe and buzzed the kitchen for some hot *kahve,* served with lots of sugar, *sekerli.*

While I drank it, I got to thinking that maybe this wasn't too bad. I could brief them very exactly. I could also force them to take, no matter how many Voltarian codes it violated, a receiver and decoder.

I went back, drinking more *kahve* and keeping them

standing. It gave me a certain satisfaction to realize they must have just come off a long plane ride and had had no sleep. It was also nice that it was a boiling hot Turkish September day and that they were probably dying for a cold drink. You have to keep such people in place—riff-raff.

"You are not going to be executed," I said, to open the conversation and put them at ease. "Unless, of course, you keep fouling up."

They shifted about uneasily.

"The agent I have trailing you is a complete madman," I said. "But I think I can hold him in check."

Karagoz and a waiter came in with a silver pitcher of *sira* that was beaded with mist, and three glasses. I sent two of the glasses and the servants away and sat there sipping the cold drink.

So far, everything I had done was just textbook. But it made the rest easier.

"There is a platen," I said. "It is about so big." And I made a motion with my hands. "It is just a sheet with slots in it. Do you know what one is?"

"A platen code sheet," said Raht.

"You put it over a piece of paper and write the real message in the slots," said Terb. "And then you fill in the rest of the letter."

"Your target has one. We must get it!" I said. "Even if it costs you your lives." Also textbook. "It is somewhere in his baggage and that baggage is in the old Secretary General's suite on the top floor of the Gracious Palms. Do I make myself clear?"

They both nodded.

"You are to disguise yourselves as diplomats. You are to pretend to buy services. You are to go to that suite. The door is never locked. He is never there during the day. You are to ransack the place and find that platen! Understood?"

They nodded.

"One more thing. Another agent tried to plant a bug there. But there is some sort of interference, some carbon disturbance. You are to find that and disable it."

They nodded.

"And one more thing," I said. "You, Raht, must shave off your mustache."

Horror went over him. "But it hides a knife scar that is very plain and identifies me!"

"All right," I said. "Then just trim it."

"My beautiful mustache!"

One must be firm. "It's better than trimming your throat," I said.

He got the point.

"Now, there are no taxis," I said.

"We just came in one."

"There are no taxis," I said. "So walk to the airport, spend the night in the waiting room and get a plane tomorrow morning."

They nodded glumly.

I swirled my glass and made the ice in it rattle and tinkle. "Any questions?"

"Those two devices you gave us with orders to keep them within two hundred miles of him are hidden on the television antenna of the Empire State Building," said Terb. "Is that all right?"

Hey, that was very all right. The units to relay the signals from Heller's bugs were right above him. "It will serve at the moment," I said, coldly. "Is that all?"

They nodded.

I gave the ice in the glass another tinkle. "Then get out. I'm busy."

They walked away in the boiling sun.

I rejoiced. I had them under control now. I would soon have the platen so that I could forge Heller's reports back to Voltar. And then BLOWIE! Dead Heller.

Life was sweet!

Chapter 4

The following morning, suddenly, abruptly and deliciously, life became much sweeter.

The taxi driver came rushing in. "Quick! Quick! Utanc will be here in two hours!"

My new Turkish dancing girl!

I had been eating breakfast. I leaped up and ran about the patio. I had overturned the *kahve* service and my feet crushed the remainder of the fragile cups.

He seemed to want to say something else. I stopped in front of him.

"There's another five thousand U.S. dollars for the camel and truck drivers. They have to have it before they will deliver her."

I pushed the five thousand at him. He took it. "Now, where is her room?" he demanded.

I ran about a bit more. The villa had plenty of rooms. There was one huge one that opened on a private area of the garden and had its own bath. "That's her room."

He looked over the locks on the inside of the doors. "I'll have to call a locksmith to rush down and strengthen these," he said. "She's very shy and afraid of things."

He called a locksmith. He came back. "He'll be here at once. That's another ten thousand Turkish lira."

I gave it to him.

"You've seen her?" I demanded. "How is she?"

"I haven't got time to talk now," he said and rushed out and drove away at high speed.

I called Melahat Hanim, the housekeeper. "Get this room ready, quick."

"I prepared another smaller room," she said.

"No, no. Prepare this room."

The staff ran around and got the best rugs moved in and set the place all up.

The locksmith arrived in an old truck and promptly started drilling and hammering and pounding. He was fastening ornate Turkish iron bars across the inside of the doors. Two helpers arrived in another truck. They had brand-new, latest-style Yale locks and started putting these in place.

With me yelling at them, the staff ran around in circles and took out what they had brought in, brought in what had been taken out, forgot the towels, couldn't find the towels, took my towels and put those in the bathroom.

The gardener rushed around and cut flowers and stuffed them into vases.

We were finally all ready.

We waited.

I went out in the road several times to look. No Utanc yet. Four hours went by. I had just decided to go to my secret room to check up on things when one of the small servant boys came screaming in, "The truck is coming, the truck is coming!"

It was a huge truck. It couldn't get in the gate. It had eight laborers on it. It was piled with metal trunks!

The eight laborers jumped down in the road and one by one began to carry the big trunks in. Karagoz directed them and got them to put them down in various spots in the new room.

The taxi driver arrived.

The foreman of the laborers came over and demanded fifteen thousand lira. The truck driver explained to me that this was a local truck and not covered in the five thousand U.S. I paid.

The truck drove away.

The taxi driver went into the room and locked the garden door from the inside. Then he set the locks on the patio door. He demanded all the spare keys. He gathered them in his palm and then threw them into the room. He then shut the patio door so that it was locked and could only be opened from within.

"Wait a minute," I said. "Where's Utanc?"

"You've got to understand," he said. "She's a shy, simple, tribal girl from the Kara Kum desert. She knows nothing of civilization. She is also terrified after the whole Russian Army tried to rape her. She is also exhausted from her long, long trek and the terror of fleeing out of Russian Turkmen, and should be allowed to rest and wash up for a day."

"But where is she?" I demanded.

"Probably in one of those trunks," he said.

"You don't *know*?" I said, incredulous.

"When I was talking to her this morning, she said not to pry because it made her blush."

"You've *seen* her then! What does she look like?"

"You really can't tell through her veil but I'd say she looked just like the photograph I showed you when you bought her. She is very shy. She not only had a veil on but she was also just peeking out of a truck tarp. Oh, yes, here's her bill of sale."

It was all in Turkish and it had a lot of seals and a notary stamp. It said one Utanc was the property of one Sultan Bey. My hands trembled as I took it. I owned a real, live, Turkish dancing girl! Body and soul!

"Maybe she'll suffocate in one of those trunks," I said.

"My advice," said the taxi driver, "is just to let her rest. She is a flower of the desert. A wild thing, really. Fragile, frail. Unused to men and a total stranger to civilization. I would just let her rest." And he left.

About ten minutes later, there was a loud clank inside the room. Then another clank. I recognized what it must be: the iron door bars were being dropped into place. I sighed with relief. She had gotten out of the trunk and locked the doors.

Well, needless to say, I wasn't much good for anything the rest of that day.

I listened at the door and once I thought I heard the shower running.

I spent hours walking about the yard and patio.

It was late evening. I became concerned that the girl had had no food. I thought I could hear some stirrings from the room. I went and got Melahat Hanim and had her prepare a tray with nice things on it.

Melahat knocked at the door of the room. An iron bar slid aside. The door opened the tiniest crack and then slammed quickly.

The housekeeper turned to me, perplexed. Then she apparently heard a whisper from the other side of the door. Melahat left the patio. The iron bar clanked back in place.

Then there was another clank!

The garden door! She had let Melahat in the garden door! Oh, of course. When Utanc had opened the patio door, she had seen a man—me. And naturally, she had withdrawn.

There were whisperings in the room and it was hard to tell they were indeed whisperings, even though I had my ear pressed to the door.

The garden portal opened and closed. I saw Melahat in the yard. She was beckoning. Two of the small boys ran up to her. She bent over and whispered to them.

The boys ran to the other side of the house. There was a clank and the garden door opened and then a clank as it was closed and barred.

Melahat came to me in the patio. "She said..."

"You've seen her?" I demanded. "How does she look?"

"She was behind a drape," said Melahat. "She said there were no servants provided for her and she'd seen the two small boys through the garden window and she wanted them to be assigned to her as servants."

"Oh, of course," I said. "A wild desert girl. She would feel lonely without servants."

"I knew you would approve," said Melahat, "so I assigned them for now."

"Oh, assign them permanently. She will be here a long time." And, indeed, she would. I owned her, body and soul.

The shower seemed to be running again. "She seems to be taking another bath," I said.

"I think it was the small boys," said Melahat. "They were pretty dirty."

And, indeed, it must have been. In about ten minutes, one of the small boys went out the garden door and came around to the patio. It was the one I had kicked most. His hair was plastered with water and he looked two shades lighter. He was wearing a pair of embroidered pants and an embroidered jacket. Where had those come from? Turkish national dress! Oh, of course, the wild people of the desert!

"Utanc," said the boy, impudently, "says that Sultan Bey better take a bath and put a turban on. That he looks too scruffy to be sung to!"

I started to kick him and then thought better of it. The meaning of the message sank in. Aha! She was going to get right on the job!

I hurried off. I took a bath. I went into my costume department and found a cloth to wind into a turban and also a caftan to wear.

Finally I went out. Melahat and Karagoz and the two small boys had been doing things to the salon. I was glad now I had let Karagoz buy all those new rugs. The servants had set up a little raised dais with cushions on it. They indicated I was to sit there. There was a pile of pillows in the middle of the floor, some distance from and lower than where I was to sit.

Karagoz, apparently on instructions, turned the lights very low. Two oil lamps were set up to drift a soft yellow-orange flame light through the room.

The staff stole away.

I sat on the dais, cross-legged, and waited for Utanc.

Chapter 5

In about twenty minutes, the salon door cracked open slightly. I was aware that an eye was at the slit. But I knew how shy, modest and bashful she must be and I was afraid to frighten her with sudden movements so I sat still.

The door opened a trifle wider. Like a shadow, she slid through it. She halted. The yellow-orange flame light reached her.

She was dressed in baggy pantaloons and a very tight vest that hid her breasts but left her throat and belly bare. She wore no slippers and her toenails were bright scarlet. She had a band of flowers around her raven-black hair. She was veiled!

But her eyes, slightly slanted, very large, were fixed on me in what might be fear.

She had one hand up under her veil and I could see that one fingertip must be gripped bashfully between her teeth.

I beckoned for her to come on in.

She very nearly fled.

I stopped my motion. A minute went by. Gradually, she seemed to gather courage and came fully into the room. In her left hand she bore a couple of musical instruments.

Timidly, she approached the pillows in the center of the room. I could see her better. Her skin was a tawny color. I could not see her face because of the veil but her eyes, downcast and flicking up only occasionally, were beautiful.

She put down one instrument—I saw that it was about eighteen inches in diameter, a sort of tambourine.

Gracefully she sank, cross-legged, on a pillow. She put the other instrument in her lap. I recognized it as a *cura irizva,* a long-necked sort of lute with three strings and frets.

"O Master," she whispered, and I could barely hear her, "with your permission and at your command, I will sing."

I waved my hand in a lordly fashion. "Sing!" I commanded.

She flinched and I realized I had spoken too loudly.

Her eyes were downcast. She tuned the *cura irizva.* Then she began to play without singing. BEAUTIFUL! Traditional Turkish music is very oriental and it ends on indefinite upbeats and usually I don't like it. But such was the dexterity of her hands and so expert her rendition that the whole place seemed transported into a dream world. What an accomplished musician!

The last chord died away. I was afraid to applaud. She was now looking at me so shyly under her eyebrows that I was sure she thought she had been too bold.

Then she whispered, "There are no recording devices in this place, are there?"

It startled me. And then I realized why she was asking. The primitive Turks have a superstition that if you record their voices, they will lose them. It proved beyond doubt she was just a Kara Kum desert wanderer, a wild thing.

I said, "No, no. Of course not."

But she got up, her movements poetry itself, and went around the room looking behind things just to be sure. She came back and sat down. She picked up her *cura irizva.* "I did not feel bold enough to sing," she whispered, "but I will sing now."

She struck several chords and then she sang:

She rose like the moon into heaven's embrace.
She opened her mouth of the dew to taste.
And then came the sun!
She retreated in haste!
All scorched with the rays of your burning!

I was entranced! Her voice was low and husky, sensuous, insinuating! Her accent was Turkmen Turkish, identifiable even though Turkish, spoken all across Russia, varies hardly at all. Her voice had a thrilling effect upon me. It set my pulse surging.

To my disappointment, she put the *cura irizva* aside. With bowed head and downcast eyes, she whispered, "O

Master, with your permission and at your command, I will dance."

"Dance!" I permitted and commanded eagerly.

Again I had spoken too loud. She cowered. But then, presently, she took up the tambourine. This was unusual. Turkish dancers usually use finger castanets. But it was a Turkish drum.

She rose so sinuously and effortlessly that I scarcely realized she had stood.

I thought for a moment she was just standing there. And then I saw the muscles of that bare stomach!

In the flame light, her belly was moving and writhing without another single motion to her body. A *real* belly dancer!

The jacket covered her breasts. The pantaloons covered her thighs. But the nakedness in between was alive!

Then, in time to the moving muscles, she began to tap the drum. She tapped it harder and her legs began to sway. Harder and her whole body began to sway. Her stomach muscles bunched and writhed and her hips began to grind!

Oh, my Gods!

It was enough to drive a man MAD!

And all the time her eyes demurely cast down.

But now what was she doing? Between each time she used her hand to strike at the drum, she was giving a tug at her face.

She was unveiling!

Little by little, as one foot lifted and then the other foot, as her hips swung wider and wider, she was disclosing more and more of her face. She began to hum a wordless song in time to the drumbeat.

Suddenly, with a yell, she leapt into the air!

The veil flew away.

She came down, her hips grinding, grinding, her

belly twitching and churning, her hands and arms writhing. Her eyes on me were steady and burning!

She was GORGEOUS!

Never had I seen such a face before!

I caught my breath. My heart was in my throat. I had never before in my life been so aroused.

She began to pick her feet up higher. The tambourine began to beat more savagely. She began to strike it against her elbow and hand alternately, and then she was AWAY!

She leaped through the flame light, turning in the air, spinning, coming down, pausing to grind—her eyes had an intensity that would drill holes in me!

She sprang in huge bounds into the air. The drum beat faster and faster. She spun and sprang faster and faster. She was a blur of motion in the yellow-orange fire!

I have never seen such dancing!

My own body began to jerk in rhythm to hers.

Suddenly, she sprang high in the air, let out a piercing cry and came down cross-legged on her pillow. Sitting, absolutely still.

But her eyes on me were like coals of fire!

I could not catch my breath.

She reached out with a fast gesture and snatched at the *cura irizva.*

She clutched it to her.

She struck a chord.

Her eyes were hot—riveted upon me!

In a throbbing, passion-congested voice she sang:

The nightingale lay trembling
In his brutal hand,
Its throat that pulsed
With fear,
Was strangled in a moment of coarse passion,

Dear—
Remember me when I am gone,
If you would kill for love!

It was too much! I screamed at her, "No! No! Oh, Gods, I would never kill you!"

That did it.

Too loud!

She cowered back. She raced to the door, crying out in fear, opened it and was gone!

I raced after her.

I was too late.

Her room door was steel-barred from within.

I sat in the patio, aching with passion unfulfilled, drowned in remorse.

I sat there until dawn, watching that door.

She did not come out.

Chapter 6

Throughout the following day, I was in a daze. I could only think of Utanc. But I couldn't think very clearly. Numerous ideas of how I might attract her attention and make amends for frightening her were all discarded.

The fence of her private garden had a small hole in it and in the afternoon I crouched there, longing for a glimpse of her.

In late afternoon, when it had become cool, she came out of her garden door. She was wearing an embroidered cloak. She was unveiled, unaware of scrutiny. Her face was so beautiful that I could not breathe. Her walk, so easy, so poised, was poetry itself.

She went back in her room.

That night I sat in vain in the salon. No boy came to inform me. She did not come.

I sat there all night, alert to the tiniest sounds.

In exhaustion, I fell into a sleep knifed with nightmares that she had only been a dream.

Around noon of the next day I woke. I took hardly any breakfast. I paced in the yard. I went in and tried to interest myself in something else. It was impossible.

About three, I went outside again.

Voices!

They were coming from her garden!

I quickly scrambled to the small hole in her fence and peered through.

There she sat!

She was unveiled. She was gorgeous. She was dressed in another cloak but it was fallen carelessly open. It revealed a brassiere and tight, short pants. Her legs and stomach were bare.

So magnetized were my eyes to her that at first I did not even notice the two small boys. They were sitting at her feet in the grass. They were wearing little embroidered jackets and pants. They were scrubbed and clean. Each was holding a little silver cup on his knee.

She said something I did not get and they both laughed. Smiling, she leaned back indolently, exposing more stomach and the inside of her thigh. She was reaching. It was toward a silver teapot and another silver cup on a silver tray.

With grace, she picked up the cup in one delicate hand and the teapot in another. She poured from the pot to the cup. Then she leaned over and poured into the cup each had on his knee.

A little tea party! How charming!

She raised her cup, the two small boys raised theirs. *"Serefe!"* she said, meaning "Here's to you" in Turkish. They all drank.

The tea must have been awfully hot and strong. The two small boys drank theirs and gasped and coughed. But they smiled and watched as she sipped hers.

"Now," said Utanc, in her low, husky voice, "we will get on with the next story."

The two small boys wriggled with delight and hitched themselves closer, fixing their eyes on her adoringly. How utterly charming she was—telling them fairy stories.

Utanc spread her arms along the top of the garden seat. "The name of this story is 'Goldilocks and the Three Commissars.'" She settled herself comfortably. "Once upon a time there was this beautiful little girl named Goldilocks. That means she had gold-colored hair. And she was ramming around in the woods getting into things. Nosy. So she came to this cottage and picked the lock and trespassed with illegal entry.

"Now this Goldilocks had a horrible appetite because she came from capitalistic parents and, as usual, she thought she was starved. And there on the table sat three bowls of porridge. So she decided it was a worker's cottage and she better exploit it.

"She sat herself down in the biggest chair and had at that porridge. But it was too hot. So she went to the next-sized chair and tried to wolf that porridge. But it was too cold. So she sat down in the smallest chair and, wow, that porridge was great. So her capitalist tendencies got the better of her and she ATE IT ALL UP. Left absolutely nothing.

"Now, actually, this cottage belonged to three commissars and they had been out to a party meeting to help the workers and it was an awful joke on this Goldilocks pig that they weren't workers at all but real rough, tough, friends-of-the-people, no-nonsense commissars. A real bad break for this kid Goldilocks, but the little pig should have known better. So she split.

"So the biggest commissar put his whip down on the table and suddenly looked at his porridge and he said, 'Who the hell has been at this porridge?' And the medium-sized commissar put his brass knuckles down on the table and said, 'Hey, what (bleepard) has been at *my* porridge?' And the smallest commissar had just hung up his handgun when he saw his own plate and it was EMPTY!"

The two small boys strained forward to get every word. Utanc leaned toward them. She continued, "So they spotted footprints in the snow and they got out their dogs and they trailed Goldilocks! They trailed her across mountains and ice packs on rivers and through forests. Wow! What a chase! And they finally got Goldilocks up a tree."

Utanc sat back. She took another sip from the silver cup. She didn't seem to be going to go on. The two small boys strained forward. "Yes?" "Yes?"

Utanc smiled dreamily. Then she said, "So they caught her and (bleeped) her and everybody had a lot of fun."

The two small boys began to laugh. They laughed and laughed and so did Utanc. The little boys got to laughing so hard they were rolling around on the grass, holding their stomachs.

Finally it calmed down. Utanc smiled at them prettily. She got the silver pot again. "Have some more tea," she said.

It was such a charming scene! Of course, Utanc had been subjected to the Russian propaganda machine. And naturally she would not be timid talking to little boys. But it was so sweet of her to be taking her time to educate these two little Turkish brats. It showed a kind, indulgent heart.

It was as she reached out with the pot that I caught sight of her naked armpit. I had not realized anything could affect me so much. I suddenly couldn't breathe.

And then that excrement named Karagoz came around the end of the inner garden wall and coughed. I got up and pretended I had lost something and walked off.

The husky, low sound of her voice haunted my ears. For the rest of that afternoon I couldn't think of anything else.

Imagine the thrill when, at eight o'clock that night, one of the small boys came to me.

"Utanc says to take a bath and get on your turban and go sit in the salon."

And believe me, I was into the turban and caftan like a shot and into that lounge zip. I sat on the cushions and waited.

Chapter 7

The yellow-orange flame light painted the room.

She slipped quietly through the door.

Like a shadow she flowed to her pillows.

She sat cross-legged in the center of the room. She put down a large, silver, mirror-shiny tray, her *cura irizva* and tambourine. She wore baggy pantaloons of gray, a silver-embroidered short jacket that hid her breasts but exposed her stomach and arms. She had a silver band around her hair. She was veiled.

Her head was down. She was not looking at me.

She just sat there. From time to time she sighed.

I was afraid to speak for fear she would run away. But after a very long time, I whispered, "Why are you downcast?"

In a very low, husky voice she said, "O Master, I am sad because I cannot tolerate the thought of being without the bare necessities of life. I sigh for the deprivation of not having silk handkerchiefs, French bubble bath, antiperspirant and Chennel Number 5. I require only minor cash to buy them—a few hundred thousand lira."

She looked so sad, slumped there. She was a wild, primitive nomad of the Kara Kum desert. It would not do to remind her she was now a slave. Naturally she needed money to buy necessities. How she must have missed them, tending camels in that sandy waste.

"They are yours," I said in a lordly manner.

At once she sat up straight. Her eyes flicked at me and then were demurely downcast.

She picked up her little drum and began to beat upon it, slowly, timidly. Then she began to hum a wordless, plaintive tune.

I knew she was encouraging herself.

The drumbeat grew stronger. Then in midbar she changed over from the drum to the silver tray and began to beat upon it instead.

The tune she hummed became stronger, faster, less plaintive.

As she sat, her body began to sway. She came to her knees. Her body swayed more.

Her bracelets were hitting the tray with a crash! The

beat became faster. In a sitting position, but sitting on nothing, she began to kick out with her feet, one after the other!

In that sitting posture, kicking out her silvered toes in rhythm, banging the flashing tray, she sailed around the room humming some savage tune! She actually seemed to float above the floor!

From one end of the room to the other she went, back and forth. Now at the end of each passage, she leaped up, came down on her heels, extended and cried, "Heigh!" And then each time, her bracelets rattled against the tray. Barbaric!

She was going in wide circles now. It was a Russian dance! She went faster. The tray crashed louder as she banged it.

My body began to jump with the rhythm of it. I was following her with my eyes but my body also began to twist to the left and to the right.

The circles were getting smaller. She was closer and closer to the center of the room.

And then she was back in the center. She was humming more intensely. She was on her knees. She was swinging the tray above her head, the flat side facing me, left and right and left and right, banging it with her hand each time.

I found my body twitching in response to the rhythm. My eyes followed the tray.

The yellow-orange flame flashed and flashed. I found myself panting in rhythm.

Her hips were grinding now. She ripped the veil from her face. Her eyes were on me like hot coals.

My body was jerking, all of its own accord, back and forth, back and forth.

Suddenly she sank on her heels. She put down the tray. She seized her *cura irizva*.

With the same tune she had been humming, she began to strike chords.

Her eyes were scorching me.

She began to sing:

Unspent kisses clog my throat,
Unspent smiles lurk
Behind my lips.
Unspent passion dams my breath
And sucks back in
The unspent tongue!
My hands
That ache
With unspent caress
Tremble
When I think
Of pouring out upon you
All my flood
Of UNSPENT LOVE!

It was unbearable! I cried out, "Oh, my darling!" I flung out my hands to her.

The cry, the gesture, startled her. She cowered away. And before I could protest, she abandoned her instruments and fled from the room!

Before I could reach her door, the iron bolt was in place.

I tried to plead. I begged. But my voice must not have been able to penetrate the door. It remained locked.

After a long time I went and got five hundred thousand lira and pushed them, one by one, through the crack under the door. The last one simply stayed there, its tip still showing. I looked at it for the rest of the night.

The next day I got bold enough to creep along the

wall of the inner garden but, alas, the hole I had found was now plugged up.

I thought I heard voices in the garden once. I could not be sure. I spent a miserable, aching day.

I did not really have too much hope. But around eight, a small boy came to me. He said, "Utanc told me to say you should take a bath and get your turban on and go into the salon."

Oh, never was a bath taken so fast.

Almost in no time, I was in the salon.

I waited.

At long, long last, the door crept open.

Softly and quietly she slipped in. She was wearing a tight jacket that left her arms and belly bare. It was of gold embroidery. She wore baggy pantaloons of gold. She had a gold band with flowers around her black hair. She was veiled in a golden veil. As she sat, I saw that her fingernails and toenails were painted gold. She was carrying a flashing sword and her *cura irizva*.

But she sat with her eyes downcast, her head bowed. From time to time, she sighed.

"Why are you sighing?" I said at last, very softly so as not to frighten her.

"O Master," she said with downcast eyes, "I cannot tolerate the thought of not being able to call Istanbul, Paris and New York to order, C.O.D., the small and vital things a poor woman has to have to preserve her beauty in her master's eyes. I need a telephone in my room with a WATS line and an unlisted number."

Well, naturally a wild and shy desert girl from the primitive and uncultured wastes of the Kara Kum desert wouldn't want to have her phone number listed.

"It is yours," I said in a lordly way.

She began to hum slowly and plaintively. She picked up the sword and began to tap the blade in rhythm, first to her right, then to her left. Her body began to move with the sword.

The sword seemed to be leading her, pulling her up little by little to her feet as it went from left to right. Her eyes were on it, following it.

Her feet began to move, steps to the left, steps to the right.

The yellow-orange flame light clashed upon the sword, rippled over her body.

Now she began to slash with the sword as she danced. The whoosh-whoosh of it blended in with the tune she was humming.

Then the sword began to spin. I was terrified she would cut herself!

Then with one hand on the tip and the other on the hilt she began to leap over the sword and back again in rhythm! And gracefully!

Suddenly she let go of the tip end and began to whirl. She had the sword extended. She became a blur of gold.

She leaped into the air and came down!

The sword lanced up!

I was certain she would stab herself!

The razor edge slit her veil!

The two halves fell apart. Her face was revealed. She seemed fixated upon the upright sword. Her head began to go back. Her hips began to work. Her belly muscles began to writhe.

The sword seemed to pump up and down.

The tune she hummed was turning into moans.

Her hips ground harder and harder. My own body was moving in rhythm to hers. I could not control it. I did not try!

Suddenly she upended the sword.

She drove it into the floor!

It quivered there!

She sat behind it.

Her eyes went from the sword to me and I was almost scalded by the passion in them.

She savagely yanked her *cura irizva* to her. But then she sighed tremulously.

She struck a chord of great longing. She sang:

Let me drink of you.
Let me drink with my eyes
The bold male beauty of your limbs!
Let me drink with my breath
The brutal male scent of you!
Let me drink with my lips
The taste of your male flesh.
Let me drink and drink and drink
Before I starve
Of longing for you!
Let me drink,
Let me drink,
Oh Allah, let me drink
Before I die of love
And EMPTINESS!

The sobbing plaint was more than I could take. "Utanc!" I shouted.

It broke the spell!

She cast away the *cura irizva* with a clatter.

She fled from the room!

And even though I was very fast, the door was locked and barred before I could reach her room.

I stood there for hours. I couldn't stop trembling. I went to my office and wrote out an order for a WATS line with an unlisted number. I slid it under her door but the edge stayed in view.

The next day I realized that I was becoming physically ill. I ached all over. Things were in a sort of a blur. I just wandered about, stopping now and then and staring and not seeing what I was looking at.

I thought to myself that this was no good, getting ill this way. I would not be fit if anything did happen to bring Utanc to my bed. Although I almost never touched the stuff, a bit of Scotch might do me good. I had been keeping a bottle to give to the captain of the *Blixo* when he arrived. I went to a cupboard to dig it out.

It was gone!

I called the waiter.

He said he didn't know anything about it.

I wandered around some more. I couldn't even sit down!

The waiter came in to serve me my supper.

He kept standing there, twisting his hands, so I looked at him. The waiter had a black eye!

"Sultan Bey," he said, shuffling his feet, "I came to confess that it was I who took the Scotch."

But really, even though this was a marvelous opportunity to punish him, I was too far gone. I simply waved him away. I couldn't eat my supper either.

Maybe I would die and simply be through with the whole thing. I had decided finally and inevitably that this was the best plan when, suddenly, there was one of the small boys.

"Utanc says that you should bathe and put on a turban and go into the salon."

Weak as I was, I made pretty good time!

I waited quite a while.

Then there was a slither at the door. It cracked wider. In she came. She was carrying a bucket, two unlit torches and her *cura irizva*.

Quietly she took her place in the center of the room.

She was dressed in red-embroidered pantaloons and vest. She had a red band with flowers in it around her black hair. Her toenails and fingernails were scarlet. And so was her veil.

But she just sat slumped, eyes downcast. She sighed deeply. She looked listless.

At length I got up courage enough to whisper, "Why are you sighing?"

"O my master, I am sad because I cannot tolerate the thought of being cooped up all day in a single room and garden. Were I to move about on foot, I would be stared at or attacked upon the roads. I feel I can never be happy without a BMW 320, fuel-injected engine, five-speed stick shift, rally-model sedan."

For the first time I felt a surge of horror. Such a car would cost a million and a half Turkish lira!

She sighed tremulously. But then, of course, she *would* feel cooped up. A wild, primitive desert girl, she was used to the limitless vistas, rolling dunes and the vast sky of Russian Turkmen. Her leg moved slightly. I was terrified she would run away.

"It is yours," I said.

She began to hum quietly. She picked up the two torches and went over to the open lamps. She lit them. She came back to the center of the room.

She stood there, a torch in each hand. Their light and the lamplight made moving shadows around her on the floor. The live flame seemed to make her body writhe.

Humming, she began to juggle the torches, tossing them and catching them, one after the other, in rhythm.

Then she sped to the right and sped to the left and back and forth. I was turning my whole body to follow her. At the end of the run, she tossed a torch high, turning and then catching it.

She narrowed the run. And then she was standing in

one place. She was still juggling the torches. But now, each time a hand was momentarily free, she was tugging at her red veil. Little by little, her face was becoming bare.

Then the veil was gone!

She stood there juggling the torches. But now there was a change. The torches were crossing from one hand to the other, both together as they spun. I turned right and left, following the flame. Her feet began to beat the rhythm of the tune.

Her body now seemed to be writhing more. Or was it just the flame shadows?

It was her body!

Her belly was moving!

She was beginning to grind with her hips. She was going from one foot to the other. The torches both together were being tossed from left to right and back again. My body moved of its own accord to follow them.

Her chin was coming down. Her eyes were fixed upon me.

Then, as she stood there, grinding her hips, moving her belly, her head began to come up. Up and up! Her eyes began to glaze!

Her mouth was open, slack. I had never noticed before that her mouth was large, that her lips were full and red. And wet.

The tune she hummed was phasing over into moans!

Left, right, my own body was jerking back and forth in time to those grinding hips and flying torches.

Then suddenly she stood still. She was shuddering. A torch was in each hand now. She was crying out faintly.

She was having an orgasm!

The two torches, one in each of her hands, held level, began to approach each other.

Suddenly the flame heads ground together!

She screamed in ecstasy!

Then she sank abruptly down, cross-legged. At the same moment she dropped the torches into the bucket where they hissed and steamed.

She seemed dejected.

Her fingers fumbled out and she found her *cura irizva.*

She struck a plaintive, quavering chord.

Her eyes came up and fixed themselves on me. There were tears in them!

The indefinite oriental music began to flow sadly from her fingers. In a voice that was a dirge of sorrow, she sang:

You have no need of me,
You beautiful man.
You do not want my arms.
You do not wish to feel
The entwine of my legs.
You have no need
Of pressures from my breasts.
You do not need
My hands with their caress.
You do not crave
To flood me
With your juice.
But OH, you brutal male,
If ONLY that you DID!

As her crying words died away in the hall, I was totally beyond the ability to react.

I sank back. I whispered, "Oh, Utanc, have pity on me. I do want you. I will *die,* Utanc, unless I have you."

There was a tiny sound beside me.

A hand was lightly caressing my cheek. The softest

whisper floating in a haze of perfume, "Lie quietly, darling."

There was the click of a light switch. Then the sound of the lamps being capped.

It was totally dark.

Another stir beside me. A delicate hand on my chest. Lips, full and soft and moist against my cheek—a delicate kiss.

I reached up to grasp her jacket to pull it off.

"No, no," she whispered. "I am much too modest to be seen undressed by a man in the dark."

She pressed my arm back against my side. She kissed my throat. "This is all for you. Do not think of me. Think only of yourself. Tonight is yours."

She was removing my turban in the dark. Then she kissed my eyes.

She removed the caftan from me and then she kissed my chest.

She pulled off my boots and kissed my feet.

Then she gently undid my belt and slowly began to pull off my pants, her lips kissing lower and lower as the flesh was bared.

Lightly she began to caress my shoulders and arms with her fingertips. She took my ear lobe between her teeth in a gentle way. Then her tongue sought the entrance of my ear.

Quivers of pleasure began to go through me. I once more sought to reach her with my hands and pull her garments away.

"No, no," she whispered. "There is no need for me to undress. I am too shy. This is your night and your pleasure."

She kissed me on the mouth!

I felt like I would faint with pleasure!

Her tongue pried my lips apart and sought the inmost reaches of my mouth.

She sucked my willing tongue out and her lips drew upon it and her teeth lightly held it.

I was going into a daze of pleasure.

Her hands were stroking me, touching spots in my body I had never suspected had any pleasure in them. I began to breathe heavily.

She stroked my breast. "Darling, darling," she was whispering. And then, "The mouth is everything."

She kissed down my throat. She kissed down my chest. She kissed down my stomach. She kissed down my thighs.

Suddenly all the blackness around me was a vortex, pulling me in as though I were being swirled right down, helpless with sensuous pleasure.

I floated suspended in joy amongst the stars.

White lightning seemed to flash across the whole universe.

I lay in an utter daze. I had never felt such a thing before. Lights were spinning in the utter blackness of the room.

My heart was pounding so hard I felt my chest was going to explode.

We lay quietly in the velvet dark.

I could feel the spent relaxedness of her.

Time passed.

Then her hands upon my cheeks. She stroked them. "That was very good," she whispered.

Weakly, with one hand, I sought to pluck at her breast. Gently she steered my hand away. "This is all for you," she said. "The mouth is everything." She kissed me. "Everything," she said. She kissed me more passionately. "The mouth is *everything*," she moaned. "Oh, darling, lie still. This is all for you. Just spread out your arms and legs and enjoy it."

Her tongue was stroking my lips. Then her whole mouth was cupping and stroking my lips. Then her mouth and tongue and hands were once more finding secret places in my body.

My passion began to stir anew.

Her hands suddenly caught my hair on either side of my head. She was gripping my head passionately. I could feel her eyes like black coals in the dark as she looked at me.

"Oh, darling," she said with choked passion. "The mouth is *EVERYTHING!*" She kissed me. She drew back. "It is many hours until dawn."

And her mouth once more began its journey down my body to culmination in sublime ecstasy. It seemed to me that never before in my life had I ever had sex. And not like this! But it was beyond anything I had ever dreamed for or of. Nothing, absolutely nothing in Heavens or on Earth had felt that good before!

Chapter 8

When I awoke it was well into the afternoon.

I showered, something new for me. I put on clean clothes. Something new for me. I smiled at Melahat Hanim. Something new for me. She was helping the waiter serve me breakfast.

The whole world smelled good, looked bright. Something *very* new for me.

"Where is my darling Utanc?" I said.

Melahat said, "When the car was delivered, she and Karagoz went off to get her driver's license."

Of course, that was easy. I had given her the proper identification and birth certificate of an actual baby girl that, had it not unreportedly died, would have been about Utanc's age by now. But Karagoz would have to teach her quite a bit before she could pass any driving test.

I went out to the cool patio and sat in a chair. One of the small boys came tearing out of Utanc's room without any clothes on, spun about and vanished. He returned with pants on and tried to sneak by me. It was too narrow a gap. I tousled his head and smiled at him. He gaped back.

I reached in my pocket and got a coin. I gave it to him. He stared at it suspiciously.

I reached into my pocket and gave him a ten-lira note. He took it and looked at it in amazement.

I reached in my pocket and gave him a hundred-lira note, almost a U.S. dollar. "Just tell Utanc, when next you see her," I said, "that the moon and sun together are dim compared to her."

He didn't know what to make of it. He went off muttering the phrase so he could remember it. Suddenly he was back. "Sultan Bey," he said, "can we eat all the grapes we want?"

I smiled indulgently. "Of course."

A little while later, there was a roar of an approaching car. I got up and looked out toward the gate.

A vehicle shot in, braked with a squeal of tires and slid exactly into the parking place.

It was a white BMW road-rally car. A sedan with a low profile and a big trunk. Plastic no-see-through glass covers had been put over the inside of the windscreen and windows. You couldn't see who was in it.

Utanc got out on the driver's side. She was garbed in a white cloak with a peaked hood, and veiled, and all that was visible of her were her sloe-black eyes and even these were shadowed by the hood.

Daintily and modestly, she crept across the yard and when I would have stopped her, turned her body and slid past me, eyes downcast, and was into her room.

I was in a state of alarm at once! Had I done something to offend her?

Karagoz was getting out. He had some bundles. A small boy grabbed them and sped to Utanc's room. The door slammed behind him.

I went over to Karagoz in alarm. "Is the car all right?"

Karagoz said, "It's fine. They had one all ready to deliver to a rich official and, for a premium, they sent it right over this morning as soon as I relayed your note. Drives great. Awful (bleeped) fast, though."

"Did she like it?"

"Oh, yes! Drooled over it."

"And when does she get her driver's test and all?"

"Oh, we got the license. I only had to show her a few things the salesman showed me. Then I showed her how to steer and so on. In about ten minutes she had it. The test man said she was the best driver he'd seen for some time. Mysterious."

"Well, of course anyone expert at driving camels would have no trouble learning to drive a road-rally, stick-shift car," I said.

"That's true," said Karagoz.

"Then what's she upset about!" I demanded.

He thought and thought. Then he said, "In the store where they sell cassettes, she wanted some Tchaikovsky—he's some composer or other—and some piece called 'The Overture of 1812'—she said she wanted the one with real cannons in it—and they didn't have either one and said they'd have to send to Istanbul for it. But she really wasn't upset. She just told them she'd take the Beatles that they did have and they could order the rest." He thought a while longer. "Oh, yes. She said the high-frequency band was missing on the audio cassette deck they tried to sell her and that they better get some decent hi-fi equipment in if they wanted her for a customer.

"But actually, she was very sweet about it. She's very shy and not forward at all. You can tell from her accent she's been raised amongst the wild nomads of Russia. Really, she's the most mannerly and demure person I ever met. Except, of course, when she gets behind the wheel of that car!"

So I had no slightest clue of how I had upset her.

The day dimmed for me.

I could hear some laughter coming from her private garden, her own throaty amusement and the high-pitched little squeals from the two small boys. So she wasn't mad at them. She had drooled over the car. She had not been mad at the merchants. She had gotten her driver's license. She was not upset with Karagoz. There was only one conclusion I could reach.

She was mad at me.

I stared for hours unseeingly into a discarded pile of shriveled grass.

I knew I could not live without Utanc.

Chapter 9

Now and then in a lifetime, somebody catches a glimpse of Heavens and then promptly plunges into Hells. And that was what was about to happen to me.

That night, there was no messenger from Utanc. I fretted away the hours fruitlessly.

In the morning, red-eyed and bushy-haired from lack of sleep and worry, I thought that if I could just speak to her and ask her what was wrong, it would all come out all right. At least I would *know.*

Accordingly, realizing it would be fruitless to knock and fearing to just get the door slammed in my face, I conceived a cunning plan. I would lie in wait in the patio and when somebody came in or out, I would be able to go in and quietly put my question to her.

Looking back on it now, it still seems sensible. Yet it was rash beyond belief.

I took a position behind a high-backed wicker chair just outside her door. The tall and curving weave of the chair hid me rather effectively, yet, kneeling there, I could peer out and keep an eye on her door.

Faintly, from within, I could hear water running and then splashes.

After a bit, suddenly the inner bar of the door was being lifted!

The door opened!

One of the small boys, stark naked, came out of the door!

He stopped!

He yelled, "Melahat!"

From within came Utanc's voice, musically calling to him, "Ask her for a back brush, too!"

The small boy dashed through the patio and out into the yard, shouting, "Melahat! We need some towels!"

My chance! He had left her bedroom door ajar!

Out I came from behind the wicker chair.

I tiptoed into the room, taking great care not to make a sudden noise and frighten her.

Water splashing was coming from the bathroom. Its door was wide open.

Silently, I crept forward. If only I could say a word or two and see her smile back, I knew everything would be all right.

Then, there she was!

She was lying in the tub! The bubble bath was white froth clear up to her chin. Only her head and the tips of her fingers were showing. Her hair was tied high upon her head to keep it out of the water. She was in profile to me. Her eyes were upon her hands and a bar of soap she was lathering.

I had passed by a low table. A small book was on it. My trousers must have brushed against it. It fell and made a small sound.

Utanc must have heard it but she did not look in my direction. She said, "Did you get the back brush?"

The sound of her voice sent a shiver of delight through me. How utterly sweet she looked, just her head and hands above the bubble froth.

The sound of her voice and sight of her in her bath was making it almost impossible to speak. My love for her welled up. I fought for control of my vocal cords. "Utanc . . ."

Her head whipped round toward me. She opened her mouth in shock. She turned bright red!

I took a step forward to reassure her, trying to find my voice.

She cowered back, trying to shrink into the bubbles. Suddenly she screamed, "Don't kill me!"

I recoiled!

I gazed in horror at how I had frightened her.

I backed up out of the bathroom!

Another voice! "Don't kill her!" It was the second small boy. He, too, was stark naked. He was standing by a dressing table that was covered with open boxes.

Suddenly he exploded into action!

With all his might he threw a powder puff!

"Don't you dare kill her!" he screamed.

He found another powder puff on the dresser. He pitched it as hard as he could throw!

The powder trailed through the air!

The puff hit my pants in a white explosion!

"Don't kill Utanc!" he screamed at the top of his lungs.

He was scrambling through the boxes to find another powder puff.

I got out of the room.

I went across the patio, totally confused.

The first small boy was racing back across the yard. He had dropped the towels and they were strewn behind him.

He was carrying something—a long-handled back brush.

Screams were still coming from the bedroom behind me.

The first small boy rushed at me from the yard, blocking my way. "Don't you dare kill Utanc!" he shouted at the top of his lungs.

He struck at me with the bath brush!

He wasn't very big. The brush could not reach

higher than my arm. But he wielded it with all his might.

I had had enough!

It was his fault anyway! He had left the door open!

I cocked my right fist.

With everything behind it, I hit him in the face!

He flew backwards about fifteen feet!

He landed with a crumpled thud!

Staff had come pouring out of other buildings, probably at the first screams.

They saw the boy land.

They saw me in the patio door.

They stopped.

They made a ring of people twenty feet back from where the boy lay.

He was twitching, lying on his side, his eyes shut, blood gushing from his nose.

The staff did not come forward to him. They knew better.

The boy's own mother started ahead toward him. Then her arm was caught by Karagoz and she halted.

The Turks were wringing their hands. They did not know what to do. But they knew me.

One by one they knelt and, slowly, moaning, they began to pound their heads against the grass of the lawn.

I stood there, glaring at the scene.

There was a sound behind me.

Something slipped past me.

It was Utanc.

She didn't look at me. She didn't stop to soothe me.

She went out onto the lawn. She was covered with a white hooded cloak and she was veiled. Her feet were bare and had left a trail of water on the flagstones.

She went straight to the small boy.

She said, "Oh, you poor little boy. You were trying to protect me."

She felt for his pulse. She looked at his limbs.

Then she picked him up and carried him toward me. Then past me. Her eyes did not even flick at me.

She took the small boy into her room.

She closed the door.

The staff melted away.

I did not know what to do. I was in a spinning confusion. I could not add it all up.

I went to a corner of the yard that was very dark and sat down under some bushes. I was sort of numb, like you feel when you are going over a cliff and are only halfway down.

After a while a bearded old doctor from the town drove up. Karagoz showed him the way to Utanc's room.

The doctor was in there a very long time.

Finally he came out.

I was instantly in front of him. I said, "How is Utanc?"

He looked at me. "Is that the boy's name? Odd name for a boy."

"No, no," I said. "Not the boy. The woman! How is she?"

"Ah, she is very upset. You see, the boy had, she says, a very pretty face. His nose is broken and his cheekbone is pushed in. She offered me real money to repair it."

I saw what it was all about now. She had some weird female concern for aesthetics. "Well! Can you? Can you?"

He hesitated. Then, "The nose, somewhat. But the cheekbone . . ."

"Fly him to Istanbul!"

He shook his head. "No reason to do that. They can't do any more than I did, no matter their fancy equipment."

He left.

I went back and sat down behind some bushes in the dark corner. I was trying to think, trying to reach some conclusions. I felt as though somebody had died—the lingering, heavy grief you can't do anything about. The awful consequences of the events were boring into me harder and harder.

Utanc would never talk to me again. She would never dance for me. She would never even look at me. I felt she was cut off from me forever.

I couldn't live with that.

I tried futilely to dredge up anything I knew in psychology that would handle any part of this. There was nothing. The grief became heavier and heavier.

All the rest of that day I sat there in the gloom. I sat there all through the night.

The next morning, base commander Faht Bey entered the yard. He was going to go into the patio but Karagoz came over and pointed to where I was sitting under the shrubs.

Faht Bey came over. "Sultan Bey," he said, "please do not murder that new girl you got. We have enough trouble without more corpses to explain away."

Dully, I said, "I didn't try to kill her."

"Well, the staff here thinks you did. And Karagoz told me that the girl is terrified for her life."

"Terrified for her life?" I said. It was so far from the way I felt, it just didn't sink in right away.

Faht Bey nodded. "Karagoz says she was already afraid she'd be attacked here. And actually, in my opinion, we ourselves are not well defended at all. We don't even have alarm systems to alert us in event of a major attack."

He looked at me for a while. Then he said, "Will you please promise me not to kill that girl and leave her body lying about? If you want to be rid of her, why, just send her away."

It was his parting shot. He left. But he might as well have used an 800-kilovolt blastick.

The thought of Utanc going away made my blood freeze in my veins!

That was the thought I had been trying not to think! That she would leave!

Oh, it was one thing not to be talked to, to be shunned. But it was quite another for her not to be around at all! I could not tolerate the idea of it!

My wits were churning.

Somehow I got the thought to come straight.

She felt undefended.

Perhaps if she felt defended, she would not get the idea of leaving!

Driven by this, I rushed to my office. I got out pen and paper.

I began to design a defense alarm system.

The more I worked at it, the more carried away I became. I would make it really good!

I started with the gate. One of the numbers outside it could be pushed. That would call the whole staff to defend the gate!

I put an alarm buzzer in her room so she would be able to press it and alert the staff if she was afraid.

And then I got to thinking about what Faht had said about the base being not well defended. So I designed an alarm-signal system for it that would assemble all the base personnel into the hangar; they would have gun emplacements in the center and be able to shoot at every entrance.

I put the signal buzzer for it in my secret office. By treading on just one tile and twisting one's foot, one could assemble the entire base to man the hangar and be ready to shoot.

I finished it up. I marked it top priority. I wrote an order that the staff would be drilled and another order that the whole base personnel would be drilled.

She would hear that the place was now defended.

It was all I could think of to do.

The heavy feeling of loss came over me again.

I knew I had been parted from Utanc and I thought it was forever.

I was crushed.

PART TWENTY-ONE

Chapter 1

More to take my mind off my troubles than as a matter of concern, that afternoon I slouched into my secret office and turned on the viewer. After all, Raht and Terb were on the job and we would soon have the platen and could end Heller.

Frankly, I was too far gone to pay much attention. But after a bit I came up to strong interest in what was going on.

Bang-Bang was taking Heller down in the Gracious Palms elevator. Heller, I could see in the elevator mirror, was dressed in a white, V-neck sweater over a sea-green silk shirt. He was wearing slacks to match the shirt. His red baseball cap was on the back of his blond head. I wondered dully how Heller always managed to look so neat and yet so casual. Maybe if I had looked like that, Utanc would have paid more attention to me.

Bang-Bang was in a severely tailored black suit, black shirt and white tie—the typical gangster setup. But he was wearing an old, leather, taxi driver's cap that looked so out of place with his suit that it seemed to be an incomplete disguise.

"But I tell you it IS important!" Bang-Bang was saying. He seemed very agitated. "I came right down here! There was your name, right on the bulletin board! It had a time and everything! PSYCHIATRIC CONSULTATION!"

"I know," said Heller. "But is that really bad?"

"Oh, Jesus Christ, yes!" said Bang-Bang. "They must think you're loopy! I see you just don't grab at the seriousness of it, Jet."

So it was Jet, now. Must have gotten it from Izzy.

"Well, I know," said Heller. "But..."

"They're mind benders!" said Bang-Bang. "Shrinks! They can put you in the slammer the rest of your life with no charges. You can't even turn state's evidence or take the Fifth! They got no sense of legality but the law and fuzz is all behind them."

They were down at the garage level now and walking through the garage.

"But if..." Heller tried to say.

"You don't get it," said Bang-Bang. "They just sign an order and put you away with the loonies. They jam you full of drugs and fry your brains! They even take your skull apart with an ice pick! They ain't happy unless you're a complete vegetable! And you don't have to have done nothing! The government depends on them completely to do away with birds they don't want around!"

"Well, well," said Heller. "That sounds pretty bad."

"It IS bad. And these shrinks are the looniest of the lot!"

They had arrived at a car.

It was the old, old Really Red cab! And it certainly looked different! It was a shining orange. It was all groomed up. It had no chipped windows. As Heller opened the door to get in back, a dome light came on and I could see shiny new leather upholstery. It looked like a brand-new antique!

Bang-Bang slammed the door behind Heller and then jumped under the wheel in front. He started the cab up. The engine roared into life and then purred as he backed it out of its stall.

They shot out of the basement garage and headed east. A big sign said:

Franklin D. Roosevelt Drive

Bang-Bang shot into the traffic stream, heading north. Heller was mainly watching the East River beside them, sparkling in the morning sun. But I could see on peripheral vision that Bang-Bang must think he was flying a whirlybird, the way he ignored imminent tail collisions and went through holes that didn't seem to exist.

He also wasn't watching his driving. He yelled back through the open divider, "Maybe they got onto us." Then he said, "Maybe they found out I was a marine. They know all marines is crazy."

He caused a limousine to dodge out of his way and seemed to be trying to part a semi-trailer from its cab. "Hey," he yelled back to Heller, "I got a great idea. Maybe we just ought to blow up the place!"

With a squeal of brakes and several skids he was onto 168th Street. He rolled to a stop in a taxi rank. He jumped out and opened the door for Heller. When Heller was on the sidewalk, Bang-Bang dropped a sign over the door label. The sign said Out of Service Until Inspected by the Bomb Squad.

Bang-Bang pointed. "It's office sixty-four, it said. Doctor Kutzbrain. I'd do this for you, kid, only I ain't got many brains to spare. Now, don't let them put any straitjacket on you. They don't even allow a phone call. So just run if it looks bad. I'll keep the engine going for a quick getaway."

Bang-Bang reached into the cab and put the flag down. A police radio at once turned on. It was a dummy meter. Illegal!

Heller went in and was shortly giving all sorts of particulars to a receptionist in nurse's costume. He showed her his student papers. Then he filled out a long form about previous mental illnesses by writing on it, *Prevailing opinion in dispute.*

"You can go in now. You don't have an appointment with Doctor Schitz, so I don't have to sedate you first." The nurse pushed him through a door.

Doctor Kutzbrain was peeling an apple at his desk. His hair stood out straight on either side of his head. His glasses were so thick they made his eyes look like black carp swimming in bowls.

"Is this Lizzie Borden?" said Doctor Kutzbrain. He cut himself and swore.

"This is Jerome Terrance Wister, the engineering student you asked to see," said the nurse. Then added, "I think." She laid the card on the desk.

"Too bad you never seem to come up with Lizzie Borden," said the doctor. "Now, I could have done a lot with that case. Could have gotten rid of thousands of parents." He cut himself again. Then he lowered his head and peered at Heller. "What did you say your name was?"

"Jerome Terrance Wister," said the nurse. "You know. *That* one. I'll leave you two now. Don't be naughty. Unless I'm here, that is." She closed the door behind her.

"Well, Borden," said the doctor. "This is pretty grave. Cutting up your parents that way with an axe. Pretty grave. Pardon the Freudian slip."

I was pretty interested, actually. I might learn something new about psychology so I paid close attention to what the doctor was saying.

"Ouch, (bleep) it," he said. He had cut himself again.

He threw the apple in the wastebasket and started to chew on the knife.

Heller pushed the card the nurse had left so it could be seen by the doctor.

"Aha!" said the doctor. "Two names! Now that is a very revealing symptom. Two names. Invites schizophrenia of the older type."

"Two names?" said Heller in a wary voice.

"Yes. It's right here on the card. Jerome and Terrance. Two names. Were you twins? No." He waved the knife at Heller. "There is no reason to beat around the bush, Jerome or Terrance or whatever you might call yourself in the next few minutes." He saw he was holding the knife. He looked at Heller sadly. "Why did you eat my apple?"

The doctor threshed around in a desk drawer for a bit. "Where is that folder? Very grave case."

He came up holding some paper and a pair of scissors. He began to cut the paper into the shape of a paper doll. Then, disgustedly, he said, "No, that wasn't what I was looking for. Why are you here, Borden?"

"You sent for me: Wister," said Heller.

"AH!" said the doctor. "That clears that up. I was looking for the *folder!* Yes." He dug into the drawer again, removed some balls of twine and with reluctance laid aside a top.

"The folder," said Heller. "Is it that one on your desk?"

"Precisely," said Doctor Kutzbrain. He found it and opened it up. He cleared his throat. He read. He said, "Now, she keeps talking about she is going to do everything to make you fail."

"Who?"

"Miss Simmons, your Nature Appreciation professor, that's who. She is in the Calming Ward just now. Now, Borden, such a reaction is, of course, the normal female reaction to a male. It is technically called the 'black widow spider gene syndrome.' You see, Borden, it is all a matter of evolution. Men evolved from reptiles. That is a scientific, indisputable fact. But women, Borden, evolved from black widow spiders and that, too, is a scientific, indisputable fact. It is proven by my own paper on it. But I see that I am talking above your head. However, those spiders you see up on the ceiling aren't mine. They were left by the last patient. Do you follow me," he consulted the card, "Jerome?"

"Quite clear," said Heller.

"Good. Now, the fact that women have this reaction to men is disturbing only because it is rational. You see," he consulted the card, "Terrance, everything a mental patient thinks or says is a delusion. When a person is in a mental ward, they are, of course, a mental patient. So anything she is saying is a delusion. Do you follow me," he consulted the card, "Empire University?"

"Very closely," said Heller.

"So obviously, if she says you are a good man, you aren't. But she is not saying you are a good man. She is saying you are an atom bomb. So, of course, you aren't. You must be some other kind of bomb. A hydrogen, perhaps? Come, tell me truthfully," he consulted the card, "Gracious Palms, you can confide in me. I am bound by the Hippocratic oath sometimes. Except in police matters, of course.

"But to get on with this interview, it says here that Miss Simmons keeps screaming you killed eight men with your bare feet and she even got loose one day and got to a call box and phoned the police."

Heller's hands tightened on the arms of the interview chair.

"They came, of course," said Doctor Kutzbrain. "Yes, it all comes back to me now even though it was several days ago. We cooperate very closely with the police.

It seems they had noticed eight bodies in a park. Now, what do you think of that?"

Heller's grip tightened on the chair arms.

"However," he consulted the card, "New York, you must remember what I told you about the black widow gene, evolutionary proven, scientific fact concerning women. It was a clear case of guilt transference. A role reversal, you know. She lured those poor, innocent men into the park and got them fighting over her so that she could enjoy both being raped and watching the mad male natural rivalry explode into mutual murder to further exploit and gratify her natural sexual appetites.

"Now, the police had another theory they had been working on which was that two rival gangs were using corpses to mark out the boundaries of mutually disputed territory. We teach the police, you know, and many wild animals mark out precise territories. But in this case, they were applying an incorrect theory.

"I pointed this out and proved it to them by showing them my own paper on the black widow gene evolution of women. They then understood that it was the natural thing for a woman to do and they marked down the findings of lure-rape-murder for sexual titillation on the case and closed it. Miss Simmons, already being in the psychopathic ward, therefore is insane and that is how the case came to be closed."

"You're going to keep Miss Simmons locked up?" said Heller.

"Oh, no! It is totally against professional ethics not to let the criminally insane loose on the public. But maybe, just this once, to oblige them down at City Hall—for we must serve them, after all, since they pay us—we will keep her inside for a while. She's given the Tactical Police Force a lot of trouble, you know. Something about bomb protests. If people want to be bombs, let them be bombs. One should never interfere with personal liberty. Do you follow," he consulted the card again. But he didn't see a name. He said, "... 'Advices'? 'Advices'? It says here you are called to an interview for advices."

He sat back and he thought. He pursed his lips and he stroked them. Then he looked at the Simmons folder and massaged his forehead. "Well," he said, at last, "the only advice I can give you is that when you find stray women lying about with broken legs, leave them alone." He thought for a moment. "Yes. Just leave them alone!"

"Is Miss Simmons going to come back on teaching staff?" said Heller.

"Why do you ask that?" said Doctor Kutzbrain.

"If she's insane, how can she teach?"

"Oh, nonsense," said the doctor. "If she's insane, it won't make any difference. All bright people have to be at least neurotic. So if she's insane, that makes her a genius, so of course she can teach!" He looked at the folder. "It says here she must be released in time to take her class in the next semester. What gave you the insane idea that insane people couldn't teach school? You'd have to be insane even to try it!"

Because the doctor had picked up the scissors and the paper again, Heller must have thought the interview was concluded for he started to get up.

Doctor Kutzbrain was instantly distracted and cut himself. He reached out a hand and urgently waved Heller to sit back down.

"I just remembered why you were sent for!" said the doctor. "My God, yes. It came to me like a flash." He pawed through the folder hurriedly. "It was important, too. It refers to us. To our own hospital staff. And they come first!"

He dredged up a huge red sheet. It had *URGENT* all across the top of it. "Aha! I knew we'd get down to this! The hospital staff is complaining about the litter you are making for them!"

"Me?"

"Indeed so!" said Doctor Kutzbrain triumphantly. "This is an important staff! They have to give drug injections every hour on the hour to themselves and the patients. They have to shock whole wards, morning, noon and night. They haven't got time to be cleaning the floor!"

The doctor leaned forward and shook an accusing finger at Heller. "She is tearing up the flowers you send to bits! She is stamping them into the concrete! She is slamming them into the toilets and clogging all the plumbing! SO, STOP SENDING HER FLOWERS AT ONCE! DO YOU HEAR?"

Heller drew back from the intimidating finger and nodded.

Doctor Kutzbrain threw the folder into the wastebasket, picked up his scissors and cut himself. "End of student psychiatric interview! NURSE SCREW! Send in Borden now!"

Heller went out, taking the interview order card with him. He firmly made the nurse sign it off as completed.

He went outside to where Bang-Bang alertly had the motor running.

Bang-Bang got out and elaborately wiped the inside of his leather cap sweatband. "You didn't *run* out, so I assume you got away." He opened the old cab's shining door. He took a bag, apparently dynamite, off the seat. "I guess we won't be blowing up the place today."

Heller got in. Bang-Bang closed the door, removed the sign, threw the bag on the front floorboards and got in. He put up the flag and the police radio went off.

Heller said, "Bang-Bang, those people are crazy!"

"So, hell, what's news? Everybody knows *that.* Where we going now?"

"If there's nothing more up here, I better get to the office."

"Heigh-ho, Silver!" said Bang-Bang and rushed the cab perilously out into the traffic. It made me kind of giddy watching the viewscreen, streets and signs and trucks flashing about.

I tried to concentrate on the interview. There must be a lot there to be learned. But actually, I myself was far too sick at heart about myself to concentrate.

Chapter 2

Heller was not paying any attention to Bang-Bang's driving. He reached into a rucksack and pulled out a textbook. It was a paper-covered text and on the top of it was written in pencil:

> *You asked what Marketing was. This simplified text is recommended.*
>
> *Izzy*

What was a combat engineer doing going off into a subject like marketing? One more thread in the crazy pattern he was weaving!

Evidently, he had already almost finished the book, for there was a marker near the end. He opened it up and while, as seen in his peripheral vision, Bang-Bang sought to separate nurses from their baby carriages and massive trailers from their cabs, Heller demolished the remainder of the text.

There was one page at the end. It only had one thing on it: a paragraph. It said, *To integrate his grasp of the subject, the student must now do a complete marketing project, getting a specific product wanted and accepted by consumers.*

Heller sat there looking out. His eyes were picking out advertising signs. He watched quite a few go by.

Then his eyes unfocused, a thing I had seen him do before when he was thinking deeply. To himself he said, "Beans? Bootleg whiskey? Seagulls? Shoes? Bunion powder? No, no, no. Oh, a survey! I haven't done a consumer survey."

He leaned forward and yelled through the mainly closed partition, "Bang-Bang! If you were a consumer, what would you really want to consume the most of?"

Bang-Bang skidded with screeching tires around a street-under-repair obstruction as he yelled back. "I'll let you in on something if you promise not to spread it around." He mounted a curb and got around a produce truck. "Everybody thinks I'm called Bang-Bang because of explosives. That ain't so." He careened past a fire truck. "Cherubino can tell you. I been called Bang-Bang since I was fourteen." He leaped the cab lightly over an open manhole cover. "The reason I'm called Bang-Bang is because of girls. If Babe knew I was going in and out of the Gracious Palms, she'd have a fit!"

"So the answer to the question of what you'd consume the most of is girls."

"And girls and girls!" Bang-Bang yelled back, narrowly missing one on a crosswalk to prove his point.

Heller sat back. "Girls. Hm." He made a note on the inside back leaf of the marketing book, *"Survey done. Item: girls."*

After that harrowing ride that violated all laws of traffic and nature, Bang-Bang let Heller out at the main entrance of the Empire State Building with a yell that he'd put the taxi in their parking lot as he drove away.

Heller looked up. It made me dizzy: the building, even though you couldn't see the top from the street or even a quarter of its height, seemed like it was going into the clouds.

He threaded his way through the hurrying throngs. He walked past the ranks of express and other kinds of elevators and entered the one that, apparently, had its first stop on his floor. No one paid him any attention.

He got out. Their hall had changed. It had more brass plates and it had palms at intervals. I had not remembered how really vast that half a floor of theirs was!

He found Izzy in the communications room. "Hi, Izzy!" he said above the roar and chatter of teletype machines. "How's it?"

Izzy smiled at him wanly, probably the most smile Izzy could manage. He was still in a Salvation Army Good Will suit. His horn-rimmed glasses accentuated his beak of a nose. "I hoped you wouldn't be in until things were better," said Izzy. He held up a sheet. "We just lost on the ruble exchange with Italy. It's an awful strain. We can't seem to get the hundred thousand up above a half million. Conditions are so uncertain."

"Well, we're paying the rent," said Heller.

"Oh, we're not just here to pay rent," said Izzy. "If corporations are to take over governments, we ought to be thinking in acceptable sums like trillions."

"We will," said Heller cheerfully. "Now, what was so urgent?"

"Oh, dear," said Izzy. "I'm afraid I'm not ready for that, either."

Heller was beckoning. They went out and walked

and walked past doors and doors with different nameplates. It gave me a melancholy pleasure to see that several girls, obviously their own employees—possibly students working part time, from their appearance—didn't even say hello to Heller but hurried on by on their errands with their burdens.

They had stopped before a door. The sign said:

Maysabongo Eastern United States Legation
Republic of Maysabongo
Long Live Dictator Ahmed Allah!

Izzy was fumbling in his case for keys. He must be carrying ten pounds of them. He opened the door, threw on the lights.

The decor was bamboo. Sets of vicious-looking swords adorned the otherwise bare white plaster walls. The obvious coat of arms—crossed assault rifles—was sitting against a desk.

"You got the vice-consular appointments, didn't you?" said Heller.

"Yes, Mr. Jet. They're there on the desk. Here's Bang-Bang's; here's mine. Ah, yes. And here is yours."

Heller took his and glanced at it. It made him a Consul of Maysabongo but I couldn't see the rest of it. He put it in his pocket.

"And you got the company formed," said Heller.

"Oh, yes. Wonderful Oil for Maysabongo, Limited, incorporated in Maysabongo, registered to do business, etc. But you aren't a director, Mr. Jet. They have to be Abie Cohen and his wife. You see, I must be firm, as I'm responsible for you, that you have no connection with any of these corporations. Not even anything a Justice Department black-bag job can find. That attorney Mr. Bury is pretty vicious, and Rockecenter controls the

Justice Department, amongst everything else. A frightening man."

"I don't see the problem."

"Well, it's the mural. The deputy delegate is demanding that it should be a portrait of Harlotta."

"I think I can get her to pose."

"It isn't the model, Mr. Jet. The model problem we have is the Tahiti mural. And we do have other model problems despite this local agency here. No, the problem, Mr. Jet, is the *painters!*"

"I thought you had some."

"I don't think you'll approve. I have some waiting and the samples are in your office but . . . but . . ."

Heller told him to lock the legation back up and walked off down a long, long, long hall past doors, doors, doors, toward his office.

Izzy was trotting along beside Heller. "I really don't think I'm ready to show you their work."

"You found some artists, didn't you?" said Jet.

"Yes. But they have a nonconventional style. They're antiestablishment, which should win friends. But they're total nonconformists. They barely squeaked through art school at Empire: their professors hated them. They tried to take up residence in Soho, the new New York art colony, and they were ostracized and ordered out.

"They won't prostitute their art by working for advertising companies, so they are starving and have no place to go."

"Prostitute their art," said Heller. "Hmm. Well, what's this art style that's so bad?"

"It's called 'neorealism.' When they paint a sailboat, it looks like a sailboat. It's pretty revolutionary! And very daring, very much into the teeth of all modern trends. Their people look like people!"

They were into Heller's office now. It looked like half an acre of white shag. Heller went over and opened an air vent. The view of lower Manhattan was brilliant in the September sun.

"Sure smells of paint," said Heller. He turned. And there, all lined up against the entrance-door wall, were dozens of canvases.

Heller looked at them. He went nearer. "But they're gorgeous!"

Actually, they were not up to Voltarian standards. But they were a lot better than most art seen on the planet.

Izzy said, "Well, technically they are quite good. But they went astray after studying pictures by Rembrandt and Vermeer and Michelangelo. They went totally out of step with the art world. One even refused to run a tricycle over paint tubes and call it a picture in spite of a handsome commission. And the others stood up for him. It's sort of a pathetic case. They're hunted now and scorned."

Heller picked up a large canvas. It was a flesh-colored girl with a red shawl about her shoulders, balancing an orange pottery jug on her head. If I'd been in a better mood, I would have called it very arousing. He picked up another. It was a painting of a beautiful girl on a sofa, naked, holding a cat up in the air with her two hands. By some trick, even on my two-dimensional screen, it looked a bit three-dimensional. He took another: it was a girl in profile biting a rose off a live-looking rose bush—just her face, her teeth and the rose.

"Where are these guys?" said Heller.

"There're eight of them. They're down in my anteroom having kittens! But Mr. Jet, I must point out. This art is not in the mode! That cat looks like a *cat!* Those girls look like *girls!* I don't . . ."

"I agree we should think this over," said Heller.

"Oh, thank heavens."

Heller sat down at his desk. "You got the school things all arranged."

"Oh, yes," said Izzy, offendedly. "You are answering all roll calls. Your quizzes are being handed in. All your lab work is being done. And we don't have to take any more notes or recordings. All of last year's lectures to those same classes are there in mimeograph form in your top file cabinet. You are even taking gym. Bang-Bang is doing well on ROTC. And here is a beeper to wear in case you are suddenly summoned." He handed it over. "I hope this is easier for you now."

"Great way to go to college," said Heller. "I handled the psychiatric interview this morning, but Miss Simmons will be riding my tail next semester."

"I am so sorry I can't help you there. I strongly advise against violence. It's really so unbusinesslike. Can she be bought off?"

"Not a chance," said Heller.

"So you may fail after all."

Bang-Bang came in.

Heller said, "Well, I've decided. Bang-Bang, will our cab hold eleven?"

"Yikes!" said Bang-Bang.

"It's illegal," said Izzy.

"And all these canvases?" said Jet.

"We'll try," said Bang-Bang.

"Collect your painters," said Heller to Izzy. "Bring them and these canvases down front."

"Where we going?" said Izzy, in dismay.

"Marketing," said Heller. "We're going marketing."

"Look," said Izzy. "I can buy anything you need. I can get it for you wholesale."

"Not that kind of marketing. We're going marketing marketing."

"Oh, the book I got you," said Izzy. "What are we going to market?"

"The survey said 'girls.'"

"But that's illegal!" said Izzy.

"You have to do class assignments honestly," said Heller. "And that's what the survey said. So, wouldn't it be illegal to try to get an illegal pass on a subject?"

"That's very true," said Izzy. "You have no choice! If the survey said girls, it will have to be girls."

A few minutes later, the canvases were lashed to the carrying rack on top and the mob somehow squeezed into the old cab.

They went rocketing up Fifth Avenue.

Chapter 3

"Now, gentlemen," said Heller to the paint-smocked mass, which was nine people in a space meant for five—Izzy and Bang-Bang were up front—"I don't want you to look on this as prostituting your art."

A nearby, bearded face drew back as much as it could. A real flinch. "We refuse to change off from neo-realism!"

"For Heavens' sake, don't!" said Heller. "But you'll see what I mean shortly."

They went roaring into the garage at the Gracious Palms. They jammed into the elevator.

Heller walked into Vantagio's office. Vantagio was sitting at his desk. He obviously had a bit of a hangover. He frowned at the mob he saw coming in behind Heller.

"We want to paint Minette," said Heller.

This was a little bit direct for Vantagio at this hour. "Good morning, kid. Would you like to introduce your friends?"

Heller did. Then he said, "We have a bare wall and it needs a bare girl. We deal only in the authentic. It's for the Beautiful Tahiti Gilt-Edged Beaches Wonder Corporation. Minette is the only beautiful Tahitian I know of."

"Well, take her along, kid. The UN session doesn't start until next week so we're not peak load. I'm sure Minette will do what you tell her so take her along to the Empire State."

"No," said Heller. "Izzy here," and he glanced at Izzy who obviously didn't know where he was or what was coming, "has a great idea. Come along."

Heller went out in the lobby. He opened a closet and rolled out a little platform they must use for something. He began to push it across the lobby. A houseman instantly jumped to help him. Heller put it in the far corner, near the street door.

Then he went and got a painter. He stood him near the platform. Then he got an easel from their gear and stood it up in front of the painter, who, seeing an easel, promptly put a framed blank canvas on it.

Heller and the houseman moved a couple of palms in pots up on the platform to the back.

Heller went to the phone and hit some numbers.

"Who ees thees?" Minette's voice. "I am not dress'. It ees too earlee!"

"You sure you got no clothes on?" said Heller.

"Oh, 'ello, pretty boy. I come right een!"

"No," said Heller. "Grab your grass skirt and some flowers for your hair and come down in the lobby!"

"Ze lobby? You mos' be jokeeng. Vantagio..."

Heller handed Vantagio the phone. Vantagio said, "The kid is changing the decor, Minette. Anything is liable to happen. Come down."

A couple of diplomats were leaving in somewhat tousled condition. They saw the painter standing there with a blank canvas. They stopped.

An early-day demander, a big black, walked in the front door. He saw the blank canvas and stopped.

A limousine drew up and spilled out three Moroccans. They entered, saw the blank canvas and stopped.

Minette arrived. She was wearing a grass skirt and had hibiscus in her hair. Heller put her on the platform. The painter posed her. He began to paint.

"Allah forbids the rendition of live figures," said a Moroccan. But he stood closer to get a better look.

A cab drew up and two diplomats got out. They started to walk to the desk but stopped and watched the painting.

Heller beckoned to Vantagio, Izzy and the other painters. He drew them back into Vantagio's office.

"You're going to cost us a fortune if you stop everybody who comes in that door," said Vantagio.

"Ah," said Heller, and he waved his hands just like an Italian, "think of the word of mouth. The advertising!"

"Maybe you better tell me this idea," said Vantagio, sitting down at his desk.

"Well," said Heller. "Izzy figured it this way. Now, this is strictly between you and Izzy but I will outline it. I told him I thought it was great.

"It goes like this. The UN is just going into session. We put an artist, easel and platform in the lobby." He turned to the painters. "How long does it take you to paint a really good, big portrait?"

They disagreed. But it seemed like anything from twelve hours to a week.

"Now, every night," Heller told Vantagio, "for one whole week, a good artist will be there in the lobby painting a nude. And every week, the painting and the nude will change. We will choose the girls who epitomize the beauty of each country. And each week, you feature a different country."

Vantagio sat up straight. Then he got up and began to pace, a bit excited.

"It has political advantages! Bargaining power!" said Vantagio. "They will push and prod to get their country featured early in the program! They will want to have a part in conceiving the subject matter."

Heller made an Italian gesture. "Ah, there you have it, Vantagio. Depend on you to grasp the nuance! This is a marketing program aimed at expansion and penetration. Your products will become known in every land. It puts a Gracious Palms commercial in every one of the top offices of every nation. And they will pay handsomely to exhibit the commercial itself! What the Gracious Palms needs is more penetration. Consumer desire will be aroused in every country on the planet and you will have a better market projection into your resources!"

Vantagio peeked out into the lobby. Heller stepped behind him. Minette, on the platform, had assumed pose after pose, despite the painter's pleas and was now exhibiting one whole leg while she cupped her breasts and smiled lasciviously at the crowd. The original ones who had paused were now feverishly signing up at the desk. Another was on the phone loudly telling his chief delegate he should drop whatever he was doing and rush over. The crowd around the easel had swelled.

"You see," said Heller, "it makes it all refined. It puts it in the world of art. The positioning of the

Gracious Palms is upgraded to number one instead of just a horizontal graph. It will be on top!"

Vantagio went back into his office. He began to pace up and down excitedly. Then he stopped and made an expansive Italian gesture. With glowing, visionary eyes, he said, "I can see it now! We've been taking it lying down! We've been guilty of practicing seasonal *interruptus.* We can spread this climax into a more bilateral approach, even multilateral. We've been practicing non-intervention! We have been underprivileging certain elite minorities!" Vantagio pounded a fist into his palm. "We need a wider spread internationally! And it will give us more consumer flow! They'll lap it up!"

Izzy said, "You can hang a whole gallery here in the lobby with the paintings for sale at very fancy prices. And you can put forms on the counter they can fill out to have girls of their choice painted for their offices and special gift forms for paintings so heads of state and leading politicians can come here and pick out a girl to be painted. And we can handle special trips for artists to go to their countries on special commission, accompanied by PRs to run beauty contests to select Miss Country Name with the grand prize of training and employment at the Gracious Palms. I just this minute formed a corporation called True Allure Fine Arts International, Incorporated—probably in Greece as we don't have one there—and these artists are all under contract to it. Our prices are high and the commission we get is twenty-five percent!"

"Excellentissimo!" cried Vantagio, lapsing into Italian from excitement. "*D'accordo!* Agreed!"

"I told you Izzy was pregnant with ideas," said Heller.

"The slack season!" said Vantagio. "Things go limp

nine months of the year! This will stiffen up foreign trade!"

"We only want ten percent of the gross increase over last year's net," said Izzy.

"Marvelous!" said Vantagio.

Heller turned to the seven remaining painters who were standing there a bit goggle-eyed. "Now, I hope you gentlemen don't think you will be prostituting your art."

"Oh, no!" said the leading painter. "The proposition is too hard to refuse!" Behind him the others cried their assent.

"The name of the program," said Heller, "is Whore of the Week."

They all cheered.

The leading painter said, "Mister, whatever your name is, you're something out of this world!"

"Keep it to yourself," said Heller.

Izzy rushed around and got contract signatures from all eight painters on blank sheets he said he'd fill in. He scribbled a *Memorandum Agreement In Principle* and Vantagio signed it.

Then they left. As Heller walked out with Izzy, he said, "So that was my marketing project. Did I pass, Izzy?"

"Oy," said Izzy. "Just plain 'oy,' Mr. Jet!"

As they climbed into the cab, Izzy and Heller in back, Heller said, "Well, that was just fun mostly. But it also has its place."

"Fun?" said Izzy. "With neorealism in demand by the tops of every government, it will sweep the world! That project is worth millions! And every real revolution has to have its own art form. Neorealism! Things that look like what they are! Absolutely revolutionary in itself! Neorealism, the art of the people!"

Bang-Bang zoomed the cab out of the garage, heading back to the office. After a bit, Heller said, "Izzy. I've been checking it over and I think we can consider Phase One of the Master Plan complete."

I instantly went into a spin. Even my dulled senses could smell danger. WHAT plan?

In haste I prepared to go back through the older recorded strips. And a moment later, I stared at my equipment in horror. In all my recent travail, I had overlooked loading the recording strip reservoir! I didn't have any back track to look at!

WHAT PLAN!?!?!

Geological surveys and a legation and a diploma and Gods knew what else. I knew Heller! This would all come together some way with a huge black eye for me. Death, even!

A sort of savage feeling began to grip me. Heller and all this success with women. Wasn't it his fault that I had gotten into all this mess in the first place? And if he hadn't been distracting me, I wouldn't be in any trouble with Utanc!

A burning, bitter hatred of Heller began to sear through me.

Chapter 4

The following day, I was wandering about after a sleepless night and bitter morning and chanced to look at the viewscreen.

I was startled to see Heller was driving along in the cab! There was no sign of Bang-Bang and, as he turned to check a sign, there was nobody in the back seat!

He was driving in New York! It was illegal! By his license, he was not yet eighteen!

I looked at my watch. It was not yet 6:00 A.M. in Heller's zone!

With a savage curse, I sat down to watch and study this. He was off on some new tack!

I watched for signs. He was on Franklin D. Roosevelt Drive and by the horizon light of dawn, he was travelling north. I got out an Octopus Oil Company map of that area. Where was he going? Why?

The old cab was really purring. Heller seemed quite happy and relaxed. He was going faster than Bang-Bang drove but he didn't seem to be having any trouble.

By the signs, he was going to the Bronx. I tried to figure out what was in the Bronx that would interest him. I couldn't come up with anything.

Now he was paying a toll. He left the bridge behind him. Now he was ignoring Bronx signs. He was spotting U.S. 278. Throg's Neck? Was he going to Throg's Neck? No. Now he was on Hutchinson River Parkway. White Plains? Was he going to White Plains? No, he passed that turnoff. Boston? Ah, New Brunswick, Canada! He must be running away to leave the country.

I instantly got up to send Raht and Terb a message. Heller would be going out of the range of the activator-receiver, to say nothing of the 831 Relayer!

I halted. My Gods, due to all the disturbance Heller was guilty of, I had forgotten to give Raht and Terb their receiver and decoder! I was not in contact with them!

Helplessly, I sat and watched the viewer.

I cursed him. This was all his fault. He hadn't gone over this cursed "Master Plan" with anyone while I was watching!

The sun was up now where he was. He seemed to

be appreciating the green trees and grass that flowed by, for he certainly wasn't paying much attention to his driving. Maybe somebody would consider that scenery beautiful if they were less under the hammer of fate than I was.

He went through a toll gate and was on a toll road, the New England Thruway. His eye lingered on a sign. Stamford! He was in Connecticut!

And then I got my first clue. Looking at some very dark green trees, he said, "Old Cap Duggan was right! You are a beautiful country."

Cap Duggan! The Geological Survey! But what had they discussed? Gold in Alaska? Maybe he was going to Alaska! But this wasn't the route to Alaska. And you wouldn't be driving a bright orange, vintage antique, New York taxicab to Alaska. You'd go in a dog sled! I knew the planet! But maybe he had some cunning deception plan in mind. I knew no good would come of his ROTC studying for the Army's G-2!

He went right on by any opportunity to turn off into Stamford. But just as my attention was beginning to relax, off to his right he went and was on a bad state highway. A sign said Noroton Point lay in that direction.

Soon, he stopped the cab and got out.

He was standing on a beach. A vast expanse of water spread before him, a solid sheet of gold in the morning sunlight. He walked along the sand. He seemed to be enjoying the flow of ocean air. He took several breaths as though it tasted good.

He said, "They haven't completely wrecked you yet, old planet." Then he walked a ways and saw an oil scum. He amended what he had said. "But they're working on it pretty hard."

He walked further. Some sandpipers did a running walk away from him. Some gulls wheeled overhead. The surf, golden-tipped, purled up the beach toward his toes.

"It's a shame," he said. "You're such a pretty planet." Then, with sudden determination, he said, "I better get to work while you're still habitable!"

He trotted north. He was looking at a place where a river emptied into the sea. "Aha," he said. "That's it!"

He ran back to the cab, jumped in and was soon roaring along. He bypassed the New England Thruway, went through a fair-sized city and continued on into a hilly countryside, green and much of it wild.

He stopped. He unrolled a Geological Survey map. It seemed to have every house on it.

He tossed down the roll and turned the cab from the state highway he had been on straight off into a cow track!

He seemed to be looking for markers. He found an aged milepost. Right there on the cow track! It was so weathered you could hardly read it. Then I worked it out. He was on an ancient, abandoned road!

With rhododendrons and laurel and weeds whipping at the old cab's fenders, he came at length to some buildings. They didn't look like a farm. What did they look like? Then a thoroughly rusted sign told all: it was an abandoned service station now doing duty, with some chicken coops in the back, as a sort of makeshift residence.

A small plume of smoke was coming from a chimney.

Heller knocked on a rickety door.

A very old woman opened it. Suddenly, from her eye misdirection, I could tell she was blind.

"I'm the young fellow who called yesterday from New York," said Heller in a gentle voice.

"Oh, sakes alive. Come in, come in and sit. Have some coffee." Heller did and she bustled about and got him some coffee.

"I am surely glad you could drive in," she said.

"There ain't been a car on that road since my husband died. How'd you find this place anyway?"

"You're still on the map, ma'am," said Heller in a strong New England accent.

"Well, I do declare it's a comfort not to be spilled off the country complete!" She groped for the chair and sat down, not quite facing him. "This used to be a busy place until they changed all the roads. Them dang-blast commissioners is always changing things. Be moving these hills off next! Some more coffee?"

I blinked. How did she know his cup had been emptied?

"No, thanks," said Heller. "Now, you said, ma'am, that the old repair shop could be locked up tightly and the roof was still sound. Could I see it?"

She got some keys and shortly had groped along a wall and around the building and had the place open. It was a space big enough for several cars, greasepits in the floor, windows sealed.

"Looks fine," said Heller. "I'd like to rent it for a few months."

"Well, a little rent would help in these inflation times. What would you be willing to pay?"

"A hundred a month."

"A hundred a month! Sakes alive! You could have the whole place for half that and the chickens, too!"

"Well, there'll be two cars here," said Heller.

"Oh."

"Off and on. Does anyone ever come here, ma'am?"

"My niece, every couple days, to see if I'm all right. But since I drivv some intruders off with a shotgun, nary a soul except my niece."

"It's a deal, then," said Heller. "Mind if I drive a car in here now? I got to make some adjustments."

"Go right ahead! There's plenty of tools if you don't mind rust."

He gave her a hundred and she gave him some keys. He drove the cab in.

And then he did something that showed the cunning and treachery I had always hated in him.

He closed up the doors from within.

He opened a bag and got out paper rolls and he taped it across all the window insides. He turned on the old electric bulbs of the place.

Then, (bleep) him, he took a small floodlight out of his bag and pointed it at the side of the cab, and the area turned BLACK!

The sign on the door vanished!

Playing the light over the whole cab, section by section, he was turning the glaring orange to a midnight ink!

Then I knew what it was. He was using a Voltarian preparation. He had had that man in Newark add it to the cab's paint! The light was giving it a color shift!

They use it in fancy Voltarian advertising signs. A beam passes over the sign and it turns blue, then a second beam of a different frequency passes over the sign and it turns red, by a shift of refraction frequency in the paint additive.

It didn't take him very long. Then he went around to the front and bent down, snapped a sort of cover off the license plate. He did the same thing in back.

Then he opened up the bag and got a little vial, put some liquid on his fingers and rubbed it over his face and into his hair. He put some on the back of his hands.

He sat in front of the rearview mirror, turned a dial on his light and played it over his head. He had black hair! Then he turned the dial again and played the light over his face and hands and he had dark brown, almost black face and hands. Then he put on a false black mustache.

The sly treachery of it!

But he wasn't that good. He still had blue eyes!

He had been wearing a black suit. He didn't change it. He got out a black slouch hat and put it on.

He stood back and looked at the cab. He got in and folded the meter down out of sight.

He opened up the garage and backed out.

At the house door, he said, "I'll be back and forth from time to time. I may be late or early."

"That's all right," said the old blind woman. "Just toot your horn twice so I'll know it's you. An' anybody else'll get drivv off with a shotgun!"

Off went a dark-brown Heller in a black car!

But he wasn't that smart. It still looked like a vintage New York cab, orange *or* black!

He seemed to know right where he was going. He drove into a town, looked at some street numbers and pulled up at an old house with a big sign:

Real Estate
Cyrus Aig

Heller knocked, was sent by a woman around to an office in the back.

"Cyrus Aig?" said Heller. "Me—English no not native tongue—got appointment?"

Cyrus Aig was a very, very old man. He turned away from his roll-top desk and eyed the stranger. "Glad you could make it. But I dunno if anything I got will suit. All the old barns and proppity like that gits bawt up by rich folks to make homes out of, y'know."

Heller had a roll of maps. "Actual, me look for mines, old."

"Oh, yes," said the aged realtor. "You did hev somethin' to say about that on the phone. Now, I done some lookin' at records. Somebody buyin' a mine here in the east is kinda out of my line. I git holt of old barns for rich folks to make homes out of. Sit down."

Heller sat in a rickety rocking chair.

"Could be a hundred years ago," said Cyrus Aig, "there might hev been a mine. But jus' because the name of the creek is Goldmine Creek ain't no reason it ever had a gold mine on it."

"This place," said Heller, pushing out the Geological Survey maps, "it show buildings on Goldmine Creek."

"Oh, that," said Cyrus. "Nobody been up in that area for years. That's wilderness. Ain't even a road in there. Wonder them government surveyors even went there. That's a valley with rocks. Cain't grow nothin' on it. Just two, three little hills. Creek runs through it. Half a century back that was the bootlegger roadhouse."

The old agent took the maps. "Yes, that's a fact. I was in there once when I was a kid. There was a highway run past it in them days. Now, see here. This creek runs down and turns here and then goes into the sea."

He got a road map. "But you can make out on that that they put a reservoir way up that creek near the source and the water didn't flow much anymore. And then they put two turnpikes across it before it reached Long Island Sound. So she don't work for bootlegging anymore."

"Me not see how . . ."

"Why, you couldn't run a shallow draft boat up it no more. Y'see, the bootleggers used to run their stuff in from the Atlantic, up the creek and to this roadhouse. Then they'd water it down, rebottle it and either serve it on the spot or run it down to New York through the gauntlet of hijackers."

He handed back the maps. "Was a time nobody'd go near that old roadhouse. Bodies! Haunted. But I even forgot it existed."

"Me mebbe buy," said Heller.

Cyrus Aig wearily got an old fishing hat. Heller followed him out. Using Cyrus Aig's rattletrap Ford they went to the courthouse and Cyrus looked into the records.

"Listed here as owned by John Smith of New York in care of this attorney they note here. Hundred and twenty acres of prime rocks."

Heller was writing down all the particulars and addresses. "If me buy, me give commission."

"Well, that's fine but you don't catch me thrashing around up there off the roads. I cain't even get out fishing lately. You sure you don't want an old barn? I got a couple of those in driving distance."

Heller went back to the house with him, jumped in the cab and was off. Thank Heavens he was still very well within the activator-receiver range. He wasn't more than thirty miles or so from New York! Whatever he was up to, I would at least know and be able to handle it if it proved dangerous.

Chapter 5

He headed north on U.S. 7. He was driving at a leisurely pace, looking about him at the hills and valleys and streams of Connecticut, apparently highly approving. A very rural scene, mostly picturesque like you see in paintings—I myself wouldn't like it at all. Too neat and serene.

Way ahead, although they probably didn't think it was visible, a police car was lying in wait for unwary speeders. Heller went by it at a crawl. It wasn't really a police car. It was a sheriff's car with a big star on the side of it. Two men were in the front seat, dressed in khaki. They had cowboy hats on. Deputy sheriffs, no doubt. They were taking it easy. From the litter on the ground around it, this was their favorite speed trap.

Heller went on. He was examining the left side of the road very carefully. Ahead, a difference showed in the embankment. I myself might have missed it.

He turned left and went on down the embankment! Right off the road into the brush! Just like that!

He must have been steering more by his sense of compass direction than whatever he thought he was driving on. He was going dead slow. Weeds were raking and whipping at the underside of the car.

A big bush was ahead. There seemed to be no way around it. He got out, took a machete from the car and cleared the bush away. Then he got back in and on he went.

It came to me that he must be following an old road not unlike the one to the ancient gas station but much more obscured. He even had to go around trees more than a third of a century old.

He went over a little rise. Ahead was what appeared to be a massive stand of maple trees and some evergreens. They were huge trees, fifty years old at least.

Just beyond them lay a streambed, only a trickle of water in it now, despite the high banks. The remains of a wooden bridge were collapsed into the stream.

Heller stopped the cab and got out. It really was a

wilderness. Several knolls were visible. There was flat ground but it was covered with rocks.

He walked around the fields. There was a flat place not too far from the trees. This seemed of interest to him.

He went down to the stream. A ledge of white outcrop with a red rust stain seemed to interest him. The stream had eaten down through it over the eons.

A small, unnatural hill caught his attention. He got a shovel and dug into it. It was just very fine white dirt. He put the shovel back in the car and took out a pack.

Only then did he pay any attention to the grove of huge trees. He walked straight into it.

Canopied and shadowed by the growth which must have matured long after the original place was built, masked by climbing vines and shrubs, there lay the roadhouse!

It sprawled. It had a veranda and wings. It was apparently built of the same rocks which lay in such abundance roundabout.

Heller walked up the stone steps to the front door. It was a big door. It was padlocked. Still, I wondered how, after nearly half a century, this place would still be there without the usual traces of vandalism. America is like that.

Heller took out a picklock and an oilcan and in almost no time at all had the padlock off! It startled me. Apparatus people weren't that fast at locks. Then I realized he was, after all, an engineer. He knew levers and tumblers intimately.

With his oilcan, he got to work on the hinges. The door, although a bit sagged, was not too hard to open. He examined its edge and then I saw why the place wasn't vandalized. That door was cored with armor plate!

He tapped a window. Bulletproof glass!

This place was a FORT!

He went back to the car and got a bag. He entered the main front room. He turned on a lamp he carried and set it down on a table.

The faded, drooping remains of what must have been the last party in the place hung forlornly from thick rafter beams. The gutted remains of Japanese waxed paper lanterns cast strange shadows against the ceiling.

He walked across what must have once been a polished dance floor, for he kicked off his spikes before he stepped on it.

He picked another lock and opened an inner door. The bar! A long piece of mahogany, little else in the way of furniture. He examined a broken mirror—a bullet hole.

There were other rooms—private party rooms and what once might have been overdecorated bedrooms. The kitchen had a big, wood-burning range—a rat had made a nest in the firebox, exiting and entering through the chimney.

The back door was also armor plate. And every outside window was bulletproof!

Heller found an office. The desk was still there. The papers were browned with age. He looked through them. Forty cases here and eighty there and an IOU for five hundred. One wondered if it had ever been paid.

There were framed photographs on the wall. Some were autographed with age-browned ink. *To Toots, Jimmy Walker* said one of a handsome young man. Jimmy Walker? The famous New York mayor?

Another attracted his attention. It was a lineup of stiffly standing young men. Four of them. They were holding submachine guns! Heller was reading the name signed under each one. Joe Corleone! He was second from the right. He looked like a kid of twenty!

Heller took a Voltar camera out of his bag, focused

in just on Joe Corleone and shot a copy, including the signature. Then he shot one of all four of them.

Ghosts indeed! "Holy Joe" had been pushing eighty-eight when he died. But he was a ghost now with all the rest of this roadhouse and this era.

Now Heller must have considered that he had amused himself enough. He began to move very fast. He took a metal bar from his pack and with great rapidity began to tap walls and floors. I knew enough about him now to know that he was echo-sounding. He must be looking for hidden rooms.

He found one. When he also found its entrance, it was just a closet.

He went on.

Then he trotted outside and began to hit the ground. He gave that up.

He got out a little meter and started to walk all around the house. He got a read. He stopped. He criss-crossed an area. He got more reads.

Heller must have worked it all out. He went straight to the bar and took soundings with his meter. It was the far end of the bar.

Using some oil, he shortly had a hinge working. The whole end of the bar slid aside and he was looking down some steps.

He went down.

He was in a cavern!

He walked along a tunnel and then shined a light down a shaft. If there had ever been any ladder there, it was gone now.

He examined the walls. "Granite," he muttered. Eventually he found some chiseled letters. They said:

Issiah Slocum
Hys Myne 1689

Heller examined some more galleries. He found some white quartz. He put it in his pocket.

There were the rotted remains of wooden cases in some of the galleries. The bootleggers had been using the mine to hide their hooch! And that's what had happened to the "lost mine" of Goldmine Creek!

Chapter 6

Heller locked the place back up but he used his own padlock on the front door. A massive lock! He wasn't learning that much from G-2. The brand-new padlock stood out with its gleaming brass!

He jumped into his car and, taking it easy, got back to the main road and ran along at normal speed back toward the town. He passed the speed trap once more. The sheriff's men were half-asleep.

Heller went into a restaurant. It was a nice place. It had a phone kiosk in its waiting room. Heller went into the phone booth. He dialed a number. Izzy answered.

"On target," said Heller. "It's A-okay!" My, he was getting slangy! With great rapidity he read off the data he had gotten at the courthouse, gave the realtor's name but added, "Not active in deal but send commission for PR value."

"Right," said Izzy. "Same corporate status as planned?"

"Right," said Heller. "Greater East Asia Co-Prosperity Sphere, Limited, of Maysabongo. My number here is . . ." and he gave it.

Heller went out of the phone booth and went to a

table. He sat down. A waitress came. "I'm afraid it's early for lunch. The stuffed shrimp won't be ready yet."

"Good," said Heller. "Five hamburgers, five Seven Ups."

I had expected there would be trouble with his black face. But he was in New England. The girl brought one hamburger and one Seven Up.

Heller ate and drank them.

The girl brought the next serving, one hamburger, one Seven Up. They were doing them one at a time! Nice place.

Heller got a paper and read it.

All the hamburgers and Seven Ups were gone and he topped it with a chocolate sundae.

The phone in the booth rang. Heller went over and answered.

Izzy's voice. "John Smith has been in a federal pen for years. He got life for negligence of bribery of J. Edgar Hoover. His mistress held on to the place for sentimental reasons but she died last year. Smith was going to let the place go for taxes as he had no way to pay them. I just phoned him and he's overjoyed. So's the warden as he's going to sell Smith a new cell. It's yours."

"Thank you," said Heller.

"Mr. Jet," said Izzy. "Don't get in any trouble, please. Connecticut is way out in the wilds. They may still have Indians there."

"Thanks for the warning," said Heller.

He paid his bill with a liberal tip and went out and jumped into his cab.

He turned north again, on the same highway.

And then, despite all Izzy had warned him of, Heller opened that cab up to eighty miles an hour!

He went *scorching* up that road.

And just before he came in sight of the speed trap, he started the cab weaving!

And just at the trap itself he veered onto the verge in a cloud of dust, shot back onto the road, went off the other side and came back on the highway!

Then he slowed to forty!

The crazy fool!

That sheriff's car came out of the trap like a fish leaping from the water after a mayfly!

Its lights went on. Its chortle racketed!

It came screaming up the road after him!

Heller went ahead just fast enough to keep a distance. But I knew that cab couldn't outrun a police car! It was geared down for sudden maneuvering!

The pursuer was almost upon him.

Heller skidded the cab to the left and plunged off the edge of the road!

He was on the same track he had been over before!

The old car bumped and lurched and swayed! It darted around trees! It swept along over the tops of weeds! It was heading toward the old roadhouse! Did Heller intend to fort up and shoot it out? What was he up to?

In the rearview mirror he caught glimpses of the police car. It was having very heavy weather of it. Heller slowed down!

Ahead was the grove which held the building.

Behind was the chortling, raving, flashing police car!

Ten yards short of the nearest trees, in an open area, Heller suddenly stopped!

He got out!

He tossed some sort of a folder on the front seat.

He adjusted his mustache.

On the left side of the cab, he planted his feet wide apart.

He put his hands out and leaned forward to support

his body against the car roof. He was assuming the classic frisk position.

With one last slither and bounce the police car jolted to a stop behind the cab. The chortling ceased with a dying snarl.

A deputy sheriff leaped out each side, guns drawn.

They stopped.

They looked around warily.

One walked up to Heller and began to frisk him.

Almost instantly he struck pay dirt!

He swept aside the tail of Heller's coat. There was a jerk. The deputy sheriff stepped around into Heller's view.

He was holding that gold damascene Llama .45!

"Ralph!" said the deputy. "Jesus Christ, look at this piece of jewelry!"

"What the hell is it?" said the other, coming closer.

"It's a God (bleeped) diamond-plated cannon, that's what."

"Lemme see that, George. Looks like one of them old-time gangster rods!"

"Naw, that ain't no Colt .45 ACP, Ralph."

"Yes, it is! It's just been engraved or something."

"Naw! Look there! This fancy picture on the side says it's a Maysabongo."

George said to Heller, "Hey, nigger. What the hell kind of a handgun is this thing?"

"Me no talk beautiful English," said Heller in a high-pitched voice. "English not native tongue."

Ralph said, "He's some kind of a foreigner."

George said, "Hey, nigger. You got a permit for this thing?"

"Look on seat," said Heller.

George leaned into the cab. He evidently found the

folder Heller had dropped there. But he continued to lean in, looking it over. He was muttering.

George backed out. "What the hell, Ralph. I can't make head or tails out of this." He walked over to his partner.

"Mebbe so you better call in on beautiful radio," said Heller. "Checkee license plate."

George said, "Oh, yeah." He went to the back of the cab, made a note and then, carrying the papers, went back to the police car and leaned in. Ralph stayed alert, holding the Llama pistol in one hand and keeping his own Colt .357 Magnum trained on Heller.

I couldn't hear the radio conversation because they'd left their motor running and George was too deep in the police car. Suddenly he backed out, microphone still in hand. "Ralph! Does that car look like a foreign limousine to you?"

Ralph pushed his cowboy hat back with the Llama barrel and then moved to get a better look at the old cab. "Yeah, George. It looks old enough to be un-American."

George ducked back inside the police car. Then suddenly he backed into plain view, pulling the microphone with him. His eyes were popped. He said, "No (bleep)?"

He leaned in and put the microphone on its hook. Holding the papers, he went over to Ralph. "Look, Ralph. These papers say this is Rangtango Blowah, Republic of Maysabongo, Consul for the State of Connecticut. Now, them tags is diplomatic tags. The dispatcher checked with Washington. This nigger has got diplomatic imboomity."

"What the hell is that?" said Ralph.

"The dispatcher says Washington says you can't put a finger on him. He can do anything he pleases. We can't arrest him no matter what he commits."

"Jesus! Diplomatic imboomity? Must mean he could

blow the whole place up and we couldn't even touch him."

"I'm afraid so," said George.

"Oh, (bleep)!" said Ralph. "Can't we even impound this handgun?"

"I'm afraid not," said George. "Give it back to him. He could even shoot us and we couldn't say a word!"

Heller took the weapon back from a reluctant Ralph. "This whole place now," he said in a high-pitched voice, "proppity of part of Republic of Maysabongo. You not in States United now. You standing in Maysabongo."

"Jesus," said Ralph. "The God (bleeped) foreigners are buying up the whole (bleeping) country!"

"I'm afraid so," said George.

"Look, nigger," said Ralph. "We saw you drive nice and peaceful by us twice. What the hell was the idea of suddenly speeding?"

"Test," said Heller. "Me see if you good alert top man fine cops. You pass test very good, please."

He reached into his wallet and took out two one-hundred-dollar bills. He gave one to each of them. "Every month, you each get one."

"Did the chief pass the test?" said George, "He's my uncle."

Heller took out two more one-hundred-dollar bills. "He good man. He pass test double. So he get same so each month, too."

They were putting the bills in their wallets. "My God," said Ralph. "We can't even get him for bribing an officer! This imboomity has advantages!"

"Hey," said George, "this is just like the old times my grandpappy used to tell me about. When the boot-leggers had this place, they paid off regular and you couldn't touch them, either!"

"No, no, no," said Heller in his high-pitched voice.

"Not bribe. Please raise left hand. Maysabongo do everything left-handed. Now say after me: 'I now part-time honorary . . .'"

The deputies both did.

"'. . . deputy sheriff in marines of Maysabongo . . . and do aforesaid promise . . . if I see anything strange going on, I look other way . . . and if I see stranger trespassing I blow heads off.'"

They repeated it all carefully.

Heller reached into his pocket and brought out three plain, gold stars with nothing on them. He handed one to each of the deputies. Then he gave George the third. "You tell uncle chief he sworn in, too. Here his badge."

"Hey!" said Ralph. "It's legal after all! You could tell he wasn't a hundred percent pure nigger. He's got blue eyes!"

"One more thing," said Heller. "Me hire whitey engineer. He very good man. He gottee pale hair. He got diplomatic imboomity, too, so he okay if you see here." And he handed them a passport picture of himself!

They looked at it gravely. George gave it and the folder back. He raised his hat very politely. "You can count on us to blow heads off anybody you say," he promised.

Ralph raised his hat.

They got into their police car and drove off.

With a horrible shock, it suddenly came to me what that (bleeped) Heller had done! He had enlisted the local constabulary! Nobody else could get near that place now!

At the place he would use for a garage, the old lady would blow people's heads off. At the roadhouse, the deputy sheriffs would blow people's heads off.

How perfectly awful of Heller! We couldn't get our noses into either place to sabotage things!

As soon as we got the platen, the bump-off of Heller would have to be done in New York!

(Bleep) him. I knew we'd be in trouble if he started studying espionage. And here it was!

PART TWENTY-TWO

Chapter 1

Fate is seldom kind. And when it starts shovelling out bad news, it seldom knows when to stop.

Heller had worked around the roadhouse for the rest of that day, mainly airing things out and making sure the stove worked—I suppose because winter was on its way. He seemed to enjoy it outside. He admired the maples, the leaves already reddening from a night frost. He trotted up to a hilltop and looked all around. He seemed to be very interested in rocks in the flat field near the roadhouse, for he took a blasting cord and levelled a couple outcrops—he just loves to explode things!

The last thing he did was post a sign. It said:

Property Trespassers
Will Be Deported to Elsewhere
with Their Heads Blown Off

Not Responsible for Damage
Done by Mine Fields

He found a place where he could get the cab across the river and was soon going deeper into the country. Abruptly, the other side of the abandoned gas station came into view. It was on the same forgotten road!

The old lady fumbled around and opened the garage door for him. Heller drove in, played his light over himself and then over the cab and in no time at all had restored everything to its original color.

He went out and fixed a sagging chicken-coop door for the old lady, cut her some firewood by playing a disintegrator gun at sections of logs, had a cup of coffee, listened to what a nice young man he was, and by twilight was rolling along back to New York.

Whatever he was doing, he was making a lot too much progress and a lot too fast!

It was well past midnight where I was. I was just crawling into my otherwise empty bed, pretty exhausted in fact, when there came a knock on the door.

It was Faht Bey. He handed me an envelope and went away.

Groggily, I opened it. I read the first two lines and sat abruptly down. It was the expected report from Raht and Terb:

AGENT UPDATE

We have good news for you.

We are in the hospital.

We did exactly what you said.

Immediately on our arrival in New York, we procured suitable credentials from the forger as UN delegates from Zimbabwe. We obtained suitable costumes. In this suitable guise we proceeded upon our assignment.

We went to the designated target area as ordered.

At the desk we made appointments with two suitable girls and paid the suitable amount, receipts attached.

Proceeding on schedule, we did not go to the

assigned rooms but instead, detoured to the top floor.

As per informant advice, the door to the subject's room was open. There was nobody in the suite.

We entered and proceeded to ransack the place. We went into every cupboard and crevice. Subject certainly has a lot of clothes.

We were just completing the search by restoring what we could when the door to the suite opened.

A high-yellow whore about five foot ten inches tall with silver finger and toenails, wearing a purple dressing gown, not tied and open in front and wearing nothing else, walked in.

Said high-yellow whore was accompanied by a tan whore about five foot two inches tall with red finger and toenails of apparent Tahitian racial extraction, wearing a small hand towel and black hair.

Said high-yellow ejaculated, "What the hell are you (bleepards) doing in Pretty Boy's room?" The voice was not modulated. No recording of it is attached.

Agent Terb, being nearer the door, sought by prescribed and standard means to seize the Tahitian. With a standard riposte and cross-slice with hand edge, said Tahitian broke said Agent Terb's arm.

Agent Raht, unable to get behind a bar which is positioned to the right of the said suite's door and which contains Seven Up and nonalcoholic Swiss beer and ice cream, raised a standard #18 cosh which contains three and a quarter pounds of birdshot and brought it down in the prescribed fashion, intending to knock out the high-yellow who was advancing with gown flying wide open.

Said high-yellow's right foot advanced and connected with said cosh which then flew into bedroom, which has a circular bed big enough, according to professional estimate, to hold six.

Seeking to use a snatch draw, said Agent Raht, bending, directed his hand toward the Colt Cobra which regulations require to be affixed to an agent's right ankle.

The maneuver, though standard, was interrupted by the left foot of said high-yellow rising in a swirl kick and connecting with the jaw of said Agent Raht, which broke.

Agent Terb, seeking to use his remaining arm on the Tahitian in a standard chop found it misdirected into the tube of the Sylvania 25-inch, by diagonal measurement, television set.

Agent Raht was hit with a bottle of Seven Up in the back of the skull by an unorthodox maneuver executed by the high-yellow.

Lying on the floor, looking up, Agents Terb and Raht saw a young man, about five foot four, dressed in a blue three-piece suit, with black hair, answering to the name of Giuseppe, which may or may not be an a.k.a., standing there holding a Beretta Model 1934 Italian Automatic pistol caliber .380 with its safety catch off.

Said young man told the said high-yellow and said Tahitian to get up off the chests of said Agents Raht and Terb respectively at which said high-yellow made a request as follows: "Let me hit the (bleepard) again, Guiseppe." A request which was ignored by said Guiseppe who was on the phone. Said high-yellow accordingly struck said Agent Raht in the solar plexus which produced paralysis.

Three and a half minutes later a second young man, five foot three inches tall, black hair, black eyes, wearing a gray suit and carrying an eighteen-inch rubber truncheon, appeared. His name is unknown as he was not addressed by name. The Tahitian requested that any further work done not be done in "Pretty Boy's" suite.

Accordingly, Agents Raht and Terb were escorted to a room in the basement, about ten feet by twelve feet, furnished by a table and two chairs.

One answering to the name of Vantagio appeared. He is about five foot two, has black hair and black eyes and was dressed in a suit of dark material, expensively cut.

The young man Giuseppe said, "Vantagio . . ." but the rest of it was in Italian. There is no recording attached.

Said Vantagio did then remove said wallets and other I.D. from the said agents and said in English, "Hold up on that rubber club until I verify."

Said Vantagio left.

Said Vantagio returned.

Said Vantagio said, "You (bleepards) aren't from the UN. The Secretary General's office never heard of you. These are forged." This remark was addressed to the said Agents Raht and Terb.

Said Vantagio said to the said Guiseppe and the other young man, "Work these (bleepards) over and find out where they really are from." He left.

Said other young man, utilizing the rubber truncheon in an experienced manner for one hour and fifteen minutes, was, however, unable to extract further information from the said agents.

When consciousness returned, said Agents Raht and Terb found themselves in the back of a delivery van, make and license number not noted. The delivery van was en route somewhere.

As Agent Raht could not talk due to jaw fractures, Agent Terb said to the young man who was riding in the back of the van, "Where are we going?"

Said young man stated, "We are taking you for a ride, you (bleepards). So say your prayers." He enforced this advice with said Beretta with which he gesticulated.

The van stopped. The roar of other traffic could be heard.

A young man came back from the front of the van.

The two young men picked up some large garbage bags. The bags were made of black plastic. They placed some concrete blocks in the bottom of said black plastic garbage bags. They then inserted Agents Raht and Terb into said black plastic garbage bags.

The back doors of the van were heard to open. Traffic roars were louder. It is agreed by both Agents Raht and Terb that they were thereupon lifted over a rail and dropped.

The fall distance was considerable.

The water impact was excessive.

Utilizing the thin-blade which is required by standard regulations to be carried in the sole of the right shoe, Agent Raht cut through the black plastic garbage bag and shortly surfaced. As there was no sign of Agent Terb, said Agent Raht dived again and located said black plastic garbage bag and cut it off Agent Terb.

Upon surfacing, both agents agreed that the bridge they saw upstream in the darkness was the Queensborough Bridge and, being competent agents, had a knowledge of the local geography. The water in this area is noted for its riptides and no one has ever been known to swim in it.

The East River at this point is divided by a long island known as Roosevelt Island. It once served as a prison without walls because nobody could swim through the riptides and make the seven-hundred-foot crossing to the mainland. It is a historic spot.

The current had carried the said agents just past the southern tip. There is a geyser there which shoots 4,000 gallons of water per minute 400 feet into the air. It is a historic spot.

The wind was carrying the geyser spray over said agents.

A backwater was located and taken advantage of. The shore is covered with barnacles and debris and oil scum.

There used to be two hospitals on Roosevelt Island, one for the chronically ill and the other for the aged. It is a historic spot.

On the southern end of the island there is also the Silverwater Memorial Hospital.

Agent Raht carried Agent Terb to said hospital and pleaded being both chronically ill and aged.

They were taken in and given treatment and,

as they had money in their shoes, are still there.

We could not write sooner because the hands of both Agents Raht and Terb are ripped to pieces from fishhooks encountered in seeking to search subject's baggage.

No platen as described was located.

However, there is good news! We have found the interference requested.

Before entering subject's room, adjacent rooms were accidentally entered. Immediately next door to the subject's suite there is a room about twenty by thirty feet. This room contains backdrops of the sea and jungle which can be interchanged. The floor of this room is made up of sand and patches of grass.

Said room also contains palm trees which spread out, making alcoves.

The purpose of said room is apparently to simulate the earliest conditions of coital contact by diplomats from jungle or sea countries. They do it lying on the sand or grass or under the palm fronds which make the alcoves.

In the exact center of this room, in an apparent effort to simulate glaring sunlight, there is a mammoth carbon arc light. This light is fed by carbon bars.

In this way the earliest sexual experiences of diplomats can be reduplicated.

There is a similar rig in a whorehouse in Hong Kong, at 116 Lotus Street, third door from the right.

So this is very good news that we can tell you. The above carbon arc is the interference.

> *You did not give us any bugs to plant so we did not plant any bugs.*
>
> *A messenger from the New York office is picking up this report in suitable guise.*
>
> *We await your further instructions. We will not be ambulant for another month. Always at your service."*

Their agent numbers followed.

The report was really a kick in the jaw. They were just doing it to spite me. That was obvious!

It was just a way to lie down on the job and take a vacation at Apparatus expense. It's happened before.

It made me even more savage at Heller! Most decent, respectable people use Doberman pinschers or Alsatians as watchdogs. He was using high-yellows and a Tahitian whore.

It just shows what can happen when you try to work with somebody who is an amateur in espionage. They go unorthodox! You can't keep up with them!

In my mood, I could sympathize even harder with that con man Izzy. Once fate gets started on you, it never knows when to stop!

What would be the next blow?

Chapter 2

Lightning is said never to strike twice in the same place. But there apparently is no law about it striking twice in the same time period.

Around 4:00 A.M., I had finally managed to get to sleep in my lonely bed.

I was brought up like a rocket by a savage pounding on my bedroom door.

I unbarred and opened it.

The new gatekeeper was standing there wild-eyed! He was pointing at the gate with a mad, jabbing finger. He stammers so I didn't wait. I raced across the yard, gripping a Mauser machine pistol, hoping there was somebody or something there I could vent my spleen on by shooting.

No such luck. It was the taxi driver.

"Sultan Bey! Come quick! There is a long-distance person-to-person phone call for you! At the Dregs Hotel!"

It spun me. Groggy from just awakening, and shocked, I could not for the life of me imagine who could be calling me. A crazy idea that it might be Lombar Hisst from Voltar insisted on splitting through my head. But that, time and spacewise, was impossible. Maybe it was somebody invalidating my bill of sale on Utanc!

He rushed me back to my room and I got some clothes on and shortly we were flying along the bumpy road to Afyon. It was just a little too early for camels and carts so we made good time.

I spilled into the hotel. The night clerk pointed urgently at the phone in the lobby. I grabbed the phone. Post, Telephone and Telegraph in Turkey—PTT—is usually not too bad. The local operator was in a spin.

"Sultan Bey. I will try to get Istanbul back. They disconnected!" I heard some muttering. Then somebody came on the line. My party? No. "Is this Sultan Bey in Afyon?"

I said, "Yes, yes!"

"This is the Istanbul overseas operator. Wait."

I waited.

Somebody else came on the line. "Is this Sultan Bey, Turkey?"

I said, "Yes, yes!"

"This is the Rome overseas operator. Wait."

I waited.

Somebody else came on the line. A British accent. "Is this Sultan Bey, Turkey?"

I said, "Yes, yes!"

"This is the London overseas operator. Wait."

I waited.

The sound of many coins gonging into a phone.

"Hello, Sultan Bey?"

By all the Gods in all the Heavens!

It was HELLER!

"Is this my old Academy friend?" he said in English.

"Yes," I said, my mind racing as how to shut him off! All long-distance calls in the world are monitored by the National Security Agency of the United States! They go by satellite!

"We'uns up in Ha'lum is having us a wedding. De date is 2 October r'aht aftuh sunset. We'uns will leave de po'ch light on."

"My Gods," I said. How could I shut him off?

"De pahty goin' be very fancy so don' bring dat ol' Miss Blueflash. She trash. You'uns bring dat Prince Caucalsia foh shuah. We goin' empty he stomach."

"Good Gods!" I said.

"Now we is countin' on you coming 'cause we got to write de cap'n you'uns is doin' jus' fine. Now de address he be griddle..."

"Good-bye!" I screamed. "Good-bye! I be there. Good-bye!"

I hung up hysterically.

The phone rang.

"This is the New York overseas operator. Did you complete your call?"

"My Gods, yes!" I screamed at her and hung up again.

The (bleeped) fool! Calling in plaintext!

"Somebody dead?" said the night clerk in Turkish. "You look awful. Want me to open up the bar?"

I went outside and got in the taxi.

"Somebody dead?" said the taxi driver.

I didn't answer and we drove off. It was the last bit of the moon for the month. It would be totally dark on October second. He had worked that out. But breaking security . . .

Such was my reaction that for the life of me at that moment, I could not remember the rest of the message.

The taxi driver dumped me at the villa. I went inside.

Then suddenly I realized I would have the message on my recorded strips. I went into the secret room.

I backtracked the strips.

There was Heller in a midtown New York restaurant. A Howard Johnson's? He was looking out of a phone kiosk into the room, waiting. I could see by the reflection in the glass that he was black-haired and black-faced. He was wearing some kind of workman's white coveralls.

I skipped ahead through his travails in placing the call.

He ordered and ate three hamburgers.

The phone rang. He went to the kiosk. He got through. He dropped a handful of money into the box.

And there was the call all over again. My ejaculations were a bit loud and I had to turn the volume down.

He was being awfully obscure. I played it through again. I didn't know any "Miss Blueflash." Then I worked it out. He meant not to flash the stunlight on landing. Well, of course. He'd be down on the field.

The "porch light" meant he had a radio beacon. I hadn't known he had taken one.

It was on the third play through that I caught "griddle." He was probably going to say "griddle cakes." And he had been about to give the Voltarian Fleet grid position for that exact spot on the planet. It would be a short series of numbers.

But of course I knew where he was.

It came to me with a big flash of comprehension why he had bought that roadhouse. It was a landing field for the tug, the *Prince Caucalsia!*

Aha. "Empty he stomach"! Heller wanted his boxes!

Oh, there was more to this than just a tug landing and a message to Captain Tars Roke. Heller was going to use that roadhouse for something else!

I went over it again carefully. Now I noticed that when he had been cut off so abruptly by me, he had stood there and blinked. And then he had stood there thoughtfully after he hung up.

I tried to work out how the call had been a Code break. I couldn't.

But the cargo was the thing. Heller wanted that cargo. He was going too (bleeped) fast!

Raht and Terb had callously gone on vacation. I had to think and think quickly.

Then it came to me. The perfect plan!

We would make the delivery. Heller would hand over the letter. I would detain departure long enough to examine the letter in a cabin. Although the first letter was long since sent, I had a copy. If this new letter matched the first letter, I would have the platen because the positions would coincide. And then I could order the Antimancos to kill him.

Wait. I must not let him get any advantage in case

I missed on the letter. How could I tamper with the cargo?

This was going to work out all right after all.

I went to bed smiling.

One way or another, Heller was going to be stopped!

Chapter 3

It was not until noon the next day that I got around. Before I retired I had sent a note to Faht Bey that the tug would be leaving on the second, which was two days hence, and I, of course, supposed that by the time I reached the hangar, the crews would be calmly sorting things out for the departure.

Such was not the case!

When I walked into the huge cavern, it looked more like things were being set up for a battle!

Every technician at the base was lined up in the middle of the hangar floor! And the four assassin pilots had their beltguns drawn and trained on them!

The noonday sun was beating down through the optical illusion, making a sort of spotlight on the assembly.

The lead assassin pilot was standing there in his garish and deadly dress with an angry face and a shaking gun!

Faht Bey was running around flapping and perspiring.

I came in through the entrance from my office. I instantly drew my own blastick. You never go unarmed amongst such people in the most peaceful times and this looked like war!

Faht Bey saw me. He screamed, "Officer Gris! By the sacred Devils! Order these assassin pilots to desist!"

I hadn't said a word. But the lead assassin pilot shouted at me. "You have no authority over us!" And one of his copilots trained a gun on me!

"Officer Gris!" wailed Faht Bey. "They claim they are going to shoot technicians one by one until they find the culprit!"

The five Antimancos were off to the side. I fingered the star which hung around my neck. Maybe I could get them to charge the assassin pilots.

I realized I might be in the line of fire. I said hastily, "What's this all about?" Better temporize.

"Sabotage and attempted murder!" shouted the lead assassin pilot. I thought, a fine one he was to be talking about murder. That was his trade.

He turned his slate-hard eyes on me. "Maybe you had a hand in this!"

"You'd better tell me what 'this' is," I said, putting a bold face on it and hoping my voice didn't quaver.

He pointed a red glove at the technicians. "One of those (bleepards) messed up our ships!" His face was as red as the explosion insignia on his collar. "They rigged it with cross wires! If we had pressed a gun trigger to do our duty, our own ship would have blown up! That's murder and willful destruction of Apparatus property!"

I could see why he was mad. He wouldn't be able to do his duty and shoot down the tug. But I walked over to the technicians.

"What do you know about this?" I said severely.

They were chalk-faced. The repair chief said, "Nothing! Those two gunships are locked! We are never allowed aboard."

I turned to the assassin pilot. "There, you see? They didn't do it."

He stamped up close to me. "Then WHO did?" He

grabbed my tunic front. "You? Yes. You'll be riding in that tug. You could be trying to save your own neck at government expense!"

My blastick was accidentally against his stomach. He backed up. "Threatening me, are you?" He caught sight of the Antimancos standing in a group in front of the tug. "Maybe you ordered them to do it!"

The Antimanco captain came forward. Bless Captain Stabb! "I haven't received any orders from Officer Gris."

The assassin pilot turned on him. "You'd lie even if you did! You're the ones that will be riding in that tug if we have to shoot it down! And now you are going on a trip!"

Captain Stabb said, "The ship is disabled for outer space. It can only travel on its auxiliaries within the solar system. It is bugged and you can find it. So what's the scream?"

Bless him!

"Then," said the assassin pilot, "I have no choice but to shoot technicians one by one until I get the answer. And if I finish with them and still no clue, I'll start on your crew!"

Faht Bey screamed, "Officer Gris! They'll paralyze the base if they shoot all the technicians! You won't be able to move with that tug if they shoot your tug crew! Please, by the fervent Gods, THINK OF SOMETHING!"

Well, I could see he had a point there.

Captain Stabb said, "The only one that isn't here now that was here when the two cannon ships arrived was that Royal officer!"

Inspiration came to me!

I said to the assassin pilot, "Oh, this wasn't done just today? Have you inspected your guns since you arrived?"

"No, why should I? My target is that tug. It hasn't moved!"

"You only inspected your ships when you thought they might be called into action by the movement of the tug?" I said.

"Yes!" the assassin pilot snapped at me.

"Oh," I said. "That accounts for everything! Now, that Royal officer is really a Crown inspector so I didn't think anything of it. But I observed him enter and leave both of your cannon ships shortly after you came."

"What?" screamed the assassin pilot. "And you didn't report it?"

"Well, he's a Crown inspector. Has orders to shoot all of you. He was snooping into everything, all your private affairs. And I knew you'd inspect everything before you flew."

"That Royal officer? The tall one with the blond hair?"

"And blue eyes," I said. "The very one."

I turned to the assembled hangar and base personnel. I said loudly, "I am very sorry that a crime of sabotage by that Royal officer put you all in danger of your lives. But you can relax. Obviously he did it. So that is all there is to it. You'd better remember to shoot him on sight if you see him again. He is a threat to your lives."

"The Royal officer," they whispered.

"That God (bleeped) Royal officer," said the assassin pilots.

"You can always count on a blasted Royal officer to make trouble!" said Captain Stabb.

Having established unanimous agreement that Heller ought to be killed on sight, I smiled at them. "Now that we have decided upon our course of action if he ever shows up again at this base, shall we get back to work?"

They drifted off.

The cream of the jest was, I was right. I was quite certain it had been Heller. That his action might have included his saving my life as well did not enter into it.

After that phone call, there was some chance he might show up here. Well, I'd taken care of that. Whatever else happened, he would never leave this planet alive. That was for sure!

Those angry and vengeful faces were a balm to my suffering! Now somebody else besides me and Lombar were frothing at Heller!

Chapter 4

In the crew salon in the tug, Captain Stabb gazed on me admiringly. "You sure handled that to perfection, Officer Gris." And his little black button eyes gleamed with good comradeship.

"It wasn't anything," I said. "Now let's get down to business." I pulled out a Voltar Fleet grid of the planet and some U.S. Geological Survey charts and pinpointed for him exactly where we would land.

"And then we kill him?" said Captain Stabb.

"That is not positive," I said.

"We torture him first?"

"Captain Stabb, I really think we understand each other. But we have a problem. He has something I have to get. If we don't get it this time, we will get it later."

"Oh," he grumbled to himself. Then he brightened. "But as soon as you get it, we kill him."

"Right."

"Right!" he said.

"Our strategy is to keep him lulled, give him no warning. Make him think we are cooperating."

"That's wise," said Stabb. "Then he can be gotten in the back."

"Right," I said. "Now, he wants those boxes down in the hold. It might be I don't get what I want this trip and we may have to deliver them. But if we do, I want to sabotage the shipment."

"I thought it was sabotaged," said Stabb.

Ah, Lombar had briefed him. "Well," I said, "not really enough. He is very tricky and dishonest."

"All Royal officers are," said Stabb. "Excepting present company, of course, meaning you."

"Well, actually," I said, "I never made it. They sent me to the Apparatus instead."

"You're not a Royal officer?"

"No," I said, telling the truth. "Just a Secondary Executive of the Apparatus."

He reached across and pumped my hand. "You're a good man, Officer Gris." Warmth flowed through the crew salon.

"The problem is," I said, "how to get Box Number 5 out of that hold."

"The hold and floorplates are locked tight!"

"I was hoping you knew of a way. We're going to remove it completely."

He thought. He called for one of the two engine sub-officers. They left. They came back.

Captain Stabb said, "There's a small engine-room escape hatch. It's mandatory in construction. You can get one man through it. It exits into the lower hold. It bypasses all his deckplate seals. In flight, the deckplates, in theory, would not be locked. One would drop from the engine room down into the hold and out through the deckplates in case of an overheat that fused the main engine-room doors. The Fleet does silly things like that."

A few minutes later I was in the hold. I played a light around. The boxes were all there, neatly lashed. Box Number 5 was just as I remembered it—on top.

I let them do the work. And it was a lot of work. We had to unpack the box piece by piece. It contained a lot of heavy pans, mostly. We passed these up into the engine room and out—or rather they did. Then we sawed the box up and passed the pieces out.

It was at this point I went to work. I got rid of every scrap of debris and packing that had drifted around. I retied every knot that secured the boxes. I even made Captain Stabb inspect. There was no trace of Box Number 5 left in that hold.

We got all the debris out of the ship and disintegrated it. I buried the heavy pans in the bottom of an old detention cell.

"What are you going to tell him?" said Stabb. "In case, that is, we don't get to kill him."

"That it was never loaded. Simplicity is best."

"You're a wonder," said Stabb. "What were those things?"

"I don't know. But I'm sure he does. And it will put an awful crimp in any plans he has."

"You really are a wonder," said Stabb.

I hung around for a bit. The Antimancos seemed to be taking a lot of pleasure in fixing things up so Heller's suspicions would be lulled. They were removing the tiniest bits of dust, eradicating every smudge, inside and out. The actions were quite foreign to their natural bent—they mostly laid around and shot dice or drank.

But now there was a sort of glee around them. They were creating the atmosphere which they were certain would disabuse a Royal officer of suspecting he was about to be stabbed in the back.

They couldn't get into the rear of the ship, of course, but Heller would not expect that. But anything he could see would be shining.

"We want," said Stabb, "a new uniform issue, all of us. We'll look like a perfect crew. And we'll want a new personal weapons issue, of course."

I stamped it gladly.

All was going along well there so I went back to my secret room. I wanted to be very sure that Heller wasn't laying any booby traps for us at his end.

But Heller was simply having breakfast in his suite and having a second chocolate sundae while he read a G-2 manual entitled *The Handling of the Trained Spy.* The interference was off, for a change, as it often was in the morning. The diplomats didn't seem to want to relive their youth under the carbon arc at that time of the day.

He was on a chapter named "The Case Officer's Dilemma." He was eating his sundae so I got a chance to read some of it without still-framing it on the second viewer. It seemed that spies often had personal intentions of their own. These included their reasons for being spies in the first place. They wanted personal revenge or wealth for their own purposes. And the case officer, which is their term for a handler, had to accommodate these personal ambitions and take advantage of them where possible.

Well, that was all kindergarten stuff. Naturally a spy had personal ambitions. It didn't mention that the case officer might have them also. Take my case: wealth and power covered it.

Then he was onto a subsection. It was entitled "Love, The Case Officer's Worst Enemy." It seemed that love was a very dangerous thing. When you sent a spy to some country, away from a lady love, he would sometimes just give the job a brushoff or turn in any old thing in order to get home.

It also covered the danger of a spy falling in love with an enemy agent and turning into a double agent. But that was of no interest to me.

I got to pondering this dangerous thing called love. In my own case, there was no menace in that direction. Utanc would simply never talk to me again, that was certain. And my heart was heavy about it.

But Heller, now, that was a different matter. He had been in love with the Countess Krak. In fact, he had even delayed his departure because of it. But he wasn't following the pattern laid down in the textbook. He was not skimping his job, (bleep) him. He was plowing right along on it.

The trouble with Heller was that he was inconsistent with the textbooks. Obviously, as I looked at it, he was planning to *do* his job *fully* and then go home, whereas, by the text, he should be *skimping* his job and *rushing* home. There was just no accounting for the man at all!

I idly speculated on all the ramifications of this. If he would just slow down and poke along *and* skimp his job, I would have nothing to worry about.

But in any event, I at last had some kind of a solution in progress.

If all went well, he would very shortly be dead. I would forge reports on and on and the whole thing could be strung out for years.

In spite of the leaden feeling I had about Utanc, some small hope was stirring in me.

Chapter 5

In the first pitch-black dark of October second, we ascended through the optical illusion and rose far above the planet.

Ringing in my ears was the last warning from the assassin-pilot leader, "We're tracking your bug with a temporary satellite that went up three hours ago. At the first hint that you're leaving the vicinity of Blito-P3, up we come and down you go, on fire. We can catch you before this tug can get up to speed. And you are not armed. We will be watching you. Be smart. Don't try anything."

So I took no joy in the flight. I wouldn't anyway. Space travel, even a local jump, makes me nervous.

Captain Stabb let the dark band on the surface drift along directly below us. It would be seven hours and I simply should have lain down on a gimbal bed and had a sleep. But I was too jumpy.

Unlike Heller, I am not a religious person. I knew too much about psychology to really believe in anything but crude matter. But in my childhood I had been exposed to it by the more decent people around me, and now and then I would suffer a lapse and feel some need to pray. I did tonight.

The strategy was all worked out. Captain Stabb assured me there would be no hitches. But an awful lot depended upon this. If Heller were actually to get loose and start accomplishing things, he could utterly smash Lombar's connections, wreck the best-laid plans for Voltar and completely block, without knowing he was doing it, Lombar's rise to the rule of all Voltar. There were tremendous stakes here. Even for me. I hardly dared speculate on what I myself would do when I became the head of all the Apparatus. For it would be an Apparatus greatly strengthened beyond even what it was now.

One thing sure. There were a lot of people I would order killed at once!

But there was one flaw in all this planning. And he was sitting down there ahead, waiting with a report to send. If that report gave me the platen...

I must have dozed off. Captain Stabb was shaking me by the shoulder. "I don't think the landing is safe."

I left my cabin and went with him to the flight deck. He pointed at the screens. He had everything turned on. Even the steel plates that cut off the eyeball-view ports were closed. Pirates take no chances.

We were about two hundred miles straight up. It was about seven in the evening of a very black autumn night.

New York lay about thirty miles to the south of our position, a vast spread of lights. One could see the planes taking off and landing at La Guardia and, further off, John F. Kennedy International Airport. The planes looked like tiny fireflies. The skyscrapers of Manhattan were clearly outlined. There was the Empire State Building! Izzy probably busy! There was the UN, and nearby, one of those high-rises must be the Gracious Palms, probably busy.

To the northeast, scattered like small sheets of light on a black velvet cloth, lay Bridgeport, Danbury, New Haven and, further away, Hartford. It was a crystal clear night.

Directly below us it was black as pitch, a hole of lightlessness.

A call-in receiver was beeping in the panel. Its grid showed the signal was coming from directly below.

I looked at Stabb. I had seen nothing alarming. But he was the accomplished smuggler and pirate.

"Watch," he said. He turned a dial to shift a screen to a different part of the spectrum. He pushed a button and let it enlarge the picture.

There was a police car sitting beside the road. The road was just east of our destination.

"Trap," said Stabb.

I laughed. "That's where they hang out," I said. "They're sheriff's men. Deputy sheriffs. That's a speed trap, not a trap for us."

"You sure?"

"If that Royal officer is down below us, he has probably conned them into seeing nothing. But they won't see anything anyway as we're not going to blueflash. Their names are George and Ralph."

"Devils!" said Stabb. "How'd you know that?"

"It's safe to land. They won't see anything."

"On your orders," said Stabb, giving the usual Fleet half-protest.

Down we went!

The New Haven Submarine Base radar indicated on our hull. They would get no blip back.

A hundred feet up, our pilot laid the tug horizontal. He scanned the ground with a screen. "Not even a sharp rock," he said.

We settled into place.

The second engineer was out through the airlock like a shot. He scanned the area for living things.

A hot spot.

It was Heller!

He came walking up. He stood in the glow from the airlock. He wasn't even disguised. He had on workman's coveralls, dark blue. He wasn't wearing his baseball cap and he wasn't even wearing those deadly spikes!

I saw he had no gun in his hand. He thought he was amongst friends, the fool. So I met him at the port.

He nodded to me and to Stabb. He went down the passageway and knelt. He unlocked the floorplates to the hold.

"If you will give me some crew," he said, "we'll move these inside. There's two dollies over in the edge of the woods."

Stabb looked to me and I nodded.

Very soon, with a lot of help from Heller, despite working in the dark, fifteen cases lay on a thick canvas he had put down to protect the dance floor.

A kerosene oil lamp spread a yellow glow across the ancient dance decorations and the Voltar cases. Heller was checking case markings.

"Where's Box Number 5?" he said.

Before I could answer, he went trotting back to the ship. He got down in the hold again.

He came out. He opened up other doors to the rear and checked there. He locked everything up once more.

"There's a box missing," he said to Stabb.

Stabb shrugged. "I never been in that hold," he said.

Heller checked the forward cabins and storage spaces. Then he left the ship. He reentered the roadhouse. He once more verified the numbers and the count.

He beckoned to me to follow him. I went into instant alarm. I was carrying a blastick, a Colt Cobra in an ankle holster and a Knife Section knife behind my neck and he was apparently unarmed. But I did not feel comfortable. I turned. Captain Stabb was at the roadhouse door. He winked at me. I followed Heller.

He had a kitchen fire going. The night was somewhat chilly. He had cleaned up the place. There was a kitchen table and a couple of chairs. Heller sat down at the far end.

I sat down but I didn't take my hand off the 800-kilovolt blastick in my pocket.

Chapter 6

Heller had taken some papers out of his pocket, a notebook and a pen. He began to look at the papers—they appeared to be old invoices. I didn't see any sign of the letter.

I looked around. The kitchen was quite clean now. He had a fire going in the old iron cookstove: a wood fire, from the way it popped occasionally and from some wisps of pungent smoke.

The place was lit with a hanging kerosene lamp. Probably the electricity was not turned on. The light glowed and flickered on some old glass jars on a shelf.

A calendar was on the wall: big picture of an elk and the words *Hartford Life Insurance*. The year was 1932!

Ordinarily I might have been very interested in this place. But I had to get that letter! If I was lucky, in a few minutes Heller would be dead and we would be sailing away.

He was going over some invoices and writing things on the piece of paper. For some reason, seeing him so calm made me very nervous.

I imagined he was reconstructing the list of things in the box.

He wasn't talking so I sort of felt I had to be talking. Maybe I could steer him around and hurry him up and get that letter. Maybe he was being silent because he suspected I had done something with the box. "I never saw those boxes," I said. "I didn't even know they were in the hold. If you remember, I was not aboard the tug at that time."

He was consulting the invoice sheets again.

I said, "I do recall, though, a Fleet lorry driving away one day. It had a box on it. I asked the sentry at that time why they were removing a box. He said he didn't know."

He didn't say anything. He was making some sort of a calculation. I wished he'd just give me that letter.

"I mailed the other letter on the first freighter out. It went just two or three days after you gave it to me," I said.

He was trying to locate some item on an invoice. I wished he would speak.

"I know how important it is," I said, "that I mail your letters to Captain Tars Roke. I know he tells the Emperor and the Grand Council. If they didn't hear from you, I know they'd send an invasion fleet right away. They'd have to, to preserve the planet. I can see it is in very bad shape. So don't think for a moment I'd let you down. I know both of us could be killed if this invasion hit. So it's in my interest, too. I'll sure make certain the letters get mailed."

He was busy with his figures. No sign of the letter. Maybe he was upset about the telephone.

"I am sorry I had to cut you off on the phone. You see, the National Security Agency monitors all long-distance calls. It was my fault really. I didn't give you a phone number you could call."

I wrote the cover phone number in Afyon on a piece of paper of my own, torn from a notebook, and put it down on the table near him.

He just kept on working.

"I should have given you a mail address, too," I

said. I wrote the mail address he could use in Turkey on another piece of my own paper and laid it on the phone number. "Future reports can just be mailed to this. I'll take the one you've got now."

He was riffling through his papers. Sort of absently, he encountered a sheet and laid it on the table halfway between us. He went on working.

I picked it up. It was a request form. It said:

Mission requirement: one professional cellologist experienced in making spores.

"Oh, I can get this for you," I said. "Just give me any note of anything you require. On this, I'll get them to send the most competent cellologist I can find." What a lie that was. "I'll send this request right along with your current report. Yes, indeed. Right along with your current report." (Bleep) you, where IS it!

He was writing more things down on the sheet. He was saying nothing.

I was getting pretty uneasy. "I know you are probably reconstructing the contents of the box. Well, you just reconstruct it and I'll put it on special order on the very next freighter. You'll have it all replaced within three months or so." And that was an even bigger lie than the cellologist one. "I'll send it out right with your *current report!*"

He was making a list of measurements. All I could see was his hand, arm and the top of his blond head. I didn't know what mood he was in at all. I didn't know what he intended, really. Maybe he had some other means or idea. I couldn't be sure.

"Really," I said, "we shouldn't wait around here too

long. Those two sheriff's deputies out there on the highway might have seen something. If you give me the report now, I'll be going."

He was adding up something. The awful thought came to me that he might be stalling me for some reason. I didn't feel it took that long to figure out just one box.

"I know they are very friendly but you can't ever trust sheriff's deputies, no matter how much you've conned them. So if you'll just give me the report, I'll be going."

Aha. I had it. He suspected that as soon as we got the report we'd kill him. That was it. He wasn't going to give me the report! That raid on the Gracious Palms suite had tipped him off!

I better calm his fears! "Look, I didn't have anything to do with the ransacking of your suite at the Gracious Palms. That happens all the time in New York. They were probably just looking for money. You can have every confidence in me, Jettero. You can trust me to faithfully mail that report for you. You can go in another room and write it. I won't look."

He was writing out a lot of figures on a new blank sheet of paper. Suddenly he handed it to me. It was the order for the replacement of Box Number 5. It had the manufacturer's name and address on it.

"Oh," I said. "I'll get this right off. Now, if you give me your monthly report . . ."

He reached into his pocket and pulled out two large envelopes.

The report! It was addressed to Captain Tars Roke!

The other one was addressed to Snelz!

"Oh, I'll get these right off for you," I said. Then my eye caught sight of the old glass jars. "Listen, I know this has been very upsetting for you. I'll make it up to you. I'll go in the crew's galley of the tug and get you some hot-jolt powder. Now you just sit there. We don't want too much activity outside. Look, I'll even thrash around and see if I can find some canisters of sparkle-water in the crew's stores—no reason to open up your own quarters in the back of the tug. I know how tired you are of drinking Seven Up. You wait right there. Let me be some help for a change."

I raced out.

With any luck, I had it and Heller would be dead in minutes! And my worries would be over!

Chapter 7

Aboard, I tore into my old cabin. I locked the door. I got out the tools necessary and in seconds had the Tars Roke letter open.

I read it avidly:

Dear Captain Tars,

Well, things are going along fair. It's a nice planet. It's too bad they don't appreciate it more.

I am mostly involved currently with basic setup. They use a fossil fuel in a most inefficient manner, even though I am certain that, even with their primitive technology, they know better. I think they may even hide efficiency inventions, as nobody could be that stupid.

It is the wasteful method of using this fuel that is causing the bulk of their atmospheric and regolithic contamination. It is also, strangely enough, the basic cause of their financial inflation, which is planetwide. I am working on this. Technically, the fuel problem is simple.

The people are a lot of them very nice people. They do have rather odd leadership and seem to easily let themselves be led into false technologies. They have a thing called "psychology" which is ridiculous. They even force schoolchildren to learn it. You won't believe this, but they think matter created life. This somehow tends to make them immoral and without honor. I have to be careful in dealing with them to keep my own honor clean. But I am making progress with people.

The political and economic aspects are under study. The job does not seem impossible. So please don't recommend the second alternative unless you cease to authentically hear from me or I have obviously failed.

But speaking of study, do you recall Isto Blin? He said there was nothing wrong with learning a dead mathematics except it was liable to take him to the tomb with it.

Please remember me to your dear wife.

I trust Their Royal Majesties are well and that the State prospers. With courteous salute,

Jettero Heller

It was written with uneven lines. Some of the words were cramped, some extended. A definite platen code.

I quickly got out the first letter copy. It was duplicated in the exact size. I laid the two large sheets over one another. I studied it for duplicate words and match.

I did it again.

I did it backwards.

I did it upside down!

Nothing matched!

My head was in a whirl. What was I holding here?

It was a platen code. But . . . Then I realized with a beaten sag that Heller was using a sequence of platens! He had a whole pad of them! I looked carefully into a corner. Yes, there it was! A number. It said *2*. So faint I could barely make it out in strong light.

Those Devils at the departure party had made up a *series* of platens!

Listlessly, I opened the second letter addressed to Snelz. It had, as I suspected, a letter in it to the Countess Krak. I scanned it without interest. Just a mushy love letter. He was looking forward to the moment they were reunited. Just mush.

A scratching came at the door. I quickly hid the letters and opened it.

Captain Stabb was there. "He's come out on the porch over there. He's a perfect target. Can we kill him now?"

I sighed. And I really was disappointed. "There's been a hitch. It will have to wait until next time."

That didn't sit well with him at all.

I myself was so upset I almost forgot the glass jars. I went to the airlock door and emptied their moldy contents on the ground. I went back to the crew's galley and found some packaged sweetbuns and some jolt powder. I put them in the jars.

Trying to seem cheerful, I went back to the roadhouse.

He was on the porch. I handed him the jars.

"I am sorry it was an upsetting trip," I said. "Possibly this will help make up for it."

He didn't say anything.

"On my honor, I will send your letters, order you

another box and a cellologist," I said. "I certainly wish you every success in the mission. And I will be more attentive in the future." I could have killed him with every word.

He didn't say anything. He was looking out at where the tug was, just a blacker blackness, only a faint glow where the airlock was open.

"Then it's good-bye for now," I said.

I raced back to the ship. I jumped in the airlock.

Stabb took off at once. He didn't even sweep the grass upright. I knew he was making Heller do that.

In the flight deck, even though I got in their way, I threw a spare viewscreen into the night band. I couldn't see the house or porch or Heller because of the trees.

We soared on upward at speed, a blackness in the blackness.

What an unlucky trip! I wished to the Gods I had been able to add his ghost to those which must be haunting that place.

To say that I was upset was an understatement.

When I had fastened myself into a gimbal bunk, I tried to take an assessment of my situation.

Although the nights were much longer than they had been a month before, and although we had plenty of time to get back while it was still dark in Turkey, Captain Stabb had the tug going at a savage speed. And jerking it about, too! He was in no pleasant mood. He had been denied his prey. I would somehow have to cope with that.

In a minor way, however, I had been successful. I certainly, on no account, would send for any replacement box. I had stalled him to that degree, whatever he had planned to do.

It was only then that I began to worry about his attitude. He had been busy with figures, true. But he had not said good-bye. Was his attitude one of hostility? Or was it just one of preoccupation?

Of course, the denial of that box had upset his plans. Had he just been making new plans or was he antagonistic to me?

Did he suspect something?

I began to shiver. Suppose he had seen through it all! Suppose he had realized we intended to kill him. Would that make him act that way?

But no. He had not been armed. He hadn't even worn those deadly spikes.

He had stood on the porch and he must have known that with a night sight he would have been an easy target. So he didn't know.

Or did his silence mean that he DID know?

Speeding back against the dawn to the base in Turkey, I vowed to carefully watch what he had done after we had left. Maybe that would give me a clue. I HAD to *know!!!*

Chapter 8

Safely landed down through the mountaintop in the dark, I made speed through the tunnel to my secret room.

Stabb had really pushed it. It was well before dawn. But in the United States, by Eastern Standard Time, it was only 9:00 P.M.

I was very anxious to gauge his reactions. Did he know?

I ignored the current picture and backtracked to the

moment of our departure. I proceeded with spot checks, ignoring unimportant bits.

He had gone inside and locked the door. With a dolly he had taken the boxes one by one into the bar. With a little block and tackle, he had lowered them through the concealed trap at the end of the bar and down into the old mine.

Evidently he had been working there before we arrived. There was a precisely measured hole in one of the galleries. Into it, he put all boxes but one.

He took two small objects out of one box and put them in a rucksack. Then he added that box to the rest. Bad light. I couldn't see the number.

He threw down the canvas and covered it with dirt. He took a machine and made some cobwebs over that gallery and one or two others.

Heller was working very fast. I could hardly follow what he was doing. The light was awful. But it showed he was being very secret. It was a bad sign. He *did* suspect something!

With water from a bottle, he put out the fire in the iron stove. He turned out the kerosene lanterns. He locked everything up. The care with which he did that indicated to me that he probably *knew.*

Playing a light over the landing place, he found a couple of weeds that had been crushed. He simply pulled them up.

He ran up the road about a hundred yards. There was an old white van standing there. Aha, he had had an escape route planned! So he *did* have suspicions!

He tossed the rucksack into the front seat. He got into the van and began to drive rapidly back to the road. The speed he was going showed his anxiety.

The van eventually came out on the highway. He turned south. Very shortly, his lights picked up the sheriff's car. He swung in. Aha! He had had them posted as a trap!

He got out and leaned into the window of the sheriff's car. It was Ralph and George. They looked half asleep. Deceptive!

George said, "Everything go all right, young feller?" Aha! So they *had* been alerted!

Ralph said, "You get your measurements?"

"Yes," said Heller.

George said, "You know, you can drive down there. You don't have to leave your car at the highway and walk. You can get a car all the way in there—I didn't know it myself until t'other day."

Ralph said, "Say, young feller, you being an engineer and all, deer season is coming right up. Sometimes we like to hunt over that way. Do you suppose the consul would mind if we hunted across that property?"

"I'm sure he'd be quite happy about it," said Heller. "He spoke very highly of you both."

George said, "You can tell your boss, Rangletangle Bowja, we're on the job."

Aha. Heller *was* suspicious that we'd been there to kill him. He had cunningly arranged to get the place patrolled by sheriffs posing as deer hunters! Oh, we'd better stay away from *there!*

When Heller pulled away, heading south, the sheriff's car pulled out and headed north. He had even arranged a rearguard action!

Suddenly I realized I had neglected another clue. I scanned back. In my hasty perusal the first time I had missed an important point. The glass jars!

He had put them down on the counter in the dance hall when he first reentered the house. Just as he removed the last box, he had picked them up and looked at them and then scraped at the inside mold. He had dumped the contents in the old iron stove. That was why it was blazing so when he had put it out. Very significant! He had been sure we were trying to poison him!

Well, there was not much need to look any further. But I did.

He had gone off the highway again and come to the old lady's house. He had put the van in the garage. He had taken off his blue coveralls. He had put on his spikes. That showed he was expecting trouble, perhaps thinking we would ambush him.

The blind old lady came out belatedly. She was carrying a shotgun. Very significant. He had tipped her off he might be pursued and have to fight a gun battle.

She said, "Oh, it's you, the young man." She offered him a cup of coffee. He apologized for disturbing her so late and she said, "That's all right."

He put on a leather taxi driver's hat, got in the old orange cab and drove away.

Only one more thing happened and was happening right this minute. He had stopped at a shore seafood restaurant and was eating two lobsters broiled in butter. Very significant. They say a condemned man is always fed a last meal. Even though he was having his late, it showed that he knew he had been condemned.

I sat back.

The conclusion, based on these collective actions of his, showed without a shadow of a doubt that Heller knew we had come there to kill him.

It must be puzzling to him why we had not done so. Yes. The way he was worrying away at a lobster claw, trying to get the meat out, showed he was under strain.

He had been alerted to my real intentions.

That meant I would have to be very careful and plan in a much more deadly way.

Tonight we had failed to do more than alert Heller.

Now I had real problems.

A wary Heller would be much more dangerous. Therefore, I had to be much more cunning.

Certainly, I could not let him go on. If he actually succeeded in this mission, Lombar would be ruined. If he didn't succeed, Earth would be ruined.

It made my head ache.

I desperately needed to untangle all this.

But how?

PART TWENTY-THREE

Chapter 1

The next day, although I should have known better, I went from my secret office through the tunnel to the hangar. My object was actually to see if the secret alarm system was going to work.

What I intended was to carry out a drill. Now that Heller suspected we had been there to kill him, we had better be prepared in case he attacked us.

Faht Bey was in the hangar. I told him I wanted a drill. He argued with me, saying it would interrupt everybody's work. I was just trying to explain to him that we were now in danger from Heller when Captain Stabb, seeing us shaking our fists at each other, came over.

I thought the Antimanco was going to take sides and defend me. But he was in a very sour mood. He paid no attention to what we were talking about.

Captain Stabb said, "I'm facing a mutiny!"

Faht Bey didn't want anything to do with mutinies and he cut out of there at what speed his fat hulk was capable of, leaving me to face Stabb.

"You're a good officer, Gris, if there is any such thing as a good officer. But you can't hold tidbits up in front of a crew and then tell them they can't have them. That ain't right. You as good as promised them they could kill that Royal officer and no questions asked, and then you call it off, just like that. It's ruined morale, that's what it's done. And besides, it isn't fair."

"What can I do?" I said.

"They're standing up for their rights. If they don't get them, I can't answer for it. So you better agree to their demands."

"What are their rights?"

"To go pirating, of course."

"Look," I said. "Be reasonable. Those assassin pilots get nervous when you take the tug out."

"Oh, that thing," said Stabb, dismissing the tug with a flick of his thick hand. "It ain't armed. It won't carry loot. Who's talking about that tug?" He beckoned.

I followed him to a recess in the main hangar. It was really a storeroom where decades of junk and crates had accumulated.

Stabb steered over to one side of the vast hill of debris. He pointed at some very large, age-discolored cases. There were an awful lot of them.

"You know what that is?"

I hadn't the faintest idea.

"That's a 'line-jumper.' Now, I been busy while certain others neglected their duty and I looked up how it came to get here. It was totally dismantled, crated and freighted here from Voltar. And," he added impressively, "it ain't never been assembled."

"What," I said, "is a 'line-jumper'?"

"It's a blazing wonder, that's what it is. They were developed by the Voltarian Army. They use them. They can pick up a hundred-ton piece of artillery, jump the enemy lines and set it and its ammunition down way back of the enemy lines and bomb them from the rear."

I was all adrift. We had no enemy lines to jump, no artillery to move.

"I think," said Stabb, "that somebody in your Apparatus office, maybe even your chief, had one of those bright ideas that officers get sometimes and figured this could be used to shift huge quantities of drugs across borders on this planet. So they got one from the Army and shipped it down here in pieces."

"Sounds like the very thing," I said, looking at the discolored cases with new respect.

"Yeah," said Stabb, "but like a lot of officers' ideas that get men killed and foul up operations, it wouldn't work. It lifts its cargo on traction beams and carries it. The cargo is totally exposed and can be picked up by the most primitive radar. It only operates in atmosphere—there's minimal pressure protection in the flight deck—and it can't go up very high. So they never assembled it."

"Then it's worthless," I said.

"Oh, no," said Captain Stabb. "It's just about the greatest pirate tool you ever heard of. It could pick up a whole village on its tractor beams and fly off with it. You could pick up a whole bank, loot it at ten thousand feet and just drop the rubbish. If it ain't carrying cargo, it is undetectable. So it ain't worthless. It's priceless!"

He patted a box. "I could even devise a curtain to cover cargo and it could be used to run guns to revolutionaries. There's a fortune in this thing! But no officer ever asked no bright, dedicated subofficer what *could* be done with it. The Army sprayed the artillery with absorbo-coat. I don't think the Apparatus knew that. It wasn't in the directions. Experience is what counts in the long run. Not book learning."

I had a marvelous inspiration on how to end this mutiny. "How long will it take to assemble this thing?"

"Well, it's all dismantled down to the last plate and adhesion joint. If we work hard in our time off from shooting dice and drinking—maybe a couple hours a day—it would only take us a few months."

"Do it," I said. "By all means, do it!"

"You're a great fellow, Gris, even if you are an officer. We will show you we mean business, that we're sincere. If we ever get it finished and operating, we'll cut you in on a handsome share of the loot." He clapped me on the back in good fellowship and rumbled off to tell his crew.

I was much relieved. I had certainly handled that mutiny in an expert way.

But Fate was not being kind, even so. I had no more than entered the tunnel which led back to my office than I was suddenly stopped by Faht Bey.

"There's something I better report," he said. I thought, oh Gods, I knew I shouldn't have come into this place.

"We're having to step up our heroin production," said Faht Bey.

"Why? You're already running at top speed!"

"I know," said Faht Bey. "I hate to have to tell you this but there's a twenty-five pound bag unaccounted for."

"So?" I said. (Bleep) these bookkeeping details.

"The security guard says it has been stolen by someone."

"Oh, somebody just miscounted!"

"No," said Faht Bey. "It has never happened before and this is the third time in the past five days. Somebody is stealing heroin supplies and in quantity! And it's happening right here inside the base."

"Well, step up production," I said impatiently. My Gods, I was in no mood for more problems.

"Just so you know," he said, fastening a peculiar eye on me. "We'll step up production."

So I had also solved that.

That would teach me to move around the hangar! You had to be armed with more than a blastick! Too bad you just couldn't throw a grenade at all these problems you met! All this thinking on top of all this grief was making my head ache.

Chapter 2

Now that Heller knew there was a plot against his life, I had to keep a very close eye on him. He might come over to the base and try to kill me.

But, as usual, the things he did didn't make much sense.

In the ensuing days after he returned from Connecticut, Heller devoted a lot of time to studying. He was covering the mimeographed class lectures of his courses to date. He studied in his office at the Empire State Building; he probably even studied in his suite—but who could tell what he did in his suite, thanks to the interference. But what worried me most was his studying in the lobby of the Gracious Palms.

On an evening, he would sit half-masked from the lobby by palm fronds but still in sight of the front door. Why he chose such a place to study, only Heller knew, for he was constantly interrupted.

He was affecting a black, silk-collared tuxedo in the lobby. The shirt had puffs of lace on the front of it and the silk cuffs were held in place with diamonds. How he got them, I don't know, maybe he had them built, but he was wearing black, patent-leather baseball spikes!

He'd get started on a lecture on differential equations or some such silliness and he'd get no farther than a page when some diplomat or another would wander over and he'd get up and shake hands and pass the time of day. The UN was apparently just starting session and there were lots of customers, all of different shades and hues.

They didn't say anything intelligent and for a bit I thought they must be talking in code. Things like "How are you, old boy?" from the diplomats and things like "Just ripping," from Heller. Unintelligible. And some diplomat, with a lift of his eyebrows, would say, "Getting any yourself?" and Heller would say, "The important people have the priorities." And they'd laugh in a sort of knowing way. Incomprehensible.

But one thing was clearly understood. He was too (bleeped) popular!

There was always a painting going on in the far corner of the lobby. Always a crowd around the artist, the girl standing, half-clothed, provocatively. I wanted to get some better looks myself and Heller never even glanced in that direction! You can't get much detail in peripheral vision.

About the only time I'd get a good look at the girl—and they were real stunners of every imaginable hue—was when one would leave the lobby. And then she had a robe on as the painting would be ended for the night. They'd stop by Heller before they got into the elevator and say, "It's going well, pretty boy. I got South Africa to say yes." Or something equally nonsensical. It was confusing. In the first place, the program called for a whore of the week and it had evidently been shifted to whore of the night! It was almost enough to give one jet lag. But he was obviously up to something, even though you couldn't keep up with him.

But it was probably better that I didn't get many looks at these girls. My own bed was empty, and although she would go out each day in her car, I saw nothing of Utanc. She had obviously erased my suffering self from her life. I did hear that the little boy was better but neither of those boys left Utanc's room.

But for all his hobnobbing with diplomats and nosing in his lecture mimeographs and texts, Heller, (bleep) him, still found time to run around.

For three whole mornings he went through the silliest routine I have ever seen.

He would take a regular cab and ride somewhere. And after a bit Bang-Bang would drive up to where Heller had alighted and come over to him and say, "Nothing." That was all.

Heller would get on a subway and ride to some station and get off. After a while, Bang-Bang would come up to him and say, "Nothing." Then Heller would walk slowly past this building or that, stopping to look in shop windows. And then Bang-Bang would come up and say, "Nothing."

I finally worked it out that they were practicing some stupid G-2 idea of tailing. But Heller was always in his red baseball cap, easy to spot. He took no evasive actions. It was either G-2 or just some silly way of exercising.

After three days Heller quit doing that. Maybe he got tired of walking and riding. Maybe he was just seeing New York. Who could follow his inane actions?

Almost two weeks had gone by with this routine of study and lobby when he made a sudden shift.

He got up early one morning. He took a train to Newark and walked into the Jiffy-Spiffy Garage. Mike Mutazione pulled his head out of an engine and they staged an effusive greeting and then chattered of this and that including a persuasive pitch by Mike to get Heller to join the Catholic Church, and Heller's defense, "How do you know my soul hasn't already been saved?" Mike didn't seem to have any textbook answer to that so they got down to business.

Heller wanted a garage to rent. And Mike told him sure, they had several nearby where they stored "hots" until they got their "faces lifted," and Mike himself drove Heller around and they looked at them and Heller chose one that could be very securely locked. And he rented it.

Then they went back to the garage and there, over to one side, was Heller's old Cadillac. It was making some progress but apparently the new engine was still being modified "for 190 miles per hour." But Heller was not interested in the new engine. He wanted the *old* engine that had been taken out and was sitting on some blocks.

Heller did Mike a little sketch in his disgustingly precise and rapid way. He wanted the old engine and a radiator mounted on a trailer. He wanted a gas tank mounted on the trailer. And he wanted a brake drum put around the old engine's crankshaft connection.

It baffled me. Why did anyone want an engine sitting on a trailer that wouldn't run the trailer?

Mike said, "Hell, that's easy. We got a trailer right over here that some (bleeped) fool stole. How can you change and sell a baggage trailer? You can have it. I got a couple guys idle. We can fix your rig this afternoon."

So Heller gave him some money and told him to finish it and move it into the rented garage. Crazy. He not only was making a rig that wouldn't run itself, he was also just putting it in a private garage! No wonder this Mike wanted to convert him to something. He was too insane the way he was.

Heller went out shopping after getting a couple addresses and he bought a huge tank of oxygen and a huge tank of hydrogen gas and had them delivered to the garage.

He went back to New York and went on with his usual routine that day, but the next morning, bright and early, he headed for Newark, carrying a huge bag of tools and whatever.

Heller went to the garage. There was the trailer and there were the oxygen and hydrogen bottles. He put on some white mechanic's coveralls and got to work.

He left the garage doors open. He put a spring balance on the brake drum behind the engine. He started the engine up and began to measure the spring-balance readings as he revved the engine up faster and faster. The roar and vibration and smoke was awful!

Playing. You can always count on Fleet people to play with machinery!

Then, using gloves to keep his fingers from scorching, he took the carburetor off the engine.

Then he connected regulators and hoses to the oxygen and hydrogen tanks.

He made a brass fitting that covered the place the carburetor had been and made two nipples into it and connected the hoses to it.

It was a pretty crude rig.

He even put on a gas mask to work with it.

He started up the engine!

It ran!

Then he began to fiddle with amounts from one tank to the other and began to put pressure on the brake. He kept writing down readings from the tank regulator gauges and the brake spring balance.

Using some kind of a gauge, he started sampling whatever was coming out of the exhaust pipe of the engine. He got the gauge meter to read zero by adjusting the two valves of the hydrogen and oxygen tanks while the gauge on the spring balance on the brake measured maximum.

It was late by that time. He dismantled everything, took off his mechanic's coveralls and left.

He also left me with another puzzle. What was that all about?

But I could tell one thing. He was happy. As he walked down the street to get on the train to New York, he was whistling. Some new trick he had learned.

He was making too much progress on something too fast! I knew he was doing it just to spite me, to mock me for having had to forego killing him.

I felt awful.

Chapter 3

Just when I was feeling that nothing could get any worse, the *Blixo* arrived. It utterly dispersed my existing confusion. It was eight o'clock in the evening, Turkish time. I had been trying to figure out what to do to avoid another sleepless night in my lonely bed when the warning panel in my secret office began to flash:

SHIP ARRIVAL

It could only be the *Blixo.* A sudden thought, "My gold!" began to lift my spirits. Then a sag. I had promised Captain Bolz a bottle of Scotch on arrival. He was an officer who remembered these things clearly. The bottle of Scotch I had gotten had been stolen. He might hang on to my gold!

I made a sudden, urgent telephone call to the taxi driver. "For Gods' sakes, bring me a bottle of Scotch quick!"

"It sounds bad!" he said.

"It is bad!" I said.

I hung up. I went tearing around trying to find a uniform. At the moment the panel flashed, I didn't have any clothes on. It would not do to go aboard that way. He might think I was so lacking in authority he could hold on to my gold. It would buy an awful lot of Scotch—six million dollars worth! I knew Captain Bolz.

I could find a uniform tunic but no pants. Then when I found the pants, I had mislaid the tunic. I found my cap underneath the mattress. I couldn't find my rank locket anywhere.

The place looked like a hurricane had struck it. But I managed to get pants, tunic, boots and cap assembled and on. Maybe he wouldn't notice the lack of a rank locket.

I heard the taxi coming. I went into my bedroom. The driver rushed in and thrust a bottle at me: Haige and Haige. Counterfeit Scotch. Made by Arabs. They can't spell.

"This is bad Scotch," I said.

"It's a bad situation," he said.

It would have to do. I got him out of there with a fistful of lira.

I went tearing down the tunnel from my secret room to the hangar.

They hadn't dollied the *Blixo* into position yet. I waited.

Finally, they got all two hundred and fifty skinny, battered feet of her off to the side of the landing pad and plunked a wobbly, far-too-tall landing ladder up to her airlock. They got another one. It didn't fit either. The *Blixo* spacers put their own landing gangway out. I got aboard.

Captain Bolz was in his cabin getting into a sloppy-looking civilian suit, ready to have a night on the town. He was buttoning a ragged shirt across his hairy chest. I handed him the Scotch. He let go of the shirt. He chomped his teeth down on the cap and tore it off. He had a long, long drink. He shuddered and went a trifle popeyed.

"Gods!" he spluttered. "Gods, but that's good." He took another swallow. He said, "Well, Gris, how are you?"

I reached into my pocket and got the key to the storeroom where I had locked in my gold.

"Your passengers arrived in great shape. Somebody named Gunsalmo Silva was in deepsleep so he wasn't heard from. Prahd Bittlestiffender, he just stayed in his cabin the whole way, studying like fury. That little (bleepard)—what's his name, Too-Too?—I had to put him in irons: it wasn't him, it was the crew, they kept trying to get at him to sleep with. So, it's all in order. So, if you'll just stamp a few papers, they're yours and so's the cargo."

I promptly got out my identoplate and began to stamp. Shortly, I noticed my wrist was getting tired so I looked at what I was stamping. The last half of the pack was blank gate passes so he could land contraband on Voltar. I stamped them.

He grinned. "We understand each other," he said. "Now if you'll let my mates do the unloading, I'm on my way. Have some Scotch. No? Then here I go and the Gods help Turkey." He was gone.

He must have shouted at his spacers as he left for here was a mate to help me. We opened the locker. And there it was! Nine beautiful cases. Eighteen fifty-troy-pound bars of gold! Allowing for difference of gravity—Earth being only about five-sixths as massive—this was only seven hundred and fifty pounds of gold. At twelve troy ounces to the pound that was nine thousand ounces. Gold at the moment was selling at seven hundred dollars an ounce. So I was looking at six million, three hundred thousand dollars worth of gold! Shows you that crime pays after all.

I grabbed a couple of hangar helpers and soon the gold was trundling up my tunnel to my secret room. I went in, threw a blanket over the viewer and then let the helpers pack it in a corner. It didn't take up as much space as you'd think. They, of course, didn't know what it was. The cases were all marked as medical and radio-active.

I was about to shut the door on them and gloat when a messenger came up.

"They want to unload the rest of the cargo! Where does it go?"

I closed my room and went back down the tunnel. They were discharging boxes and boxes and boxes of Zanco material.

Oh, Hells! The hospital! I had forgotten to check if the hospital was complete!

I found a phone and got the contractor. "Of course it's complete!" he said. "I've been trying to get in touch with you for days."

Aha! So I was rich there, too! I got my mind off it. "Where's the keys?"

"Faht Bey has them."

Better and better. I sent a messenger for Faht Bey.

"Trucks," I said. "I need trucks! All this goes to the new hospital!"

"All that?"

I looked again. They were still unloading! They had a mountain-sized pile already and they were still unloading! This was not correct.

I grabbed an invoice sheet out of the hands of a mate. It turned out to be three invoice sheets. One from the goods used at the Widow Tayl's, one from my original purchase and then a third!

My Gods! There was no end to what crooked things superiors will do. Lombar had quadrupled the Zanco order to make another million and a half credits in graft for himself! There were enough cellological supplies here to take care of an army. Two armies! And they had quadrupled all the extra odd bits I had ordered blind as well. There was no telling what was in this growing pile. It must have strained the tonnage capacity of the *Blixo!*

Then it suddenly struck me. The dirty crooks. They hadn't given me my extra thirty-thousand-credit personal rake-off! I was about to rush off and write them an angry letter but Faht Bey said, "You mean all this goes to the hospital?"

"Yes, yes. Overpaste the labels. Get your hangar crews on it."

"But you'll mess up all the markings," he said.

Oh, Hells. Details, details.

I said to a mate, "Where's that Prahd Bittlestiffender?"

The name was unknown to him but I described him and the mate went up and let him out of his cabin. Tall and spindly, he came gawkily down the gangway, burdened with recorders and baggage.

"You're in charge of the hospital! These labels can't

be seen in public. Change all the labels and get this stuff into trucks."

"Hello, Officer Gris," he said. "I can speak Turkish. Listen. I'm speaking Turkish now. Does my pay start now?"

I started to rush off again to write my angry letter.

A mate stopped me. "Where do we put this one?"

They were carrying a stretcher. Somebody in deepsleep. The vicious face of Gunsalmo Silva, no better in repose. "A cell. Any cell. Don't wake him up. I'll take care of him later."

I tried to rush off again. Two spacers were leading somebody out. He was in chains, wrapped up in cloth with a lock on it. He could barely walk. He had a sack over his head.

The mate asked, "What do we do with him?" He pulled the sack off his head. It was Twolah, Too-Too, from my office. The second he saw me, he started to cry.

"Put him in a cell," I said. "They'll show you where the detention cells are. Incommunicado, completely."

I tried to rush off again. A spacer said, "He's got about two hundred pounds of papers in his cabin. What do we do with those?"

"Put them in my office. And don't produce anybody else out of that ship. I'm busy!"

Finally I got away.

I went and wrote the nastiest burning letter I could possibly write! To Zanco. They owed me thirty thousand credits and were trying to gyp me out of it! Not only that, I told them they had denied me the opportunity to buy gold with it! Villains!

And only then did I feel better. The *Blixo* had arrived. I foolishly thought my troubles were over. They were just beginning!

Chapter 4

My gold had arrived so I was sleeping peacefully in the dawn.

Karagoz was shaking my shoulder violently.

"Sultan Bey!" he was saying. "Come quick. Maybe riot!"

I got out of bed, got on some pants and boots and a turtleneck sweater. I went tearing out after Karagoz.

Faht Bey was in a car by the gate. He was holding the door open. It was barely light enough to see his face but what I saw was ashen.

"The hospital!" he said and the driver raced toward it.

"They've been gathering since before dawn. They heard the hospital would be opened today."

"Who?"

"The mothers."

"Why?"

"Because of the sign."

I said, "That doesn't sound like much trouble to me."

"No?" he said. "If we lose the support of mothers in this district our supply of birth certificates will dry up! So be careful how you handle them."

"Me handle them?" I said. "What about the rest of the Apparatus here? Isn't that your job?"

"It's your hospital. You didn't clear it with the Officer's Council."

"I have to do everything!" I wailed.

"And be careful how you handle the picket line," he said.

"*What* picket line?"

"The local doctors and their assistants."

When we arrived at the hospital, there was a huge mob. They were mostly mothers and children. They were standing there docilely the way Turkish people do. They are a very docile people, particularly just before they explode. They are obedient to the will of Allah. But Allah apparently wants holy wars at the first chance.

I pushed my way through them. There was a lot of coughing. Tuberculosis is endemic in Turkey. Eyes turned my way. Diseased eyes. Trachoma is also endemic in Turkey. There was the occasional twisted limb and the inevitable sores.

The hospital was surrounded by mounds of raw earth—it had not been landscaped. But the building itself was imposing—spreading and low. It was approached by some broad steps and a wide walk and a big front door.

A huge white board was nearby. It had a red crescent moon on it. On most of Earth they use a red cross on ambulances and such, but in Turkey it's a crescent, the symbol of rebirth.

There was another big sign. It said:

WORLD UNITED CHARITIES MERCY AND
BENEVOLENT HOSPITAL
Mudlick Construction Company

I could see nothing wrong with this. What riot? Faht Bey always exaggerates so.

I went up the broad steps, pushing through the crowd standing on them. I collided with the picket line!

"Stop!" said an overbearing man carrying a placard.

"Anyone crossing this picket line is an enemy of the Turkish national pride." He pointed at the placards they were carrying.

The crude placards said:

UNFAIR TO ORGANIZED MEDICINE!
NO SCABS!
DOWN WITH CHARITY!

The doctors and assistants carrying them looked very tough.

There was a pedestal on the flat place at the top of the steps. Probably it was for a statue not yet arrived. Faht Bey was pushing at me from behind to get up on the pedestal. I had no choice. I mounted up.

What a sea of faces!

What a lot of coughs and sick eyes.

What a lot of limbs and other ailments being held up!

I knew the Ministry of Health and Social Welfare of Turkey was very active against disease. Also the Ministry of Labor. Also a lot of philanthropic organizations. But handling Turkey was a big job. I hadn't realized there were so many sick people about. Riffraff.

I opened my mouth. I was going to tell them all to go home. I didn't get a chance.

The big doctor on the picket line shouted, "I was trained in the United States. I know how doctoring must be run. THERE MUST BE NO FREE CLINIC!"

Instantly, the picket line closed against the bottom of the pedestal and began to hit me with their placards and sticks!

I dodged, I ducked, I tried to defend myself.

The others in the picket line began to chant, hitting at me to keep time, "NO FREE CLINIC! NO FREE CLINIC!"

I screamed, "Of course there will be no free clinic!"

The crowd went into instant action. They had mud clods! The air was suddenly dark with them! They were throwing the mud at ME!

The doctors let up first. The huge one turned to the crowd. "You see! There will be no free clinic!"

Instantly, the crowd began to throw at both me *and* the doctors! The jeers rose to a savage roar.

"Where are the security troops?" I screamed at Faht Bey.

He was cowering at the far end of the steps. "It's your hospital!" he shouted above the din.

A mud clod hit me in the face!

It knocked me off the pedestal!

The blood started to pour out of my nose!

Suddenly, a tall, gawky figure in a white coat leaped up on the pedestal, holding up his arms. It was Prahd Bittlestiffender!

The crowd stopped throwing to see what he would say.

In purist, scholarly Turkish, Prahd bellowed, "Fellow citizens! Fellow Turks! I come before you today to issue the clarion call to freedom! It is time, due time, that we, the children of Allah, rose as one and cast from off our necks the iron heel of the foreign oppressor!"

My nose was bleeding so much, I thought I would bleed to death. There must be cold water in that hospital. I scrabbled backwards to the door. I got into a hall.

Prahd's voice carried. "A United Turkey facing outward against her rapacious enemies . . ." I was too far away to hear more.

I got into a bathroom, closed the door and found cold water. I sat on a toilet seat and held wet toilet paper against the back of my neck.

I half expected the mob, at any moment, to tear

down the door and rip me limb from limb. But my nose and precious blood came first.

At long last, the bleeding stopped.

It was awfully quiet outside. Had the security guards arrived and shot them all?

I risked a peek. I was looking into a big waiting room. There were lines of mothers there, all quiet, all orderly.

Tables had been set up.

The local doctors were working around the tables, doing the various things doctors do. They seemed very cheerful as they handled people one by one. I didn't see any money being passed over by the mothers. I couldn't understand it.

Afraid that I would be seen and pelted again, I crept down a hall.

A hand on my shoulder. I jumped.

"I was just coming to find you." It was young Doctor Prahd Bittlestiffender. He led me into a small operating room. He began to examine my nose.

"What did you do?" I said. "What was that speech?"

"That was a speech made by Kemal Ataturk at the beginning of the revolution," said Prahd.

Ah, Kemal Ataturk. The Turks worshipped him. They'd recognized the speech and so they'd stopped to listen.

"Ouch," I said. He was probing up into my nose.

"Hold still, please."

"What about the free clinic?" I said, shuddering at the idea of the expense.

"Oh," said Prahd, putting a probe in deeper, "I told them it was all free."

"Ouch," I said.

"I told them it was, after all, their hospital, so they ought to volunteer and fix up the grounds and act as nurses and things. They thought that was wonderful."

"Ouch," I said. "But those doctors?"

"I appointed them all part-time staff to serve a couple hours a day at high salary."

"Ouch," I said. And not because he'd stabbed me. This hospital was suddenly a liability, not a profit! "Where do you think you got authority to do that?"

"Last night, you told me I was in charge of the hospital," said Prahd. "So I did exactly what I knew you would want me to do, Officer Gris. Cure the sick. Help the poor and needy. Better relations with the tribes of this primitive outpost. I admire you for your broad grasp of interstellar relations. Does my salary start now?"

"Oh, my Gods!" I said.

"I can speak Italian, too," he said persuasively.

"How do I know you can cure anybody?" I snarled. "Your test has just begun! It is just barely possible you will get paid when this hospital starts to make money. Real money!" He was jabbing harder at my nose. "Ouch!"

Chapter 5

Because my sweater was all clogged up with mud, Prahd took a white coat he'd brought and put it on me. "I want to show you the place because it has problems," he said.

I bristled. How could it have problems? I had designed it myself. Spent a long time at it, too.

I followed him out. The lines were moving in the main room and it seemed peaceful.

We went down a hall. An operating room, equipment not fully set up. Interview rooms not wholly set up. Then a lot of doors. Wards. A vast number of them. I started to go in one.

"No," said Prahd. "It's full."

"That many patients already?"

"No, no. All these ward rooms and all these private rooms are full of equipment and stores. The base crew and I worked all night. We didn't get further than changing the labels and moving it over here. There's enough equipment and supplies here to operate several hospitals and operate them for years. That's what I wanted to show you. We've got no room for patients. It's all in use for storage space. I need another building just to store things! And a big refrigerated room when I start to build up cultures and cell banks."

He didn't know. I pressed a panel. A stairway was revealed. I took him down to the basement.

It was a whole hospital complex in itself. It had innumerable private rooms as well.

He was amazed. "What's this? A secret hospital under a hospital!"

"Precisely," I said. And I told him about the master plan of changing the identity of wanted men and gangsters.

"They look like prison cells," he said.

"That's to make them feel at home," I said. "Can you do it?"

"Oh, no difficulty with that. It's just that the upstairs hospital should run, too."

"That's for cover," I said.

"That still doesn't solve the storage space, Officer Gris. Nor the refrigeration. It will be all the more necessary because of the increased cultures I will have to make, changing fingerprints and larynxes and so on."

I could see he was being mulish. We went back upstairs to where he had established his office. And a nice office it was. The phone was in and connected. I phoned Mudlick Construction Company and was shortly talking to the contractor.

"I think we had a financial transaction that was not complete," I said.

"There was a cost overrun," he said.

"I will need a huge storage addition and a refrigeration building," I said.

"There was no cost overrun," he said, "if it comes to another half a million U.S."

My Gods, this hospital was expensive!

"Same terms," I said.

"Same terms," he said.

"Make the plans with the man in charge," I said, "and get started on it."

"You're rich," he said.

"You better not get too rich," I said. "There's an awful lot of mud around here." I hung up. But oh, well—charity hospitals had their good points. My rip-off would now be half a million, U.S.

I got ready to leave. My nose was still hurting. "Just tell the Mudlick people what you want when they come and get them started on it. I've got other things to do."

Prahd was making no effort to get up. "Don't you want to hear the news from Voltar?" he said. "I know how you have the welfare of your country at heart."

People will be chatty and social. I sat back down.

"Everything on Voltar is fine," said Prahd. "The weather was nice. All the flowering shrubs were doing beautifully." I knew he was talking about the Widow Tayl's place. I was wary.

"You know that I had some work going on the Widow Tayl," he said. "I'm sure you'll be happy to know it was all concluded successfully before the *Blixo* left."

It was more suspicion than interest that prompted me to ask, "What work was that?"

"I knew your interest in her place and your obvious concern about her. So I did exactly what you would have wanted me to do, Officer Gris. The problem was nymphomania—an obsession with sex."

Oh Gods, was he ever right!

"So I enlarged her ovaries, as a beginning. She can now have three times as many orgasms as before and much more strongly."

Devils! No man in Pausch Hills would be safe! Thank Heavens I was down here on Earth! But wait, he had used the word *beginning*. "You did more?"

"Why, of course. As you are part of the famous Gyrant Slahb family, I did not want to be remiss in my professional activities in your employ."

I waited with my eyes getting narrower. Suspicion is a built-in fact in the Apparatus.

"Nymphomania," he said learnedly, "is often caused by sterility. So I checked and, sure enough, there was an ovulation blockage—the ovum could not come down to be fertilized. So I removed the blockage."

Aha. Maybe he had handled the situation. If the Widow Tayl started having babies, maybe it would slow her down.

Prahd was smiling happily, the true professional. "Well, remember the first day I had the honor of meeting you? You had intercourse with her in the house? Well, I took some of your semen . . ."

"Wait!" I said in sudden alarm, "You'd been having intercourse with her for a day and a half! How do you know it wasn't yours?"

"Oh," he said, waving it away, "it's against the ethics of the profession to use my own." He gave a pitying, professional smile. "What cellologist does not know his own sperm configuration? Easy to tell. Anyway, she was ready to ovulate, even if blocked, so I put one of her ova in a test tube with one of your sperm. And here is the good news: they 'took' very successfully. And so just before I left, I made sure there was nothing else in her womb and I inserted the established embryo."

Horror was going through me in waves. The Widow Tayl! "Does she know whose it is?" I said with dimming hope.

"Oh, yes! She said that as long as it couldn't be Heller's, yours would have to do. She was very happy about it, really. She will be seven weeks along by now. It will be a boy."

I had gone through horror and was into savageness.

"I was so appreciative for all you had done for me," said Prahd, "that I did it all for you. And imagine! It will carry along the line of your great uncle, Gyrant Slahb! It will have the blood of the most famous cellologist on Voltar! Doesn't that make you proud?"

My fists were clenched. "You can't make this stick! There's no evidence I'm the father!"

"Oh, yes," said Prahd. "I filed the medical parental certificate with the authorities. Have no fear you'll lose it. I made very sure you could claim the parentage."

Oh, Gods and Devils! This fellow was a fiend! I surged up. "Why have you done this?"

At last he was intimidated. He began to stammer. "All . . . all . . . all r . . . r . . . right. There was another reason. Y . . . y . . . you said you were going to burn down that b . . . b . . . b . . . beautiful estate! I couldn't bear the . . . the . . . the thought of it. So I knew . . . knew that if you knew . . . knew you had a son there, you would not burn it down!"

I slumped back down into the chair. Oh Gods, Devils and Hells. Here he had tied me to the worst nympho on Voltar! Maybe, if she pressed the demand, I would even have to marry her!

Prahd recovered somewhat. "It has its good side. It *is* a beautiful estate. And she sent you a card."

He reached into his pocket and pulled it out. On one side it had a statue of a naked nymph leering at the viewer while hiding her nakedness in such a way that it was flagrantly displayed. On the other side there was a scrawl. It said:

> *To Soltan,*
>
> *Yoo-hoo, wherever you are. I'm just coming great! It's just coming great. Will you be coming soon? I hope so.*
>
> *Your cuddly Taylsy-Waylsy*
> *Ooooooh*

I went home.

I lay down in my bed and wept.

It was too bad Prahd was officially dead. Otherwise, I could have killed him on the spot.

Chapter 6

Fate didn't have me on rations that day. It was being very liberal. It was even insisting on me taking all the bad luck I could hold and then some.

Midafternoon, Karagoz came into my bedroom. It seems when there is bad news, he brings it. When it is good news he doesn't even send anybody with it.

"There's a horrible-looking man out on the lawn," he said.

I got up. You can't hide a weapon in a sweater—besides, it was muddy. I changed to a windbreaker and put a Colt Cobra in my pocket. Watchfully, I went out.

It was Jimmy "The Gutter" Tavilnasty. He was playing mumbletypeg with a stiletto.

He turned his pockmarked face to me. He looked at me with his beady black eyes. He said, "You got my man?"

"No gun play around here!" I said in alarm.

He juggled the stiletto. "I never use guns. Why do you think they call me 'The Gutter'?"

He looked all around to make sure we weren't being overheard. He seemed to talk mainly out of the side of his mouth. "I got the guys you want right here." He tapped his pocket. "When you finger my man, you get these."

The candidates for altered identities! With us paying the local doctors to work and telling the world it was all free, this new income was not just good. It was vital!

"You come back in a little while," I said.

"I stay right here until you finger Gunsalmo Silva. We got the latest on it. He was the trigger man on 'Holy Joe' after he became 'Holy Joe' Corleone's bodyguard. He ain't honest. We want Gunsalmo Silva *bad.* So these names I got is really *good.* But if the trade is off, say the word and I use you instead. I need practice."

"No, wait! You got me wrong! I just meant it will take a phone call to set it up away from here. You sit right there. I'll have one of my men bring you a shot of something and . . ."

"I never drink on the job. It's illegal for cops so it's illegal for me. Square is square. Make your phone call!"

"What hotel are you staying at?"

"None. I just drove in from Istanbul in a rented car."

"That's all I need to know," I said.

I raced into my bedroom and locked the door. I got Faht Bey on the base internal system. "That *Blixo* deepsleeper," I said. "Get him in an unidentifiable car that will seem to be coming in from Istanbul. Take him to the Saglanmak Rooms. Put him in the room at the exact top of the stairs. Register him as 'John Smith' and tell the clerk he had too much to drink en route. Turn the deepsleep current off in the car so he won't know where he's been. Make sure there are no identifying marks or equipment on him."

Faht Bey said that he would. But he added, "No commotions, Officer Gris. A riot is enough trouble for one day."

I picked up a night infrared scope. I went outside. I persuaded Jimmy "The Gutter" to get up off the grass and sit at a lawn table. I got him served some soft drink. He gave some to a cat that was wandering around and then watched the cat.

He was not very good company. "How's Babe?" I said at length.

"Why do you want to know?"

"Well, an old flame, after all."

"She says she never heard of you."

"I don't always use the same name," I said.

"Oh."

"How's Geovani?" I said.

"Why do you want to know?"

Well, it was not what is called a chummy get-together.

I thought I'd given Faht Bey enough time to get organized.

We went out to Jimmy "The Gutter's" rented car.

I told him where to go.

In a few minutes, I had him park on a back street. We went to the house across the road from the Saglanmak Rooms. It was a flat-topped house. There was an old Turk that we know. I said, "I'm a roof inspector." I handed him a five-hundred-lira note. "We don't want to alarm people by making our inspections public."

He let us through a trap door. The roof had a parapet around it. On hands and knees, we went over to the edge of the flat roof, hidden from the Saglanmak by the parapet.

We were looking straight into the indicated room of the hotel. I showed Jimmy "The Gutter" the stairway which led up to the outside porch. But he knew it already, to his sorrow.

Even though it was autumn now, it was a bit hot on the roof. But Jimmy "The Gutter" didn't seem to mind. He was apparently well conditioned into lying in wait. A properly trained hit man.

The sun went down. We did not make any conversation. Some stars came out. This occasioned no comment.

A car drove up in front of the hotel. Three men got out. The one in the middle seemed to be sagging. They went into the hotel.

Shortly, the light went on in the room.

"Oh, boy!" said Jimmy "The Gutter."

Gunsalmo Silva, very recognizable through the window, was half carried through the door. He seemed to be out cold.

The two men got his clothes off. They put him in the bed and threw the covers over him. We could see the end of the bed.

Jimmy "The Gutter" was checking his stiletto and

a gun. He was so intent on his job, I had to remind him. "The list," I said.

He reached into his jacket. I had the Cobra on him in my pocket in case he drew something else.

It was the list. "Two hunnert names," he said. "All good ones, ready and waiting to come. The last on the list is my brother in Hoboken. You send the commissions to him. He's the straight member of the family, a garbage man. If you forget to pay, I'll be back for you next trip."

"Honesty is the best policy," I said. "It's a pleasure to do business with you."

He grunted.

We went down through the trap.

Jimmy "The Gutter" headed for the outside stairway to that room.

Although I have been known to be a devotee of spectator sports, I thought it would be wiser to have an alibi.

I went down the street and walked into a bar. I ordered a Coke. I was prepared to stay there half an hour talking with the barman about the weather. I didn't.

With a battering roar a shot racketed up the street!

Then two more shots!

My Gods, what was Jimmy using? A cannon?

I stayed right where I was. A police car sounded. There were running feet in the street. Voices and shouts.

"Awfully loud out tonight," I said to the barman.

"Can't understand it," said the barman. "You were standing right here, Sultan Bey."

"I sure was," I said. I shortchanged him so he would remember it.

After our argument died down, I went out on the street. A lot of people were standing outside the Saglanmak. A cop was at the door.

I walked the other way and found a taxi.

The driver let me out at the hospital.

I went in.

I was sort of amazed to see a white-uniformed nurse at the reception counter. It was a very competent-looking girl, good-looking, a Turkish brunette. But she seemed awfully young. "Whom did you wish to see?" she said professionally.

I almost said "Prahd." Then I recalled he had been given papers of a dead male baby and "had been overseas being educated." What name was it? I couldn't remember. "The new head man," I said.

"Ah, Doktor Muhammed Ataturk! You have an appointment? Perhaps I should direct you to a resident intern instead?"

"He's a friend," I said hastily.

"That will be three hundred lira," she said. "We can adjust the amount after your examination. It is a deposit."

"I thought this was a free clinic!"

"Only to those who cannot pay. You obviously can pay. You came in a taxi. No lira, no appointment."

"Get him out here!" I said in a deadly voice.

It must have been kind of loud. Prahd stuck his head out of his office. He said, "That's all right, Nurse Bildirjin. It is a business appointment."

She reluctantly let me pass. In his office, I said, "What the Hells is that?"

"Her name means 'quail.' I thought it kind of pretty," said Prahd.

"More payroll?" I demanded.

"Why, yes. She's the daughter of the town's leading practitioner. His son is coming in from Istanbul in the morning to finish his internship here. But only five more nurses are coming down from the Istanbul training school."

"Who's this 'resident intern'?" I demanded.

"Oh, that's me when they don't have money."

I noticed he had a big tray on a side table, a finished dinner that must have been enormous. "Are you running up bills at the restaurants, too?" I demanded.

"Oh, no," he said. "You told me to be economical. So I only hired two cooks, three dishwashers, a laundress and a chef. They don't want much money. Just plenty of food to carry home."

"Look," I said, "that girl out there will steal your patients for her father. That son when he comes . . ."

"Oh, I mean to train him in cellology!" His eyes suddenly glowed. "Officer Gris, I think I can clean up all the TB and trachoma in this district! And then go on to all of Turkey! And then the whole Middle . . ."

"Doctor Bittlestiffender!" I said sharply. "They obviously omitted from your training a course in finance. Doctor Gyrant Slahb often said, 'Where the Hells would cellology be without money'! So there!"

"She did try to collect a fee off you," he said weakly.

I sat down. "Prahd, I think you need basic orientation in the facts of life. It isn't money *from* me you're after. It's money *for* me, young Doctor Prahd."

I saw he looked shocked.

I am quick at these things. "So that I can finance cleaning up diseases," I added.

His eyes instantly glowed worshipfully. "Then it was all right that I ordered two new ambulances and have drivers coming in."

Gods!

There was no use talking to him about some things. He was too stupid. I whipped out Jimmy "The Gutter's" list. "Here are two hundred names. You will find phone numbers on this list. They are in Paris and New York and Las Vegas and Rio and Gods know where else. Schedule them to come in here a couple dozen at a time and get busy!"

He took the list. He looked confused.

"*Now* what's the matter?"

"I don't know how to use one of these phones!"

I snatched the list back. I knew a balk when I saw it. "I'll do it myself!"

I started out the door.

"There's no need to walk back to your villa," he called after me. "My car and driver will take you!"

And, (bleep) him, there was a new Omni waiting on the front drive and a uniformed chauffeur opened the door for me. "To where did you wish to go, Sultan Bey?" he said.

I told him he could go to any Hell Moslems went to and walked back to my villa. That would show them!

The walk cooled me off. Prahd was pouring out money in rivers. (Bleep)-all was coming in.

I sat down with the list. What to do with it. I got to thinking. The National Security Agency monitored all long-distance calls. Perhaps it wasn't wise to phone from here. It might even bring in hit men on their trail or even CIA hit men, which is worse, and I had had a bellyful of hit men for the night.

Ah. I wrote explicit instructions to use messengers and not to use the phone at all. I wrote exactly what to do. I coded these and the lists up. I ran down the long tunnel to Faht's office.

"Send this to our New York organization," I said. "Right away!"

He took it. "I hope you know what you're doing, Sultan Bey. We're having about all the commotion we can stand. There was a shooting in town a little while ago. I just got a call. Where were you?"

"In a bar, having a Coke, and I can prove it," I said.

"I bet you can," he said.

But he took the list over to his machine and sent it.

Chapter 7

But fate was not through dribbling on me yet.

As I turned to go, Faht Bey said, "You have another prisoner in the detention cells. Captain Bolz phoned from an Istanbul whorehouse this afternoon and told me he had orders to take the person back with him when he left and he wanted to make sure we had an extra set of irons for him."

Too-Too! Oh Gods, would duty never cease to nag! "All right," I said impatiently. "I'll go interview him now."

I went out. I had no car so I walked through the chilly night to the archaeological workers' barracks. I got the duty officer and we entered the hangar.

At the cell, the guard officer said, "You want me to stay? They brought him in, in chains. He must be pretty violent."

It was an opportunity to show how tough I was. "I can handle him," I said. "I'm heavily armed."

The officer unlocked the cell door for me and left.

I turned on the cell glowplates.

Too-Too woke up, saw me and started crying.

He was pretty rumpled. "Six horrible weeks in a horrible spaceship with a horrible crew trying to get at me," he said. "And now *you!*" The tears streamed down his pretty face.

I slapped him. I hate homos. They make me sick at my stomach. The very thought of a man making love to a man makes me turn green!

"I've got two postcards," I said. "One for you and one for Oh Dear. If you don't mail them on return, your mothers will automatically be killed."

The tears turned into rivers.

"So if you want those cards to continue to hold the magic mail," I said, "you will stop blubbering and tell all—clearly and distinctly."

He begged permission to go to the toilet.

There is not much privacy in a detention cell. He made me turn my back.

Finally, he composed himself on the stone ledge—which is to say, he sat there drawing long, shuddering sobs.

Now that he was relaxed, I said, "I want to know everything Lord Endow has been saying or doing since I left. Start talking!"

"I was only there ten days after you left!" he wailed.

"No equivocations. Begin!"

"The minute he saw me, he said, 'Oh, how darling!' Then he said, 'Your trousers seem a little tight. Come into my bathroom so I can . . .'"

"No, no, no!" I stormed at him. I hate homos! Men making love to each other curdles my blood! "I want you to tell me the essentials! The important information!"

"Oh. The important things. He said I was much more beautiful than his orderly so he transferred the fellow back to the Fleet at once. And I *am* lovely! Endow said one night . . ."

"Too-Too," I said in my most deadly voice. "Political. I want political, not homosexual, data!"

He started crying again and I had to slap him.

Finally, with my knee on his chest and him lying

back on the stone ledge and a stungun held to his throat, I began to get data.

It seemed that Lombar, through Endow, had begun to get several of the Grand Council on uppers and downers—methedrine and morphine—to "help their rheumatism." The physicians in Palace City were all pushing drugs and success was looked for.

With a few more slaps and jabs, I got more data. Lombar had heard of the U.S. Congress's Harrison Act of 1914, Earth date, which regulated narcotics, and was pushing it to get it passed by the Grand Council so that anybody else pushing drugs that hurt Lombar's monopoly would be instantly jailed. The growing of poppies on any planet in the Voltar Confederacy would be punishable by total confiscation of the land, the poppies, heavy fines and imprisonment for life. Synthesizing speed or any other such drug would carry the death penalty. There would be one license for all types of drugs and that would be Lombar's.

Very smart. Just like I. G. Barben and Rockecenter had done. Lombar had studied the primitives very well.

Aside from some odds and ends, that was really all Too-Too knew about the Grand Council.

I let him up. I was almost reaching for the postcards when a sudden suspicion took me. He looked smug, the way homos will. I hate homos. You can't trust them.

I took out the cards all right. And then I put my hands on them in a position that indicated I was about to tear them up.

"No!" he screamed at me.

"You know more," I said.

He thought wildly. Then he said, "All I can think of doesn't concern the Grand Council or Endow. It's only Bawtch."

Aha! He was holding back. I made my hands look tense.

"No, no," he screamed. "I'll tell you! Just the day after you left, I saw Bawtch sitting in his office. He was laughing to himself. And he said something."

Good Gods! Bawtch laughing? That silly old chief clerk never laughed in his life. This must be something terrible! "What did he say?"

"It didn't make any sense to me. But it concerned you. Bawtch said, talking to himself, 'Forgery. Oh my. Oh my. It's wonderful. Forgery! They'll execute Gris for it!' "

I went cold. What did Bawtch have on me?

The only forgery you could instantly be executed for was forging the Emperor's name on a document!

And then it came to me. Those two (bleeped) forgers in Section 451 had talked!

They had told Bawtch about those two documents I had used to con the Countess Krak into persuading Heller to leave!

Yes! They could execute me!

Bawtch was getting his jealous revenge!

What could I do?

Those two documents, the only copies, were on the body of the Countess Krak!

The deadly Countess Krak, that would let nobody touch her! That killed, if anyone but Heller reached toward her.

My head was in a whirl.

I needed time to think!

I put the two postcards back in my pocket.

Too-Too screamed in anguish.

I left the cell. The guard officer was waiting. He said, "Devils! I've heard some brawls in my time but that one in there . . . No wonder they brought him in chains!"

I said, "Lock him up again but hold him ready."

I went up the tunnel to my room. This was a real emergency. Fate had just been playing with me until it hit me with an axe!

What could I do?

Chapter 8

My old Apparatus school professor in Wits Utilization used to say, "When the natives have you lowered in boiling oil and are sticking spears into you, it's time to accumulate data." I heeded his advice.

The night was getting on. I sat there trying to think. My eye was attracted to the viewscreen.

The interference was off in the suite. I usually kept the sound off when I was away. I turned it on.

Vantagio, Izzy, Bang-Bang and, of course, Heller were lolling around in Heller's suite. It must be just before dinner there.

Vantagio had a huge atlas on his lap. He had it open to a map of the world. At first I just thought he was riding his hobbyhorse—political science.

". . . so that's what the 'democratic process' is: the politicians give the people things the politicians don't own in order to get elected. Got that, kid?"

Heller nodded. Bang-Bang said he wished they had some Scotch.

"Now, communism," continued Vantagio, "is where

the people are forbidden to own anything so the commissars can grab it all for themselves. These are the essential differences between democracy and communism. You got that, kid?"

Heller said, "Yes. Political science is a wonderful subject."

"Yes," agreed Vantagio. "Politics is mostly grabbing and political science gives you a good chance to grab first."

Izzy looked around at them apologetically. "Could we please get back to the Master Plan?"

I became alert. Spinning though I was, the "Master Plan" was something I knew I had better know about. I had missed it before.

Izzy continued. "How many of these countries have to depend on voter appeal?"

Vantagio picked up the atlas and turned it toward them. He pointed. "Let's take England first. . . ."

On went the interference. Some (bleeped) diplomat was reliving his youth in hot, synthetic sunlight on artificial grass! I hoped he got sand in his hair!

I turned off the sound and was about to throw a blanket over the viewer when the import of what I had heard struck me.

You understand that I was in a very nervous state. I was in the hands of Bawtch, which was bad enough, but I conceived that I was also in danger of being executed by the Emperor. One might have thought these were sufficient threats for one night. But here, I realized abruptly, was another one!

Heller could get at me!

They were actually conspiring, there in that suite. Heller was studying political science and there could only be one reason. If they were taking over every country in the world—and Vantagio had clearly stated they were about to take England—Heller could then control the combined military forces of the planet, and now that he knew I had tried to kill him, he would use them for only one purpose—to capture *me!*

It tipped the scales utterly.

I made up my mind.

I woke up Karagoz. He told me the Ford station wagon was able to run.

I was too shaky to drive. I made him get in, ignoring his plea that he had no pants or shoes on, and forced him to drive me to the hospital.

On those inventories I had seen a hypnohelmet. When I had asked Zanco for all the other new bits they had, that appeared to have been one of them.

At the hospital I pushed my way right by the old woman asleep at the desk. I made my way noisily to Prahd's bedroom.

I was not noisy enough. He was in bed with Nurse Bildirjin. Their heads popped up.

"My father!" said Nurse Bildirjin.

"It's not your father," said Prahd. "Sultan Bey, I think you have met Nurse Bildirjin? Please don't blow up the hospital."

Nurse Bildirjin professionally started to get into her uniform. "You should register at the outer desk. The first examination is three hundred lira."

I kicked her out. "Where are the inventories?"

Prahd got some pants over his skinny legs. He got on a doctor's coat, and barefoot, led the way to his office. He had the inventories in a safe.

I looked at them. There were two lots. It took me a while.

Then I was chilled. There were sixteen hypnohelmets in these shipments! My own horrible experience with them made me shudder. Sixteen of those things on the loose! I only wanted one. But fifteen more were going to go out of circulation right away!

Well, the problem was that Prahd had not had time enough to list the boxes per room. He and the hangar crew had only managed to change the labels.

I made Prahd do most of the work. It was hard to get through and between things, hard to lift up and look under things. Ward after ward crammed full of boxes.

One after another, however, due to my persistence, we unearthed them. The last one was in a bigger box along with electric slicing machines.

It was a chilly night but Prahd was really sweating when he finally had sixteen hypnohelmets in a stack out by the station wagon.

"But what *are* they?" Prahd pleaded as Karagoz stuffed the boxes into the wagon.

"The most deadly contrivance known to any sentient species," I said. "The thermonuclear bomb is nothing compared to them. And there you had them right in plain sight!"

He didn't look contrite enough.

"Because of this insecurity, I am not going to start your pay yet."

That made him look pretty contrite. Sort of gnashing his teeth. It would have to do.

I drove off and went back to my villa.

I have a vault opening off my bedroom that nobody knew about. I sent Karagoz back to bed. I carried the boxes in there myself, all but one.

I got it out of its carton. It smelled very new. I checked its power supply. I was careful not to be anywhere near it and I did it with a stick. It was live.

I sorted through its spares. I found the recording-strip blanks.

With great care, I put a recording strip in my

machine and made the suggestion-command. I got it all ready to slide into the slot of the helmet.

I then sat down and wrote a letter to Lombar. I did not say too much. Only cheerful generalities. And then one request.

I wrote another letter to Snelz.

With great care I packaged them with Heller's last report so they would all go on the *Blixo.*

Now I was ready for the next stage. If this all worked, it would save my life in more ways than one.

I felt confident.

I was going to combine both the cunning skill of Earth psychology with the police techniques of the FBI. How could I miss?

Chapter 9

It was time I turned against fate.

I phoned the taxi driver. He was in bed.

"You know that fat, dirty old whore that lives north of town—Fatima Hanim? Get her and bring her here at once." It greatly alarmed him. "Hey, what's the matter with you know who?"

I couldn't let him think there was anything wrong with my own sexual prowess or ability to control women. "She's wonderful. Fatima is for somebody else."

"I'm so relieved. There's no money-back guarantee, you know. I'll be right there with Fatima."

I opened up a spare bedroom. I threw some pillows on the floor. I fixed some lamps just right. Then I went to my lockers and got a strip camera. I put it in the corner of the room, hooked it to remote and put the remote switch in my pocket.

I picked up the hypnohelmet and went through the tunnel to the hangar.

The guard officer let me into Too-Too's cell.

Too-Too woke up. "Oh, no!" he screamed just at seeing me.

"Be calm," I said. "It is going to get worse. Put this on."

"NO!" he screamed.

The guard officer and I got it on him and chained him down.

I took the guard officer outside. "What's that we put on him?" he asked.

"Something to muffle the screams," I said.

"Oh," he said. "It's about time!"

"Now listen," I said. "What base personnel has been disciplined for molesting small Turkish boys?"

"Half a dozen," he said.

"The worst one," I said.

"Oh, he's doing ninety days right this minute. Cell thirteen."

We went to cell thirteen. The fellow sat up groggily when we put the glowplates on. He was a huge, hulking monster, with muscles like balloons.

"You do exactly what I tell you," I told him, "and your sentence is finished."

"What is it?"

"Sex," I said.

"I won't have nothing to do with girls," he said.

"Not girls," I said. "Is it agreed?"

"Okay," he said. "You want to do it here, right now?"

I almost slapped him. I hate homos. But I had more important things to do.

"Keep him right here," I said to the guard officer.

I went back to Too-Too's cell. I put the recorded strip in the helmet slot. I took a stick I had brought and standing well away from any field from it, I turned the helmet on.

Too-Too stopped threshing about.

I took the stick and turned the helmet off.

I undid his chains.

I removed the helmet from his head. I took out a Colt Cobra. I marched him out into the corridor.

From my pocket I took two bandages. I told the guard officer to blind their eyes. He did.

At a pistol point I made them walk up the tunnel, through my secret room, through my bedroom, across the patio and into the prepared spare room.

"Sit down on the pillows," I said. "Don't take those bandages off. I'll be right back."

I went outside. The taxi driver was there with Fatima Hanim. I told the driver to wait in his cab.

Fatima Hanim was mostly quivering flesh and stink. I said, "You do exactly what I tell you and you get paid five hundred lira."

"On the grass here?" she said.

I shut her up. I told her what she was supposed to do. She was a bit puzzled but nodded.

I took her in the spare room.

I had trouble. The big brute had slipped his bandage and was trying to get the clothes off Too-Too.

At gun point, I made the huge bird stand back. And it took a lot of gun pointing!

"Now, Too-Too," I said, bending over and whispering in his ear, for he only spoke Voltarian, "you get your reward for being such a good messenger."

I stood back and motioned to Fatima.

I went outside and pushed the remote button that started the camera.

From behind the closed door, I heard Fatima begin to croon a soothing lullaby:

Poor little baby,
Hungry as a cat.
Come to mama, darling,
So she can fix that.
Put your little fingers
In hair as fine as silk.
Mmm, mmm, mmm,
Mmm, mmm, mm!
Inhale mama's milk!

There was a sudden screech from Too-Too!

A curse came from the big bird, an order to lie still.

I curled my lip in disgust as Too-Too began to moan.

The lullaby started up again. It went on and on.

Then there was an explosive curse from the big bird.

Too-Too screeched in ecstasy.

Then I heard a scramble and a loud kiss!

"Oh!" came Too-Too's voice in Voltarian. "You are ever so much better than Endow!"

Instantly, I shut off the camera-recorder.

I opened the door.

Too-Too was standing there with his arms around the big brute.

Too-Too looked stunned. "Why did I say that?" he said. "It isn't true. You're not better than Endow!"

I smiled thinly. He had said that because he had been told to on the hypnostrip.

"Time's up," I said.

"What language is he speaking?" said Fatima.

"Baby talk," I said.

"Oh," she said. Then, "Isn't anybody going to take *me?*"

I got her out of there. I gave the taxi driver a thousand lira to pay himself and her.

I went back.

The brute was pawing Too-Too again, who wasn't complaining. I kicked them apart. I hate homos.

Punching them with the Colt Cobra, I got their clothes and the bandages on them. I marched them back through and down to the hangar and the detention cells in the passage to the right.

"Go okay?" said the guard officer.

"Just fine," I said.

We started to put Too-Too back in his cell.

I said to the hulking brute, "You can go now. You're free."

"Can't I do another ninety days with him?" said the brute, trying to get past us.

I made the guard captain take him away to the barracks.

I set Too-Too down on the ledge. He was still drooling.

"You've had your fun," I said.

"Oh, yes," he said, rolling his eyes.

"Now there's a price."

He went wary. "You said it was a reward."

"The reward was the woman. You haven't paid for the man. Now listen carefully."

I took three objects out of my pocket, chosen from my routine Apparatus kit. "You often serve the office staff their hot jolt and a sweetbun in the morning. Here in my palm you see three capsules. Each of these contains a concentric molecular powder. The core is a molecule of a deadly poison."

He quivered and his eyes shot wide in horror. Psychology is right. What you say to them right after intercourse is itself hypnotic.

"This molecule of poison," I continued, "is enclosed in a molecule of copper which shields it. The molecule of copper is enclosed in a molecule of sugar. When these arrive in a person's stomach, it takes two hours for the stomach acid to eat away the copper. Then the person dies. Do you understand?"

He did. But just to spite me, he fainted. There was a water can in the cell. I threw some in his face and brought him around.

He moaned, "Give them to me. You are going to order something terrible. I will take all three at once!"

"No," I said patiently. "The poison produces one of the most painful and agonizing deaths ever devised. It took Apparatus chemists years to develop something this painful. So you would never be able to survive taking them."

He was beginning to cry so I slapped his face to get him back on the subject.

"Now pay heed," I said. "You know the two forgers in Section 451."

He groaned.

"You are to serve their snack. You are to empty one of these capsules into each of their sweetbuns and cover it so it just looks like more sugar."

"Oh," he moaned. "You are proposing murder!"

"Stop quibbling," I said. "When you have served the two forgers, you are then to serve Bawtch. You are to put the third capsule in Bawtch's . . ."

"BAWTCH?" he cried and fainted.

I threw more water on him. I got him around eventually.

"Now," I said, "if you do not do this, I will not

give Oh Dear your magic mail card when he comes in three months. The Commander of the Knife Section on Mistin will get an order. And that will be the end of your mother."

He fainted again. There was no more water so I kicked him back to life.

"One more thing," I said. "I have written some orders to Lombar but I want to make sure. You are to make very certain, using all your influence with Endow, that two people come with Odur next trip—without fail. They are to arrive here, straight up, happy and intact. The first of these persons is the Countess Krak. The second of these persons is Doctor Crobe."

He was crying and wailing and threshing about, beating his fists on the ledge. I knew this would be his effort to refuse. I was ready for it.

I took a small viewer from my pocket. I set it up. I held his head so he would have to look at it.

The whole sex scene ran off. It ended with the kiss and the classic remark he had been made to make by posthypnotic suggestion. "Oh, you are ever so much better than Endow!" We psychologists know our business.

"Endow will kill me! He'll imprison me for life! With maniacs!"

"Precisely," I said. Yes, indeed, we psychologists know our business. "And if those three people on Voltar aren't dead and if the two named do not arrive with Odur, these strips go straight to Endow! Understood?"

When I got him conscious again, he understood.

After, with some trouble, I had made him rehearse it over and over, he had fainted one more time. His heart palpitations had been getting worse. I couldn't think of any other way to torture him at the moment, so I left.

It was a masterly stroke!

Heller had asked for a cellologist. Crobe had been aching to ruin anybody as good-looking as Heller. So I would give him Crobe.

The Countess Krak was wearing those two forgeries on her body. When she arrived, I would simply pluck them off with suitable guise.

The Countess Krak would rave at Heller and upset him so for living in a whorehouse that he would never get anything done. She would slow him to a walk and maybe, as I had told Lombar, she would kill Heller. Lombar would listen to my needing a hit woman.

And when I finished off Heller, however it was done, there would be no Countess Krak waiting to take revenge at the other end. I would see to it that she never left Earth once here.

All witnesses dead. The forgeries of the Emperor's name safely in my hands. Really a masterly stroke!

I knew that Earth psychology had not failed me and the use of FBI evidence-gathering, frame-up know-how had been flawlessly executed.

I went to bed comfortable for the first time in many, many days.

PART TWENTY-FOUR

Chapter 1

For some reason, possibly understandable, I wanted to see the *Blixo* unquestionably gone. Other ships come and go but the *Blixo* apparently had its own brand of cargo—bad news. Accordingly, when I awoke from my well-earned sleep, I tackled two hundred pounds of papers that had to be stamped. Captain Bolz could take them away, thank you.

It was too much to ask of one to read them so I sat in my office and stamped away. My arm got tired. How, in just ten days, could Bawtch accumulate so much paper to be stamped? But, oh well, he was cared for. In another few weeks they would give him a nonmilitary funeral—probably the coffin would be carried between two lines of clerks making an arch with pens, and his tombstone would read STAMP HERE.

I tried to tie the identoplate to my foot but my back got tired bending over to change the sheets. I toyed with the idea of going out and finding a blind beggar to do the stamping—but they whine so and I had had my fill of whining lately.

It was ten o'clock in the evening when I finished. I got a dolly and pushed the papers down the tunnel from my office and into the hangar. A couple of hangar men loaded them into the ship.

Bolz had a terrible hangover, fortunately, and there was no social chitchat. He had encased Too-Too in irons and locked him into a strongroom to which there was only one key. He had made sure the cartoned balls of opium were lashed down, the heroin bags wouldn't leak or roll about and that the cases upon cases of I. G. Barben speed wouldn't crush at high acceleration. He gave me a wincing farewell—I shook his hand too hard (I was so glad to see him go)—and went to his flight deck.

The trundle dolly rolled. The airlocks clanged shut. The *Blixo* lifted its skinny, battered length up through the mountaintop illusion and was gone into the dark night. Six weeks from now it would, I hope, land uneventfully on Voltar and my main troubles would be solved.

Exhausted from my stamping labors, I went back to bed and slept the sleep of the cunning and the just.

It was almost ten o'clock the next morning when I got around, much refreshed. I lolled over breakfast in my room, and when the waiter had gone, I decided to take a turn in the yard.

I was expecting nothing. My mood was optimistic. As I looked up from the patio at the open sky above, I could see that it was a fine autumn day.

The door from the patio to the yard was shut. It had a small port in it—the Romans were cautious people. More from habit than from fear, I glanced through the small port before I opened the yard door.

I froze!

Sitting on the grass! Sitting on the grass, tossing an object into the air and catching it! Sitting on the grass was GUNSALMO SILVA!

I flinched back!

My world went topsy-turvy!

What was HE doing there? HE was supposed to be DEAD!

I peeked cautiously. He had not seen me. He was

just sitting there tossing whatever it was. But what was it? It was about fourteen inches long, it was narrow, it was black.

A sawed-off shotgun! I think they are called a "leopard" by U.S. gangsters. They saw off the barrel and they saw off the stock and it leaves a sort of pistol. But what an awful pistol! A double-barrelled, twelve-gauge smoothbore! It could blow a hole in a man a dog could jump through and do it twice!

What was he doing here?

Only one conclusion could be reached. He knew I had put the finger on him and he had come here to kill me!

I abandoned all thought of going for a walk!

Silently I withdrew to my room.

I closed and double-barred my bedroom door.

I opened the passage to Faht's office and went tearing down it as fast as I could run.

Somewhat out of breath, I burst in upon Faht.

"There's a man in my front yard!" I said without preamble.

Faht Bey was going over some accounts. He looked up tiredly. "Probably it's part of this mess with the American consul." He saw I didn't understand. "The shooting," he explained. "The one you got the alibi for. Things were very calm here before you arrived."

"What American consul?" I shouted at him.

"Don't you know about American consuls? They got two main duties. One of them is to claim the bodies of dead Americans. The other is to protect live Americans from justice and make sure they get thrown in any foreign jail that's handy. And of course, there's the other secret duty of running the CIA."

"What's going on?" I screamed at him.

"There's no use to pretend you don't know," he said.

"Couple of days ago, there was a shooting in a local rooming house. A guy named Jimmy 'The Gutter' Tavilnasty went into a room and got shot to pieces. A man named Gunsalmo Silva was arrested. He's been on our lines, Gris. He came in on the *Blixo* and you know it. You ordered us to deliver him to that rooming house and we did. And he killed this Tavilnasty."

"What happened?" I pleaded.

"The police arrested this Silva and threw him in the jug. The American consul from Ankara came in here to claim the body and ship it home and Silva heard there was an American consul in town and he insisted on seeing him, claiming to be an American citizen. We got scared they would take Silva and maybe interrogate him but that didn't happen. The American consul verified Silva was an American citizen, so of course they demanded the court put him in prison on bread and water. But the local police said it was self-defense and they let Silva go. They don't like foreign interference. The consul was awfully mad at the lack of international cooperation but he left on the morning plane with the body of Tavilnasty. Now do you understand?" He didn't really want to know. "If the man on your front lawn is squat, very muscular, black hair, black eyes, swarthy complexion, then that's Gunsalmo Silva. But it's all handled." He fixed a beady eye on me. "How is it there always seems to be trouble where you've been and how come you always show up later when everything is handled?"

Handled? "My Gods, what do you mean, handled? He's sitting on my front lawn with a sawed-off shotgun!"

"Oh, well," said Faht Bey. "Details, details."

I saw I wasn't going to get any help there. I turned to leave and I swear I heard Faht Bey mutter, "And good luck to him." But I was shaking too hard to take it up at that moment.

Going back through the long, long tunnel, I regained my room.

A thousand plans began to race through my head and tangle with each other.

I half-loaded a ten-gauge shotgun and then left it. I couldn't splatter Silva all over the front lawn. It would leave evidence. And besides, if I stuck my head out that yard door, he might shoot first!

I could not cower here in my room for weeks. I had to work this out!

Sitting down, I took a piece of paper and a pen. I began to write down everything I knew about Gunsalmo Silva. It is a last-ditch sort of exercise. Out of it can come a masterstroke.

The first thing that hit me was that I didn't have to pay Tavilnasty any commissions. That was on the good side of the ledger.

The next thing was that Gunsalmo Silva was sitting on my front lawn. That was not on the good side of the ledger.

What did I really know about this gangster? He had been "Holy Joe" Corleone's bodyguard but had acted as the triggerman in wasting him. He had had some trifling information that the Spiteos interrogator had gotten out of him about senators in the pay of organized crime. Ah. And he didn't have very good sense: he had called for an American consul.

But there was something else. It was eluding me. Then I had it. He was now hypnotrained in Apparatus techniques! A graduate of that school! Yikes! He was deadly!

I cursed Bawtch for having delayed his execution

order to be stamped. Leave it to Bawtch to mess things up. But then, Bawtch was cared for.

That was all I could come up with. I paced. I went back and forth. There wasn't much space to pace in and I barked my shins.

Hypnotraining! That was it! I knew I could come up with something masterly!

Right there in that very room were sixteen hypno-helmets. If I could get some guards to shoot a paralysis dart into him from a distance, I could get a helmet on him and untrain him!

Now, let's see. What did I know about hypnosis? Actually, I had never studied it very much. I wanted to be very sure of what I was doing.

I got out my Earth psychology textbooks. I looked the subject up. Psychologists on Earth use hypnotism all the time. They are the masters.

It said that hypnotism was known to most primitive races and that it was used by priests in ancient times, which proved religion was no good—psychologists don't like religion, it is a threat to their racket.

But hypnotism, it continued, was of great use to the psychologist. You could use it to seduce girls. As that was its primary use, it got me off on another track. It opened some new vistas. Thoughts of Utanc were never far away and I began to wonder if maybe I couldn't hypnotize Utanc and make her be sensible, which is to say, get into my bed.

Then my attention fell upon something awful. The text said that hypnotism was of very limited use because only about 22 percent of the people were potential hypnotic subjects and the rest couldn't be hypnotized. And as the psychologist had as his goal the mastery and puppetizing of ALL the people, the tool was in disrepute.

It was a sad blow. Even if I mastered spinning spirals

in front of Utanc's face or got her to look at a swinging bright object, she might be one of the 78 percent. And I doubted I could make her stand still that long.

But wait! Hypnohelmets! Hadn't I seen some literature? I opened the vault. I fished around in the box of the one I'd used on Too-Too. When I had made the strip, I had just done what I had seen Krak do. There was probably more to this.

Aha! A little manual! I opened it.

Hypnotism, it said, was a tool applicable in the reenforcement or eradication of memory, or the substitution of false memories for actual ones. Now we were getting somewhere!

It said any emotion could be suppressed or heightened. Aha! I could order Utanc to love me!

Then it said that primitive hypnotism only worked on about 18 percent of the subjects. This was a discrepancy and it bothered me. Earth psychologists never lie. At least not about statistics.

However, the manual plunged on. It seemed that the mind had several wavelengths. The helmet approximated two of these. First was the sleep wave, and by parallelling this, one could produce a trance state. The second wave the helmet employed was the thought wave. Anything carried along on this wave—from a recorded strip or direct speech to the helmeted subject—was accepted by the subject as his own thought and was retained. Thus, hypnotism became effective on 100 percent of the subjects. Subjects were at the total effect of the helmet. You could do anything with the helmet that could be done in any hypnotism. However, its primary use was speed-training. Any skill or language . . . I had learned my languages with such a helmet under Krak. . . .

Suddenly, with a wave of horror, I recalled the terrible experience I had had after Krak had put a helmet on me and told me I would feel sick if I harmed Heller! What agony!

I dropped the manual as though it were spouting fire!

These helmets were DANGEROUS!

I had ordered Krak to arrive.

Supposing she put another helmet on me!

The thought was so awful that I almost ran out of the room to get away from the helmets.

I checked myself in time. I must not go out on that lawn!

I made myself sit down on the other side of the room from the helmets. I had to think.

Maybe I should destroy them. I could get a disintegrator from the hangar shops. . . . No, wait! These helmets were valuable. I could use them to seduce any girl I wanted. I could get the staff to bow and slaver whenever I appeared. I could make Utanc love me and that was the important thing.

Oh, yes. And I could untrain Gunsalmo Silva and make him get the idea he was needed at the North Pole. Under the ice.

No, I mustn't destroy these helmets. Maybe I'd never get out of this room unless I used them. Gunsalmo had gotten Tavilnasty. Apparatus trained, maybe he'd get me no matter what I did.

Obviously, the right answer was to hit him with a paralysis dart, get a helmet on him and send him off to burrow in the ice.

Good.

But under no circumstances did I want to take any chance of MY getting a helmet put on me by Krak or anybody else!

I got nerve enough to examine a helmet again. There was a little light in front that showed it was on.

Wait! That light was not part of the mind-wave circuit.

INSPIRATION!

I would be able to get out of this room through the yard, seduce all the girls I wanted, make people bow to me and make Utanc love me with devotion!

With no risk to myself!

Chapter 2

Using the communicator system to the hangar, I sent for the technician who had installed the new emergency-alarm system. He soon came in through the hangar tunnel.

He was a cocky, self-confident type, a little runt named Flip, product of Wiggo, one of the Voltar planets. Nobody had ever persuaded him to comb his hair Earth style: it stood up in two spirals, like twin antennae.

"Alarm system don't work?" he said.

I sat him down. I handed him the hypnohelmet and the box it came in. "There is a grave emergency," I said. "These just came in on the *Blixo.* They work on everybody."

He looked the hypnohelmet over. Count on a technician. They never look on the outside of anything. He instantly began to look inside and open up the guts. Then he paused. "If they work, what am I doing fixing it?"

"You don't understand," I said patiently. "I've got sixteen of these. I want them fixed so that they only work when I want them to work. I want them fixed so that on *some* people, they appear to be working when they are not working at all."

He probed around in it. "Well, that's easy. The light on the front that shows the operator it is working isn't part of the main circuit. It can go on independently. So we just put a switch on it and it goes on but the main circuit doesn't."

"It's more complicated than that," I said. "I want the operator to turn the helmet on and think that it is working but on some people it works and some it doesn't. Now, I thought if you could put some kind of a secret switch inside the helmet that only the one it is put on can turn off, it would solve the problem."

"Oh, you mean the guy inside the helmet should be able to turn it off while the operator thinks it is still on. Right?"

"Right. Now, I was thinking that very few people can wiggle their ears. I can wiggle my ears. It is a talent I have. So if the operator put a helmet on me and I wiggled my ears—let's say three times—the helmet would be off when the operator thought it was still on."

"I can't wiggle my ears," said Flip.

"Precisely," I said. "So the helmet would work on you but, as I *can* wiggle my ears, it would not work on *me*."

"Can't be done," he said. "Not with the state of the art. There are no ear-wiggling switches."

"Not even a tip of an ear?" I pleaded.

He saw I was pretty desperate. He thought. Then he looked at the little manual I had been reading. "Huh," he snorted disparagingly, "a scaled-down operator's manual. Worthless." He reached down to the bottom of the carton and he brought out a huge, thick manual, enough to break a man's arm: *Design, Theory, Maintenance and Repair Manual for Technicians.*

In a moment he was absorbed in huge, spread-out schematics. "Aha!" said Flip. "A multimanifold, bypass-input, shunt circuit!" He put a finger on it impressively. "Right there!"

I sat hoping.

He looked into the helmet. He unfastened a small cover and looked in. "These are Yippee-Zip Manufacturing Company components. You're lucky. They're standard in computers. We got their stuff by the ton."

"You can do something?" I said breathlessly.

"If I put a mutual-proximity breaker switch in this circuit right here, and if it is activated, the front light will go on but the helmet will be null and void."

Although the chart was huge, the part he was pointing at—and the whole setup in there actually—was no bigger than my thumbnail. I said, "But I can't get the tip of my ear in there! It would be too risky!"

"No, no, no. A mutual-proximity breaker switch is in two parts. They use them on spaceships. When one spaceship gets too close to another spaceship, it trips a switch in the other's computers and shunts in an avoidance direction."

"I don't understand."

"Look, I put Part A of the switch in the helmet circuit. The subject it isn't supposed to work on wears Part B in his hair. When they come together, Part B interacts with Part A and the helmet, she don't work but she looks like she is working." He saw I was befuddled. "I'll get some," he said and rushed out.

In about ten minutes he came back up through the tunnel. He had sixteen cartons. They were small but *heavy*.

"You can't wear anything too big in your hair," I protested.

He laughed. He opened one carton. There were two

little lead boxes in it, each marked differently. "This one," said Flip, "goes in the helmet. This one the guy puts in his hair."

"They'd be noticed!" I protested.

"No, no, no," he said. "You don't get it." He opened up the box for the helmet side. In it, carefully positioned by tiny prongs, was the tiniest speck I have seen in some time. He opened up the other one. Same thing. "Mini-micro circuitry components," he said.

"But why the heavy lead boxes?" I said. "Are they radioactive?"

"Oh, no, no, no," said Flip. "If you keep them in the parts store unshielded, they activate other components around them. Computers won't work that have these in them. The computer field hits one of these in the parts store and all it will register is collision! So they put sets of them in shielded boxes."

He got right to work. He put the helmet part of the switch into the helmet. It was very delicate work, done with a huge magnifier and a little screw-adjustable set of prongs and snips. Indeed, it never would be detected! It was like working with molecules.

It took him a long time. Finally he had it. "Now, I will show you," he said.

He put the helmet on a chair. He put one of his innumerable meters under it. He turned it on. The meter read like mad. That helmet was really putting out! I shuddered.

Then he opened the little lead box of Part B and with prongs put the tiny bit on the chair. The meter went dead. The front light of the helmet glowed brightly. He hit the helmet switch several times. On and off went the light but the meter did nothing. Then he put the tiny bit back in its lead box, turned the helmet on and the meter went mad!

I had been thinking very hard. I knew what I would have to do. And I also knew what I would have to do with Flip. The secret must not get out.

"Fix them all!" I said.

Happily he went to work.

I dozed and read some comic books. The day wore on. I saw he was getting down to the last helmet. It was sunset.

My original plan had been, when he was finished, to pretend I wanted the illusion inspected on the mountain-top and then push him through it. But Faht Bey was so touchy these days. A dead technician splattered all over the hangar floor might also excite the appetites of the assassin pilots—they earlier had wanted to kill technicians.

No, I had a better plan by far. I excused myself and went into the bedroom. I closed the door. Out of his sight and hearing, I fished a recorder from the vault. I studied the manual on how to make a hypnostrip.

I made a strip. I said, "When you are finished with the hypnohelmets you will forget everything about these hypnohelmets being in my room. You will forget you changed them. You will think you were called for to repair the alarm system and that while you were here, that is all you did. When I remove the helmet from your head, you will see nothing and feel nothing until I say 'Thank you.' You will then ask me if the alarm system is all right. Then you will be awake and normal. You will forget you have heard this recording."

I went back in where he was working. I had the strip in my pocket.

He finished the last helmet. "All done," said Flip. He carried the helmets, back in their boxes, to the vault and cleaned everything up.

I brought back the last helmet and one Part B box. "All done but the test," I said.

"The meter tells you that."

"I don't know about meters. Tests should be live. Do you mind?"

"Sure, go ahead," said Flip. "But if it don't work, then spaceships will be crashing all over the place. Those things are reliable."

I opened up the lead Part B box. I took the tiny scrap out and put it in his hair. I put the helmet on his head. I turned on the switch.

He went out like a light! The thing I had put in his hair was a dust speck! The real Part B was doubled in a lead box in the other room!

I slipped the recorded strip into the helmet slot. It went right through, just like it was supposed to.

I took the helmet off his head. He just sat there with his eyes shut. I took the dust speck out of his hair.

I removed the helmet and lead box from the room. I closed the vault. I came back and laid some of his tools beside the trick floor plate in the secret office where he'd been working.

All was ready. I said, "Thank you."

He looked at me, his eyes still kind of glazed, and he said, "Is the alarm system all right?"

"I sure appreciate your coming here to fix it," I said.

"Yeah," said Flip, looking perfectly normal, "there wasn't much wrong with it after all. You got to step on that floor plate real hard and twist your foot to set the alarm off in the hangar. Just remember that."

He gathered up his tools and, humming to himself, left.

I had stolen one of his test meters. I went and got a helmet. I got a real Part B of the switch. I took it out of the lead box. I put it under the helmet. I turned the helmet on.

The meter was DEAD!

Hurray! Oh, was I the right one now!

Shortly I would be in a position to seduce any girl, make my whole staff bow down on sight, maybe even get somebody to rob a bank for me. I could untrain Silva. But above all I could order Utanc to love me and get into my bed!

But there was one more thing to do.

Chapter 3

I wrote a hasty note. I stamped it so it would look official.

I got out a Colt .45 and made sure it was loaded just in case I ran into Silva—which I surely didn't intend to do.

With flying and jubilant feet, I raced down the passageway to Faht Bey's office.

He wasn't there, I was happy to note. I got on his phone and called the taxi driver. I had trouble finding him but after three calls around town, made it. He was in a bar, gambling. He said he was losing a bit and wanted to get even first. I was very tolerant. He said he'd be along shortly.

Faht Bey's wife came in, saw me and went out hurriedly.

Faht Bey finally came in. I didn't want to see him. He didn't want to see me. I could tell. He sat down. He looked at me.

"Those heroin thefts are continuing," he said.

"Why tell me?"

"Are you sure you don't know?" And I could tell from the way he looked at me that he thought *I* was taking it!

"You better be more respectful," I said with a steely tone. Oh, would I get him. He was going to be an early candidate on those hypnohelmets.

"We're pretty broke," he said. "That hospital is costing the planet! The Lebanese banker is very upset."

"Why tell me?" I said.

"You're the Inspector General Overlord," said Faht.

"Yes, I am. And don't you forget it," I said.

"We owe I. G. Barben for the last shipment of speed," he said. "The one that went on the *Blixo*."

"To Hells with the *Blixo*," I said and meant it.

"The Lebanese will have to borrow money from the bank to buy the current poppy crop. Interest is 30 percent."

Oh, Gods, was he ever a candidate for a hypnohelmet!

"We were solvent until you came," he said.

Two hypnohelmets a day! I'd show him!

Finally the taxi driver came. It was ten o'clock. I looked around carefully for Silva before I went outside.

"I lost my roll," the taxi driver said. "Could you lend me a few bucks?"

Angrily, I told him to drive me to the hospital. He was going to get a hypnohelmet, too!

We got to the hospital. I told him to wait and keep his eye open for a swarthy Sicilian.

I went inside. It was deserted except for an old woman doing night duty at the counter. I pushed right on by her. I crashed open the door to Prahd's bedroom.

Two heads popped up.

"My father!" cried Nurse Bildirjin.

"Has my pay started yet?" said Prahd.

Evidently they had been halfway through something.

They seemed to be under a strain.

"Get up out of that bed!" I ordered. Here were two more candidates for hypnohelmets for sure. No respect. Her father is a fat slob.

They knew menace when they heard it. Nurse Bildirjin got out of bed. She didn't have much in the way of breasts, being maybe only fifteen. She got into her professional nurse's uniform. She seemed to be swearing under her breath.

Prahd got up. This time he was smart. He put on his shoes first.

I hauled him into his office. I showed him the official-looking forgery. "Here is an order I just received. It must be complied with instantly."

It said:

> *BY ORDERS. You are to be bugged instantly. If you were ever put in one of those cells in the basement or in some grave, we would never be able to find you unless you had a responding bug in your skull. This is secret, official and anybody mentioning it will never get his pay started.*
>
> *The Powers Above*

I took the order back.

I handed him the Part B lead box.

He opened it and squinted to see it. "This is a bug?"

"A mini-micro responder," I said. "It buzzes back when a searching beam is scattered around."

"Oh, yes," he said. "One of those."

"Right. I want it implanted in the top of my skull

in such a way nobody will know it is there. That's the order."

"And then does my pay start?"

"We'll see," I said.

He sort of looked at me strangely. But he yelled for Nurse Bildirjin. She raced up. She was muttering under her breath. "Get the operating room ready," he said.

She raced away. She was still muttering. We followed her at a more leisurely pace. He had set up the operating room. Lights glared. A table with straps was in the middle of the room.

"Is it for him?" said Nurse Bildirjin.

"Yes," said Prahd.

She promptly grabbed me by the arm and threw me down on the operating table. I was amazed at her strength.

She got me laid out and began to buckle straps. She encased my feet, she encased my stomach, she put big heavy straps across my chest and arms. Then she took one final strap and fastened it across my throat. It was too tight. I was having trouble breathing.

She was muttering under her breath. Sort of savagely.

"Wait!" I said. The way these two were looking at me, I didn't want to go unconscious. I might wake up with the lancet sticking out of the wrong place. "No general anesthetic!! Just a local. It's not much of a job."

"There is no Novocaine," said Nurse Bildirjin.

I turned my head. "That's a bottle with *Novocaine* written on it right there!"

She picked it up and put it in her pocket. "It's empty. And there are no pharmacies open at this time of night."

"That's true," said Prahd.

She went over to a drawer and got something. She came back and said, "Open your mouth wide."

I did, expecting her to look at my teeth. She jammed a huge roll of bandage into it and gave it a final shove.

She got up on my chest with both knees. As she was young and a bit bony, they were quite sharp. She pulled up her skirt, leaving her thighs naked. She braced her elbows and took my face in her hands. The fingernails were quite sharp, too. She held my head as though it was in a vice.

"Go ahead, doc," she said. "And I hope those tools are dull! Young girls have tender feelings."

I realized that she had an Elektra complex. A fixation on her father. I tried to open my mouth and tell her that I wasn't her father but the bandage roll was in the way.

Nurse Bildirjin's knees were digging in so hard I didn't feel the first slice. I felt the second!

Prahd—I could roll my eyes enough to see—was using a Zanco electric knife. He had a pan catching some blood. He had opened my scalp! I didn't need to see to know that! It stung like mad!

Nurse Bildirjin held my head very steady with her fingernails. "Maybe it's not a good idea to go around interrupting things right in the middle," she said. "Maybe doing it once was okay but when it happens twice, it starts looking intentional. Young girls have tender feelings!"

Prahd was putting some blood in a test tube and warming up a catalyzer. Things buzzed and metal pans clattered. Burners were hissing.

He came back over. He had a little spade sort of instrument. I couldn't see.

FLASH! Pain went through me like a javelin. Worse!

He backed up. He had taken a little piece of skull!

He put it in a test tube. He put the test tube in the catalyzer. Burners sizzled. So did my skull!

"Did you ever do it halfway?" said Nurse Bildirjin. "Did you ever do it halfway and then have to stop?"

I couldn't feel her fingernails. My skull hurt too much.

Prahd now had a drill. He started it up.

YEEOW! The noise of it going into my skull was almost as bad as the living agony! The room spun!

"It was going all so nice," said Nurse Bildirjin. "Nice and slow and even. Making it last. Oh, it was good!"

Prahd had the drill going sideways. I fainted.

When I came to, Nurse Bildirjin said, "It was the first one for the night. I had been looking forward to it all day. I could feel it clear to the top of my head! And then my father came in!"

I tried to tell her, "Nurse Bildirjin, I am not your father. That is an Elektra complex. You have a secret passion for your father and it expresses itself in hate." But the gag was in my mouth.

Prahd was holding the lead box. "Please verify the object."

She let my head go for an instant. It was the object. I nodded sufferingly.

He took it in some tweezers and dropped it in a solution. He fished it out. She grabbed my head again. Her knees dug.

YEEOW! YEEOW! YEEOW! He had put it in my skull none too gently.

"You ever get stopped halfway through?" said Nurse Bildirjin. "Just when it is going wonderful?"

He was taking a mass of bone cells out of the test tube he had catalyzed. Like a plasterer, he was pasting it into the hole he had made.

At every touch it felt like he was yanking on every nerve!

"You see," said Nurse Bildirjin, "I am a young girl. I am just starting out. All this is new and wonderful to me. I had heard, but I never knew it could be so good, so good, so good!"

He was tugging scalp down now. It hurt like blazes. Stung!

"You should be very careful of young girls who have never had any before," said Nurse Bildirjin. "It is their most delightful time of life!"

Prahd was smearing something around the edges of the scalp wound. It was agony at every stroke!

"You don't stop young girls halfway," said Nurse Bildirjin. "You go right on and let them finish! Young girls have tender feelings, and don't you forget it!"

Prahd had a light he was shining on my skull. It was so hot I could hear my hair sizzling.

He stepped back. "You can let him up now, Nurse Bildirjin," he said professionally.

She got off me. I hurt so bad elsewhere, I didn't even feel her knees gouging me, leaving bruises.

She picked up a lancet, apparently just to have it handy in case she had any afterthoughts. She undid my throat strap so I could breath again. She unfastened the rest.

"Well," said Prahd. "You're bugged. Does my pay start now?"

I got the roll of bandage out of my mouth. "Get out of here!" I yelled.

They were very obedient. As she left, Nurse Bildirjin was already unbuttoning her uniform. She was looking adoringly up at Prahd.

"Oh, I just love practicing medicine, don't you, doctor? It's SO stimulating!"

I got off the table somehow. The room was spinning.

I didn't know if I'd been (bleeped) or operated on!

Chapter 4

The taxi driver woke up as I approached the cab. He stared at me. In a shocked tone, he said, "Gee, did that swarthy Sicilian catch up with you?"

I made him drive me to the barracks: I couldn't confront more whining by Faht Bey. I went through the hangar. The guard officer said, "A gang beat up on you?"

I went up the tunnel to my secret room. I fumbled through the closet entrance to my bedroom.

I collapsed. I didn't really go to sleep—I just went unconscious.

The following morning I awoke very late. My sweater collar had blood on it. My hair was caked. It called for extreme measures. I took a shower. I was surprised when I found my head didn't gush further blood. I was even more surprised when I touched the spot: it almost killed me.

However, getting into a shirt I didn't have to pull over my head, I began to savor what I had accomplished. None of the hypnohelmets would work on me. There would be no more nightmares complete with Manco spike-tailed Devils. I was safe from Krak. And nobody on this planet was safe from me. It was a nice feeling.

The waiter brought me in some hot *kahve sade*—without sugar. I drank it in sips between great gulps of water. That is the proper way to drink it, though I seldom did it. But the wounded get thirsty. I ignored utterly the *baklava* sweet pastry.

As the waiter seemed to have gotten in and out without being blown apart by a double-barrelled leopard, I tiptoed across the patio to the yard door: I wanted to plan from where I would get a guard to shoot the paralysis dart at the intruder. I put my eye to the peephole.

My Gods!

Utanc was just leaving in her BMW.

And sitting right beside her in the front seat, chummy as you please, was GUNSALMO SILVA!

The car vanished from the gate.

I stepped out into the yard.

Karagoz was helping the gardener plant a flower bed. I beckoned and then pointed mutely at the gate—I was speechless.

"Oh, him?" said Karagoz. "He was waiting for you."

I nodded numbly.

Karagoz said, "There were some strange men in town the last couple days. They scared Utanc. So this morning she hired Silva as a bodyguard."

Worse and worse! Not only was he gunning for me, he was stealing my darling dancing girl! And who knows but what they'd both plot against me!

It was a good thing I had it all planned out with the hypnohelmets.

Karagoz said, "He's broke, you know. The American consul took away all the cash he got off the dead gangster—said it was a consular fee. We been feeding him."

Even the staff were in league on this!

I started to go to the gate. Then I realized that I stupidly had come out here unarmed. I turned to go back to my room.

There was a rush and a roar!

Utanc slammed the BMW into the yard!

It stopped in its usual place in a scream of tires.

I froze.

I looked at the car like a snake-fixated bird.

This was the end.

Gunsalmo Silva was getting out. He had the leopard in his hand.

Utanc, hooded, cloaked and veiled, swept by me without even a flick of eyes in my direction, as though I didn't exist. She had obviously written me off. In a moment her room door slammed behind her and the metal bars clanged into place.

Silva was just standing there, half in and half out of the car. He was looking at me.

I have never felt quite so naked. No gun to draw. And he would have plenty of time to shoot me before I could draw it if I had one. And he was Apparatus hypno-trained now, capable of anything.

He was walking toward me slowly, leopard in hand. He was squat, muscular, very Sicilian, terrible. He was frowning.

He stopped five feet from me. He raised the leopard. He scratched his head with the muzzle.

"Now, where the (bleep) have I seen you before?" he said.

I said nothing.

He frowned harder. Then his face brightened up to a dark cloud. "Oh, I know. It's that God (bleeped) nightmare I get. You're the guy in it! I'm standing there in a barn full of flying saucers!"

Silva looked me up and down and nodded. "Well, that clears that up. Can we go some place private and sit down? It's kind of public here."

Tricky. Just what you'd expect after Apparatus training. He didn't want the execution to be public.

My bedroom was closer to my guns.

I found my voice. "Come with me," I said and led

the way to the bedroom. Then I got even more clever. "You want something to drink first? Some Scotch?"

"Never touch it," he said. "God (bleep) ulcers."

Well, try again, my old professors used to say. If you're not dead yet, there's always a slim chance you won't be right away.

I got him into my bedroom. I sat him down in a chair. I toyed with the idea of going in the secret room and stepping on the floor plate with a twist, which would assemble the whole crew in the hangar. Then I thought, they'd be in the hangar, not here where they are needed.

I tried a ploy. I said, "I understand Utanc hired you as a bodyguard."

"Yeah," he grunted.

"This is pretty wild country. Are you qualified? How'd you kill Tavilnasty?"

He gave a short, barking laugh. "Child's play. When them two (bleepers) took me to that God (bleeped) room I come to and I said, 'This is a setup for a God (bleeped) hit.' You get me? That's what I said—'A setup for a God (bleeped) hit.' You unnerstan' me?"

I understood him. This was his threat to me.

"So, when they put me in the God (bleeped) bed, I said, 'Some God (bleeped) (bleeper) is going to be in here in a couple minutes to rub me out.' So soon as these (bleepers) left, I just balled up the blankets like it was a body and rolled under the bed. Child's play.

"Couple minutes later I'll be God (bleeped) if I wasn't right. The (bleeper) comes quiet in through the window. He walks over cat-foot to the God (bleeped) bed. He's got a God (bleeped) stiletto in his hand. He's also got this leopard in a holster inside his God (bleeped) left leg.

"He jams the stiletto into the God (bleeped) roll of

blankets like he's God (bleeped) upset. So I just reached out and grabbed the God (bleeped) leopard off his God (bleeped) leg.

"Before he could bend down to see what was under the God (bleeped) bed, I blew his God (bleeped) left leg off. And then he fell down, so I blew his crotch apart.

"He wasn't so God (bleeped) interested in killing anybody then, so I got out from under the God (bleeped) bed. I seen he had a crappy .38 Saturday night special so I took it and though it was a awful God (bleeped) risk to shoot the God (bleeped) thing—they blow up—I put a bullet in the blankets and wiped the God (bleeped) gun off and put it back in his God (bleeped) hand that had stopped twitchin'.

"I frisked him for his God (bleeped) money and I found four extra loads. So I dumped the leopard and the loads for it in the God (bleeped) toilet trap.

"The God (bleeped) police come. They thought the guy had tried to use a bomb and it had gone off too God (bleeped) quick. But seein' I was American they put me in the jug.

"Like a God (bleeped) fool, I yelled for the God (bleeped) American consul and he come down the next day and demanded they give me life but they said to hell with you, go (bleep) yourself. And that's the last God (bleeped) time I ever call for an American consul. He took all my dough.

"So I went back to the hotel the next day and fished this leopard out of the toilet trap." He sat pensive for a moment. "I dimly remember in a nightmare I was calling for an American consul. I'm a dumb (bleepard). But I somehow feel I'm a lot smarter about business these days. I seem to know what to do just like that. Which brings us to you."

"Just a minute," I said. "You seem to be qualified. But this is pretty wild country. If you're going to be a bodyguard, you'll need this."

I had left a hypnohelmet out. I picked it up. I put it on his head and turned the switch. The front light glowed brightly.

I waited.

He just sat there.

I waited for his eyes to glaze and close.

He just sat there.

Bright awake!

"Hell," he said, "I don't need no helmet." He reached up and took it off. "It don't look bulletproof anyway." He put it on his lap.

My Gods! It wasn't working! The helmet wasn't working!

I reached over and took it away. I was thinking awfully fast. I had a hypnotrained Apparatus hit man sitting right here!

"I got this strange idea," he said, "that I'm supposed to see the God (bleeped) head man in Turkey, and people tell me you are it. I got this God (bleeped) fool notion that you got something for me to do."

My pent breath wheezed out. So that was what they had told him under hypnosis after he'd been hypnotrained!

"This dame you got here—what's her name, Utanc? Funny name. Anyway, she offered me a job. But I don't think it's what I'm supposed to do and I don't think it's permanent.

"Just a few minutes ago, we started up the God (bleeped) road for town. And she told me how scared she'd been with all the non-Turks in town last couple days but she didn't want no hassle with heaters. And then she asked me..."

"Wait a minute," I said. "You don't talk Turkish."

"Oh, I know. God (bleeped) lousy language. Her English has got a funny accent."

Oh, the darling had been studying English. Maybe to please me! I saw her with lots of textbooks being carried in. How sweet of her.

"She's God (bleeped) hard to unnerstan' sometimes. She uses too many God (bleep) big words. But anyway we're driving up the road to town just a while ago and she wants to know who I thought these birds was. She didn't call them birds. She said . . . oh yes. She said 'foreign intruders.' And I knew, of course, and I told her those God (bleeped) (bleepards) was the American consul from Ankara and three, four other CIA men. And bang, she turns right around—one hell of a U-turn—and she come back here. I don't think she thinks she's safe."

Well, of course, she didn't. Poor little wild desert girl.

"And she must have changed her mind," he continued. " 'Cause first she's talkin' about no God (bleeped) hassle and then she wants to know how much hits cost. Women!" he added disgustedly. "Always changin' their (bleeping) minds!"

Yes, women were a trial. I could agree with that.

"Now," he said, "hitting the American consul from Ankara is awful God (bleeped) close to home!"

Desperation is often father to inspiration. I had to get rid of this Silva. He was not only a menace to the base, he was also a threat to my continued possession of Utanc. He might persuade her to run off with him!

What was the most dangerous thing I could ask him to do? One that would be sure to get him killed. Who was the best-protected person on the planet?

"How about hitting the president of the U.S.?" I suggested.

He shook his head. "Hell, I don't want to be no hero like Oswald."

Then I had it. This would *surely* get Silva killed! "How about the director of the CIA?"

He thought about it. He scratched his chin with the muzzle of the leopard. "Has its points. (Bleepards) and their American consuls. Has its points." Then he fixed me with his opaque eyes. "All right," he said. "I'll do it for a hunnert big ones." Then he added, "And expenses."

I did a rapid calculation. I was slightly hazy on whether "big one" meant one hundred or one thousand. But let's say it did mean one thousand. One hundred thousand Turkish lira was probably only about a thousand dollars U.S. And besides, he'd never make it. They'd shoot him to Swiss cheese.

"It's a deal," I said. Anything to get him away from Utanc. Even money. I reached into my pocket and got out a fistful of lira. I handed it to him. "You go get a room in town. And stay away from here so as not to compromise the plan. Sign in at the Castle Hotel: we haven't shot the place up lately. Tomorrow you'll receive money and a ticket to the United States."

"You got some loads for this leopard?" he said. "I think the loads got wet in that God (bleeped) toilet bowl."

I had some number-twelve-shot shotgun shells that would fit his gun. A dealer had been selling them cheap because number twelve shot is so tiny a pellet it is useful for nothing, not even canaries. I told him to go out in the yard. I got to my gun racks. I found the box. I even put a piece of lead in the side of it to make sure it showed up on aircraft detectors.

I went out. I gave him the box. I shook him by the hand. "Good luck," I said fervently. But I did not say good luck to whom.

I told Karagoz to drive him to town.

Good riddance! Trying to steal Utanc!

I went into my office and wrote the order for the money and ticket to Faht Bey. I knew he'd squeal but this was an emergency. GOOD-BYE GUNSALMO SILVA!

Chapter 5

WHY hadn't that helmet worked?

I examined it. I put the stolen meter under it. Sure enough, it was dead! The light went on but no waves went through the helmet itself.

Just as I was about to call the technician, Flip, I remembered he'd been given a posthypnotic suggestion to forget it.

Something was definitely wrong here. But if I am good at languages, circuit diagrams and such are gibberish to me.

I laboriously got out all the other helmets. I tested each one with a meter.

They were all dead! The lights went on but they didn't work!

My roseate dreams of controlling everybody on this planet with hypnotism were at stake.

Carefully, I went back over what had been done to them. They had all worked when he first fixed them.

Aha! I still had the cartons and boxes for the switches. I got one out. It said Mutual-Proximity Breaker Switch. Wait. It had some small print: Yippee-Zip Manufacturing Co., Industrial City, Voltar. No, no. Not that. The other side of the box. More small print. It said:

> *Warning:*
> *Minimum-Range Model. For Use Only in Spacevessels Operating in Formation. Active range: 2 miles.*

The world fell in. Spacevessels travel so fast that a two-mile warning zone was nothing. Probably these switches were here in such abundance because they used a longer range switch normally—maybe a thousand miles.

But two miles!

Any time I was within two miles of one of these helmets it wouldn't work!

Forlornly, I tried to figure out how to put a helmet on somebody and then drive more than two miles away.... No, it was quite impossible.

Get the thing taken out of my head?

Oh, no, never! Not with Nurse Bildirjin sitting on my chest! Not any of that agony again! That Part B was in my skull from here on out!

Sadly, I put the helmets back in the vault.

And then, being of an optimistic temperament, I brightened. There was one thing very sure.

Krak would never be able to use a hypnohelmet on me again.

No more Manco Devils!

It had all turned out successfully after all!

The *Blixo* was gone. Gunsalmo Silva was gone. Bawtch and the forgers would be dead. Heller had been set up to get his brains bashed in by Krak.

Maybe I could take a long snooze. And maybe go hunting. I had done splendidly well, really. The Apparatus would be proud of me. I had really earned a rest!

If only I could think of something that would please Utanc and bring her once again into my lonely bed.

PART TWENTY-FIVE

Chapter 1

In an optimistic mood, I conceived of a plan to make things even more all right.

My nights were pretty lonely and miserable without Utanc. I was certain I knew of something that would appeal to her.

I was planning a nice, quiet hunting trip. I had bought a Franchi Deluxe Automatic Shotgun during my last visit—twelve-gauge, thirty-two-inch barrel, full choke, three-inch magnum loads, five-shot magazine. I had never fired it. With No. 00 buckshot, each one .33 inches in diameter, it was the very thing for songbirds.

That shooting songbirds is illegal in Turkey goes without saying. They have odd ideas. But it is open season all year round for wolf, lynx and wild boar. And the season was open now for wildcat, fox, hare, rabbit, duck, partridge, woodcock and quail. The trick is to pretend you are hunting one of these and then, turning quick, shoot a songbird and say it got in the road.

My permit was all in order.

The Ford station wagon was running, if a bit oddly.

There would be sparkling campfires in the wilds. And where did Utanc fit in? As a wild girl from the Kara Kum desert, she, of course, would greatly admire a man who could go out, go bang and bring home game to fill the old stew pot, while she sat beside the campfire. I could just see the adoring look come into her eyes as I came up loaded down with wild canaries or such. The primitive instinct. In my Earth psychology textbooks, it is called *atavism*. Everybody is a caveman, even though Freud passed a law against it, and gets thrown back to primitive instincts like any other beast or animal. So you see, my hopes were not founded on nothing.

There are also bear to be hunted in Turkey, and while it sounded attractive to drag a bear into camp and stand there and sort of beat my chest to show her what a great hunter I was, bear are pretty tricky things to shoot. If you only graze them, you've probably had it. I thought I'd better stick to impressing her with wild canaries—maybe shoot lots of them to make a show.

As I saw it, it was all carefully thought out. I had earned the rest. The Apparatus doesn't give medals in public so I thought I'd better pin this trip on myself as a sort of substitute for labors well done. I spent two nice days planning it.

Undoubtedly she had forgiven me by this time over the little boy. He was still in her room and so was the other one. But frankly, who cares about a little tap on the nose? You can't cry about it forever.

I checked with Karagoz. No, Utanc had not come out of her room for two days now. Not since Silva had left.

I listened outside her garden wall. No laughter in the garden.

Ah, well. She really should be cheered up.

I wrote a note. On it I said, "Utanc, you adorable, beautiful creature. You are invited to go on a nice long hunting trip. I will shoot songbirds and you can boil them in the wilds." I knew it would appeal to her atavism.

I slid it under her door.

Aha! The corner of it vanished instantly!

Breathlessly, I listened. After several minutes, I heard the iron bar lifting.

Success! I knew atavism would be stirred. Throwback to cave days. Works every time!

The knob rattled!

The door swung open!

And suddenly a torrent of everything female you could name started to hurl out of that door at me! Shoes! Cups! A potted plant! A looking glass soared through the air and shattered against the far patio wall!

She was standing there, her nostrils flaring, her hands clenching and unclenching like they wanted to get into some hair!

In pure venom her words lashed out, "You dirty (bleepard)! It's not enough to ruin forever a beautiful boy! Now, (bleep) you, you want to kill SONGBIRDS!"

A small hand boosted something up behind her. It was a chair!

She launched it at me like a cannon shot! It shattered into splinters!

I only got the edge of it. I ducked into my room.

I had aroused atavism all right. The wrong kind!

I locked my door very thoroughly. I sat down and pondered this.

Amazing as it might seem, she was still upset about that (bleeped) little boy. Imagine it!

Well, women are funny. You really can't ever tell. I thought she might get over it.

Well, she hadn't. My first conclusion had been right. She would never forgive me. And all over one (bleeped), useless, small boy.

Gloom settled over me. Actually, it was only Utanc that had motivated my desire for a hunting trip.

Chapter 2

I wandered into my secret office. I slumped in the chair. The viewer was in front of me, untouched for days. Maybe Heller was in some kind of trouble that would cheer me up. Listlessly I turned it on.

It seemed sort of dim. I turned up the picture gain.

A cathedral!

An awfully big cathedral!

Something was going on.

A funeral!

It was a big crowd. There were gowned priests going through various motions. A choir was singing beautifully.

It fitted squarely in my mood. What soulful music! So sad. So beautifully sad!

Heller was sitting on a bench. He was holding somebody's hand. Somebody in a black veil. Babe Corleone! She was sobbing! Heller patted her hand.

There was some sort of casket lying in state. Evidently there had been a file-by already.

Then I understood. Jimmy "The Gutter" Tavilnasty. It was his funeral! In possibly the biggest cathedral in America? St. John the Divine? St. Patrick's? It was awfully big. All gold and glittering candles and high, imposing arches.

The music swelled in majesty.

And here came somebody to a lower altar or pulpit. A choir boy. A hush fell. He was speaking into the great vaulted room, his clear, tenor voice trembling with emotion.

He said, "If it had not been for our dear, departed Jimmy, I never would have learned to let the other boys love me!"

And then he raised his voice in the saddest song I have ever heard. The choir swelled in solemn beauty behind him.

The Latin music faded away. Here came another to the small pulpit, an elderly man, stooped with age.

"As head of the reform school, I counted Jimmy as my friend. My fondest memories of him are those when he organized, all by himself and out of charity, the greatest riots the youth prison has ever experienced. And today, without his coaching, we would have hardly any new prisoners at all. A great man, idol of a thousand street gangs. He will be missed."

The choir lifted their voices in saintly chords that faded away into the vaulted dome toward heaven.

And here was another man coming to the pulpit. He bowed his head reverently, and there were tears in his voice as he spoke. "I was his prison psychologist many times. Jimmy Tavilnasty was a model patient. I have never seen a man who took to behavior modification therapy so well. He went from bad to worse and finally, under my careful coaching, became the very embodiment of American crime." His voice broke with emotion. "He was the All American Boy that became the hit man we will never forget."

The choir swelled in reverence and awe.

Oh, it was beautiful.

The funeral progressed. Eight pallbearers bore the casket. They were dressed in black. They were all Sicilians. They all had bulges where their guns would be beneath their coats.

And then I saw why my screen had been dim. Everyone was wearing heavy, dark glasses, including Heller. I noticed this because the screen got even darker than it had been and once more I had to turn up the brightness. A gloomy, gloomy day! It was raining!

The casket was carried through an arch of switch-blades made by twenty street gangs.

At the cemetery, there were wreaths and wreaths and flowers everywhere. A huge horseshoe of lilies had a banner on it:

Jimmy Our Pal

Another stand of flowers was in the shape of a stiletto. Its banner said:

To Jimmy from the Faustino Narcotici Mob

It got kicked down and trampled under solemn feet.

Five chorus girls in widow's weeds stood weeping at the grave, pressing black handkerchiefs to their sobbing mouths.

The reason for the dark glasses appeared. The whole funeral was being covered by TV crews that had the good grace to wear black armbands at the last. The bands were being handed out by a mobster who held a gun in his other hand.

The huge procession wound down into a crypt. It said:

Family Crypt
Corleone

Jimmy's casket was slid into a vault. The sobbing was much louder.

Babe's fingers were trailing over a stone:

"Holy Joe" Corleone

She was breaking down. Heller led her toward a limousine. He gently got her away from people who were trying to touch her hand or kiss her cheek in sympathy. She was really crying hard.

Heller got her in the back. He closed the door. She clung to him.

"I'm losing all my boys," she sobbed.

He patted her gently and gave her another handkerchief. She sat back, more quietly. Bodyguards were gently pushing the crowd away from the car with sawed-off shotguns. At last the limousine was moving.

Babe was clenching and unclenching her hands. They were going across a bridge. "Jerome," she said brokenly. "I have heard you are learning to drive race cars. Jerome, promise me, please promise me not to do anything dangerous."

Heller seemed unwilling to speak. Then he said, "Life is a chancy thing, Mrs. Corleone. I cannot promise that."

She looked at him suddenly. "Good," she said. "Then if you ever see that God (bleeped) Silva, promise me you'll rub the (bleepard) out."

He said he would.

But I was haunted by that cathedral music, the choir boys, the Latin solemnity and tragedy of it all. I turned the viewscreen off.

The music continued to haunt me. How lovely. What a gorgeous funeral.

There crept into my mind the vision of my own funeral.

And there was Utanc kneeling beside my grave, withered flowers in her hand, in the rain. She was weeping because she had been so mean to me.

Oh, what a gorgeous vision. I felt like crying myself.

Dim-eyed, I stumbled into my bedroom.

I collapsed on the bed.

Something was under my head. The operation was still sore but I let it hurt. The vision of Utanc kneeling at my grave was still with me.

The pain hurt worse and I brushed at it because it was interrupting my mood.

Something flew out onto the other pillow. I turned my head.

Face to face, I saw a note. It said:

> *Just to remind you that idleness don't pay. Lombar was sure you would slack off. So this serves notice that if you haven't handled Heller, it will be my duty to terminate you.*

It had only a bloody dagger as signature.

Ah, so my vision was going to come true after all.

After a little while, I sat up. The beautiful cathedral music still haunted me.

I picked up the note. The rear side of it was blank.

I found a pen. I wrote on it *Go ahead.* I signed my name. I left it on the pillow.

It seemed the right thing to do.

Utanc would kneel in the rain. She would be sorry. At least I'd have her precious tears in mud spots on my grave.

I made sure I had no weapons in my pockets.

I walked out across the shattered mess in the patio—how similar it was to my shattered life.

With the cathedral music sounding in my ears, I walked alone through the dusk, hoping for a fatal shot that would end a life that no longer was worth living.

Perhaps, as she wept, she would sing some sad song and realize she should have been much nicer to me while I still lived.

How beautiful.

Chapter 3

I walked all night and nobody shot me.

In the cold dawn, I went to my bedroom, disappointed.

The note I had left was gone. Whoever it was that had Lombar's assignment to kill me must be pretty skilled at getting in and out of places, but I had gone all over that.

Exhausted, I got out of my clothes and got into bed. Maybe there was still hope. Maybe I would die in my sleep.

In the late afternoon, I awoke. I was disappointed to find I was still alive.

Somewhat petulantly I turned over to get out of bed.

And there, on the other pillow, not five inches in front of my eyes, was a new note! Maybe it was an apology for not having killed me last night.

I sat up. I disinterestedly turned it right way to.

It said:

While it would be a pleasure to kill you, that isn't the sequence. If Heller is not stopped, Utanc will be killed first.

A surge of shock went through me!

A scream of protest struggled to escape my constricted throat!

Without even grabbing a towel, I rushed into the patio and pressed my ear to Utanc's door.

Silence!

Maybe they had killed her already!

I dashed into the yard.

Melahat was cutting some flowers. She averted her eyes.

"Have they killed Utanc?" I demanded.

She stared at me. Then she averted her eyes again. "She was all right a few minutes ago when I took in some towels."

I wheezed with relief. Then I thought I'd better take precautions. I lifted my head and yelled real loud, "I'm working!"

Maybe that would hold them!

It seemed to confuse Melahat. But this was no time for parlor manners.

I rushed back into my room. I struggled into some clothes. I tried to think. It was difficult. What was the reason for this sudden attack?

They must know something I didn't know!

Heller. Heller was up to something!

I rushed into my secret room. I turned on the viewer. I braced myself and stood watching it. I couldn't see it well from that angle. I sat down.

Just some old parts on a table.

He looked up at that moment. He was in his office at the Empire State Building. The office had some people in it. The decor was different!

Ah, the walls. Huge murals of oil refineries decorated the walls now. They were in color. They were belching smoke. Vast vistas of tall stacks coating the sky black.

No. They were not all of refineries. One wall had a montage. Hard to make out in peripheral vision but it seemed to be birds drowning in pools of oil, flowers wilting, trees dying.

Wait. That wasn't all of them. As he turned his head I saw another mural. It seemed to be a planet festooned with hydrogen-bomb explosions.

He turned his head again. There was another one! It was a sort of fantasy drawing. Dimly seen spaceships were firing barrages at a planet that looked like Earth. Maybe the original of a magazine cover?

The people. There seemed to be quite a few people in that huge office. I still-framed the record strip so I could see how many and who. People can be dangerous.

Over at the bar, behind it, was a white-coated bartender. He was just sitting there, reading the *Daily Racing Form.*

There was a girl sitting on a stool at the office bar. She was dressed in a very skimpy-back gown of sequins. She had very dark, seductive eyes. She was toying with an ice-cream soda. His secretary?

Three girls were standing to Heller's right. Their skirts barely covered their hips. They had little pillbox caps at an angle on their heads. They had on short boots. Their clothing—what there was of it—was all in sparkling white, matching the shag rug. They seemed to be holding pens. His secretaries?

In my nervousness, I had had the sound off. I turned it up. In the background could be heard a very hot band playing atmosphere music. Lots of kettledrums and rolling snares, a strident trumpet rolling over the top of it.

I began to relax. My fears were not well founded. Nobody could work in that much commotion. Heller was just playing around as usual.

He seemed to be fiddling with two metal objects. He

had a thick canvas spread out under them. He turned his head further. Izzy was sitting on his left.

Con man Izzy. He was in his Salvation Army suit and he had the battered briefcase on his knees. His horn-rimmed glasses flashed away on either side of his beaked nose.

"You have lost me, Mr. Jet," Izzy was saying. "I just am not very bright about engineering. I know you explained it yesterday but with so many things worrying me, I couldn't retain it. I had a headache all night. My health isn't good, you know."

Heller handed a screwdriver to one of the three girls. She spun it expertly in a baton twist and slipped it into a case.

Heller made some kind of a mysterious signal. I watched it closely. A code of some sort. The barman put down his *Daily Racing Form,* picked up a tall glass—crystal?—and expertly began to toss a fizzing stream into another matching glass, back and forth in an arc. He put it on a silver tray and brought it to Izzy. Did Heller have Izzy on drugs?

Izzy drank it, leaving a white fizz mustache on his upper lip. The bartender courteously took the crystal back. "Was the Bromo Seltzer to the right strength, sir?"

Izzy nodded and thanked him.

Meanwhile, the slinky girl at the bar had finished her soda and left. A girl wearing almost absolutely nothing in bright red came in. She sat down on a stool. The bartender on his return started to serve her some ice cream. Another secretary?

Oh, nobody could work in an area like this. No real danger. Engineering work is very painstaking and tense. An engineering lab is stark and steely. An engineer doesn't work like this. I had been unduly alarmed.

"Your headache better?" said Heller to Izzy.

"I'm afraid it's gone," said Izzy.

"All right," said Heller. "I will explain it again. It all boils down to whether or not a society can handle *force*. This one doesn't seem to be able to.

"Now, pay attention. You must be able to convert matter to energy. Then you can use energy to move matter.

"Politically, financially and every other way, you have to know how to handle *force*. If you don't, you can blow up the whole society.

"Now, for some screwball reason, this society considers *life* junior to *force*. This is a nutty philosophy called *materialism* or *mechanism*. It is false.

"Unless this society snaps out of it and gets rid of that philosophy, which is just primitive nonsense, this society will never be able to survive.

"The fact is, it is *life* that handles *force!* Only life gives things direction. Matter cannot control matter—it has no intentions. Life is NOT a product of matter. It is its boss!

"You want this society to get into space? Start considering that *life* can handle force. You want this culture to survive, realize it is *life* that handles force.

"Anybody telling you otherwise is not only trapping you on this planet, he is also trying to destroy it."

"Oh, dear," said Izzy. "Do you mean we'd better shoot all the psychologists and other materialists?"

"I'm not talking about shooting anybody, but it might be a good idea. They've got you trapped on this planet!"

"I abhor violence," said Izzy. "Excuse me, Mr. Jet, but you said you wanted to see me about matter conversion."

Heller looked back at his huge desk and waved his

hand at it. "Well, for starters, here are a couple of matter converters."

Lying there were two metal objects, duplicates. They had a lot of parts and intricate curves. Oh, those were just those two elementary-school demonstration machines he had taken out of the box in Connecticut—the educational models. They were even all there. The rods for electrical discharge and the bags to catch the gas were included. Heller picked one up. The three girls promptly did baton twirls with three screwdrivers and presented them. He took one. The other two twirled theirs and put them back in their bags.

He started dismantling the object. He extended his hand, more baton twirls and he got more tools.

He began to shed parts all over in front of Izzy.

"I've got two," said Heller, as he worked. "So dismantling one is all right."

Izzy was staring at about forty parts, spread before him.

Heller took the one he had not dismantled. "Now, see here." He pointed to the top. "You put a rod of pure carbon in the top. The machine then reduces it by atomic conversion. Oxygen comes out this side and hydrogen comes out the other side. Electrical charge comes out on these two wires."

"Oh, dear," said Izzy.

Heller put out his hand and, after the baton twirl, got a pen.

"It's simple chemistry," said Heller. And he began to write. "Carbon has six electrons. Oxygen has eight electrons. Hydrogen has one electron. The machine simply shifts electrons in the atoms. Carbon loses its identity as carbon. Its electrons shift up and down on the periodic chart and you get oxygen and hydrogen. You then have the formula $C_2 \rightarrow H_4 + O$."

He tossed the paper at Izzy. "Oxygen and hydrogen burn when combined. Got it?"

"But . . . but . . . " floundered Izzy.

"Actually," said Heller, "the amount of energy available is higher in terms of electrical potential and the planet needs electrical engines. But nearly everything right now is powered by internal-combustion engines—cars and all that. It's a silly sort of engine. You put fuel in to get heat and then you have a cooling system to take the heat away and waste it. But people seem addicted to it so we will use it. This machine makes oxygen and hydrogen out of carbon and there's an almost unlimited supply of carbon on this planet so we're in."

"Any kind of carbon?" gaped Izzy.

"Sure. Oil, asphalt, old weeds, rags. The amount of gas volume—and I mean *gas,* not gasoline—you get out of solid matter approaches a billion to one. Gas is awfully full of space. So you can put a chunk of carbon in the top here. You put a pressure tank on each side of this machine to catch the gas. You put a lever to feed the amount of carbon in the top, you put a valve to use as an accelerator to regulate the gas flow into the engine itself, and you've got it."

"I haven't got it," mourned Izzy. "I'd need full engineering drawings showing every part."

Heller sighed. He held out his hand, some kind of a finger signal. One of the girls set up a drawing board with a flourish. The second waved a piece of drawing paper like a flag and pinned it on the board. The third baton-twirled two pens.

Heller went smoothly and rapidly to work. With motions so fast his hand blurred, he began to freehand perfect engineering drawings using Earth symbols.

More paper was waved and put on the board, more pens twirled and offered.

He shortly had fifteen complete engineering drawings. All of the general and particular parts of the device.

Izzy seemed suddenly to be all business. He was rolling the drawings up. "Can I have one of these models?"

Screwdrivers were baton-twirled, wrenches spun. Parts grew and the device was reassembled.

Izzy took it and put it carefully in a box.

"I'll get all this patented," he said. "I'll attribute it to an anonymous team of engineers. We don't want your name associated with anything here—because of Bury, you know." He paused. "I think the patents should be in the name of Multinational. I control that."

"Patent away," said Heller. Didn't he realize Izzy was stealing his patent? The fool. "I've got to work on this other one. I have to make the tanks and fit it on the car once I've got the car tested with its own fuel."

"You go right ahead, Mr. Jet," said Izzy. "But don't connect any part of that activity with these companies or Multinational."

"I promise," said Heller.

The three girls did a sort of dance and one of them said, "Can we have some ice-cream sodas now? We've got to get back to baton-twirling school."

"Give them some sodas," said Heller and the bartender went to work.

"Gee, ain't he cute?" said one of the girls as she sat down on a stool.

Bah, they weren't his secretaries at all, just some students from a school on the same floor. And the slinky girls who had been at the bar must be just from the model school. They were cadging ice-cream sodas. Typically New York. Decadent.

The bartender brought Heller a nonalcoholic Swiss beer.

Just as he was about to drink it, a man came bursting in the door, followed by some others with cases. The tailor!

"I'm so sorry, sir," the tailor said. "I would have waited until you were back at your rooms. But the whole production line stalled."

Heller drank some nonalcoholic beer.

A tailor's assistant came up. He had a costume. It was blue. It was like a jump suit but the front lapel buckled across the front very boldly. Another one came up. He was holding an incomplete suit just like it.

"The color," said the tailor. "We got into a dispute about the color. Blue is more ethereal. But then it suddenly occurred to us about the blood."

"Blood?" said Heller.

"Yes, you see, racing is a dangerous sport. And you want to be very suitably dressed. TV cameras are always around at racing wrecks and if you wore red, it won't show the blood. So we had to get your opinion. Don't you think red is best?"

Heller sort of snorted into his beer. Maybe it was too strong for him. "Maybe you better put some padding across the front flap. It will absorb the blood better."

"Ah," said the tailor. "Make a note of that, Threadneedle. More padding on the front. Then red will do?"

"The car is red," said Heller.

"Ah, that's such a relief. Forgive us for bothering you." They all rushed off.

Izzy had not left. He was nervously wringing his hands. "Mr. Jet. He spoke of blood. Are you sure I had not better hire security guards for you twenty-four hours a day?"

"Nonsense," said Heller. "I've got weeks of work ahead of me. Nobody will get wind of this."

"Mark my words, Mr. Jet," said Izzy. "I am responsible for you even if the companies have no connection. Rockecenter will be put right out of business if you popularize that carburetor. It could be the end of the oil industry."

"No, no," said Heller. "It can burn oil, it just won't burn much of it. And it will be totally clean."

"It could ruin him just the same," said Izzy.

I went cold. Suddenly I understood what Heller was about to do! Those (bleeped) children's demonstration kits. He was using it for a carburetor! For any car or engine!

My Gods! The very worst was happening! If Delbert John Rockecenter lost a fortune, he could also lose his control of I. G. Barben Pharmaceutical! Lombar was right! Our arrangements with I. G. Barben would vanish! And that would be the end of Lombar's fondest dreams on Voltar!

It WAS an emergency!

And I had not caught it!

This would not wait for Krak! I had only a few weeks!

I must ACT!

Chapter 4

I had to get something effective going on this at once. Up to now, I realized, I hadn't been heavy enough on Heller.

On flying feet, I sprinted down the long, long tunnel to the office of Faht Bey.

I burst in. "Get Raht and Terb on this at once!"

He wasn't at his desk.

I tore into his living area. He was stuffing himself at the table. His wife was just getting ready to hand him another platter of *kadin budu*—"woman's thigh," a dish of meatballs and rice. I snatched at his arm. His wife leaped back and the platter spilled all over the floor.

Urgently, I dragged him into his office. "There's trouble in New York!" I shouted at him. "I've got to get Raht and Terb on this at once!"

He was wiping at his mouth with a napkin. He didn't look very cooperative.

"I'm working on it!" I shouted into the air.

Faht Bey said, "Raht and Terb are still in the hospital, thanks to whatever you did. They won't be out for two weeks and you know it."

Oh Gods! That was true.

"The New York office!" I cried. "You've got to send something out to the New York office. They can begin to work on it at once!" Then I lifted my head and yelled, "I'm being industrious!"

Faht Bey heard his wife crying as she tried to scrape the food off the other room's floor. It made him scowl. "Every person in the New York office is gone. They're flying all over the world trying to locate people on that list of criminals you sent. You knocked them right out of operation!"

I raised my head and shouted at the top of my lungs, "I'll think of something!"

"Why are you yelling up in the air like that?" said Faht Bey.

"In case somebody is listening," I said. Stupid fool, didn't he realize this was a national emergency?

I didn't wait for his answer. He was no use. He'd gummed it all up by leaving the New York office unmanned. His fault!

I fled back up the tunnel.

I flew around in circles in my room.

Karagoz was in the yard. I rushed out and asked him if Utanc was still alive.

He tried to answer me but I couldn't wait. I raised my head and yelled, "It will all be handled!"

Karagoz was looking at me very strangely. He said, "The waiter just took out her supper dishes and she was fine."

"She wasn't writhing around the floor from poison?" I begged him.

He looked at me and shook his head. Somewhat sadly, I thought. No help from him.

I rushed back to my room.

I couldn't think. I paced.

Then I got smart. I got a bag of hand grenades out of my locker and went out in the patio. I sat down in a wicker chair. I would sit there all night and if I heard the slightest sound of anybody trying to sneak up on Utanc, I would let them have it.

It was pretty cold as night wore on. The breath of coming winter was in the air.

It cooled me.

I also realized I couldn't sit there every night for months. It was too cold.

I had just dozed when, in a flash, it came to me, totally and completely, how to stop Heller. An entire plan!

A few minor details were missing but they could be filled in as I went along.

I would go to New York, personally, myself.

I would cook Heller's goose by recruiting the most powerful opponents possible.

Wait!
I did not dare leave Utanc here!
I would take her with me!
Another hour of shivering.
I dozed off again.
I woke up with a flash of inspiration!
I knew exactly how I could make Utanc go with me.
Dire emergencies can spawn some hefty ideas!

Chapter 5

With daylight and the staff about, there was less risk of an attack upon her. I lay down on the floor of my bedroom, keeping the door slightly cracked open so I could watch the patio and the further door into the yard.

I had a long time to wait and I must have dozed. The sound of a car starting woke me.

Utanc! As I supposed she would, her fear had worn off and she was going into town. By the sun, it must be around ten o'clock. Usually she was gone for about two hours.

Now was the time!

Those two (bleeping) little boys would be alone! And I was going to handle them once and for all.

I knew they were dangerous. One of them might have a gun. This time, I wasn't underestimating them. I must not fail.

In my earlier visit to Earth, I had bought a Colt .44 Magnum Single Action Peacemaker in a hock shop. It was a huge handgun, enough to break your wrist. I loaded it.

I had also acquired a Mannlicher "Safari," over-and-under double-barrelled .458 caliber elephant rifle. Its barrels were so big that when you looked down them, you got the feeling you could fall through them without touching the sides. I loaded it.

Melahat was in the yard cutting flowers. I walked up behind her and shoved the elephant-rifle muzzle under her chin. When I had brought her to, I hissed, "You're going to get that door open and get me into Utanc's room."

She was white as paper. She wasn't moving, her eyes fixated on the muzzle. Crossed.

"If you don't do it," I grated, "I will shoot the whole staff!"

She rose to the occasion, if a little shakily.

With me right beside her and the elephant gun close under her chin, after a couple tries she found her voice. She called out, "Boys! Utanc said when she left you were to have your present now to amuse you while she was gone."

Silence.

Then a tiny, piping voice. "What is it?"

A jab of the elephant rifle.

"Open the doors and see."

Curiosity won the day. The sound of the inside bar sliding up. The lock being turned. The creak of hinges as the door opened a crack.

CRASH! I was into that room like the New York Tactical Police Force!

The boy at the door went tumbling like a ball across the room. The other was in bed, sitting up, his face cased in bandages. He began to scream!

I kept the elephant rifle on the one on the floor. I pulled out the Colt .44 Magnum and trained it on the one in bed.

"Stand up against that wall!" I ordered. "Put your feet well away from it. Put your palms flat against the wall!"

They looked for help from Melahat. She was sprawled across the door in a dead faint.

The two boys did as they were told, even though they were shaking and crying and one of them had developed hiccups.

I frisked them, keeping a foot ready to pull their feet from under them if they tried anything rough. They were clean. This wasn't odd as they were wearing only pants.

I breathed a sigh of relief. So far so good.

I looked around the room. Utanc had laid rugs on top of rugs decoratively. Musical instruments were on racks. She had a bunch of framed pictures.

Keeping one eye on the little boys, I walked over to the pictures. They weren't real photographs. They were magazine cutouts she had framed in golden frames. Movie stars! Male movie stars! Actors from all down the years.

Some books. I had often seen her bringing in books. Watchful that the boys didn't pull anything, I pawed over the volumes. Odds and ends. But a whole series of hard-cover volumes called *The Illustrated Lives of Famous Stars.*

Suddenly my plans got even better.

I turned on the boys. They were shivering and shaking. Both of them had hiccups now. Good. They'd cooperate. I brandished the Colt .44 Magnum. Then I cocked it.

"Which one of these movie stars does she like best?"

The one who wasn't vomiting stopped his hiccups long enough to say, in a thin scream, "Those two on the end!" He pointed, lost his balance and hit his head on the wall.

I went over and looked. Sure enough, the two on the end were smeared with the lipstick of kisses!

Rudolph Valentino and James Cagney!

I went over and grabbed their well-thumbed copies of *Illustrated Lives.*

Out of my pocket, I took a roll of two-inch-wide adhesive tape. I grabbed the wrists of the first boy and taped them together. I kicked his ankles together and taped them. I slapped adhesive tape across his mouth.

I grabbed the second boy and did the same.

I kicked Melahat to her feet. "Get me two blankets!"

She tottered off and came back with them. I spread them on the floor. I dumped one boy per blanket. I picked up the corners and threw them over my shoulder, two bundles, not even squirming.

"Melahat, you camel's dung," I said in a deadly voice. "You will clean up this room. When Utanc returns you will tell her the two boys' grandmothers are ill and calling for them and that they'll be gone for many days."

She kept opening and closing her mouth, possibly trying to speak.

"If you don't and if Utanc suspects or hears one word that I took the boys, I'll slaughter the whole staff!"

She collapsed to the floor and started bumping her head against it. Aha, I didn't need hypnohelmets. All I needed was an elephant rifle!

I stuck the Colt in my belt. I went out to the station wagon and dumped my bundles in the back.

It had to work!

Chapter 6

I drove to the hospital. I threw the bundles over my shoulder. I went in by the secret entrance that led into the basement.

On the intercom, I summoned Prahd.

He came running down in some alarm. There was nobody housed in the basement yet.

I had dumped the bundles on a table. "I've brought the first two criminals," I said.

"Oh, wait!" said Prahd. "I'm not set up! Not down here. I've been working on a microorganism that uses the trachoma organism to spawn in. It then eats up the trachoma and becomes benign and furnishes the victim with vitamins. It's also contagious. When I've finished that, I am going to get to work on TB."

"This is more important!" I said sternly.

"Oh. Well, there's my whole project on infant mortality. I think I can reduce it to zero!"

Gods, this Prahd had no sense. Faht Bey would die if you dried up his source of birth certificates of dead babies. "Get your head screwed on," I told him.

"Oh. Well, there's another project I have in outline. I think I can make all women have triplets. Isn't that important?"

Gods, the government would go mad! They already had an oversupply of people who had to emigrate to get work! "You'll overstrain their food supply," I said brutally.

"No, no, I thought of that! I sketched a design for

a new intestinal organism that lets the body utilize 94 percent of its food intake. It will stretch the food supply way out. And also there's a way to fix their grain so its yield will quintuple!"

"Prahd!" I said in a loud voice to jar him. "Grow up! This is Earth! The food suppliers would kill us if we did that! And the U.S. couldn't export its surplus grain! Their bigwigs make a fortune out of it! Be practical! Criminals are your best product!"

He didn't look convinced. One blanket had begun to wiggle and he looked at it with alarm. He opened it up. Then he opened up the second. The two small boys looked at him above the tape gags, eyes terror-wide.

"Be careful of them," I said. "They're vicious. Put them apart, in two cells. Keep them locked up and don't take your eyes off them. Their presence here is absolutely secret!"

"But I don't have any jailers!"

"You're good at hiring. Employ half a dozen deaf-mutes to man this place. Get it set up! Get a full cellological operating room going right where we're standing."

"And then my pay starts," he said insinuatingly.

"Prahd, if you do this job perfectly, we will give it very grave consideration."

I handed him the two *Illustrated Lives.* "I want you to fix one of these boys so he looks like Rudolph Valentino and the other one so he looks like James Cagney!"

"Wait," he said. "They're too young to put adult faces on."

I compromised, "Make them so they look like they will grow up to look like those two men."

He was opening the *Illustrated Lives.* It suddenly took his interest. "Ah, there are pictures here of how they looked when they were young."

"Now you have it," I said.

He was lifting bandages on the injured one. "You should have brought him here sooner. Somebody smashed him up."

"Ran into a tree," I said.

"Never mind," said Prahd. "The bone structure has to be altered anyway."

"You can do it?"

"Oh, yes. Means perhaps some gene alteration, some pigment reorganization. A bit extensive but nothing difficult."

"How long?" I demanded.

"Until my pay starts?"

"Until they are completed and healed up," I corrected.

He considered very carefully. Then he said, "It will take until my pay starts."

"Cellogically!" I thundered at him. "How long?"

He rubbed his chin. He seemed to be making some calculations. "One week if my pay starts then."

"One week!" I howled.

"That's as fast as it can be done."

I was being defeated. How could I hold the fort for a week? I would have to think of something. "All right. One week."

"And my pay starts?"

"You do a perfect job in one week and your pay will start!"

"Ah," he said. He went over and picked up the two little boys. He put one in one maximum security cell and one in another. He began to rip the tape off the last one.

I left.

The shrieking hurt my ears.

I somehow had to bridge this gap. One week delay! Something. I would think of something!

Chapter 7

My self-confidence, after so many cruel knocks, was returning. My id had been battered to a very low point of ego. The exact instant of resurgence had commenced with that inspiration about the little boys.

My original idea had been to just get the boy patched up and restored to new condition. But this banal and unimaginative idea had stepped aside before the onslaught of true inspiration. The moment I saw those photographs all smeared with lipstick, my true genius had asserted itself.

What a present! One little boy looking like Rudolph Valentino, the other looking like James Cagney! Instead of flat, uninteresting, two-dimensional photographs, she could have these two to put on a shelf, the way you do with any other knickknack. One could admire them from time to time and keep them dusted and otherwise forget about them.

How she would admire me! And now she would do what I said!

The delay was, of course, a bit chancy. But with my id chasing my ego to new altitude records, this seemed child's play.

I planned it with care. The unseen killer was some part of the base crew, that was for sure. Thus, I must get broad coverage so whoever it was would know I was busy.

Wherever I was, I would raise my voice from time to time and shout how busy I was. But this could only go on for so long: my throat was getting hoarse.

The next day, I awoke with a brilliant plan. I dressed and got a list of everyone at the base. I then proceeded to ferret out each one.

The plot was to question them in such a way that each would realize how active I was and how dedicated to my job. I knew that people talk to one another and the word would get around. Thus, I could consume at least three days doing this.

The action consisted of searchingly and lengthily questioning each person about poison. I did not intend to poison Heller—I did not have the platen—but it would show my heart was in the right place.

From each I wanted to know everything they knew about poisons, particularly rare, violent and undetectable ones. I didn't have to say who I was going to poison as the one with the mission of killing me—and now Utanc—would understand I was really taking my job seriously.

Oddly, I didn't get too many answers. I got a lot of averted eyes and foot shuffling. And by the third day I was aware of quite a few strange looks coming my way.

On the fourth day, I could no longer continue the project. Everyone in sight walked hurriedly off when I appeared. Also I began to suspect everything I ate or drank. But the project was serving its purpose. Utanc was still alive.

When the fifth day came, I realized that if I didn't seem industrious, bad consequences could result. So I had another inspiration.

I went into my secret room. Right at the lunch hour—so Faht Bey could not accuse me of interrupting vital work—I put my foot down upon the secret floor tile by the tunnel door and gave it the proper twist.

Instantly, of course, alarm signals, silent in the office

but awfully loud and bright everywhere else, clanged and flashed throughout the base.

I gave them time. When I was quite sure everyone must have responded, I sauntered down the tunnel.

They were all gathered in the center, crouched behind sandbags, gun muzzles sweeping nervously about. I almost got shot.

I explained to them that this was just a drill. I told them that some very important things were going on elsewhere, that I had to take care of a "certain person" and that I would be away for several weeks.

Instant cheering!

Enormous volume! Some of it even hysterical! They waved their caps and cheered and cheered.

I hadn't realized I was so popular. Quite touching, really. Brought tears to my eyes.

Most important of all, I had bought time. I could now prepare to take care of Heller once and for all without being stabbed in the back.

I sorted out passports. I chose one from the United Arab League. It would give me diplomatic status, pass through all my baggage uninspected and let me designate any entourage that I chose. As it required a trip to Istanbul, which I made very speedily, it consumed two days. I was almost up to deadline and I would have to hurry.

It occurred to me that I might need bugs. There were lots of bugs in the Spurk Eyes and Ears of Voltar stuff so I tore over to the hospital.

Prahd was down in the basement and I didn't want to be plagued with nonsense talk about curing all the diseases in the world and wrecking the capitalistic system, so I tried to do the search myself. The store warehouses were not ready, the materials were still jamming the wards. I got keys and began. You never saw so many boxes piled in places where you couldn't get at other boxes.

Although the Spurk stuff was undoubtedly there, I could only find one small box that was get-at-able without lifting things.

In it there was a compact telescope. It seemed to be able to see through walls. Apparently, it used a distant solid wall as an extension of its front lens. By utilizing the space between molecules, it could get a picture and sound waves through a solid. One had to be at least a hundred feet away from the solid. Aha! The very thing! I could use this to look into Heller's suite! Interference or no interference! I knew there were roofs nearby. Here was a way to see what he did in his rooms and where he hid things! I took it.

There was also a common bug in the box that picked up sound. It was the size of a speck of dust. Maybe I could plant it in Utanc's room. I took it.

I was exhausted at the thought of lifting anything so I got out of there.

Now, money.

I have found that when one is travelling around, money is very necessary. If my plans worked out all right, it would be very necessary.

I went to the radiation-marked boxes in the corner of my secret room. I had not really checked my gold. More lifting.

Bar by bar, I lined it up. I got my thumbnail into each one, even my teeth. Nice and soft. Beautiful gold. Eighteen lovely fifty-pound bars of it! It lay there glowing.

Suddenly, I could not bear to part with any of it! I would find other means of financing my trip! Reverently, I put it all away.

I went down the tunnel to see Faht Bey. I explained to him how urgent the trip was and that it could and would be very expensive.

Faht Bey sat there at his desk, holding his head in his hands. Try as I might, I couldn't shake him loose from any money. I did manage to get a mutter that the Lebanese was over at the hospital.

Well, it was time I had a showdown with this Lebanese! He'd helped wreck the banking business in Beirut and now he was wrecking mine!

He was in the basement!

There was a little office just inside the secret entrance—it had heavy bars and wire nets across it, something new! You couldn't get into it with a blastgun! A maze of bulletproof glass to push things through, a big swing basket for heavy objects. You had to get down and shout through the glass maze to communicate with the cashier! Something, I guessed, that he'd learned in the Lebanon revolt!

"I want some money!" I yelled through the maze.

He sat there behind it and looked awfully deadly. He was bright yellow, no hair and only a couple of fangs left. "No money!"

Right on his desk, in plain view where he'd been counting it, were stacks and stacks of money! I never saw so much money in one pile. U.S. dollars, British pounds. Even some diamonds!

"Some gangsters have arrived!" I yelled at him. "I see the evidence!"

He threw some blank account sheets on top of the money. "Only ten so far!"

"There were two hundred on that list!" I yelled through the maze.

"They're scheduled, spaced into the future. Some of them had to rob banks before they arrived!"

"But ten," I yelled through the maze, "must mean you have collected a million so far! The price was a hundred thousand U.S."

"This place cost a million!" he snarled back through the maze. "We're not covering running expenses yet!"

I heard something to my left and right. I looked up. Two automatic-shotgun muzzles protruded from remote-control turrets. They were pointing straight at me. The Lebanese had his hand on a button that apparently controlled them.

I left.

I sat outside in the dilapidated Ford station wagon. The unfairness of it was very plain. I was making money for the base in rivers! They still had one hundred and ninety gangsters still to remodel! They had nineteen million U.S. in plain sight over the coming weeks or months and already had a whole million!

Aha! Mudlick Construction!

I drove madly to their office. I told the manager to fork over.

"They've got money?" he said.

"They can pay you in cash for the first job this minute!"

He drove madly to the hospital.

He came back.

He handed me a quarter of a million!

I madly stuffed it into a paper sack. A big one. It was half what I was due but he had only been paid half.

We shook hands beamingly.

I drove home.

Chapter 8

Utanc was out. Melahat was cleaning her room. Utanc apparently had swallowed the tale about grandmothers. Her attitude toward me during the past week was as usual—nonexistent. Ah, all that would change!

Melahat was sort of hanging around to lock up the room and I didn't have a chance to plant the bug well. I pretended to be inspecting for cleanliness and kicked it under the carpet.

I went to my room and set up the audio-transmitter-responder for it. I fiddled a bit with the telescope but the directions were right. I could see through a wall a hundred feet away but no closer. Ah, well, it would do for New York!

I phoned Prahd. Tomorrow morning, bright and early, he said. There had been a little delay, other business coming in. But if I would be there around eight, he would deliver "the two packages." He said the bandages were ready to come off. I said to leave them on.

I fended his query about pay. Later, if the job was perfect.

That night I dreamed of Heller being dropped from high places, being squashed between two trains engaged in a head-on collision and being boiled in oil by Manco Devils. Wonderful dreams!

And then, just before dawn, the most beautiful dream of all: lovely Utanc stealing into my bed. It was a dream I meant to become reality!

At eight on the dot, I was at the hospital side entrance. The two little boys were brought out by two deaf-mutes Prahd had hired.

I was quite surprised. The two little boys simply sat down in the front seat where a pointed finger told them to sit. They were all wrapped up in bandages. They seemed very still.

I was prepared. Down the road in a quiet place I stopped. "Which is Rudy?" I said.

They didn't answer. So I did an eenie-meenie-minee-mo. I had the photos from *Illustrated Lives* that Prahd had used. I put the photo of Rudolph Valentino on one and the photo of James Cagney on the other.

I had some colored ribbons and some tags. I wrote *To my darling Utanc. Unwrap carefully. From Sultan Bey,* on each tag.

Although I had brought the .44 Magnum Colt, there didn't seem to be any need of it. The two little boys just sat there in their bandages, very quiet.

I drove into the yard. Utanc's BMW was sitting there—she was home.

I took the two little boys quietly into the patio. I stood them by the fountain. I made a final adjustment of the gay ribbons. Then I kicked them!

They screamed!

I withdrew.

Utanc's bars came off with a clang.

Her door opened!

The two little boys fled to her like streaks!

Gleefully, I made my way to the audio activating unit. I turned it on.

Silence!

No, some slight background sound. I thought the rig wasn't working. I hastily got out the directions—I had not read them before.

This bug was designed to be put on top of picture frames. It said never put it under muffling objects. Gods, I'd put it under a rug! Blast!

I turned up the gain all the way. Just an occasional sound when a voice was raised sharply. Blast! I could get no data on her reaction!

She didn't come speeding to my room to thank me. Not enough coming through on this bug to determine anything.

Almost an hour passed and a tense hour it was!

Then, what was that sound? Water running? Yes, water running.

Then, suddenly, a song. Utanc was singing! She sang:

Come wash my back, little Rudy.
Hand me the soap, little James.
Kiss me and make me less moody.
Hug me and call me sweet names.
Then we will go in the bedroom,
And I'll teach you more lovely games.

I almost sobbed with relief. They obviously had some youthful resemblance to the movie stars. Everything was all right!

I had been under such a strain, I had hardly eaten at all the whole week. I made them bring me a marvelous early lunch. Platters of *hunkar begendi* ("His Majesty liked it"), stewed lamb with chopped eggplant, *kadin gobegi* ("woman's navel") for dessert. I washed it all down with pitchers of *sira* and then sat back to drink my *kahve.* Marvelous.

About two in the afternoon, the bug went live again. I hung over the receiver. A cymbal clash? Yes, another and another and another. Some kind of a dance!

And then Utanc's voice came through very loudly. She *was* pleased. She was singing:

One little kiss went to market,
One little sigh stayed home.
One little hug went, "Weep, weep, weep!"
And all of them gasped in the foam.

I didn't know quite what to make of it. Maybe the bug was defective. I had never heard that nursery rhyme before.

With lots of preparatory things to do such as costumes and counting money, I whiled away the time, expecting Utanc would come flying in at any moment to thank me.

Evening came. Well, shy as she was, she would be waiting for night. I took a bath. I held dinner. Then, at length, I ate it by myself. It didn't taste very good.

I checked the bug from time to time. Suddenly a clashing sound. Swords? A sword dance? Must be from the foot thuds and clashes.

And then her voice, raised high in song, came through:

Little, little feet on my tum, tum, tum.
Dancing like fairies, run, run, run.
Up and down, up and down, leap, leap, leap.
Get it in, get it in, deep, deep, deep.
Up you go, up you go, bloom, bloom, bloom.
Now you come, now you come, boom, boom, BOOM!

What in blazes was going on in there? Were the boys dead? Was she dancing a funeral dance?

No. I could hear some little squeals. Laughter? Delight? They surely weren't squeals of pain! Too cheerful.

More like ecstasy? Delight. It *was* delight.

I gave it up. It was nine. I had had a hard day. I turned out my light and without much hope, I left my door open. I went to bed.

It must have been half an hour later. I was jerked awake by a rustling sound.

My bed moved slightly.

Hands.

It was Utanc!

She was fully clothed but her lips were warm as they touched my cheek. Then they were blazing hot as they crushed against my mouth!

Her hands were all over me. She pushed the bed-clothes back to get at me better.

"Utanc," I whispered.

"Sssh. This is all for you. The mouth is everything!"

Her hands!

I started to turn into fire with passion.

It went on and on!

After a long time, I was lying there, gasping, spent.

Her arm was across my naked chest.

Joy began to well up in me.

I had WON!

"I am so glad you came," I whispered.

She whispered back. "I get so aroused." Then after a bit, "They don't have much endurance and you're the only other man around, such as you are."

"Do they look like Rudolph Valentino and James Cagney?"

She gave a shuddering sigh. "Oh, yes. I thought it was just makeup at first but it didn't wash off. They look like them when they were little boys." She sighed again. Then, "As the years go on they will become like them exactly! I compared the pictures." She sighed again and shuddered.

Once more she was all over me, her mouth searing my flesh in beautiful ecstasy. It went on and on. And then I felt like the whole world had exploded!

She lay there panting. Gradually she quieted down in the darkness.

After a bit, I got very brave. I came to a momentous decision. I decided to be honest with her at least just this once.

Utanc," I said. "I have to go away."

No response.

"Utanc, you are in danger here."

A slight stiffening of limbs?

"I have procured a diplomatic passport. I want you to come with me, posing as my wife. I have had the photo taken already—just a veiled woman. And you can go veiled."

"You have money?"

"Yes."

"You will let me take care of the money and bills on the trip?"

"Well . . ."

Was she going to get up and leave? Hastily, I added, "Yes."

"And you will go where?"

"New York."

Swiftly she asked, "I have no clothes. You can stop over in Rome, Paris, London en route?"

I considered. Was she getting up to leave again? "Yes," I said quickly.

"And I can take twenty trunks under diplomatic seal?"

Yikes! At the cost of air freight? "One trunk."

"Five trunks."

"*Five* trunks?"

She said firmly, "Five trunks."

I knew when to give in. "Five trunks," I said.

"Good," she said. "And we will have separate rooms in hotels, of course."

Well, naturally she'd want separate rooms, she was so shy. I nodded, then realized she couldn't see me in the dark. "Agreed," I said.

"And you promise to bring me back to these dear, darling little boys in a few weeks?"

The boys? She suddenly seemed totally fixated on those two little boys! I realized she wasn't going to put them on a shelf as knickknacks the way I had planned! But I said, faintly, "Yes."

"Good, then I will go with you."

My joy surged!

"Thinking about the little boys, I had better go back now and make sure they are sleeping peacefully in my bed." She got up quite abruptly and hurried out.

I lay back. It suddenly occurred to me that as time went on, as she had said, those two (bleeping) boys were going to look more and more like Rudolph Valentino and James Cagney. I had miscalculated just a little bit. I had two little boys as rivals right now and it would get much worse.

But then I stretched, luxuriating. I had really won. She had come to my bed. And she would come to my bed again and again!

Not a single thing now stood between me and the total wreckage and demise of Heller.

How sweet life was!

How sweet!

PART TWENTY-SIX

Chapter 1

Although I pushed, we could not get off the very next day. Utanc had to take the two little boys to a photographer in town to get their portraits and gold frames for them.

They did resemble the actors quite a bit, or at least the way those actors had looked at that age, if a small boy can be said to resemble anything. They were insufferably smug about their new looks. Even their own mothers didn't know them and claimed Devils had been at work. I thought so, too, to get them born in the first place!

Utanc also had to pack and Gods, when she finished, were those heavy trunks!

True to my promise that she should handle the money, I gave her one hundred thousand dollars U.S. and told her that was all I had. It seemed a fortune but I was cautious: I told her to take it easy on the bills so we'd have money left when we got home.

And so, with much fuss and hurry and scurry, the following day she, I and five trunks took off in a cloud of jet fuel.

Now, to give you some idea of how hard it was to get to Washington—the capital of the United States where I had my first business to conduct—and to give you some idea of the trials an Apparatus officer faces in his efforts to do his duty, I should touch briefly on that trip.

Our first stop was Rome. Apparently Utanc had telephoned on ahead for reservations. And while one could understand that a shy, wild desert girl was tired of privation, I hardly expected that we would stay at the Hotel Salvatore Magnifico Cosioso, the jewel of the city's center. In fact, I would have been kind of lost trying to find the city itself! But Utanc, peering over her veil, seemed to be looking at road signposts and she seemed to get the idea that the Italian taxi driver was going round about to run up the fare.

In purest Italian and in purest vitriol, she told the driver, "Listen, you emasculated rooster, if you think you can swindle me just because I am the helpless wife of a sheik, you got another think coming! If you don't get on the right road instantly, I'll shove a stiletto up your (bleep) so high you'll think you're having a tonsillectomy!"

It was something she must have learned in a tourist phrase book, of course, but it startled me.

At the Salvatore Magnifico Cosioso, we were promptly introduced into the bridal suite—which the reservation seemed to call for. It was magnificent—gold and white! Huge! Awe inspiring! She kicked me and my baggage into its sitting room and locked the bedroom door on me.

After wondering for three hours what she was doing in there with her five trunks, I decided I wasn't going to find out and decided to go to the bar and see what I could see.

In the corridor, I beheld the most beautiful European woman I have ever seen. She was walking toward our suite. She was dressed in the latest feminine mode, wearing stilt-heeled shoes and twirling a handbag to match.

It was Utanc!

She went by me and into the bedroom and locked the door. And that was my stay in Rome—two days of it.

In Paris, we had reservations for the bridal suite at the Chateau Le Beau Grand Cher. It was gorgeous, spacious, gold and white. The manager himself showed us in. Utanc pointed at the champagne bucket that was courtesy of the hotel and in what I recognized must be French, said something that must have been very disdainful. The manager picked up the bottle and looked closely at the year and then went quite white. For ten solid minutes she lectured him before she let him stumble off to return with a wine steward. She found what she was looking for on the wine list and they hastily came back with a different bottle. And also a bottle of Malcolm Fraser Scotch.

Well, naturally, a shy desert girl would object to out-of-date champagne. But I hadn't seen her studying any tourist phrase book. I must be getting unobservant.

To say the least, I got neither champagne nor Scotch. I spent those two days sleeping on the sitting-room couch and wondering what all the laughing was about in the bedroom. She came and went, of course, as she had in Rome. And I saw someone delivering a mountain of shopping packages the last afternoon. Was she buying the town out?

In London there was a change. The reservation was the Royal Suite of the Savoy Hotel. It was a magnificent suite. The sofa in the sitting room was even harder than those of Rome and Paris.

For three days in London, Utanc came and went at all hours. I didn't see her, however. I only heard her corridor door opening and closing and the noisy elevator. She must be buying London out. But when we met at the plane again, there she was in her veil and hooded cloak, shy and demure, if a bit hollow-eyed.

The direct fight first-class to Washington was fairly swift but the ride in from the airport was quite long. I found we had a reservation for the Presidential Suite at the Willard Hotel, a landmark in the city's center. Her five trunks were no more moved into the bedroom than she threw herself on the bed and said to the manager, who had escorted us in, "Please send up a cold supper. Chicken salad and Liebfraumilch '54. And perhaps some orange sherbet. Oh, yes, order me a limousine, preferably a Cadillac, for 9:00 A.M. And now, be off. I am completely exhausted." She said it in purest English. But I had her. The tourist phrase book was peeping out of her bag. That mystery was solved!

I went in to the sitting room with my baggage so she could lock the door. After all, she must be tired after all that travel and shopping. I had arrived!

I could get to work!

Chapter 2

The ease with which you can get to see a United States Senator is mind boggling. You just tell his secretary that you are the head of a local labor union from his home state and bango, there you are in his presence!

I was no longer garbed as a sheik, of course. I looked far more Sicilian in my tight and modish three-piece suit and dark slouch hat, even though I would be a pretty big Sicilian.

Senator Twiddle sat at his desk, flanked on one side by the American flag and on the other by that of his home state, New Jersey. He was the very picture of a noble politician—blond, swept-back hair, a patrician if somewhat alcoholized countenance, upright of bearing and deep and resonant of voice. A man in whom you could have confidence. He was the Mafia contact given us by Gunsalmo Silva. He was also Rockecenter's man.

"Sit down, sit down," he said. "And what can we do for you? Always glad to meet men from the unions."

"Senator," I said, taking a chair and refusing the cigar that would gas me flat, "what would you say if I told you that the Rockecenter oil interests—in fact, all of Octopus—was in dire peril of competition?"

"Aha!" he said. "I'd get right on that phone and call his attorneys!"

"Well, Senator," I said, "it's too delicate to go on the phone, monitored as they are. And even a bit too delicate to put to his attorneys."

"You mean you want to talk to the man himself?" He was stunned.

He fiddled with his cigar. He put it down. He opened a drawer and got out a pint of Jack Daniels. He took a bottle of sparkling water that is furnished the Senate free by the company. He poured two drinks. I pretended to drink at mine. He tossed his off.

He sat back, "Young fellow, I like your looks. It's obvious you don't know danger when you see it. And it's obvious that you don't know the man in question. Not that he would ever *be* in question, understand, so don't quote me."

He scrubbed his chin with a puffy hand. He tipped out another drink to sip. He sat back. "Young fellow, I like your looks. And any favor to Rockecenter is a favor to me. You understand? Don't quote me."

I nodded.

"You know any part of that family?" he asked. I shook my head. "Well, educating the young is a sacred mission of the experienced. I vote affirmative on all education bills. And on all union-sponsored bills," he added hastily. "And there are some things that aren't in the Rockecenter account in *Who's Who.* If you don't know them, you won't get anywhere with Delbert John Rockecenter. But don't quote me.

"Off the record, that family goes way back. They were emigrants from Germany in the 1800s. The right name is Roachengender. The family founder in this country sold crude oil as a quack cancer cure and was a wanted criminal for rape. Don't quote me. I'll deny everything. And you've got too frank a face to be from the FBI.

"The family proceeded to go downhill while their finances went uphill. The first generation in America changed its name to Rockecenter and expanded into crude oil and, with the advent of the automobile, got a monopoly on the nation's petroleum. Congress itself tried to break up that monopoly in 1911 but it just dodged.

"The next generation controlled oil and drug companies. The third generation controlled oil and drugs and politics. The fourth generation started to go to pieces.

"Now usually, great fortunes only last three generations. The socialists have seen to that, mostly. But the wealth of the Rockecenters was so great it went into the fourth generation. But it was wobbly. Politically, it stumbled. The third generation only got to the vice-presidency but the fourth generation appeared to fade even below that.

"Then out of this fourth generation and onto the world stage stepped Delbert John Rockecenter. A dark horse. A candidate nobody even noticed until they were buried in landslides! He apparently had read up and followed all the principles of the original American Rockecenter. And I quote: 'Be moderate. Be very moderate.

Don't let good fellowship get the least hold on you.' Another is 'Trust nobody!'

"In short, young gentleman, he resurrected the basic Rockecenter policies. Gouge everybody. Don't tolerate competition of any kind. Do everybody down including your own family. Don't quote me. This is off the record.

"That Delbert John grabbed all the holdings of all the other Rockecenters and lumped them up again in one huge pile. He even had his Aunt Timantha murdered to get her inheritance. He mended all the ropes they had ever had on anything—banks, governments, fuel, drugs, you name it. And he took those ropes into his own hands. Alone and personal. Single. Never married. Not about to. Why should he when the whole world is his to (bleep)!

"Now, you may think he's old to look at him. But don't let that fool you. He's a powerhouse of cunning! He's the most rapacious (bleepard) I have ever met. He is as crooked as a corkscrew. He has my undying support!"

He finished off his drink. He sat forward. "And that's the man you're asking to see personally." He shook his head. "Not even heads of state get to see Delbert John Rockecenter when they want." He sat back and smiled a politician's smile, totally false. "And so, you tell me all about it and I'll tell his attorneys."

"Well, sir," I said. "I can talk to his attorneys myself. A Mafia chief assured me that you could help."

Oh, that shot told. I had hoped I wouldn't have to use it. In a sort of haggard way, he said, "The unions and the Mafia. I should have known. Are you sure this is in the Rockecenter interests?"

"A new cheap fuel that threatens his monopoly is of great interest," I said. "I'm only trying to help."

"All right," he glanced at the note which his secretary had made and which bore the name I had I.D. for at the moment, "All right, Inkswitch. What do you want?"

"Credentials as a Senate Investigator," I said. "Full, complete and bona fide. He'll see me." Then I added the clincher. "Off the record, you can take the pay for yourself."

His face brightened. "Aha! You'll go far, Inkswitch. I head the Senate Energy Crisis Committee. I do favors for him all the time, keeping down excess supplies of fuel. He'll see my name and know I'm in there pitching for the old Rockecenter interests come next election time! A new cheap fuel, eh? Well, that *is* a crisis!" And he promptly wrote the order to issue me what I needed.

I was glad to see somebody else writing orders for a change.

We parted the firmest of friends.

And two hours later I had all the I.D. anyone could ask for, a Senate Investigator, including the right to bully any official in the land and even the right to carry and shoot a gun—limited only by an oath not to shoot any Senators.

Heller, I said to myself, your chin is almost under. All you need is one firm push to grease your hair with boiling oil.

Now all I had to do was pry Utanc out of Washington.

Chapter 3

After two days, when Utanc showed no signs of moving on, I resorted to a masterstroke. Using Washington cabs, I tailed her limousine. It was easy to do: I would jump in a cab and flash my credentials as a Senate Investigator and say, "Follow that limousine!" and the cabby would say, "Oh, you God (bleeped) Feds!" and follow the limousine.

I got to see quite a bit of Washington. I several times passed the huge advertising sign that dominates Pennsylvania Avenue:

J. EDGAR HOOVER

I decided not to buy any. But I did toy with the idea of going in and finding Stupewitz and Maulin and telling them, as one Federal to another, how Heller had tricked them, but as sneering laughter might arouse professional jealousy—leading to their shooting Senator Twiddle and leaving me without credentials—I forbore.

Utanc was covering museums and things. She was easy to spot, she was so well dressed and chic.

In late afternoon I found the limousine stopped in Potomac Park. It was almost in the exact place where Heller had been grabbed. I even recognized the mounted park patrolman as the same one who had spotted him. Seemed like old times.

A brief scout found Utanc. She was standing on the

steps of the Lincoln Memorial. She had her finger in her mouth and was looking east toward the great, tall obelisk of the Washington Monument. The leaves of fall were already blowing around and the wind was on the surface of the long mirror pool so the monument didn't reflect in it. At this time of year it really wasn't even a very scenic scene. I couldn't imagine why she was just standing there, looking at the monument. Nothing much to see. Just a white shaft.

I was fifty feet away from her, dressed in clothes she had never seen me in. My tailing had been very secret. She gave a shuddering sigh. She took her finger out of her mouth and turned to me and said, "Isn't it beautiful, Sultan Bey?"

I walked over to her. I might as well, now that she had spotted me. My curiosity was aroused. "What's so beautiful about it?"

"So tall, so white, so *hard.*" She put her finger in her mouth and looked at it again.

Inspiration! I said, "That's only 550 feet high. In New York City, the Empire State Building is 1,472 feet high, close to three times as tall!"

"It is?" she said, incredulous.

"Indeed, it is," I said. "It even has a spike on top." And we left that very night for New York City. It takes real genius to operate in the Apparatus!

We checked into the Bentley Bucks Deluxe Hotel, the penthouse. In the 50s, it had a clear-shot view of the Empire State Building to the south and Central Park to the north. But that wasn't what was good about it: it had *two* bedrooms! Marvelous! I could sleep on an actual bed, not a living-room sofa! And this was especially good, as I expected we would be here for quite a while. My luck was already good and now it was improving!

Bright and early the following morning, all

refreshed and with no crick in my back, I had breakfast and, as soon as the numerous waiters and maids had cleared out, unlimbered my receiver and viewer. Before I went into action, I had better have a good look at what (bleeping) progress Heller had made lately.

Flare out!

Maybe my equipment had been damaged in transit. I checked the various indicators. It seemed to be all right.

Then I realized what was wrong. The 831 Relayer was coupled to the activator-receiver! It was boosting the signal so it could be seen thousands of miles away. Until it was turned off, I would get no views in this area!

Where had Raht and Terb said they had put it? Aha! On the TV mast of the Empire State Building. I walked out on the terrace and looked south. I was in straight view of it.

Well! Nothing easier. I would get it turned off.

I phoned the New York office.

It rang and rang. No answer. Then I remembered Faht Bey's complaint that they were all out chasing criminal prospects.

Gods. One had to do everything himself. I dressed in ordinary street clothes, puzzled over the subway system, and took a cab.

We were only a score or so of blocks north of the Empire State Building, and in no time at all I entered through the 34th Street entrance, bought my observatory ticket and went flying up to the 80th floor. The elevator takes less than a minute and I left my stomach on the first floor!

Nevertheless, as it was all in line of duty and one must never quail at that, I took the second elevator to the 86th floor observatory.

Without thinking, I actually walked out on the public platform. There is a ten-foot fence around it to keep people from using it for casual suicides, but this doesn't block any views. Although I might have been able to look all around for fifty miles—it was a clear autumn day, relatively speaking, for New York—I hastily backed inside again to the snack bar and nervously had a Coke. This place was HIGH!

Cokes apparently don't calm your nerves. You'd need a telescope to see the people on the street below from that platform.

Where was the (bleeped) TV antenna? A guide said, "Oh, that's the upper platform. The circular observatory on the 102nd floor." He pointed up.

"The 102nd floor?" I wailed.

"Oh, it's perfectly safe. Glass enclosed."

Duty, remorseless duty, called.

So up I went to the 102nd floor.

Well, to be brief, that isn't the top. There's another 222 feet on top of *it!* The literature said they built it to be a dirigible mast but never used it after one near-fatal attempt. And now it was a TV antenna.

The activator-receiver and 831 Relayer were up there somewhere!

There was glass all around me. Yes, I could see for fifty miles. And I could also see 1,250 feet DOWN!

There was a trap in the ceiling.

I began to shake. I hate heights. I knew in my soul that trying to get up there wouldn't result in a *near*-fatal attempt. It would be TOTALLY fatal!

I controlled my vertigo enough to get into the elevator. And though I had protested the speed of those three consecutive elevators going up, I blessed it going down!

When I arrived once more on 34th Street, I bent over and reverently patted the sidewalk!

Silly situation. Thousands of miles away, in Turkey,

I could track Heller easily. Now here he was, only a few hundred feet up in that same building and I couldn't track him at all! (Bleep) Spurk!

Raht and Terb!

I did know where they must be—the Silverwater Memorial Hospital over on Roosevelt Island. But I did not know what names they were registered under.

I couldn't figure out the subway system on how to get there. I took a cab.

Only because I knew their approximate date of entry and the state they had been in was I able to run them down in the wards "as a caring friend."

And there they were. Ambulant! They weren't even in bed! They were sitting by themselves in a patients lounge, watching TV! The nerve of them. I knew they had done all that just to get a vacation at Voltar government expense!

They became aware that somebody was standing there in a deadly manner.

"Officer Gris!" gasped Terb. He raised the casts on his arms protectively.

Raht didn't speak. His jaws were still wired up.

"What are you doing here?" said Terb somewhat unnecessarily.

"I am doing your jobs!" I thundered at them.

"Sssh!" said Terb, waving his casts about.

"Why 'sssh'?" I demanded. And indeed, why? There were only some old and chronically ill people in the lounge. Riffraff. "You are neglecting your government duties! You left the 831 Relayer on! Negligence!"

A nurse came tearing in from the hall with a what's-wrong, what's-wrong, this-is-a-hospital look on her face. I stopped her! I flipped out my Federal credentials and in minutes I was talking to a chief administrator.

"Those two men are malingerers," I said. "They

are evading the draft. They have been recalled to service. When can you get them out of here?"

He was impressed. He said, "The records here show compound fractures. They have some time to go before they can be unwired and have the casts sawed off. It would be dangerous to just discharge them."

"If you don't cooperate, I'll cut off your Medicaid," I said. "The government must be served."

He knew that. I didn't tell him which government. He grovelled and said he'd do the best he could.

I went back and told Raht and Terb to get that 831 Relayer turned off as soon as possible. I gave them my phone number at the Bentley Bucks Deluxe Hotel and told them, acidly, that when they'd caught up on their TV, they were to phone me that they were on duty once more and that, until then, their pay was suspended.

I left. I was pretty cross, actually. Here I was working my skull to the bone while others just lay about.

But it didn't solve my problem. I had to know what Heller was doing.

I returned at vast expense by taxi to the hotel.

Before I undertook my next step, I should surely check on Heller.

Utanc was out. I had missed lunch. I ordered room service to send me up three shrimp cocktails and ate them moodily.

Then inspiration! Food sometimes has that effect on one. I remembered the telescope.

I unpacked it and went out on the terrace. Certainly one of those rooms in the Empire State Building was his.

There was trouble with the image. Unclear. Sort of yellow. I went and read the instructions.

This telescope, when you turned it on, wasn't really a telescope as such. It threw a beam. The beam sensed the *other* side of a wall by going through the spaces between molecules *of* a wall and then not finding any. When it didn't find any more to go through, it made a patch of energy which acted as a mirror. And the image on that mirror was what came back to the viewer. It also had an audio pickup. Well, well. It sure looked like a telescope.

I tried again and then saw what it was. Smog. The poor telescope thought the smog was a solid wall and tried to construct reflective mirrors all along the way. Too much smog. Too much distance. I did get a vague impression of stenographers on people's desks and things but nothing useful. Heller's office, I suddenly remembered, faced south anyway! The other side of the building. (Bleep)! I had to get on the job right away. Duty demanded it! No possible delay could be tolerated!

Utanc came back, followed by two bellboys who looked more like mountains under her purchases. I saw signs on the wrappers: Saks, Lord and Taylor, Tiffany. I hoped we would have enough money to get home!

She came out on the veranda.

"We got to stay here for some time," I said. "I hope we will have money enough to get home!"

She opened her purse. "Almost all of the hundred thousand left," she said. I gaped. After Rome, Paris, London and Washington? What a money manager this wild creature from the Kara Kum desert was! Amazing!

She was friendly, too. Talking to me even.

"My goodness, look at that!" she said, putting her finger in her mouth. She was staring at the Empire State Building bathed in the setting sun. "My, it's tall and bold and hard! So HIGH! It's a sight that goes right through you!"

"Indeed, it does," I said with a shudder, thinking of my horrible experience with it.

She had something on her mind. She looked at me

prettily. "Sultan Bey, do you suppose that when we've had some supper and it is nice and dark in your room, I might come in and . . . well . . . you know."

Oh, joy!

Never before in my life had I heard such a wonderful plan!

Duty could wait!

More than my spirits rose to the occasion!

Chapter 4

Of course, it was wonderful.

But Utanc, about 10:00 P.M., seemed a bit restless. She got up and went to her room. I myself felt too exhilarated to go to sleep. I heard her moving around and, presently, the penthouse elevator arrived and departed.

Curious, I picked the lock of the door to her bedroom.

She was gone!

Oh, well, probably out for a walk to get some fresh air.

I myself felt masterful. Suddenly I realized that my luck had changed, that it had been changed for some time in fact. The thing to do is ride the crest of good luck. I would take this telescope and go over, right now, and have a look at Heller's suite.

I looked at a street map, found I was only a mile or so from the Gracious Palms. I got dressed in dark clothes. The telescope was in a thin, long case with a carrying handle, so I picked it up.

Shortly, in a cab, I arrived at an apartment house

just north of the Gracious Palms. It was a very quiet street. The apartment house seemed old. There was no doorman I could bribe to let me on the roof. There was only a vast array of polished brass mailboxes and buzzers.

Genius. I would choose a name on the top floor, get entrance and then, agilely, get onto the roof.

A top-floor apartment—22B. And what a name, "Margarita Pompom Pizzazz." What an attractive name! Probably a showgirl with lots of boyfriends, used to being buzzed late at night. I buzzed.

Apparently you got a phone call back and you had to answer the phone. It rang. I answered.

"Who is it?" said a voice—the quality of the phone was bad.

"An old flame," I said, hoping the quality was equally as bad on the way back up the wires.

The door clicker clicked promptly. I pushed it open, got in the elevator and got out on the 22nd floor. There was a stairway emergency escape to the roof at the end of the hall. I headed for it.

Halfway there, I became aware of a door cracked open on a chain. It was 22B. A voice said, "Who *are* you?" Musically.

Through the three-inch crack I could see part of a woman's face. She must be about sixty! Welcome still registered on it.

"Roof inspector," I said.

"What?" No welcome.

"Roof inspector," I repeated. "Got to inspect the roof."

"You mean you didn't come up here for a fling?"

No, no. I was a lot too spent! "Roof inspector," I said, tapping the case I held.

The door slammed. Loudly!

Oh well, I'd heard it takes all kinds to make this

planet. I went on up the stairs. The emergency exit door was locked. I picked it expertly. It opened upon a roof festooned with tall air-conditioner units which blocked clear views.

In two minutes or less I had oriented myself and had the telescope out of its case. I went over to the parapet and, from what I knew of the view from inside his suite, tried to pick out which building and which suite. It was a little confusing until I found I was looking north instead of south. I corrected this.

After that, it was easy. I turned on and tuned in the telescope. It did everything the late Mr. Spurk claimed. I was looking into the synthetic-jungle/synthetic-beach room. A small brown diplomat, with his top hat still on, was really making a score with a coal-black girl! They were rolling over and over in the synthetic grass while the synthetic sunlight scorched them. But there was nothing synthetic about that lovemaking!

Finally, from somewhere he produced a rope and managed to get it around her ankles and her wrists. And then he really gave it to her!

I thought I had been satisfied this evening. I began to get aroused. He was going to kill her for sure!

But suddenly it was all over. She shucked off the rope as though it had not existed. She said, "Was that the way it was, Mr. Boola?"

He said, "Exactly! Let's do it all again!"

Ah, well. I hadn't come here for recreation. I moved the telescope along. I was looking into Heller's sitting room. It was quite dim.

Everything was very neat except for some ice-cream dishes sitting on the bar and they were stacked just right and ready for a houseman to take. Leave it to Heller. His neatness grated on you if nothing else did!

It sure was a beautiful living room, even seen in the half-light.

I moved the telescope along. I was looking into his bedroom. It was confusing! Mirrors! For a moment I couldn't tell which was the bed and which was any one of fifty multiplying images. I found the bed. Huge, circular; enough bed for a half-dozen people.

There was Heller! Lying on his side, blond head pillowed on one upflung arm. Sleeping peacefully. Without a care in the world for all the trouble he was causing me!

He was all alone in bed!

Not a trace of anyone else!

And then the telescope slipped and tipped up at the ceiling mirror. Was that someone on the other pillow? A face? A small, three-dimensional face?

I increased the magnification.

A Voltar three-dimensional bust picture!

THE COUNTESS KRAK!

I was stunned. Perhaps it was because those pictures look so lifelike despite their cloud and sky backgrounds, but it was sort of like the Countess Krak was looking at me! There she was, blond hair, gray-blue eyes, perfect features. He must have sneaked a portraitist in one night on the tug in Voltar.

He had been carrying her picture in his baggage!

And there it was, lying on the pillow next to him.

For some reason, I knew not why, it made me uneasy. Then I threw it off. What a dog he was, having all these women every day and still putting out Countess Krak's picture!

But that wasn't why I was here. By adjusting focus, I began to inspect closets.

He sure had a lot of clothes!

And there sure were a lot of bass plugs in those cabinets! Death traps!

But the telescope couldn't comb through stacks of sweaters and other things.

One door was very tightly barred and locked. I had a ray of hope. Maybe he only locked it when he went to bed. Maybe, had I been earlier, he would have opened it.

It occurred to me that we were approaching the time when he would be writing his third report. If I got very, very lucky and got here earlier tomorrow night before he went to bed, he might be writing his report or at least have that closet open.

I resisted the temptation to look in on more diplomats at play. I went into the stairwell, locked the door, walked down to the 22nd floor and was shortly back in the street again. How easy! Nothing to it when you're Apparatus trained.

Back at the hotel, Utanc still wasn't in. But I went to bed. It had been a busy night!

Chapter 5

I idled through the following day. I did not see Utanc, but then, I didn't expect to. I was getting conditioned to hanging around hotel rooms alone.

The afternoon papers had an item of interest. Rockecenter had roared in from a conference with kings and dictators and things in the Middle East where he had settled the world problems of energy forever until next week when the price was going up again. Nice front-page picture of him being handed a bouquet of calla lilies by Miss Peace. The photographer had had a bit of trouble shooting around and through the two or three hundred soldiers carrying cocked guns. I hadn't known he had been out of town. My luck was surely in. Tomorrow I would make an appointment and see him. But Senator Twiddle surely had been right about it being hard to get close to Delbert John Rockecenter. Those soldiers. And even while the ceremony was going on, apparently, Miss Peace was being frisked by a personal bodyguard.

As to this night's planned work, I knew that Heller would probably be up and around in his suite about nine. Earlier observations on the viewer told me that. And he was not well enough trained to know that safety lay in not repeating habit patterns.

Accordingly, I had dinner in my room and, carrying my case, at 8:45 P.M. stood once more in the lobby of the apartment house.

It had worked once. It would work twice. I boldly pushed the button of Margarita Pompom Pizzazz.

The voice on the phone. "Well?"

I opted to be charming. "I was in too much of a hurry last night. I was impolite. Could you let me in again?"

The door clicked. In I went and up I went in the elevator. I headed for the emergency exit. Her door was cracked open again.

"Roof inspector," I said.

"And?" said the voice in the door.

"And nothing," I said. "Roof inspector!"

The door really slammed!

I went up the stairwell, picked the lock and shortly there I was, training the telescope on Heller's walls.

He was up!

Unfortunately, as a swift side glance showed, the target closet was shut tight. I swivelled the telescope back.

Heller was sitting on the couch reading something.

Bang-Bang was watching TV. Heller got up and got himself a Seven Up. There was a knock on the door.

Vantagio came in. He had a girl by the arm. She was in street clothes. "This is Margie," said Vantagio. "The girl I phoned up about."

"Have a seat, Vantagio," said Heller.

"No, no. Busy night. Listen, kid, I just want you and Bang-Bang to break this Margie in. She just came on. She doesn't know. She's new."

Oho, so Heller broke in the new girls, did he! Oh, Krak would love to know about this!

Heller looked at the girl. "You really want to do this? It's kind of rough the first time."

The girl said, "Oh, yes! I heard you really had something big going!"

Bang-Bang said, "I'm leaving. I can only stand to do this just so often! It wears me out. I get sore!"

Vantagio said, "Shut up, Bang-Bang. Please, kid. Just one more girl. It helps their morale. The other girls feel pretty cocky when you're through with them."

Bang-Bang was trying to leave. "Stay right where you are, Bang-Bang," said Heller.

Vantagio said, "Do you want her stripped, kid? Lying down or standing up?" He turned to the girl. "Take off your coat and skirt." He started to help her.

Heller said, "Vantagio, you better watch it or I'll use you!"

The Sicilian got the girl's skirt off but he withdrew to the door. "No, you won't. I'm getting too old. I'm going right now," he said and left.

Heller turned to the girl. She was standing there in her slip now. She was looking at Heller adoringly. "Sit there," he said. "Now, how much experience have you had?"

The girl sat down, her knees apart. She decided she

had too much on and shucked the slip over her head, leaving herself with just panties and a bra.

"Oh," she said. "A few boys in Duluth. Just high-school stuff, mainly. In a car, back of the gym. One or two professors. And my brother, of course. Nothing important."

Heller said, "Ever get battered around?"

The girl thought it over. "Oh, yeah. Once. A drunk raped me."

Heller said, "Now we're getting somewhere. What did you do?"

"I tried to hold him off and then he just knocked me out, ripped my clothes off and raped me."

"Okay, Bang-Bang," said Heller. "Start to rape her! You get started. I'll finish up."

Bang-Bang groaned. But he got up. He grabbed the girl by the arms and threw her down on the floor. He ripped her bra off. He grabbed the band of the panties and pulled them down and off and threw them away.

Heller said, "That's enough. Now listen, Margie. Why did you let him do that?"

"You told him to," said the girl.

"No, no, no!" said Heller. "Now you grab Bang-Bang's arms and start to rape *him!*"

The girl rose up and seized Bang-Bang with a will.

Bang-Bang simply threw his wrists up and the girl sailed halfway across the room!

Heller caught her in midair. He put her down and said to her, "Now, you do that."

Bang-Bang grabbed her. The girl threw her wrists up the same way Bang-Bang had. Bang-Bang went staggering.

"Hey!" the girl said. "He couldn't keep hold of me!"

Heller sat the girl down in a chair. He said, "Now,

listen. The main trouble whores have is getting abused physically. Getting beat up."

"According to Vantagio," said Bang-Bang, "it makes them amortize too fast. But he never thinks of guys like me!"

Heller ignored him. He said to the girl, "Now, what we're going to teach you first is how to shake any grip any man can put on you. Then we'll teach you how to attack. It's not easy."

"Especially on me," said Bang-Bang morosely.

Heller said to the girl, "With practice you can not only learn those things, you can also learn to *appear* to be under a man's control but actually remain completely able to handle him, drunk or sober. Get it?"

The girl's eyes were gleaming with enthusiasm. "Oh, yes! I promise I will study and practice hard! The other girls here absolutely love it! They say they never get beat up anymore."

"It's only me that gets beat up," said Bang-Bang with a groan.

Heller went over to pour them some Seven Up. The girl said to Bang-Bang in a low voice, "I should think he must have invented these tricks himself just to beat off all the girls. He's awful cute, Mr. Bang-Bang. Is it true like they say he's a virgin?"

I was in total, utter disgust. How Heller was conning them! Pretending these were things he had dreamed up! He was teaching them Voltarian unarmed combat! And he was a dithering fool, too! A whole houseful of beautiful women and he had been wasting his time teaching them how to protect themselves! A traitor to all men everywhere! How about all those who only got their kicks beating up whores? How about them? Thoughtless (bleepard).

A man must be masterful!

A tiny sound behind me!

My head whirled away from the telescope!

Standing on the roof just outside the access door, bathed in red light from below, was Margarita Pompom Pizzazz!

She was in a flowered bathrobe!

She looked like a sixty-year-old Demon from Hells!

What was that in her hand? A huge, lethal-looking weapon! A BB pistol!

She saw she was detected!

She raised the BB airgun!

In a snarling voice of hate she said, "Put up your hands, you Peeping Tom! This is your last chance or I'll shoot! Trifling with my affections! Breaching your promises!"

She gestured ferociously with the BB gun. "You're finished! I phoned the police there was a sniper on the roof! A SWAT team will arrive any minute and blow you to bits! So this is your last chance!"

I flinched. There were huge, standing air-conditioner units in place all around on the roof. If I could withdraw behind one . . .

I moved back!

She fired!

The pellet struck the side of the fragile telescope! Sparks from its electronics flew!

So did I!

I backed in a flash behind an air-conditioner stack.

She fired again!

I held on to the telescope. I might need it as a weapon!

Going crabwise, I drew further away, taking advantage of every square inch of cover!

She was following me up!

My head was in view for an instant.

The deadly *pffft!* of the air pistol coupled with the *clang* of the pellet striking sheet metal right beside my head!

She was a deadly marksman! A killer! Maybe a hit woman in her youth!

I skittered further! I took another peek. Bathrobe flaring like the cloak of an avenging horseman, she was following me up!

Another lethal *pffft!* and deadly *clang!*

Oh, this called for top Class A strategy! And a SWAT team on its way? This called for Joint Chiefs of Staff Maximum National Emergency Plan Triple X! Maybe atomic bombs!

I drew back in a wide circle through the maze of air conditioners.

In full cry, shouting, "Surrender now, you (bleepard)!" and "Geronimo!" each time she shot, she was following me up.

To get back to the roof-access door and escape, I had to cross three open spaces. I screwed up my courage. I dashed across the first one!

She fired! A miss.

I poised to cross the second. She was circling away from the access door to get a cleaner shot. I measured my timing perfectly. I dashed!

She fired! A miss!

I crouched behind an air conditioner. I looked at that last open area. Dangerous! I was taking my life in my hands! But I couldn't stay on that roof with this yowling Demon!

I braced myself. I dashed!

My rump was struck a mighty blow! It stung!

Seeing I had not received a mortal wound, I leaped into the stairwell!

I got the door closed just as another BB crashed against it!

I locked it from inside. Six steps at a time, I flew down the stairs!

Hammering on the roof door above! Frustrated howls of rage! They lent wings to my feet!

Twenty-two flights down, I burst into the lobby.

There was no one there. The commotion was all upstairs.

I snatched the door open, thankful that they were never locked from inside.

Into the dark street I sped. I crossed it.

Police cars!

Three abreast they were coming up the street!

My way was blocked!

I dived into a handy basement stairway.

Only then did I dare look up and back.

She was standing on the roof edge! She had the pistol in one hand and was waving something in the other. The telescope case! I had forgotten it! She looked like some Demon twenty-two stories up against the sky.

She was screaming something. Too far away to get the words. She had spotted me crossing the street! She was pointing and howling.

I still had the telescope in my hand. Evidence! It was ruined. I hastily dumped it into a garbage can close by and resumed my cover.

She had seen me again!

I couldn't tell what she was screaming. She was pointing down toward me, waving the case and pistol.

The SWAT team!

They spilled out of the cars. They rushed into position.

I recognized the man in the third police car! It was Inspector Bulldog Grafferty!

This required triple think! That demented creature up there was pointing down at me. She could still see me! She was waving the BB pistol and the telescope case.

Genius came to my rescue. At the top of my lungs, I shouted, "Take cover! That's Mad Maggie, the Times Square Sniper!"

The SWAT team scattered like a puff of dust!

There was a shattering blast of rifle fire!

Margarita Pompom Pizzazz, riddled with bullets, came off the roof in a long, slow, high dive and went *thunk* on the pavement.

You can always count on the police to do their duty. Particularly when they think their own necks are out!

Grafferty made sure there were no other snipers on the roof. Then he walked up to the corpse and turned it over with his foot.

"Fellow citizens," he said with a hand bullhorn to the empty street in general, "you can come out now and go about your business. The first interest of the police is to protect its taxpayers. The streets are safe once again, thanks to Bulldog Grafferty." Was he running for office or just getting ready to hit the town for higher pay?

I sauntered off.

Some Earth poet once said that Hells had no fury like a woman scorned. He must have had Margarita in mind.

It was a bit hard to saunter with that BB in my butt.

Chapter 6

It was time for strong measures. The hour had arrived to bring in the troops, the tanks and the artillery. It was plain that Heller was dangerous beyond belief. Even trying to put his room under surveillance was as much as your life was worth. My behind attested to that. Until I got to the privacy of my hotel bathroom I was certain the wound was near mortal, and I had envisioned a tender scene of getting Utanc to draw the lethal bullet out while I stoically groaned just a bit. But unfortunately the pellet had not penetrated flesh, and simply dropped out of my pants when I took them off. But it was bruised! Tender! The red spot was a quarter of an inch in diameter!

No, I couldn't go around risking death on Heller's account. So, sitting lopsided in the ornate hotel chair, I picked up the ornate white and gold phone and called Rockecenter's office.

That produced quite a spin at the hotel switchboard. I told them who I wanted to speak with and they didn't believe me. They acted like I was trying to call a God.

Finally the hotel switchboard supervisor got the telephone company emergency-assistance supervisor who got onto the chief information supervisor of the city of New York. They kept saying one had to call the Octopus Oil Company in Ohio. I argued this down and they said you called the Octopus Oil Company in New Jersey. They were arguing with one another over the phone like it was a conference call. After a while somebody thought of getting the emergency assistance information supervisor of the Continental Telephone Company and he got the idea maybe the International Phone Company would know. More and more people kept getting added on to this conference call. It appeared no one had ever before tried to telephone Delbert John Rockecenter and they weren't sure that it wasn't sort of sacrilegious.

Eventually they included in an Arab emergency assistance supervisor in Saudi Yemen and in broken English he said they should query the local operator at Hairytown, New York, because he had heard his king went there once, and he had had to phone him about a palace revolution. So that local operator got added to the babble on the lines and she said, why, yes, she'd ask the butler at the Rockecenter Estate near there—Pokantickle, it was called—and maybe he'd know how you could phone Delbert John Rockecenter. The fourth assistant butler got on the line and said, in a lofty tone, that if it wasn't Miss Agnes calling, all such calls should be referred to the attorneys, Swindle and Crouch of Wall Street.

So the receptionist at Swindle and Crouch was added and she was horrified. Nobody ever called Delbert John Rockecenter! It should be reported to the police!

I had an inspiration. In a tough voice I said, "Put Mr. Bury on the line!"

She said, "Oh, I am sorry, but Mr. Bury is at his special office in the Octopus Oil Building at Rockecenter Plaza. He has an appointment with Mr. Rockecenter at ten and won't be in today."

A wheeze of relief went from New York to London to Saudi Yemen. They had run God to his lair. I am sure most of them had a coffee break to celebrate the instant they went off the line.

The hotel switchboard girl said, "That's only a few blocks down the street! I'll connect you."

Magic. The fourth assistant receptionist in Mr. Bury's Octopus Oil Building office had an open moment at one o'clock sharp and would see me.

Of course, I took a bath, put a Band-Aid on the red spot to cushion it and got all dressed up in my most Federal-looking investigator suit. I polished up my credentials and at one o'clock sharp was sitting, slouch hat in hand, before the iron-barred and bulletproof glass-protected desk of the fourth assistant receptionist in Mr. Bury's special office in the Octopus Building. At one-fifteen he came in from lunch.

I lifted my credentials up so he could see them through the glass.

He sat down at his desk. He said, "I'm sorry. We don't have any orders for the Senate today."

I said, "You better let me see Mr. Bury or you really will be sorry!"

He looked closely at my credentials again.

"The servant's entrance is in the basement," he said.

"I want to see Mr. Bury," I said firmly.

"Mr. Bury has just come back from an important appointment," he said. "He is exhausted! I'm scandalized that you would presume such a tone!"

I said, "You get on that blower, sonny, and tell Mr. Bury that Delbert John Rockecenter will be the one that's scandalized if I don't get to him."

"Are you threatening me?" He was pushing a buzzer. Two armed guards, carrying riot shotguns at port, burst in the door behind me.

"You tell Bury that I came here to avert a scandal!" I said, "or it will be bursting all over the papers!"

The guards grabbed me.

"What kind of a scandal?" said the fourth assistant receptionist.

"Family!" I said, struggling.

Hastily the fourth assistant receptionist held up his hand to the guards. It was time, too. They almost had me out the door.

Magic!

Two minutes later, the guards had me standing in the middle of Mr. Bury's office.

Mr. Bury was even more dried up. Life was being hard on him. He had more wrinkles than a prune.

"Now, what's this about a scandal?" he said.

I glanced either way at the guards. Bury nodded. They frisked me and took my gun. They left.

"Cheap fuel," I said.

"That's not a family scandal."

"It will be if I don't get to see Delbert John Rockecenter. Cheap fuel could wipe out the whole family fortune."

The Wall Street lawyer thought it over. "That cheap?"

"Cheaper," I said. "The dastardly plot was revealed in a long and careful investigation."

"Who knows about it?"

"Twiddle and me. And he knows no details. I came straight to headquarters with it when I was sure."

"What is this fuel?"

"That's what I'll tell Delbert John Rockecenter."

"No, no," said Mr. Bury. "You tell me and I'll tell him."

"That's what everybody says," I grated. "This stuff is as cheap as sand. You think I'd tell anyone else? Would Rockecenter want me to tell anyone else? It violates the old family policy, 'Trust nobody!' "

"Ah," he said contemplatively. "I see what you mean. Mr. Rockecenter is a stickler in adhering to family policy. But what's your own payoff? I've got to be sure this is honest dealing."

"Enemy," I said. "Personal revenge."

That made sense. That was something he could understand. But he hesitated. "Actually, I think you had better tell me. You have no other route to Mr. Rockecenter. There are none."

"There's Miss Agnes," I said, taking my cue from the fourth assistant butler at Pokantickle Estate.

"Oh, God (bleep)!" said Mr. Bury. "I told him and told him to ship that (bleepch) off!" He recovered from his unlawyerlike outburst. He passed a tired hand across his prune wrinkles. "All right," he said at last. "If you're up to it, I'll put you through the mill. But you'll be wearing concrete shoes in the East River if this is not on the level."

He saw I was determined. He pushed a buzzer and shortly two different guards came in. Bury pushed some more buttons and spoke rapidly into an interoffice phone. A huge, apelike fellow in very expensive clothes came in.

Bury said, "Take him through the precautionary sector and then take him to see Mr. Rockecenter."

"What?" yelled the apelike man, incredulously.

"That's what I said," frowned Bury. And to me, he added, "If I never see you again, don't come back."

Heller, I said to myself, write your will. You're as good as dead! Maybe worse!

And then, thinking of all this security and precaution, I amended my optimism: Heller was in the soup only if I could actually get to and handle Rockecenter!

Chapter 7

We left the black onyx and silver aluminum front of the Octopus Building. We walked through its landscaped plaza. We crossed the Avenue of the Americas. The alert guards kept a firm grip on me.

We passed the City Musical Hall. We walked through a whole street made into gardens and which ended with all the United Nations flags. We crossed Fifth Avenue. We walked below a bronze statue of Atlas bearing a huge skeletal world upon his back and I wondered if Delbert John Rockecenter must feel that way. We went north a block, passing St. Patrick's Cathedral.

The guards marched sternly on both sides of me.

I wondered what this strange promenade was all about. Were they trying to confuse me or lose me? Or was this a guided tour to show me all the buildings Rockecenter owned personally?

The apelike man stopped in a shop and bought a quart of goat's milk and a bag of popcorn.

We went all the way back, the way we had come, I supposed, though I was totally lost. We went into an ornate lobby, huge murals all around. We stepped through a small door which had been a blank wall an instant before. We were in an elevator.

We went up. It opened. We got out.

I was transferred to the burly guards in the front room and the original guards gave the new guards my gun and left. The ape-man stayed on, carrying the bag of popcorn and quart of goat's milk.

The burly guards frisked me. They shoved me through a barricade—rather tight, getting past two machine guns, manned.

Guards in the new room took over. They frisked me. They took my new I.D. Then they phoned Senator Twiddle's office and verified it.

They passed me through another barrier. They also passed them my gun. New guards there took the serial numbers off the gun. They also fired a round in a soundproof box. They phoned the results through to somebody. A sign flashed on a computer:

> Weapon has not been used in the assassination of heads of state lately.

They passed me through another barrier. New guards took over. They frisked me. They took my fingerprints and an instant photograph. They punched it into the FBI's National Crime Index Computer. It went to Washington. It came back. The screen said:

> Not wanted yet.

They put the fingerprint card and photograph in a shredder.

All this time, the ape-man was coming along with the bag of popcorn and quart of goat's milk.

They pushed me through a barrier to a new set of guards. There was a dental chair. They X-rayed my teeth for poison capsules. They X-rayed my body for any implanted bombs.

They passed me along to the next room and a new set of guards. They examined my wallet for concealed knives. They examined my keys for trick blades. They X-rayed my shoe soles.

They passed me along between two howitzer cannons—a tight squeeze—and I found myself in a room all dark except for one pool of light in the center. There was a desk over to the side. A sign said:

Chief Psychologist

I knew I was amongst friends.

He took me under the light, made me sit on a stool. He examined the bumps on my head. He drew back and nodded.

The ape-man pushed me to a revolving door. I went through. It was a miniature hospital operating room. Two attendants in blue-green gowns put out their cigarettes and donned masks.

They stripped me of all my clothes. They took my temperature and blood pressure. They got samples of sputum and put it under a microscope. They took a blood sample and examined that.

The senior of the two nodded and the other rammed me into a sort of glassed closet. They seemed to be filling bottles.

"Hey," I said to the ape-man. "Is all this necessary?"

"Listen," he said, "if the Prime Minister of England can go through this without a beef, so can you!"

They had their bottles full. They hit some knobs. I was sprayed with antiseptic.

I came out. They threw my clothes in and they, too, were sprayed with antiseptic.

They stood me and my clothes in front of a dryer.

As soon as I was dressed, the ape-man pointed at the next door. It had steel teeth on both sides that, apparently, could be closed instantly.

A girl was sitting with her feet on the desk, chewing

gum. I recognized "Miss Peace" from the news photograph. Aha! He used his own staff for greeting ceremonies. How wise!

The ape-man said, "It's cleared so far."

She took her feet off the desk. She opened a gigantic drawer. It was lined with stocks of badges. They were huge. They said, "King" and "Banker" and such things across the top and had a blank line for a name to be filled in under the title.

"Oh, (bleep)," said Miss Peace. "I'm totally out of 'Unwanted Guest' buttons. I don't want *him* to think I'm inefficient."

"Give him anything," said the ape-man. "This milk is liable to go sour and I'm late already."

She picked up "Derby Winner" and dropped it. She picked up "Hit Man of the Year" and dropped it. She was dithering. "(Bleep)! If I don't put a button on this guy *he* won't know who he's talking to!"

Apparatus training tells. My quick eye spotted "Undercover Operator Up for Promotion to Family Spy." I said, "That is the only one you've got that covers it. I'm not a king."

"That's right," she said, glancing at me. "You sure ain't no king."

"Hurry up, will you," said the ape-man. "This popcorn will get cold, too! You want me to lose my job?"

She grabbed my I.D. and scrawled Inkswitch on the "Undercover Operator Up for Promotion to Family Spy" one. She jabbed it into my lapel and into me.

What a man this Rockecenter must be to have such a loyal and dedicated staff!

There was an arched church door on the other side of the office. The ape-man pushed me through it.

I was in an enormous room. It had a vaulted ceiling

of cathedral height. It had saint niches with votive candles burning under each saint. The statues were all of Delbert John Rockecenter. There was a big desk—actually an altar.

He was not, however, sitting at his desk. He was in a gilded throne chair, staring at a wall I could not see. Ah, I thought, Delbert John Rockecenter was deep in thought, sorting out the cares of the world with his mighty brain.

I was pushed further into the room. Then I saw what he was looking at. It was a one-way mirror. On the other side of it was the dressing room and toilet of chorus girls. They were taking off their costumes and getting into even scantier costumes. They were also going to the toilet.

Delbert John Rockecenter became aware that somebody had entered his office. He leaped forward, turned and glared. He was a tall man, past middle age, not much hair. His features were unmistakably those of a Rockecenter—a cross between a politician and a hungry hawk. But it was hard to tell. The whole cathedral office illumination was red.

"Can't you see I'm having my afternoon snack!" he roared at us.

"I brought it," said the ape-man, holding out the popcorn and goat's milk.

"You shouldn't come in here while I'm concentrating," said Delbert John. Then he saw me.

He stepped closer. He peered at the big button. "You haven't been sworn in yet," he said, "but you might as well start apprenticing." He waved a hand at the one-way mirror. "I'm just making sure none of those girls are pregnant. I hate babies. You've heard of my abortion and infanticide programs, of course. Got to keep the population down. Riffraff!"

He quickly forgot about me. He sat down and resumed his close inspection of the possible pregnancy of the chorus girls. He began on the goat's milk and popcorn.

This office was apparently parallel with the back of a theater, disguised, perhaps, by the height of the theater stage loft. It was certainly big. The other end of the cathedral room had a balcony that overlooked the parks and city. Its doors were heavy glass, possibly bulletproof.

The ape-man had vanished.

After a while, Rockecenter sighed and punched a button on the side of his huge chair. With a whirr, curtains closed to obscure the one-way mirror. He tossed off the last of the popcorn and then drained the last drops of goat's milk. "Great stuff," he sighed. "This is what made Ghandi a world leader."

He peered at my badge again. "Inkswitch, eh? Well, Inkswitch, what have you done to get yourself promoted to be a family spy? It's a pretty important post, Inkswitch. Families really can be (bleepards)."

"I've always been one of your most trusted undercover men," I said. And I drew upon our file on him. "I covered up leaks of your links to I. G. Barben. *And* I covered up its links to Faustino 'The Noose' Narcotici's mob. What is an undercover man for if not to cover up links and leaks?"

I had his interest. I was taking no great risk: he had hundreds of millions of people sweating out their lives for him. He could not be expected to know even a millionth of his staff.

"Earlier," I said, "I befriended the family itself but never wanted to mention it. I was even a member of the burial party of Aunt Timantha."

"Well, well," he said. "I can see your promotion is long overdue."

"But I don't come empty-handed," I said. "Lately, I have been serving your interests as a Senate Investigator for Senator Twiddle's Energy Crisis Committee. And when I learned of my promotion, I made a point of gathering up every scrap of data of the most heinous skulduggery anyone could imagine. Senator Twiddle was utterly outraged. When I called it to his attention, he said it was the energy crisis of the century."

"One of our best men, Twiddle," said Rockecenter. "Sound. Always consults me before he casts a single vote! So what is this crisis?"

"I know of a plot to introduce a new, cheap energy source on this planet, completely independent of yourself, that would be in total competition to you."

Nothing else had gotten to him, really. The last word did. "By God! Inkswitch, the only good competition is dead competition!"

"Amen," I said devoutly, in keeping with this cathedral-like atmosphere.

"We've got thousands of patents," he said, "on devices to make fuel more efficient. We buy them up and throw them in the permanently closed file. Why couldn't this new development have been put on regular channels?"

"It's more dastardly than any of those," I said. "It makes fuel cheap as dirt. And they'll have a monopoly on the device."

"Who is this inventor?"

"The name is Jerome Terrance Wister."

"And he can't be bought off?"

"I'm absolutely certain he can't."

"And he can't be rubbed out the way some say my great-grandfather disposed of Rudolph Diesel? Into the English Channel in the dark?"

"It's been tried."

Rockecenter went over to his desk. The red desk lamps made his face pretty eerie. He punched a button. "Bury! Come over here."

He gave his throne chair a punch so it swivelled toward the balcony. He looked down at me. "Inkswitch," he said. "While we are waiting for Bury, I may as well swear you in as a family spy. Raise your right hand. Repeat after me: I hereby do solemnly swear to utilize, support and keep sacred the following family policies..."

I raised my right hand. What's another oath to an Apparatus officer? I repeated after him.

"One: Competition strangles the free enterprise system. Two: The world must continue to believe that as long as D. J. Rockecenter owns everything, they are safe from destructive rivalries. Three: Governments must continue to understand that as long as they do as D. J. Rockecenter orders, they will have plenty of conflicts. Four: The banks must continue to know that as long as D. J. Rockecenter makes a profit, nobody else matters. Five: We stand for democracy so long as it doesn't get in the way of communism. Six: The population must be educated into the need of euthanasia and wholesale abortion, and cooperate in its own humanocide. Seven: Only what is good for D. J. Rockecenter is good for everybody. Eight: D. J. Rockecenter is the only family member that matters. And Nine: Trust nobody. I hereby faithfully swear to see that these policies are rammed down everybody's throat, so help me, Rockecenter."

I had repeated it all.

"Well, that's done," he said. "I can't trust anybody else to do it. I have to be sure."

Bury came in at that moment. It was through another door. He appeared a bit haggard and worried.

"Bury," said Rockecenter, sitting down at his altar

desk, eerie in the red light, "Inkswitch here says somebody has been running around loose lately, inventing a cheap fuel. You ever hear of a Jerome Terrance Wister?"

The family lawyer turned chalk white!

I grasped the situation in an instant. Bury had never told Rockecenter about that incident! Bury thought the man was dead!

But Apparatus training is smooth stuff. I said quickly, "I can't imagine how Mr. Bury ever would have heard of him. He's just an upstart student." I closed my right eye to Bury out of Rockecenter's sight.

Bury stood there watching me like a Wall Street attorney sizing up the prosecution.

"This Wister," said Rockecenter, "seems to be a dangerous menace to society. Invented a cheap fuel and refused to sell out." He turned to me, "Do you know anything you haven't told me?"

I could feel Bury go tense. I said, "He's obviously going to demonstrate it in racing."

"Ah," said Rockecenter. He stroked his chin and frowned. Then he lit up and said something I couldn't for the life of me work out. He said, "Bury! Speak of this invention to nobody. Hire this Wister a public relations man."

"Yes, sir," said Bury.

Maybe it was not a loud enough "Yes, sir." Rockecenter got up and walked very close to Bury. He said, "Ride this thing! Get on it and pump! Ride this until you (bleep) it all up. Understood?"

I was a little bit jolted. The tone of voice! The posture! The only thing missing was the lapel jerk and the "stinger" to be Lombar!

Bury was even more haggard. "Yes, sir."

That was apparently loud enough. Rockecenter drew back. He pointed at me. "Inkswitch has just been sworn in as a family spy. He's undercover as a Federal Investigator and I'm assigning him at once to this case!"

Bury looked at me. He suddenly made up his mind. "I'm sure he'll make a marvelous family spy," he said. "It will be a pleasure to work with him."

Bury was gone. I myself rose to leave. But Rockecenter was looking at his watch. "No," he said. "It will only be a few minutes."

He walked to the balcony and opened the doors. The soft whirr of traffic came into the cathedral-like room. He waved his arm at the splendid arches.

"You may think this too plain and unpretentious, Inkswitch, now that you're a family spy. But I'm a modest man. I do not need much. My foundation of doctors was just telling me the other day how pleased they were to have made me immortal. It's such a good thing for the world to have just one man own it forever. They couldn't possibly pay the inheritance tax.

"When you came in, I saw that you were wondering why I didn't marry one of those girls. You've been so closely connected to the family—Aunt Timantha and all—that you really have a right to know and won't go wandering off getting close to any of my God (bleeped) relatives. I don't have to get married, Inkswitch. That foundation assures me that I'm going to live forever and I don't need any God (bleeped) son to add to the competition. You understand me, Inkswitch? So don't go being nice to any other family members. Got it?"

I nodded but he wasn't looking at me. Evening was sweeping the city which, like the planet, he owned.

He looked at his watch. He looked up. An ecstatic expression came across his face. "Don't you hear the harp music? It happens every day at this time. Now listen! Listen carefully!"

He paused. Bliss bathed his face. "There! Right on

time! There it was! Ah, what beautiful words: 'The one true God is Delbert John Rockecenter!' "

He turned and rushed to his desk. He came back holding a pen and a piece of paper on a golden tablet. "Oh, I'm so glad to have another witness! Sign this attestation please."

I signed but I felt the world was spinning around me.

Audio hallucination! Paranoid schizophrenia! Megalomania!

Just like Lombar!

Delbert John Rockecenter was a stark, staring lunatic!

I was working for TWO crazy men!

PART TWENTY-SEVEN

Chapter 1

The next few days were a liberal education in how well a great and powerful organization like Rockecenter's, a juggernaut of efficiency, could (bleep) up a planet. I was overawed with admiration. No wonder Lombar studied Rockecenter so hard! I took notes wherever possible so I could send them through and curry favor with my chief. Earth might be deficient and primitive in many of its technologies but the Rockecenter organization was light-years beyond anything like it in outer space. Five generations of diabolical cunning had made it what it was today: a colossus! A whole planet dancing to the tune of one psychotic man! Magnificent! Compared to this, Heller was a puny nothing! And I would launch the avalanche upon him!

It started the moment I stepped out of Rockecenter's place of self-worship and back into the office of Miss Peace.

"(Bleep)!" she said, raising her pretty head, "It's five o'clock and I'm overdue at the abortion clinic! You sure took your God (bleeped) time!"

Discipline, tight schedules! That's what it takes to make a great empire!

"Open up your God (bleeped) shirt!" she ordered. She had her hat and coat on. She was tearing through her desk, throwing things in all directions. "Where's the God (bleeped) stamp!"

I had my shirt open. I was studying her every move.

She found what she was looking for under a stale peanut-butter sandwich. What a cunning way to hide a secret stamp!

It was a big disc with a handle and a trigger. She brought it up and, with a bent paper clip, shoved furiously at the changeable letters on the front of it.

I could read what she was making it say: *Rockecenter Family Spi.* It had a date and initial space. How efficient!

She started to advance upon me with such speed and fury, for a second I was alarmed. Her finger was on its trigger. "Are you sure," I began, "that 'spy' isn't spelled with a *y*, not an *i*?"

"Don't you question codes!" she snapped at me. "When that light panel," she gestured toward a flashing board in the wall, "flashes purple with twelve dots, he means 'Sworn in family spi.' You ain't going to get very far, buster, if you start questioning *him!* Hold your God (bleeped) shirt out of the way!"

Well, what could I do? A code is a code. I opened my shirt wider.

She slammed the stamp against my bare chest and pulled the trigger. It stung!

She grabbed a weird-looking stylus off her desk and, with her tongue gripped firmly between her teeth to the side of her mouth and concentrating very hard, she jammed the stylus into my chest and very laboriously wrote what must be her initials. She stepped back and threw the stylus over a peg on the coat rack.

I looked down at my chest.

There was nothing on it!

Well, it wasn't up to me to question. Buttoning my shirt, I started to move toward the door with the huge teeth.

"No, no, Christ!" she said in exasperation. "They've

all gone home. Use this door!" And, muttering something about new, unindoctrinated staff, she herself went through a side door. I followed but she was going so fast I lost her at once.

I was in an ordinary office building hall, crowded with people going home. They sure kept tight schedules here. I made a note of the anxious strain on the faces as the employees sought to get away.

Thinking perhaps I should report to Bury, I wandered through a rush hour of people quitting work, pouring out of building after building. What an enthusiastic tide of humanity! What a thrill to see how well they kept their schedule!

By the time I had battered my way through the torrent to the Octopus Building, it was locked up tight!

As I was now a dedicated Rockecenter employee, I realized I would now be expected to enthusiastically rush home. I did. Fortunately, it was not far, as the security men had taken the five hundred dollars I had had in my wallet, leaving me only with my gun and Federal I.D.

After a bath to get the stench of antiseptic off of me, I spent some time in front of the mirror trying to see the stamp. Nothing there at all.

I called a bellboy to take away the antisepticized clothes and he called the public health service which sent a special truck. I dug some money out of the mattress and tipped him five dollars. He was very grateful.

As Utanc was nowhere to be seen, I had a huge and splendid dinner in my room, watched some TV and gratefully went to bed.

It had been quite a day, but I was duty bound now to be fresh and alert to report in at nine sharp the following morning.

Things were in motion now. Not even the Gods could help Heller!

Chapter 2

At 9:00 A.M. sharp, nattily dressed in a brand-new suit and slouch hat, I presented myself at Mr. Bury's special office.

Nobody was there.

I waited for some time in the hall.

About 9:45, a janitor opened the door to clean the place up and I went in. I sat in the waiting room. About 10:00 a security team came in to check the offices and make sure they were safe. They didn't speak to me.

About 10:30, the fourth assistant receptionist came in, turned off the burglar-alarm system, unlocked his barricaded, bulletproof cage and sat down to read *The Daily Racing Form.*

At 11:00, I approached him. "I think I'm supposed to see Mr. Bury."

"Well, why cry on my shoulder?" he said. "Bad luck is bad luck." He went back to reading his racing form.

At 12:00 I heard a tremendous rush in the hall. It sounded like a riot! Alert to my duties, I sped out. It was a horde of people pouring out of offices going to lunch. I almost got trampled in the stampede. Dutifully, I went to lunch.

At 1:00 P.M. I came in. The fourth assistant receptionist entered about 1:15. He eyed me with distaste. He went into his cage and pushed a button.

Five security guards came crashing through the door, guns drawn. The fourth assistant receptionist was pointing at me. So were the guns of the security guards!

"Wait!" I yelled. "My name is Inkswitch! I'm supposed to see Mr. Bury!"

The chief security man pointed through the glass of the fourth assistant receptionist. "Is he on that wanted list?"

It was hard to see what was going on because they had me with my palms flat against the wall, feet outstretched.

I heard the fourth assistant receptionist say, "No, he ain't on the wanted list. I can't understand it. Must be some mistake."

"You got another list there," said the chief security guard. "Is that a hit list?"

"Well, well," said the fourth assistant receptionist. "It's a note from Bury." He yelled at me through the glass. "Hey, you dumb (bleepard). You were due in Personnel at ten o'clock! Can't you get anything straight? You're late!"

The security guards rushed me over to an office marked:

Personnel

They dumped me inside and left.

"Inkswitch?" said a girl. "You're not on the combat team list for Venezuela. What are you doing here? Don't you realize that government is supposed to be overthrown by 4:00 P.M.?" It really caused an upset. The personnel manager himself came out to see what the flap was all about, snarling that he couldn't hear his favorite radio program with all this babble going on. He straightened them out. The Venezuela job had been turned over to the Russians. The staff looked very contrite that they had not been informed.

The personnel manager pushed a button. Six different security guards rushed in. The personnel manager was pointing at me. "He upset the whole office!"

They seized me.

"Wait a minute!" I screamed—my voice was sharpened by them pulling my arms up behind my back and trying to lift me to throw me out. "I'm an employee! I was just signed on by Mr. Rockecenter himself!"

They dropped me in a pile in the middle of the floor. The leading security man said, "I'll bet!"

The personnel manager said, "You're on! Five dollars!"

The leading security man said, "You're on! Rip open his shirt!"

They did, with buttons flying about.

A security man got out a strange-looking light. He shined it on my chest. I looked down.

Glowing in fluorescent green was *Rockecenter Family Spi* with date and initials.

"Jesus," said the leading security man. "You lose, Throgmorton."

"No, *you* lose," said the personnel manager.

They got in a dreadful wrangle. Somebody called the Psychiatric Department and a psychiatrist came in and told them they had both lost and were overreacting. He made them pay each other five dollars and then, sort of absently, took both bills and left.

I found myself with a personnel consultant in a cubicle. She was punching out computer cards. It was very lengthy. She was taking the data from my Federal credentials.

Finally she pushed all the cards into a computer. She pressed a test button to recall the data to a screen. Nothing happened. The screen remained blank.

"So that's that," she said. "You've been processed."

"Wait," I said. "The computer screen stayed blank."

"Of course," she said. "You wouldn't want to have your cover blown, would you?"

I left.

Mr. Bury's office door was ajar. I pushed it open and walked in.

"Where the hell have you been?" he said. "They've been waiting for us for an hour!"

We rushed out and got a cab.

At last things were happening!

Chapter 3

As we rode along, blocked from time to time with traffic jams, Mr. Bury seemed very quiet. Once in a while his eyes flicked at me.

Finally, he spoke. "How much do you know about this Wister?"

"Not as much as you," I lied. "I just saw you were taken aback so I covered for you." No use to have Bury gunning for me because I knew too much.

"Hmmm," he said. "I don't like this way of handling this Wister thing, Inkswitch. The right way is usually pretty tortuous but in this case, a direct hit would seem more like it."

I stiffened with alarm. I did not have that platen. And I sure wasn't going to get myself blown up in a Voltar invasion. With the planet in this state, they'd wipe out every living thing on it, rebuild an ecology and colonize. That "every living thing" included *me*.

How could I handle this? Ah. "Torpedo Fiaccola wasn't very lucky," I said.

It was his turn to stiffen—and Wall Street lawyers are pretty expert at hiding their feelings—what feelings they have, that is, if any.

"Jesus!" he said. He was looking at me in sort of shock. Then curiosity got the better of him. "Did the (bleepard) talk to you?"

"No," I said. "Wister sent him to the North Pole. Probably all he can talk now is polar bear." It was time to take his mind off me. "It was Wister that collected the hundred G's, not Fiaccola."

"JESUS!" said Bury.

"Yes," I said, pleasantly. "Wister is using your hit money to finance this cheap fuel invention."

"Oh, my God!"

"I know," I said, "that you are thinking that if that got back to Mr. Rockecenter, he would do something awfully nasty."

Bury was staring at me in horror. I might as well drive it home.

"But, there is something you can tell me," I said. "Why is Mr. Rockecenter so dead set against having a son?"

His face looked like a white prune.

Finally he said, "He's impotent. Just a voyeur. He's been unable to perform for years."

"Oh, come, come, Mr. Bury," I said. "Let's not squirm around. I stood up for you in his office when I could have let you have it to the hilt. Now admit that that shows you can trust me. There's more to this than that."

"Inkswitch, I do not know how in hell you have gotten any information you have. But it is VERY dangerous information. I would betray professional confidence if I told you one word more! The defense rests!"

We rode along through two more traffic jams. Then he looked at me and smiled a sort of wintry smile—a twitch at either corner of his mouth below bleak eyes. "Inkswitch, after taking consultation with myself, I have come to the conclusion that you're one of the wiliest, craftiest sons of (bleepches) I have ever met. No, let me enter a correction on the record. You ARE the wiliest, craftiest son of a (bleepch) I ever met. I think our partnership will justify the findings of the highest court!"

"And you, Mr. Bury, are the most vicious, conniving (bleepard) I have ever had the privilege of working with."

We shook hands solemnly in mutual admiration.

We had arrived at our destination. "Now," said Mr. Bury, "let's go get this Wister's life so (bleeped) up and ruined, he'll never again be able to lift his head! Let's do it beyond any appeal and carry it straight through to total condemnation!"

With what enthusiasm we alighted!

Bury lifted his hand slightly, indicating the skyscrapers which reared imposingly all about us. "We are in the advertising center of the world. We are about to call on F.F.B.O., the largest advertising and public relations firm in America. Let me do *all* the talking."

"F.F.B.O.?" I said. "What does that stand for?"

"Fatten, Farten, Burstein and Ooze. It is the prime test of the qualified advertising man to be able to say it quickly and without stammering. That means you're in the know. But, I repeat, let me do all the talking. As I'm a lawyer, they can't hold me for perjury or defamation."

We went into a huge, ornate lobby. Metal fish swam around the murals. They appeared to be suckers.

Our elevator shot up. It spilled us into a small room.

There were no chairs. People were idling about, obviously not belonging there, looking frustrated. A high, bulletproof glass cage was in one corner with a single girl behind the maze hole. The walls of the room were dark red. There was an upper port and I could see a sawed-off shotgun muzzle with an alert eye behind it. There were no signs or directions.

Bury took a card out of his wallet. He put it against the bulletproof glass. The girl flinched.

"Foreign public relations vice-president," demanded Bury.

The girl snatched a phone. She barked into it hysterically. She instantly shouted through the maze hole, "Floor 50! Go right up, Mr. Bury!"

The people in the room flinched, crowded back to get out of our way.

We got into an elevator. Out of the corner of his mouth, without moving his lips, Mr. Bury said, "I didn't like the slow response. I understand their corporate delay tactics very well: there's something wrong here. This may require the third degree. Pull your hat down over your eyes. Now, when I cough, look very tough. When I stamp my foot, put your hand inside your coat as though you are going to draw a gun. Got that?"

I was learning the world of corporate expertise. I said I had it.

Bury suddenly added, "But on no account draw or shoot anybody. We own the insurance company that has their policy and we don't want to be paying damages. Let any recourse to mayhem be theirs. Then the policy will lapse."

We had arrived. The elevator door slid open. A beautiful waiting room stretched on either side.

Two girls, scantily dressed like ushers, had a roll of carpet between them on a rod. The carpet was red.

Marching backwards, they began to unroll the carpet so that we could walk forward on it.

Two flower girls, dressed in gauzy white, leaping this way and that, daintily strewed flowers from their baskets in our path.

Two violinists in Hungarian costume walked along with us playing seductive melodies.

"I hate these (bleeped) advertising formalities," said Bury.

"Do they always do this?"

"No. Only for me. They know I despise it."

We went down a long hall. Two young men with herald's trumpets blew a blast, then made an arch of their trumpets.

A girl in a lamb's costume prettily opened a door that said on it:

J. P. Flagrant
Vice-President
Foreign Public Relations Department

The office was banked with flowers.

A rather fat man in a scarlet tuxedo was bowing and scrubbing his hands. "I am J. P. Flagrant, Mr. Bury. Welcome. Welcome. Welcome."

Three little girls raised their angelic faces on the other side of the room and began to sing:

Happy welcome to you,
Happy welcome to you.
Happy welcome, dear Mr. Bury,
JELO scrubs and rinses, too.

They bowed and tripped prettily out, throwing

kisses and doing a shuffle-off-to-Buffalo at the same time. Difficult.

Flagrant scrubbed his hands some more. "Now what would you like, Mr. Bury and guest? A Havana Havana Havana cigar? Some 1650 Vintage Raire Champagne? Or perhaps a nice, ripe secretary to refresh you? That door leads to a bedroom and there's one in there now all waiting in JELO!"

"If you will tell this court to recess," said Bury acidly, "we can get down to business."

Flagrant slapped his fat hands together and, still beaming, made shooing motions. The violin music stopped. People in the hall scattered frantically in all directions.

Bury picked a flower petal off his dark suit as though it were smut. He dropped it on the floor and cleaned his fingers on his handkerchief. He said, "We are here to retain you as a public relations account. But we demand the right to select our own public relations man."

"Oh, my goodness, Mr. Bury. We are honored. Anyone from the Rockecenter interests has only to command us and we will do anything, anything, anything at all to be of total satisfactory and agreeable service number one position to you."

He swatted his hands together.

A secretary raced in with her notebook ready for dictation in one hand and a bag of contraceptives in the other.

Flagrant swatted his hands three times. A young man in a severely cut Ivy League suit raced in holding an enormous book. At Flagrant's command, the young man, holding the book to us, began to show us smiling photographs of PR men with graphs and biographies.

Bury coughed.

On cue, instantly, I looked my toughest.

"We want, on this case," said Bury, "no other than J. Walter Madison."

The young man flinched.

The secretary flinched.

J. P. Flagrant went white. "Oh, my God, no, Mr. Bury!"

"I insist!" hissed Bury, looking deadly.

Flagrant got down on his knees. The young man got down on his knees. The secretary got down on her knees.

All three of them raised their hands in supplication. They said in chorus, "*NOT* J. WARBLER MADMAN!"

Out of the side of his mouth, Bury said to me. "We've got to have the man. He's an artist beyond compare." He stamped his foot.

I dived my hand into my coat as though I were about to draw a gun.

They screamed!

Pounding feet in the hall.

A huge, portly man in a purple pinstripe suit came rushing into the room. "What's going on here?" he roared. He saw Bury. He flinched.

"These idiots," said Bury, in a thin, acid voice, "are refusing the Rockecenter account. And, to you, Mr. Buhlshot, as chairman of F.F.B.O., that should serve as Exhibit A!"

Mr. Buhlshot got down on his knees in an attitude of prayer. "Please, God, don't cost us that account! Please, Mr. Bury!"

Flagrant wailed to Mr. Buhlshot, "He's demanding we put J. Walter Madison on it!"

"Oh, my God," said Mr. Buhlshot. He was wringing his hands in desperation. "Please don't do that to us, Mr. Bury! On his last job for you, he wrecked all the international PR of the Republic of Patagonia! He caused a revolution! Every scrap of Octopus property was seized and nationalized! The president committed suicide! And J. Walter Madison did it all himself!"

Bury said out of the corner of his mouth to me. "It's not working. Step back to the wall and cover me with your gun. This could get rough."

I did what he said. They all screamed! Doors in the hall could be heard being slammed and hastily locked.

Bury said in a deadly voice, "You will not accede to these reasonable demands, Buhlshot?"

"No, my God, Bury! Have a heart! You could cost F.F.B.O. its reputation!"

"You will not let us have J. Walter Madison?"

Mr. Buhlshot, on his knees, hitched himself forward, bent over and began to lick Mr. Bury's shoes. Bury stepped back. "You leave me only one alternative, Mr. Buhlshot."

Bury stepped to the phone. He picked it up. He said, "Get me the Grabbe-Manhattan Bank."

The four kneeling on the floor stared at him, unbelieving.

"Bury here. Put Mr. Caesar of the Delinquent Loan Department on please."

Buhlshot screamed! "Oh, my God, Bury. Don't call in the loans of F.F.B.O.! We're in a cash deficiency!"

Bury was calmly waiting on the line for Mr. Caesar. I suddenly grasped the scene. Rockecenter owns Grabbe-Manhattan Bank! One of the biggest banks in the world! And it controls most of the other banks! What a ploy! I swelled with pride at being part of such an efficient colossus! But I kept my gun on them.

Buhlshot suddenly howled, "But all our loans aren't delinquent!"

"They will be shortly," said Bury.

"Wait! Wait! Wait!" said Buhlshot. "You've reached market saturation!"

Bury covered the phone mouthpiece with his hand.

"I'll try to get him!" said Buhlshot.

The young man and the secretary prevented Flagrant from trying to open the window and jumping out.

Buhlshot rushed off.

He came back in thirty seconds. He looked haggard. "Nobody knows where he is!"

A loudspeaker was calling all staff, all floors. It said, "An immediate inspiration conference is called in Hall Five!"

Staff began to crowd into the hall. An excited buzz of voices. Looks of shock when they heard the name J. Warbler Madman.

Buhlshot rushed among them. "I need an instant response! Where is J. Walter Madison? Come up with a slogan and you get a month's paid vacation in the Bahamas!"

Bury was still holding his hand over the phone. He looked my way, slit-eyed. "I told you it might get rough," he said. "But we've got to have that man!"

They were barking instant responses. "Death to Madison!" "(Bleep) Madison." "Loan Madison five bucks today and lose your girl tomorrow!" "Position Madison as Number One above the Four Horsemen." "Show Madison sitting laughing on a world in flames." "Montage Madison killing his mother, but I think it's been done." "Two Madisons in the furnace is better than one in the fist."

A high, clear voice cried, "Miss Dicey might know where he is!"

There was a rush. They got Miss Dicey out of a mop closet where she had been hiding and, passing her over the tops of their heads, dropped her into Flagrant's office.

She was a frail-looking brunette, mostly eyes, and they stared at us in terror.

Buhlshot towered over her. "Miss Dicey! They say you were the last model to be used by J. Walter Madison. Where is he?"

She was shaking with fear.

"An all-expense tour to the top of the Washington Monument if you tell us," wheedled Buhlshot.

Miss Dicey was trying to shrink into the floor and wasn't making it.

"You'll be fired unless you tell me this minute," said Buhlshot.

"I promised not to!" screamed Miss Dicey, terror making her voice crack. "He knows you want to kill him and if I tell, he'll come back and PR me! I know it! Even his ghost would be dangerous!"

Buhlshot snapped his fingers. Two young account executives in bright yellow afternoon dress stepped in. One picked up Miss Dicey's wrists. The other picked up her ankles. They stretched her out horizontally between them. A third account executive went to the window and opened it wide. Fifty stories of space gaped. I went giddy.

The two account executives at her head and feet began to swing her back and forth, ready to sail her out into space when they got the arc going high enough.

"Wait! Wait!" said Buhlshot. "The lighting is all wrong! Get me a director from the Commercials Film Department!"

There was a scurry. A middle-aged man in a beret elbowed through the crowd. He was carrying a small megaphone. Somebody brought him a chair. It had *Director* across the back. A gaffer came in carrying lights. He set them up with rapidity and decision.

Buhlshot said to the girl, "Are you going to tell us where he is?"

She shook her head. "There is no fate worse than J. Walter Madison," she said. Although she was frail and frightened, she meant it.

"Over to you, Lemley," said Buhlshot to the director.

"All right," said Director Lemley. "This is MOS—Middout Sound. I want violins!"

A violinist appeared and began to play "Hearts and Flowers."

"Now, what I want here," said Lemley, through his little megaphone, "is cool, detached naturalness. This isn't Hollywood, you know. No mugging. And that goes for you, Miss Dicey. I want you to look perfectly natural and smile. The public has to WANT to buy the product. All right. Let's make this a cut and print the first time. Film costs the Earth. All set? Lights! Camera!"

Somebody rushed in with a clapboard and said very rapidly, "JELO Ad. Shot 1. Take 1!" They slapped the top of the board and dashed out. Confusing as there was no camera.

"ACTION!" cried Mr. Lemley.

The two young men began to swing Miss Dicey back and forth in wider and wider arcs, glancing toward the window at the end of each swing toward it.

"Cut! Cut! Cut!" said Lemley. "Jesus Christ, Dicey, keep your God (bleeped) eyes open. How can you register with your eyes shut!"

"She fainted," said one of the young men.

Buhlshot rose to the occasion. "Where the hell is a props man!"

A props man rushed in. He picked up the champagne bucket. He upended it, ice, 1650 Vintage Raire Champagne, tongs and all over Miss Dicey's face.

Miss Dicey came around.

"Retake," said Lemley. "Now, this time, the models holding her head and wrists should keep their faces toward the camera. Smile. Look pleased. Got it? All right! Here we go. Lights! Camera!"

Somebody rushed in with the clapboard. "JELO Ad. final Shot 1, Take 2!" The clapper banged.

"Action!" cried Lemley.

"I'll tell! I'll tell!" shouted Dicey. "My makeup is too ruined for a shot! What would my public think!"

"Cut!" said Lemley. "Ad lib dialogue. Not in the script."

"Take five!" shouted Buhlshot. And everyone rushed off to take their five-minute break. He sternly stopped Dicey from going out the door.

"Do I get a trip to China?" said Miss Dicey.

"Yes," said Buhlshot.

"And attached thereafter to offices behind the Iron Curtain?" said Dicey.

"Yes," said Buhlshot.

"All right. He's hiding out at Pier 92. It's the new Free Zone and he's outside territorial limits. He's sleeping in his car and it's in a box marked 'Export.' His mother is feeding him every night at nine o'clock. Now let me out of here. I've got to pack my bag!"

Bury hung up the phone. He gave me a thin, pessimistic nod. I put away my gun.

Buhlshot said, "Flagrant, you're fired for risking the Rockecenter account!"

"You're not out of the woods," Bury whispered to me. "We've got to capture him now. We will handle it as it's a matter of international law."

As we left, the two violinists walked beside us playing mood music, the flower girls tossed small paper goodbye banners across our way. The two uniformed ushers rolled the red carpet up behind us.

Buhlshot, in the hall, was mopping his face with a

purple, silk handkerchief. He said, "Jesus, what it takes to salvage some accounts!"

Chapter 4

The second we emerged into the street, I knew we were in trouble. Rush hour! The advertising district was rushing home! We were buffeted by torrents of people. There were no cabs.

"Oh, dear!" said Bury. He looked at his watch. "We have so little time! Only four hours to 9:00 P.M.! Inkswitch, we've got to have Madison, no matter what the cost or difficulties."

We hurried down the avenue. We couldn't do much else as it was like being caught in an avalanche of people.

"We're up against international legalities," he worried as we were swept along. "It just shows you what a cunning (bleepard) Madison is: he's got himself down there on Pier 92 in the Free Trade end of the shed! Right out at the end! He's beyond the territorial jurisdiction of the United States authorities."

We dodged a liquor store delivery boy who was bashing through the crowd on a delivery tricycle. I reached back and with my foot upended the vehicle.

The smashing of bottles seemed to make Bury feel better. "Hatchetheimer!" he said. "If this were simply a legal problem, I would know what to do. But it's military, Inkswitch. Raw force! Hatchetheimer is the last surviving officer of Hitler's general staff. He was a mere child then. He must be pushing ninety now. I've got to contact Hatchetheimer and get his advice. A telephone.

I've got to get to a telephone. It's absolutely vital we get Madison: we have no other appeals left!"

The nearest thing was a Jewish delicatessen. It was jammed with people. But that wasn't all that was wrong with it: a score of Ku Klux Klan members in white robes and hoods were picketing the place, marching back and forth with poles which bore signs:

DOWN WITH THE JEWS

"You can't pass a picket line," said Bury. "We own the unions. There! The subway station!"

Just beyond the Klansmen, steps led down through the walk. With Bury leading anxiously, we plowed through the crowd.

The underground platform was a milling turmoil. Bury, an accomplished New Yorker, elbowed his way through them. I saw a young black decorating the white tile with graffiti. He had two spray cans, red and blue. He was drawing an American flag with *(Bleep) You* across it. I thought Bury was heading for him, perhaps to correct the drawing, and then I saw Bury's target was an underground telephone kiosk.

There was a woman in it, using the phone. Bury banged on the glass door. The woman glared at him ferociously and went on with her conversation.

"Look, Inkswitch," said Bury. "I'd appreciate it if you could keep this area clear while I'm phoning. I will be on that phone some time and people bang on the glass the way I am doing."

I said I'd try.

"Do you have some dimes?" said Bury. "I don't seem to have any change."

I didn't either. But I was thinking fast on the other

problem of keeping this area clear. Bury started off toward the subway change booth.

I raced up the stairs. The KKK was still picketing. Their placards! I had to have a couple of those placards! "Make do with whatever is to hand," the Apparatus professors used to drum into us. Now was the time to apply that advice.

At the top of my lungs, I screamed, "Cheese it! The New York Tactical Police Force is coming!"

I drew my gun and fired twice!

The Klansmen ran frantically away!

The two I had winged dropped their placards.

I picked the picketing signs up and rushed back down the stairs.

Bury was just leaving the back door of the change booth. He had a huge sack of change in his hand. "It all takes so much time!" he mourned. "They didn't believe at first that we owned the subway!" He plunged his hand into the bag and stuffed change in his overcoat pocket. He handed me the rest of the bag. "Hold on to this. We'll have to turn the balance in to the IRT Subway accountants!"

He rushed over to the phone booth. The woman was just finishing. He banged on the glass anyway.

Quickly, I went over behind the young man. I swung the bag of change expertly. It came down on his head. He collapsed. I grabbed the two spray cans and got to work.

I ripped the placard off one pole and reversed it to the unused side. I quickly and neatly sprayed, in blue, CIA MAN. I looked around on the platform, found some used chewing gum and plastered it to the underside.

I took the other placard and changed the writing on it to DOWN WITH THE CIA!

The woman was calling Bury names. I could see

what he meant about the dangers of a kiosk being undefended.

The woman left. As Bury started to go into the kiosk, I slapped the CIA MAN sign on his back. He didn't notice.

"My God, it stinks in here!" said Bury. "She must have been chewing garlic!" He left the door open.

I began to parade up and down with my placard, DOWN WITH THE CIA! People veered off sharply.

Bury put coins in the phone. He said, "Operator? Get me the Chief Operator of the New York Telephone Company at once. . . . Chief Operator? This is Bury of Swindle and Crouch. Patch this pay phone, KLondike 5-9721, into Unlimited International WATS Line Number 1. . . . Of course I know it is a secret line. I ought to: We own the phone company. . . . What is your name, please? Goog?"

He was writing in his little notebook on the ledge. "G-O-O-G. Thank you, Miss Goog. . . . My phone credit card number is IT&T Number 1. . . . Yes, we do own the phone company, Miss Goog. . . . All right. Now, patch this pay phone into the WATS line. You stay on this line personally to shift connections. Keep this line open. Keep all other calls off this pay phone. Clear any and all calls off the board if they get in your way."

He listened for a moment. Then he underscored Miss Goog's name in his little notebook. "No, Miss Goog. I don't care if the President is talking on it, clear him off the line. . . ."

The crowd was staying very clear of us. I marched up and down with my placard, DOWN WITH THE CIA!

Bury said to himself, "Dumb (bleepch). Trying to plug me into the hot line. Who the hell wants to talk to the President at a time like this?" He was fanning the kiosk door open and shut. "My God, it stinks in here!" He suddenly gave his attention to the phone. "All right, Miss Goog. Now connect me, direct line, to the Senior Monitoring Officer, National Security Agency.... Yes, Miss Goog, I know it is a secret government line.... Hello. Who is this? Peeksnoop? Ah, how are you, Peeksnoop? This is Bury of Swindle and Crouch.... Yes, the wife is fine.... Listen, Peeksnoop, are you monitoring calls made by General Hatchetheimer?... Ah, that is fine. You verify that...."

A train pulled in. The passengers saw the signs and stayed on.

Bury said to me, "We're in luck. Hatchetheimer is heading a terrorist group in Cairo and they think he's planning to blow up the U.S. Embassy there tomorrow morning. He's confirming the satellite connections. Hatchetheimer is pretty agile for a man his ... Ah, Peeksnoop. Well, reverse the surveillance monitor system and patch me into Hatchetheimer's phone. Just ring it. That's a good fellow."

The crowd was very clear of us. I marched a bit with my placard. Bury fanned the door and left it open.

He went back on the phone. "Hatchetheimer? Ah, there you are. This is Bury.... Yes, I'm fine.... He's fine, too.... Oh, dear, you don't tell me.... Well, I'm sorry about that. I faithfully promise to see that the defective firebombs are replaced right away. Yes, you have my word on it.... Now, listen, General. I have a military problem I need your advice on. Down at Pier 92..."

A train came in. The doors opened. Passengers started to get off, saw the signs and stayed aboard. Passengers trying to get on jammed the cars. The doors clanged shut and the train roared on.

I could hear Bury again. "...oh, not the New York police. God, no.... We save the New York National

Guard for real emergencies. . . . The U.S. Army would use it to up their defense budget. Listen, General . . . Yes. International Zone at the end of Pier 92. It's an international problem. . . ."

The young black was coming around, probably from being stepped on. He got up groggily, saw his paint spray cans, came over and picked them up and got back to work on his graffiti.

Bury was saying, "Oh, yes, that is splendid, General. And I do thank you for your time. Good luck on the embassy." He jiggled the phone hook. He looked at me. "There's hope. Hatchetheimer is a brilliant man."

The phone rang suddenly. He put the receiver to his ear. He listened, then he spoke. "No, (bleep) it, this is *not* the Horseburger Delicatessen! . . . No, I will *not* send you three Ponies Supreme!" He jiggled the hook agitatedly. "Miss Goog! God (bleep) it, keep this line clear! All right. I'm glad you are sorry. Now connect me to the Joint Chiefs of Staff, Washington, Strategic Duty Officer. . . . Yes, I know it is a secret line, Miss Goog. Connect the God (bleeped) connection!" He sighed deeply and then fanned the door. "I hate garlic!"

He had his call. "This is Bury of Swindle and Crouch. What NATO units do you have right this minute in the New York area? . . . What? . . . What is your name? . . . Sheridan. General Sheridan." He was writing in his notebook. "I don't think you heard me, General Sheridan. This is Bury of Swindle and Crouch. . . . Oh. . . . Well, match your (bleeping) voice print, then. My God!" He underscored what he had written in the notebook.

He fanned the door. He looked out at me. "We're going to get this Madison yet, Inkswitch."

Some gawkers weren't as cowardly as the rest. I pushed them on, poking them somewhat with my placard.

Bury was talking again. "All right, I'm glad you are satisfied it is really me. Now answer my God (bleeped) question.... Ah. A NATO tank squadron giving a show at the 7th Regiment Armory tonight. They will have to do. Have them meet me three blocks south of Pier 92 at 8:30 tonight, all equipment, tanks and combat ready.... General, I don't happen to care if it wrecks their show. And I don't care if they are British. Get onto the Supreme NATO Commander at Strasbourg at once and get your clearance and right now! Issue the God (bleeped) order!"

He underscored something in his notebook. "All right, General. There is now one more thing. Do you have an aircraft carrier in the Brooklyn Navy Yard?... You do?... The U.S.S. *Saratoga*.... General, I don't care if she is in dry dock. Issue orders at once transferring her for the next twenty-four hours to NATO command, Europe.... Well, get the God (bleeped) Secretary of the Navy out of the God (bleeped) dinner party and get it done!... No, I haven't got time to tell you why.... Yes, it is in the national interest! Good!"

He jiggled the phone hook. He turned sideways to me. "We're making progress on Madison." Then he was back on the phone. "Miss Goog? No, God (bleep) it, your pants are not ready and this isn't the Yorkville Dry Cleaners! Miss GOOG!... Listen, (bleep) it, stay on this line. Now connect me at once to the Commanding Officer of the U.S.S. *Saratoga* in the Brooklyn Navy Yard."

Bury looked at his watch. "Time, time," he said sideways to me. "All this is taking time. But we're making progress on Madis... Hello. This is Bury of Swindle and Crouch.... How do you do, Captain Jinx. Captain, you will shortly be receiving confirmation from the Secretary of the Navy but you are not to wait for it. You and all your crew have been transferred to NATO command for the next . . ."

A train roared in. Bury shut the door so he could talk.

A mob seemed to be gathering. There were two tough-looking fellows who wanted to get through the picket line and at Bury who still wore the sign on his back. Some others tried to join the picket line.

I fended them off with various pokes and sorties. One timid-looking fellow seemed to have gotten caught between the mob and the phone booth. He had an overcoat the same color as Bury's. I hoped Bury would finish up quickly. This was getting tight. The mob was increasing. Instead of the placards fending them off, they seemed to be attracting them. These were a different crowd—blue-collar workers. An ugly situation was in the making.

Bury finished!

He hung up the phone and opened the kiosk door.

I acted, quick as a wink.

I took the sign covertly off Bury's back and put it on the timid man's back. I hissed into his ear, "They're after *you!* Run for your life!"

My, did he run! He went tearing down the platform and away!

The crowd, confused in the dim light, attracted as they should be by the motion, saw the CIA MAN sign vanishing out of their clutches!

They sped in a howling torrent after their quarry!

Their savage cries were deafening! They receded.

"What was that?" said Bury.

"Joggers," I said.

We left the impromptu emergency world-command post of the Rockecenter planetary proprietorship.

The phone was ringing. Probably Miss Goog wanted more quarters. We ignored it and left.

Chapter 5

Mr. Bury glanced at his watch. "We had better take time to eat. This schedule will be pretty tight later."

We went into the Jewish delicatessen at the top of the subway stairs. There was a greasy, white-topped table at the back. Mr. Bury said, "I hate these places normally. I'm dead set against Jews making money, but that applies generally to other races, of course."

We sat down and he looked at the menu in big letters on the wall. The Klan had spray-painted a swastika with a *KKK* over it. "I think all they have here is kosher hot dogs. No wonder our Ku Klux Klan attacks them."

"You finance the Klan?" I said.

"Of course. They make social trouble, don't they? Hey!" he yelled at the little Jew back of the counter, "two hottee doggies, you savvy?

"Blasted foreigners, they don't speak English, you know. But they're all right if you put a dash of bicarbonate of soda on them."

I was very contrite. I realized I had shot two of their Klansmen. Not very brotherly of me. Well, I wouldn't tell Bury.

We got our kosher hot dogs. Mr. Bury, eating one, was working on his notebook. I didn't interrupt him. He was being very careful and neat about it, making his rough notes written in the kiosk legible. I knew he must be rounding off the administration details to make it all right with the powers that be.

"I think we have a very good chance of getting Madison," he said. "Hatchetheimer sure is bright. I just hope we have enough firepower." He made a couple more notes. "Well, that will suffice to give my office staff something to handle. Got to keep them busy. How does this look to you?" He turned the notes around so I could read them. I was touched by his confidence and his seeking my opinion.

The notes said:

1. Send Peeksnoop's wife a box of chocolates.
2. Account for one bag of change, IRT Subway System.
3. Rebuild Fort Apache using taxpayer's money, order one squadron of horse cavalry to it, transfer General Sheridan to command it and order him to chase Geronimo until he reaches retirement age.
4. Demote Miss Goog, Chief Operator New York Telephone Company, to track polisher New York Subway.
5. Debit three hot dogs to expense account.
6. Promote Captain Jinx of the U.S.S. Saratoga *to rear admiral if he comes through on time.*
7. Tell the British they can choose the next NATO commander if their tank squadron does its job.
8. Send the mayor's wife a dozen long-stemmed American Beauty roses and appoint her president of the Metropolitan Opera.

I said, "It seems all right to me. But I don't get this last one."

He looked at it. "Oh, heavens. You're right, Inkswitch. I forgot to call the mayor." He hastily stuffed the last of his hot dogs in his mouth and rushed to the pay phone.

I didn't hear what he was saying. He came back looking the usual disillusioned look of a Wall Street lawyer.

"It was just as I suspected. I hate politicians. All I asked him to do was use every squad car in Manhattan to block all entrances and exits to Twelfth Avenue and the West Side Elevated Highway from West 17th Street to West 79th and prohibit all other traffic on it between 8:30 and 9:30 tonight. That's territorial U.S. so it's all legal to use them as long as they are not actively engaged in the assault—we have to close all loopholes to a possible Madison appeal on technicalities."

He thumped his fist on the table. "And (bleep) him, I knew he would balk. So I had already figured my way around it. That's what the flowers were for. I told him we were after a member of the Corleone mob. It's his wife, you see. She and Babe Corleone were chorus girls together at the Roxy Theater and they *hate* each other. You have to know the ins and outs of local politics as well, Inkswitch. So, of course, he issued the order instantly and Madison won't escape on any side streets. So we leave the flowers on the list."

Bury rubbed his hand wearily over his prune face. Then he gave his narrow, snap-brim New Yorker's hat a tug. "We might as well be going, Inkswitch. This is likely to be a pretty violent assault and I told my wife I'd be home by ten."

He paid for the hot dogs with a handful of change out of the IRT bag. I noticed he had forgotten his sheet of notes. I caught up with him outside. I gave them to him. He wadded them up and threw them in the litter basket by a lamppost. "Don't litter, Inkswitch. We have a campaign going right now. 'No Littering.' Lets us pick up all the anti-Rockecenter leaflets and jail the offenders, without being charged with violating the First Amendment of Free Speech and Press. You have to know these things, now that you're a member of the family. But I will say that you won't find it easy. People like us, we work and slave, cogwheels in the machines of the mighty, unappreciated and ignored no matter how devoted to our duties. I think I have indigestion. Did I put bicarbonate of soda on my hot dog?"

I didn't recall that he had and he settled it by remembering he didn't have any with him.

We made our way to the rendezvous with the Gods of battle.

Chapter 6

It was about 8:20 P.M. The deadly zero hour was rushing upon us.

Bury and I alighted from a cab: it could not get any closer than a block away. We sped on foot toward our rendezvous with fate.

Ahead were masses of vehicles. The black night was foggy blue with glowing lights. The Hudson River lay to our left hand like a plain of pitch.

Bury was muttering, "Aircraft carrier, sixteen M-20 latest model battle tanks, assault rifles, bazookas . . . I hope we have assembled enough firepower to handle

Madison. But one cannot actually tell. He's tricky beyond belief!"

We were going through police lines, squad cars blocking everyone off the coming battleground. A huge hulking figure barred our way. It was Police Inspector Grafferty.

He looked closely at us and then he backed up with a smart salute. "I see it's you, Mr. Bury. I had a notion it might be. No one else could take every squad car in New York off its patrols. Want us to look the other way at anything?"

Bury was concentrated on getting through the squad cars and police mob and to our first destination. But he answered, "No, this is all legal tonight."

"Oh?" said Grafferty, honestly stunned with surprise.

"It's an international matter so don't let your men get involved in anything but the traffic block. I wouldn't want any Americans up before the International Court of Human Rights."

Grafferty agreed hastily. "No. They wouldn't stand a chance on that one."

We got through. Ahead was what Bury wanted.

Grouped in battle formation were sixteen M-20 tanks, hulking monsters, all polished up and ready for a show.

Standing about them were their crews, all in dress uniforms, very British and smart.

NATO pennons flew from their aerials and a huge NATO flag was staffed behind the turret of the lead one.

It was a thrilling and martial sight!

A brigadier in his dress uniform and beret, swagger stick tucked under his arm, came up. "I say, are you the chaps to whom we were told to report?" He gave his military mustache a twirl. There was obviously a question in his voice: possibly he had expected a high-ranking, be-medalled NATO general.

I filled in the breach quickly. "This is Mr. Bury of Swindle and Crouch. He represents the Rockecenter interests."

Oh, my Lords! That brigadier came to a salute so stiff his arm vibrated and quivered. Without turning, he cried, "Crews, Ho-o! Sa-loot fohmahtion! Roy-yall!"

There was a shattering hammer of boots upon the pavement. The mob turned into a tight, impressive formation behind him, every eye stiffly front, every body at tense attention.

"Roy-all sa-loot! HUP!" cried the brigadier.

Every hand rose as one in the most impressive salute I have ever seen.

"TWO!" cried the brigadier. All hands and his own came down.

"At yo' ser-vice, SUH!" cried the brigadier and did a one-two-three-four foot stamp the way the British do.

Bury stood there in his narrow, snap-brim, New York hat and civilian overcoat. He raised his right hand ever so slightiy. "If you would call your officers," he said, "we will have a consultation *in camera*."

On the brigadier's crisp command, they were shortly clustered. They synchronized their watches. Bury took out an Octopus map of Manhattan. He issued orders so fast, it was a blur to me. He told them exactly what he wanted them to do.

The brigadier barked. Crews of fifteen tanks raced to their monsters and with military precision, scrambled in.

The brigadier produced a small walkie-talkie from his blouse. He barked orders into it by the number.

With roaring, snarling engines, fifteen tanks surged ahead and rushed northward on Twelfth Avenue.

The brigadier then courteously handed the walkie-talkie to Bury and with gestures and a salute, offered Bury the sixteenth tank.

Presently, with the brigadier somewhere inside, with Bury standing in his little snap-brim hat in the open command turret and with me standing on an exterior tread cover, we began to roll slowly northward.

There was a handhold on the turret side. I held on with some misgivings. But Bury had no misgivings. He was standing there in the turret, his Wall Street lawyer eyes alert to everything ahead, the walkie-talkie held in his left hand.

We stealthily crept to a position about fifty feet short of the entrance to Pier 92. We stopped.

To our left rolled the black river. Before us stretched the deserted street. And there was the silent lair of our quarry, the blackly gaping warehouse.

Bury looked at his watch. We were in plenty of time. Bury looked down at me perched precariously on the tread cover. "Brilliant man, Hatchetheimer. He rapped off this plan, just like that. A masterpiece. I hope it works. Too bad he chose the wrong side more than three-quarters of a century ago. A loss to the world. Eighteen different countries want him as a war criminal. It makes it difficult to send him supplies for his terrorist activities. In the next half hour, we'll know the best or the worst. The loosing of the dogs of war is always a chancy thing. But 'Cry havoc,' I say. When the courts fail to return a favorable verdict, there is always the bazooka to decide the last event. You should remember that, Inkswitch. In your present position you have to get used to these times that try men's souls. In minutes now, the case goes to the final judge and we either stand, weapon-shorn, before the last tribunal or we will have that God (bleeped) Madison safely in our clutches. The prosecution rests."

His attention was now fixed upon the center of the river and so I looked in that direction.

Someone from below in the tank passed him up some infrared binoculars. He began to sweep the river with them.

"Ah!" he said at last. He handed the binoculars to me.

Speed launches! But they were not speeding. They were creeping into position out on the black water. They had U.S.S. *Saratoga* on them. There was some activity on the far side of them. I could not make it out.

Bury looked at his watch. He took the glasses back and began to watch the end of Pier 92. Then suddenly he began to nod. He handed me the glasses.

Out of the water, lines were shooting. Grapnels were clutching at the far edge of the pier.

Then black figures were slithering out of the water, going quietly up the lines. They had assault rifles across their backs! And a bazooka!

Bury took back the glasses. "Frogmen," he said. "U.S. Navy SEALS. The carrier must have had a contingent of them aboard. Clever Hatchetheimer!"

He had evidently signalled the brigadier in the armored guts below. We rolled silently ahead, very slowly.

"My main worry now," said Bury, "is his God (bleeped) car. It's an Excalibur. It's a replica of a 1930 open touring phaeton, mostly chrome. But totally deceptive. Just like Madison. An Excalibur's total machinery is as modern as a jet. Cadillac engine, biggest ever built. It can outrun this tank like a rabbit can outrun a turtle! Ah, I hope this works."

We had halted again. We were just beyond the south edge of the open door of Pier 92. It was dark where we were. I could see inside. Lights showed a sign at the far end:

FREE ZONE!

INTERNATIONAL TERRITORY!

KEEP OUT!

Cargos could be unloaded into it and picked up without ever entering U.S. Customs.

A huge case, the kind you ship autos in, a big sign on it:

EXPORT

It bulked in the dimness at the extreme outward end. There seemed to be a frail, small figure advancing toward it. His mother! She had a lunch basket in her hand.

One could not see any U.S. Navy SEALS in the far darkness, but one knew they must be there, getting into position, getting ready, cocking and pointing weapons.

Bury had his eye on his watch.

Zero!

With a stuttering roar a wall of savage flame burst out of the far dark! Automatic weapons! Deafening!

I cringed down!

My Gods, we were right in their line of fire!

Bury was not ducking! What a brave man!

To keep me from running, Bury barked at me, "Those are blanks. Stay still!"

The rush, flash and roar of a bazooka! It wasn't a blank! It hit the back side of the huge case!

Above the shattering din, a car engine burst into a roar!

The front of the box burst apart!

The Excalibur hurtled out!

The flame from the guns flashed upon its chrome exhausts!

Blue flame was shooting out behind it!

The frail woman went down! The lunch basket flew!

The open touring phaeton roared toward us!

The automatic weapon fire redoubled!

Out of Pier 92 came the car!

"NOW!" Bury shouted.

The four forward machine guns of the tank opened up!

The concussions almost knocked me flat!

The car veered away from us!

With a scream of tires, it turned. It sought to escape to a side street. Banked squad cars turned on their chortling cacophony!

The car tires screamed.

The Excalibur raced up Twelfth Avenue.

Under me the tank got into motion. Faster and faster we went.

I held on to the handhold desperately.

Bury was barking into the walkie-talkie. The wind was tugging at his snap-brim. The NATO flag streamed out.

We were really going!

Eighty? Ninety? A hundred!

The car ahead of us began to draw away, its huge power plant beginning to assert its mastery!

We were on the West Side Elevated Highway. The British tank driver was driving on the wrong side!

The rails and lampposts fled by in a giddy blur. All New York seemed to be turning.

I could barely hold on!

Now, in sudden bursts, the tank's guns were firing

once more! The concussion almost finished the job of knocking me loose.

Bury, framed against the bowed antenna pennons, backed by the cracking, whipping flag, leaned forward in his snap-brim hat.

"Any moment now!" he roared into the wind.

It happened!

Ahead of us the Excalibur gave a jerk. It abruptly slowed!

The tank slued and skittered sideways on its treads. The scream was deafening!

The Excalibur had mysteriously come to a stop!

So had the tank! Halfway over a rail!

More roars!

Fifteen tanks in a double line surged out of the highway entrance roads left and right.

Fifteen deadly muzzles cranked down and centered upon the driver of the car!

"Hatchetheimer is a genius," Bury was saying. "The aircraft-landing-arrest gear worked perfectly!"

And then I saw what he meant. The U.S.S. *Saratoga* had installed the trip wires and arrests they use to brake a landing plane in each lane of the highway. The Excalibur had tripped one!

Bury was clambering down.

We approached the car.

There was a huddled figure behind the wheel.

A voice! It was speaking in a dull monotone. "Banner Headline Obituary 18-point type quote MADISON DIES BEGGING FORGIVENESS unquote subhead 12-point ROCKECENTER FOREVER LAST WORDS unquote text quote Yesterday on West Side Elevated Highway comma J. Walter Madison comma misunderstood publicist comma gave up the unwilling ghost period. He will be buried in Bideawee Cemetery at 4:00

P.M. today period. Public will probably demand removal of body from consecrated ground. . . ."

The poor man was composing his obituary notice!

Bury stood beside the car, close to where Madison could see him. "Shut up, Madison!"

The fellow looked up and went white. "Oh, my God! Bury! Hold the press. Change type size to billboard quote MADISON MURDERED exclamation point unquote subhead quote MANGLED BODY . . ."

Bury said, "Shut up. You're not in trouble."

Madison gaped. "But the president of Patagonia committed suicide! All Octopus holdings were expropriated—a loss of eighteen billion dollars!"

"Tut, tut," said Bury.

"But I just ran over my very own mother! I'll be up for motherslaughter!"

Bury said, "Your mother is all right. The Navy crew is right this minute treating her for shock. They just wanted to know on my radio, does she always demand canned heat when her heart acts up?"

"But . . . but . . . how about all the other jobs I've failed on? How about the time I was supposed to popularize the American Indians for Octopus and they were all exiled to Canada?"

"Pish, pish," said Bury. "Octopus has a big heart. Small errors can be overlooked. I forgive you. Rockecenter forgives you and God forgives you, which is mostly the same thing."

"You mean the headlines should read quote MADISON MIRACULOUSLY RESURRECTS unquote?"

"A last minute, motorcycle-rushed reprieve just arrived from the governor. Here." He handed Madison an envelope. "You are back on F.F.B.O. staff. You can move back into your mother's condo. Be at the enclosed address at ten o'clock tomorrow morning."

"Oh, thank you, thank you!" wept Madison. "Next time I will justify everything you have ever thought of me!"

Bury walked down an entrance road and I went with him. A New York squad car was blocking it. Bury climbed in. I sat down beside him.

"Take me home," said Bury to the driver. "And then drop this man off wherever he wants to go."

"Yessir, Mr. Bury," said the cop and quickly drove away with us.

I said to Bury, "Wasn't it pretty kind of you to forgive him after all that loss?"

"No, no," said Bury. "We never tell him the truth. You've got to see behind these things. As soon as he got the Indians driven out, we grabbed their oil lands. And on this Patagonia thing, he was sent to the republic to ruin our PR. The government there, on public demand, expropriated all Octopus properties and refineries. The Patagonian Central Bank, to preserve its international credit, had to try to pay for them. It couldn't, of course, so Grabbe-Manhattan foreclosed and we now own the whole country. He has ably created the same havoc on other jobs. But don't tell him what we really expect him to do or accomplish. Hide it. He actually believes he is a great PR man. So don't ruin his morale. Cheer him on with only a tip or two. He's a genius. I don't know how he does it!"

We shortly arrived at his West Side condo. "Thank heavens," he said, "I got home on time. I couldn't stand a real fight after tonight. Be at the office early."

He was gone.

Riding back to the Bentley Bucks Deluxe, I knew I had been right. It had taken an aircraft carrier and tanks and the whole New York police force to get this thing started.

Not even the Gods could help Heller now!

Chapter 7

Quivering with anxiousness now to get on the job, I reported in bright and early the following morning. I wanted to really be up to handle Madison: I didn't have any office to work out of.

I made my way through the unenthusiastic throng of fellow workers on their way to work. Slow going. But I found an office labelled New Personnel Assignments and went in.

A beefy office-manager type was at a desk. He looked at me curiously.

"Inkswitch," I said. "I . . ."

He held up his hand to halt me. He turned to a computer and punched it. It came up blank.

"Ah," he said. "A family spy! Well, I have one word of advice for you. Don't punch any time clocks around here even if you see your name on them. It would blow your cover."

"Wait," I said. "I have work to do. Don't I even get an office?"

"Oh, no!" he said, aghast. "Somebody could find you to shoot or poison you. It's promoting crime and that's illegal."

"Hey," I said, "how do I get paid?"

"Oh, that's easy. But let me warn you. Don't endorse any checks they may give you. IRS would nail you for sure."

"No pay at all?"

He said, "Of course you're entitled to pay. It comes out of Petty Cash. That's Window Thirteen. But don't sign any voucher with your real name or they'll ask for your receipts for reimbursement."

"Well, all right," I said, "so long as I don't get in trouble with my superior."

"Oh, you don't have any boss. And don't look at me. You're a *family* spy."

"I do thank you for all you've done," I said.

"Well, I've never seen you so I'll forget that you weren't here."

I went at once to Window Thirteen. It was labelled Petty Cash Disbursements. A very prim old lady was sitting behind the wicket. "Name?" she said.

"Inkswitch," I said.

She pressed her computer keys. The screen came up blank. She nodded a severe nod. Must be one of the firm's most honest employees to hold such a post of trust. She said, "How much?"

I picked a number out of the air. "Ten thousand dollars," I said.

She extended a disbursement voucher in triplicate. Mindful of the advice just received, I signed it *John Smith.*

She took the voucher back. She reached into a drawer and counted out ten thousand in small bills. Her actions were meticulous, her mouth was prim. She gave me five thousand and put the other five thousand in her purse.

I was awed. What an efficient organization. Their spies didn't exist! And they had developed a graft system unbelievably simple! I would have to write Lombar about this! No wonder he made such a study of Earth culture!

Hurrying now, I rushed down the hall to Bury's office. His door was ajar. But to be polite, I knocked.

He came to the door. He scowled. "What the hell are you doing, Inkswitch, knocking! You scared me half to death! I thought it was some enemy that didn't know his way around!" It was only then I noticed the sign on his door:

Benevolent Association

He was putting a flat Beretta M-84, .380 Auto pistol in his shoulder holster. "We've got a date with Madison right away."

"Is that for Madison?" I said and instantly started checking the Colt Python .357 Magnum-.38 Special I was now carrying.

"No, no!" said Bury. "There isn't an ounce of violence in him. This is for the Slime-Tripe Magazine Building across the way. Dangerous place: they always have people they have featured, hanging around killing editors! Come on. That's where we meet Madison!"

He rushed out with me following him.

Chapter 8

We didn't have any distance to go at all. The forty-eight-story building was right across the way from the Octopus Building. We crossed a two-tone terrazzo pavement set with fountains. The building reared in limestone, aluminum and glass splendor. We entered a huge lobby done in polished and dulled stainless steel.

We stood before an enormous abstract mural, entered an elevator and shot skyward. It spilled us into an enormous room.

A huge ladder of signs confronted us. The top one said:

Owner-Publisher Inspiration Floor

It was followed with the list of magazines published in the building: *Slime, Tripe, Riffraff, Dirt Illustrated* and *Misfortune.*

The atmosphere of the room was hazy thick. It smelled like marijuana and opium smoke. There were some people moving about: they were wearing blindfolds, being led by people wearing blindfolds.

We went further into the vast room. I saw numerous posted signs:

All the News That Gives You Fits

Unreality Is the Only Reality

Slime, the Magazine That Doesn't Lie or Cheat Anyone but Its Public

Always Check Your Facts in the Cloakroom and Then Write Your Story

They Want Blood,
Give It to Them—Even If It Is Your Own

There were some doors opening off: *Libeller in Chief, Scurrility Editor,* and *Head Pervert.*

But we were not heading for any of these. Parting the clouds of smoke, we went to a mammoth door at the end of the room. It said:

Owner-Publisher
Private
Sacred

Bury barged right on in.

Where the desk should be, there was a couch. There was no one on it.

I became aware of lights flashing on the wall over to my right. I saw that there was an organist seated at a huge console organ. It was a woman of middle age in a tail-coated suit—complete, male, white-tie evening dress. She was playing with elaborate gestures on the organ keys. But there was no music!

I noticed that the vast panorama of pictures on the wall were flashing on and mingling in rhythm. She was playing the pictures!

I looked at them. One had to stand back, they were so big. It was a flowing, flashing montage in full color. The pictures were of dead bodies, train wrecks, aircraft crashes, murdered children and graves. And through it all flowed, rhythmically, decay and blood. A symphony of disaster. Rather appealing, I thought.

Bury walked over to the woman. He said, "Get out."

She protested, aghast. "But how can you dream up imaginary news if you don't have substance before you?"

"Beat it," said Bury.

She picked up her baton and top hat, very miffed, muttering about people who did not have a true reporter's soul. But a final look at Bury's face took her out the door quickly.

"Are we here to meet the owner-publisher?" I said.

"Oh, no," said Bury. "He's an LSD addict and always off having an affair with his male psychiatrist. It's always empty, so I use it for meetings."

"Then we own this place?"

"What? And inherit all its libel suits? I should say not. Sit down, Inkswitch, and I'll fill you in."

There was no place to sit but the color-montage organ bench. I sat on it. I accidentally touched a key and a nude body being strangled flashed on the wall. Not a bad looking girl, I thought.

Bury was pacing about restlessly. "We don't have to own any newspapers or magazines. It's done this way: they're all in debt; they and their TV and radio stations are into the banks for billions. So when they want to renew or borrow, the banks tell them they have to put a bank-selected director or six on their boards of directors. And they do it in order to get the money. Then, whatever we want to appear in the press, we simply pass it to a director and he tells the editors and they tell the reporters and they (bleep) well print whatever they're told."

How wise, I thought. Lombar would be fascinated.

But there was more: "Then, if the government gets out of hand, we release stories into the press to embarrass them or get them kicked out. So the government always releases the press releases that we tell them to. It's a very tight system. We control all the banks, you see."

Oho! Lombar indeed would be interested. A masterful system! Closed-circuit propaganda! The truth couldn't even get into it edgewise! So that was how the Rockecenters had remained in control so long and now owned so much! That and chicanery, of course. Totally controlled free enterprise!

I tried to play "Saint James Infirmary" on the organ with one finger. I got a series of Japanese movie monsters smashing and gobbling people. Then I found one good key: when you tremoloed it, rivers of blood gushed down the wall in rhythmic waves.

The door opened.

It was Madison!

I had not gotten a good look at him in his car last night under the mercury-vapor highway lights and all.

I was amazed!

Here was a clean-looking, rather handsome young man. He was impeccably dressed, quite conservatively. He had brown hair and very appealing brown eyes. He might well have been a model for a shirt ad. He seemed quiet, well-mannered, totally presentable.

He said, "Social notices. Madison arrived late and was deeply apologetic. Unquote."

Bury, I noticed, backed up a bit as though talking to a bomb. "Did you get your credentials?" he said.

"Oh, yes. Today, Madison received the supreme award of the very best credentials of a Slime-Tripe reporter. Deeply honored, he expressed his gratitude. . . ."

"And you are now on special independent assignment?" asked Bury.

"Quote Credentials Department Unaccountably Pleased that no Direct Assignment Contemplated. News spread rapidly throughout buildings. Thousands cheered. . . ."

Bury said, "This is Smith, John. You will be receiving tips from him. Give him your mother's phone number and that of the F.F.B.O. office."

Madison bowed and then walked over and gave me the most sincere and genuine handshake I have ever had. Then he got out a notebook, wrote the numbers on a page and gave them over.

Then Madison walked over toward Bury—who stepped back—and looked at the attorney with appealing courtesy. "What am I supposed to do?"

Bury reached into his pocket. He took out one of the passport pictures of Wister. He handed it over.

Madison took it and gazed upon it in a friendly way. "He looks like a very nice fellow."

"He is, he is," said Bury. "His name is Jerome Terrance Wister."

Bury glanced toward me. I took my cue. "He has an office in the Empire State Building." I gave him the number. "He has developed a new fuel. He will try to get it known through racing."

"And?" said Madison.

Bury spoke. "You will act in the capacity of a Slime-Tripe reporter on special assignment. Actually, he is a modest man. He would not hire a PR directly. But as his friends, we know he needs one to help him on his way. Really, he would not accept our help so we must be nameless. It is a charitable way to contribute to this great society, to have this fellow and his invention helped. Do you understand, Madison? That is your sole assignment."

Instantly Madison became ecstatic. "You mean I am to really, truly help him?"

"Indeed so," said Bury. "Make his name a household word, make him immortal!"

"Oh," said Madison. "Glorious, Stupendous and Gala! Mr. Bury," he said with eyes glowing, "I can make him the most immortal man you ever heard of! One way or another his name will be known forever!" He could not contain himself for joy. He walked around the room, almost bouncing.

He stopped, "Quote Labor Negotiations Today Hit Snag. It was learned from unimpeachable sources that Madison wished to know what budget..."

"The sky is the limit," said Bury. "Within reason, of course."

Madison glowed. "Oh, I can see it now! Immortal! His name known everywhere by everyone forever!" Joy and enthusiasm leaped out of every pore. He couldn't stand still. Had he been wearing a hat, he would have thrown it in the air!

Bury pulled me out of the room. We waded through the clouds of marijuana smoke and stench of opium. We held steady as reporters bumped into us. We got to the elevator.

Bury looked around for any snipers as we left. He got us safely outside the building. We stood beside a tinkling fountain and breathed deeply to get rid of the stench.

He tucked his Beretta more securely into its holster. "Inkswitch, it's all in your hands now. If you lose his number, you'll find his mother in the phone book. He is on his way. I've got to go off for a few days—the Governor General of Canada is being balky about carrying out genocide on the French population there and we simply have to clear out Nova Scotia to take over the new oil fields: it has a lot of legal angles. But I'll be back well before the fireworks begin in case stronger measures are needed. You just feed Madison a tip or two as you think best. Give him his head. And we'll be rid of Wister! Good luck to you."

He hurried off upon his busy duties.

Beside the splashing fountain, in that quiet place, I was a little bit troubled.

This Madison was obviously the nicest fellow you ever wanted to meet. He seemed even naive, taking a liking to Heller at once.

I wondered if Bury hadn't exaggerated the dangers in this fine young man. Maybe he would make Heller famous and successful after all!

PART TWENTY-EIGHT

Chapter 1

That evening was no time to be out-of-doors. With sunset, a drizzle had begun that gave an acid rain. If it got on your clothes, it ate holes in them. A nasty night: the low clouds masked even the penthouse terrace at the Bentley Bucks Deluxe. Autumn was upon New York like a polluted sponge.

Accordingly, I was careful to go nowhere and instead phoned Senator Twiddle. I told him how much Rockecenter thought of him and he was certainly pleased.

I had just laid down the phone when it rang again. An operator's voice, in that curious sing-song they use, said, "Mr. Smith? This is Manhattan Air Terminal Telephone Exchange. A man has just come to the desk and handed me a slip of paper with your name on it, indicating I should call. Here is your PARty."

The line clicked. Then something said, "Mmmmmfffff."

I said, "Speak up. I do not understand you."

"Mmmmmfffff."

I hung up in disgust. But I was puzzled too. I did not know a soul in New York named "Mmmmmfffff." Hungarian?

I busied myself ordering a splendid dinner. Utanc was not around as usual. I hoped the rain wouldn't burn her beautiful face if she was prancing around in it.

The phone rang. A voice said, "Mmmmmfffff."

"Who are you?" I demanded. "I don't know a single Mmmmmfffff anywhere."

A more distant voice on the phone said, "You hold it to my ear and I'll talk." The voice became abruptly louder. "You, sir, this is us. Raht tried to phone you earlier but he still has the wires in his jaws. (Hold the phone closer.) My arms are still in casts. The doctor refused to take out the wires or break off the casts or release us for another two weeks."

"Phaugh!" I said. "Loaf, loaf, loaf! Anything to get a little more time off!"

"Well, sir, we knew how anxious you were about a certain thing. So Raht sneaked by the nurses and the desk. I couldn't go because my arms are still in casts and it's conspicuous and I can't climb. But Raht's jaws are the only thing he has that is still immobilized. . . ."

"What in Hells are you trying to tell me?" I snapped.

"(Hold the phone closer.) But he had to wait until the guards and sightseeing guides left for the night. The weather is so bad both the lower and upper towers were closed, fortunately. So Raht climbed up the TV mast as best he could. It was awfully slippery because of the rain. We'll have to get him new pajamas because of the acid eating through. But it was awfully windy and he skinned his shins. . . ."

"My Gods!" I said. "Come to the point!"

"Well, he turned it off, sir. And we wanted to tell you we can't get back on the job for another two weeks. The doctor refuses. . . ."

"You two will do anything, anything to loaf! Believe me, I'll make sure your pay is docked!"

I hung up. I was so exasperated at the flimsy pretext

they were using that, for a moment, the import of the news did not sink in.

The 831 Relayer! It was off! I could once more see what Heller was doing! And in the nick of time, too. Madison would need this information!

I quickly broke out and set up my viewer and equipment. I turned it on.

It worked!

A dinner party!

It was in some private dining room in some restaurant. It was very posh. It was made to look like an old English inn with dark oak, mounted boars' heads, a log fire. The waiters were in red hunting coats.

But what was this? I really didn't recognize the people! They all had on flat mortarboard hats and black gowns! All of them!

They were apparently just finishing a roast beef dinner with plum pudding and chatting away.

As Heller glanced around, speaking to this one and that or answering or laughing at some joke, I tried to identify the people.

Bang-Bang! What was he doing in a mortarboard and black gown? He hadn't graduated from anything. And there was Vantagio! He had long since graduated. And there was the leading painter and several other painters all in mortarboard hats and gowns.

Izzy was there, sort of shrunk back. He was dressed like the rest.

They were finished with the main dinner now. Suddenly the far doors opened and eight waiters came in, four on one side and four on the other, bearing a huge cake in a peculiar way.

Everyone cheered.

They sang:

Happy doctorate to you,
Happy doctorate to you.
Happy doctorate, dear Izzy,
Your dream has come true.

The waiters put the cake down. It was in the shape of a coffin! On the top it said "Here lies DOCTOR IZZY EPSTEIN."

"Oh, dear," said Izzy.

"It's just like you wanted it," said Vantagio.

"Speech! Speech!" the others were shouting.

Heller forced Izzy to stand up.

Izzy, squirming with embarrassment, cleared his throat several times, adjusted his glasses and said, "My good and tolerant friends, it is true that this is a lucky day. My thesis was at last accepted after three horrible years. At the graduation ceremony, thanks to your moral support, I did not trip on my gown going down the aisle. When I accepted my diploma from the president, no snake jumped out of it. I even found my seat once more, thanks to your forming ranks so I couldn't miss it.

"But I must tell you that it is very unlucky to have such good luck. Fate always lurks with sharpened teeth and can strike most unexpectedly.

"As I can now devote my full time to the corporations, any market and financial analyst can predict with ease that they will surely crash.

"You are unwise to have any confidence in me. It could bring you bad luck too. I thank you."

He sat down. They all applauded. They made him cut the coffin with a provided spade.

After a while, after his third piece of cake, Heller said, "I hope this rain goes away by tomorrow. I want to take the Caddy to Spreeport, Long Island, and do a few turns on the track."

Izzy said, "Oh, dear. I wish you wouldn't do such dangerous things. I'm still responsible for you, you know."

"Well, this isn't very dangerous, Izzy. The speedway there is quite new. I'm not trying out the carburetor. I'm just breaking the Caddy in. The engine is still stiff."

"Mr. Jet, please don't connect any racing activity or your name with the corporations. Please. I have an awful feeling about it. Fate can be pretty treacherous." Heller laughed.

But so did I. Izzy could be righter than he knew, I hoped.

I had all I needed to know. I instantly phoned J. Walter Madison.

"This is Smith. Wister will be at the Spreeport, Long Island, Speedway tomorrow if the rain stops. You can begin to work him over."

"Work him over?" said Madison. "That is a strange way to put it, Mr. Smith."

"I mean, do what you do," I corrected.

"Mr. Smith, I hope you don't think I mean anything but good for this fine young man. Please don't insist that I use anything but the most standard PR on him."

"And what is that?" I said.

"Well," said Madison, delight creeping into his voice, "first is CONFIDENCE. One must go to any lengths to build up the client's Confidence in one. You see, clients do not know the skills of PR and they often get strange ideas and balk and know best and all that. One has to be VERY careful they do not put their foot in it and get off on the wrong track.

"The next is COVERAGE. One has to get maximum exposure. This gives name-awareness to the public. And one simply gets Coverage, Coverage, Coverage! One has to achieve saturation of all media and publicity channels."

The enthusiasm of the true professional was giving his voice a lilting tone. "Then third is CONTROVERSY. The public and media will not print or touch anything that does not have Controversy in it. To get the press or TV to accept the simplest story, it must imply conflict."

"Sounds pretty straightforward to me," I said a bit dubiously. If Madison did just those things, Heller might succeed. He hadn't mentioned any shooting at all. I had my doubts. Bury must have a personal bias against this sincere and dedicated public relations expert.

"Oh, it IS straightforward," said Madison. "You will see. I will do nothing, absolutely nothing shady or underhanded. My personal ethics won't allow it. I will simply build up Wister's Confidence in me, get him maximum Coverage and make sure the press gets their Controversy. The three C's, Mr. Smith. Standard PR to standard press. You'll see. Oh, Wister will win on this one. But really, I must ring off. I see right now I have some other calls to make. I do appreciate your help. Leave the professionalism to me. I won't let you down."

He hung up. I sat there quite a while. The three C's. It did sound awfully standard. I began to worry. Maybe Heller really *was* going to win! Awful thought!

Chapter 2

Now that I knew I didn't have any office, superior or any time clock to punch, I lolled around the penthouse sitting room the next morning. The rain had cleared and I now and then glanced at the viewer.

Heller drove a semi—a trailer pulled by diesel tractor—along State Highway 27. The Atlantic Ocean was visible on his right occasionally. Signs pointed the way to Jones Beach, one of the largest recreation areas around New York. There was lots of sand.

But he didn't turn off to Jones Beach. He went along the scattered main street of Spreeport, not very impressive. There seemed to be an awful lot of fish food restaurants and motels.

He neared an area of new construction. A huge sign:

SPREEPORT SPEEDWAY
Spreeport Stock Car Association
Saturday Nights: Stock Cars and Bombers

The parking lots were vast. A grandstand sprouted flags. Heller drove up to a gate. A security guard came out and looked at his cards. Somehow he had become a member of NASCAR—the National Association of Stock Car Racing—a member of the Spreeport Racing Club and a lot of other things. He had been busy! Or Izzy or Bang-Bang had.

The guard said, "Mr. Stampi said you could use Pit 13, Mr. Wister. There ain't nobody else out today. Track pretty wet."

Heller drove on through to an area behind Pit 13 and got out of the cab of the tractor.

He was all alone! No Bang-Bang. Then I realized Bang-Bang must have a drill or ROTC class or something.

And there was the Cadillac on the trailer. It was now gleaming red. It really hurt the eyes even in that dim ocean sunlight.

Heller pulled the wheel chocks and let off the brake and rolled the car down off the trailer.

He checked the gas. There were additional instruments on the panel. The steering wheel was leather wrapped. The white seats were gleaming! Mike Mutazione had certainly done a job on that interior!

Heller climbed in, gave his Voltar engineer's gloves a tug, each one, and started the car up. It thundered with a controlled storm of power. Mike Mutazione had certainly done something under the hood, too!

He tooled the Caddy around to the pit and then, in a very leisurely fashion, began to drive around the track. It was asphalt. It was not banked very much. It was wet after the rain. He wasn't driving fast enough to skid. He was, as he had said, simply breaking in the engine. He was watching a heat gauge and oil pressure.

I didn't know how long the circle of the track was. Not too much. Maybe half a mile. Oval—two turns and two straightaways.

He began to make the car surge and slow, maybe running the engine at different speeds. It skidded once. He began to work his accelerator against his brake.

Something was worrying him. He coasted into the pit area and stopped. He got out and looked at the tires.

There was a noise behind him. He turned.

A tough-looking camera crew was descending upon him! Five men. They were carrying rather old-looking equipment. They were filthy and unshaven. The obvious leader was a very hard egg.

"Your name Wister?" he bellowed.

I flinched. Was this Madison's idea of building his first C—Confidence? That crew looked like they were going to beat Heller up!

"We got a tip you gotta new fuel!" said the leader,

maybe a reporter. "You better tell us all about it or we'll knock the hell out of you!"

I had caught a glimpse of Heller's feet as he drove and he was not wearing his baseball shoes! He was obviously not armed. He wasn't even holding a wrench.

"Are you from some paper?" said Heller.

"You said it, bud. We're sent here by 'Screw News' and you better start talking before we start hitting!"

"Where did you hear about any new fuel?" said Heller.

"Secretaries talk, bud, and don't you forget it! And it's time you commenced!"

"I don't wish to talk to you," said Heller.

"Jambo!" barked the leader. "Let him have it!"

The man carrying the battered old TV camera lowered it and charged Heller!

Heller's hand came up. The camera soared! Heller lashed out with one foot and Jambo's body went down the track so fast he looked like he was competing in a race! He fell in a heap.

The rest of the crew suddenly produced lead pipes!

"Wait a minute!" cried a voice. "Wait a minute! Desist, you rowdies!" It was Madison!

Neat, presentable, impeccably dressed, he suddenly interposed himself between the crew and Heller.

"You awful people go away and leave him alone!" said Madison. "Go on, at once, shoo, shoo, or I shall have to report you to the Reporter Ethics Committee!"

The crew slunk off. They picked up the camera and Jambo as they departed.

Madison turned to Heller. He dusted him off saying, "Oh, my," and "what thoroughly nasty oafs some reporters are." He did a good job of dusting even though there wasn't a speck on Heller's red racing suit.

"It was terribly fortunate I chanced to happen

along," said Madison. "What paper did they say they were from?"

"'Screw News,'" said Heller.

"Dear, dear," said Madison. He was looking at Heller now in a sort of appealing way. "They did mention something about a new fuel. I couldn't help but overhear them. Is there a new fuel?"

"Who are you?" said Heller.

"Oh, I do apologize. I am J. Walter Madison, a mere freelance reporter. I write for *Chemistry Today*, a very conservative little paper. Just a freelance. But I can see that you have a problem. There has been a leak of news. The thing to do is make some little statement about it, something disparaging, then they'll stop bothering you. And you don't want to be bothered all the time by oafs such as *those*, I am sure."

"I sure don't," said Heller.

"I am fortunately in a position to help," said Madison. "I'm afraid I don't know your name."

"They call me Wister."

"Is that your full name?"

"Jerome Terrance Wister is that full name."

"Ah, well. I certainly do not want to force my attention on you, Mr. Wister. But I am afraid that now it has leaked, you will be bothered no end until you make some disparaging little statement. Is there a fuel?"

"Well, yes," said Heller. "But I was going to wait until I had graduated and people would listen to me."

"Oh, I quite understand. Of course they won't listen to just a student. So, to get them off you, why don't I make some little tut-tut statement in a conservative paper like *Chemistry Today* and they'll not bother you right now."

"Sounds sensible," said Heller.

"Good," said Madison. "Now, I was down here to

do an interview on the effects of Non-Skid paint on asphalt. The asphalt has just been painted, you know. And I have a crew over there to take some pictures of the track. It would really be no trouble to rattle off some little story about some student who chanced upon the possibility of a new fuel—very low-key—and you'll be safe to go along and do your work and finish your education without press all over you. May I call over my crew?"

Heller shrugged. Madison took out a whistle and blew it.

Instantly a huge sound truck and three station wagons roared out from behind the grandstand and raced up. They were polished. They had signs on them, very modest, *Chemistry Today.* The crew alighted. They were clean, well groomed and professional. Very polite. Madison introduced them courteously and explained it wasn't an important story, just a favor he was doing. Maybe a little picture and a two-inch notice. The crew nodded understandingly.

The cameramen prepared to snap off a still.

Suddenly Madison raised his hand. "Wait, wait!" He turned to Heller. "Mr. Wister, you don't wear glasses. People associate glasses with learning. Would you mind if we put some glasses on you? To make you look learned? It's just a little snapshot."

Heller was amused.

"MAKEUP!" cried Madison.

Instantly a makeup man and two girl assistants came out of the huge truck. They set up a table with lighted mirrors. Madison took a pair of glasses. He put his finger through them, laughing. "See, no glass. But it makes you look studious." He put them on Heller. He stood back. "The jaw. It is too regular. It will arouse jealousy or women. MAKEUP!"

They quickly went to work on Heller's jaw. They

made it protruding and pugnacious. Then the makeup man slid some large teeth into Heller's mouth.

Lighting men had been setting up.

"Just a little candid snapshot," said Madison. "The crew needs practice, you know. The paper probably won't even run it."

A backdrop was produced. Madison said, "Oh, dear, I'm late for my interview with Mr. Stampi. Do you mind, Mr. Wister, if my crew just practices a bit? They're a bit green. I won't be long." He left.

The crew posed Heller. They began to shoot with a high-powered, strobe-connected camera. They put a variety of hats on him, different helmets, a mortarboard. They asked for different expressions. Heller was mainly amused. But at their request, he was serious when they shot.

"We always make a little library of shots when we shoot and we lack practice," said the photographer. "You won't mind if we make some of these available on request?"

Heller looked at himself in their makeup mirror. He certainly didn't look like Heller. "Why not," he said.

The photographer gave him a model release to sign.

Then the crew chief said, "Mr. Madison is certainly taking his time."

"We could use it to practice our TV setup. The new one we never assembled," said their props man.

Quicker than a wink, they had what looked like an interior TV stage, backdrops, platform, mikes, all erected. They got Heller into some different coats—lab coats, street coats. And each time fired away with a TV camera.

Madison came running back, puffing. "I'm sorry I'm late. Oh, dear, what are you amateurs up to? Mr. Wister, I do apologize." He sat down in a chair on the platform. "They are so enthusiastic in their practicing. Well, as long as we're sitting here, you can tell me about the new fuel."

"Well," said Heller, "the planet does need one."

They chatted amiably. The camera appeared to be all on Heller and grinding!

Madison talked about anything and everything, all very banal. Heller answered conversationally. Now and then a costume man rushed in and changed his coat.

Finally, Madison turned to the crew. "That's enough practice today. We have work to do. Scrap all that film."

"Oh, it's expensive!" said the photographer. "Can't I keep it for my personal library?"

"Good heavens," said Madison, "I hope you have film left for the real reason we came!" He looked sad suddenly.

"I'm afraid I will be in trouble. We came to shoot Non-Skid paint and Mr. Stampi has no cars. All we can shoot is just black paint. It doesn't make much of a picture."

Madison got up. "Put all this away," he ordered. "Start shooting pictures of the black track."

"Oh, that won't make any picture!" said the photographer. "We'll all get ourselves fired!"

Suddenly Madison snapped his fingers. "Mr. Wister, I know it's a lot to ask. It won't take but a moment. Could you drive your car along there and put on the brakes a little bit and make it skid?"

Heller shrugged. Madison looked so honest and so appealing, sort of like a spaniel, that Heller said, "All right."

He drove the Cadillac out on the track. The crew took positions. Heller did as he was told.

"Didn't get it!" said the camera operator. "I need more speed. More zip."

Heller was amused. He wanted to try some driving anyway. He made the Caddy skid and spin. He amused himself.

They were having trouble getting the right angles.

Heller stopped at the pit. Madison wanted some pictures of the tires. Then Heller went out again.

He did a whole circle of the track. Just in front of the cameras, he slammed on the brakes. He was only doing about sixty.

Sideways went the Caddy!

Rubber screamed!

BANG!

The front left tire blew!

The Caddy careened, lurched, almost overturned!

Heller fought the wheel!

He came to a stop inches from a barricade. Smoke from the wrecked rubber rose.

He got out and looked. There was rubber all over the track, not much to tell from it.

He got a jack and a new wheel from his truck. He was working on changing the tire.

"Is it all right if we keep that for our library?" the photographer asked him.

"You shouldn't say yes," said Madison to Heller. "They pool everything they shoot with every photo library in town. I don't have any control over what they do with their films."

The chief cameraman began to rave. "(Bleep) you, Madison! That was a good shot! If I don't get some shots today, I'll be fired!"

Heller shrugged.

"Well, all right," Madison told him. "But you should be careful, Mr. Wister. Oh, yes. One thing. You can keep those glasses and those teeth. For your own safety, you should wear them if other photographers come around. I don't think they will, of course. I do thank you for your help today."

"Thank you for yours," said Heller.

They shook hands.

Madison and his crew left.

Me? I didn't get it. This Madison was mild as milk. I couldn't for the life of me figure out what he was up to. Then I had a clue. Confidence. He had spent all that time building Heller's confidence in him. I thought it was pretty inane. Bury had overestimated the danger in Madison, that was for sure.

Chapter 3

For two whole days, watching the viewer or replaying its strips, there was no slightest sign of J. Walter Madison. I began to think he was just a fizzle and that I myself would have to get in there.

Heller was working on his carburetor. He had stored the Caddy and trailer in a garage in Spreeport. He had brought over the old Caddy engine on its trailer and put together a little shop. It was not very far from New York and Bang-Bang was happily driving him back and forth in the old cab. He usually got to his Empire State Building office around four each day.

He was making too much progress. I was worried.

On the third afternoon, just as he sat down at his desk, J. Walter Madison sailed in. He was very conservatively dressed, very mild of manner, smooth of voice:

an epitome of the most socially acceptable young man you ever cared to meet.

He greeted Heller politely. He said he was sorry to bother him but Heller might be interested in the *Chemistry Today*, just out, and here were a dozen copies for his files.

Heller opened it. The item was a two-inch-square picture on the next to last page, down at the bottom. It said, *Jerome Terrance Wister, a young student, plans to make a career of finding a cheap fuel.* That was all. The picture, however, was one of Heller in glasses with a pugnacious jaw and buckteeth. It did not look the least like Heller. It amused him.

In reply to thanks, Madison said, "It was a great temptation to say more. There are rumors all around about this new fuel. I don't know where they are coming from. My editors wanted me to put it more strongly because of tips they'd gotten. But I said no. Mr. Wister, if you need any help or advice about publicity, be sure to phone me. I fear someone is getting excited about this fuel." He gave Heller a card with a phone number on it. "Papers can get quite hyperbolical. I don't have any influence, being just a freelance, but I may be able to give you some tips to keep you from straying into some of the pits and traps of the press." They shook hands warmly and Madison was on his way.

I thought I had better have a copy myself. I went down to the newsstand. "*Chemistry Today*?" said the hotel-lobby news vendor. "Never heard of it." He looked up in a big book they apparently kept for out-of-town guest queries. He phoned Hotaling's Foreign Newspaper Center down on 42nd Street. "Can't find it," he said. "And they never heard of it. Must be some little, tiny house organ."

I was relieved. Heller's "great discovery" was buried in a newspaper nobody had ever heard of. Great! I saw Madison's strategy now. It was simply to prevent a whisper of news. Clever. He, I supposed, would lay all over the media like a blanket. Good man! I was sorry I had doubted him.

The next morning, having ascertained that Utanc apparently was not up, I was breakfasting in the penthouse sitting room, the hazy autumn sun warm through the glass, feeling at peace. I opened up the *Daily Fits* to find Bugs Bunny.

I gaped!

On page two, there was that weird picture of Heller.

> **STUDENT DISCOVERS CHEAP FUEL**
>
> **SAYS WILL REVOLUTIONIZE AUTOS**
>
> J. T. Wister, an undergraduate, claims to have found a magic fuel. It is very cheap.
>
> Known to his classmates as the "Whiz Kid," a twist on the name "Wister," he already has a considerable reputation for brilliance.
>
> When asked about the fuel, he modestly said, "It will revolutionize the whole industrial world, the whole automotive industry, as well as our entire culture."

I seethed! (Bleep) that Madison! This was one story he hadn't blanketed. The worst of it was, it was TRUE!

If Heller began to use atomic conversion, it wasn't one cheap fuel he'd have but thousands!

I rushed down to the news vendor and got every daily paper they had! On page two or page three in every one of them, same story! Varied in word formation. But the same story!

I tried to call Madison. His mother said he was out. I raged. I paced back and forth. This was the thing which mustn't happen! He really was going to make Heller famous!

A walk in Central Park cooled me off somewhat. I returned and passed the lobby newsstand.

Slime Weekly News Magazine had just been delivered. The vendor was opening the packet.

And there on the front cover was Heller! Glasses, buckteeth and all!

Same story! It was now going national!

Believe me, I didn't sleep well that night!

In the morning, it was worse!

The out-of-town papers were carrying it. And the New York papers had moved him up to page one!

They were all calling Heller the "Whiz Kid" now!

Gods! Madison had blown it!

I phoned. His mother said he was still out. I said in a deadly voice, "He better not be out!"

"Oh, is this Mr. Smith?" she said. "Mr. Smith, he wants you to come to 42 Mess Street, the loft!"

I made sure my Colt Python .357 Magnum-.38 Special was fully loaded. No wonder people wanted to shoot this Madison! He was incompetent! And now he must be hiding out!

A cab rushed me downtown into the industrial west side. Gritting my teeth, I went down an alley. There sat that Excalibur! The chrome exhaust pipes were all polished. A man was sitting in it. He had one arm in a sling. It was Jambo! The one that had tried to attack Heller with the camera!

"You Smith?" he said, holding a sawed-off leopard in his good hand. This was a strange turn of events. I eased sideways and got ready to draw, wondering if I could beat that leopard.

"Hey, Smith!" yelled a voice from above. It was Madison leaning out one of those tipped industrial windows.

"You're expected," said Jambo.

I went up some dirty flights. I entered a huge loft.

It was JAMMED with people and typewriters and desks. Birds with their hats on the back of their heads and cigarettes drooping from their mouths were giving typewriters a pounding. Others were rushing about, some with mail sacks sealed to go. News teleprinters were chattering against one wall. BUSY!

Madison was standing just inside the door to an office at the end. I walked through the turmoil, choked a bit by the marijuana smoke but more choked with rage.

He was bright and hot-eyed. "How do you like it? It was all I could get at a moment's notice!"

"You're making him FAMOUS!" I shouted at him.

He looked a little puzzled. "Why, of course! Quote Madison always does his job unquote subhead Famous Public Relations Expert . . ." He broke off. Then he said, "You still seem cross!"

"Of course I'm cross!" I screamed at him.

"My mother said you sounded cross this morning on the phone. So I thought I had better show you. Those men out there are thirty of the most imaginative reporters I could find out of work on short notice. They're writing and sending out news releases about the 'Whiz Kid' to every paper in the world. I've got Wister's confidence. I am giving him lots of coverage. You don't approve?"

"You know what you were really hired for," I grated.

He frowned. He sat down in a rickety chair. Then he said, "I understand, Mr. Smith. I will mend my ways. You'll see tomorrow!"

I went off. I was glad he had gotten the point.

The (bleeping) fool would have made Heller a folk hero or something if he had kept going on with his stupid campaign! A famous Heller was something we DID NOT NEED!

Chapter 4

Confident that all would now be well, I retired that night and slept peacefully.

The Bentley Bucks Deluxe always put a morning paper on any breakfast tray—perhaps to take attention off the fact that the two-dollar ounce of orange juice was out of a tin can. I was developing what psychologists call a newspaper-anxiety syndrome, a common ailment on Earth these days, one which is responsible for the majority of commitments to mental institutions. The symptoms are you feel fine and cheerful and then you catch a glimpse of any corner of a newspaper, like under a dog's dish, and you begin to shake; it is only after you look at some of the type that *vertigo extremis* sets in.

That was exactly what happened to me. The ounce of orange juice was halfway to my lips when I saw the lead story:

WHIZ KID
CHALLENGES
OIL COMPANIES

In an exclusive statement to the *New York Yuk*, the Whiz Kid today asked, "How come America and the world is letting itself get gypped by the oil companies?"

Spokesmen for the Seven Brothers, which includes Octopus Oil Company as their acknowledged senior, said, "We are only public service organizations. The cost of oil is such that we have done everything possible to cut it. Such accusations are common."

The story went on. I was shaking so that I couldn't see the type to finish it.

I rushed into the hall, realized I had no bathrobe on, rushed back and put on an overcoat and then phoned for a bellhop to bring up a copy of every newspaper in the stand.

Crouched on the floor, I went over them. They all carried the story. The only difference was that the name of the paper had been changed in the first line. The Whiz Kid had made the statement exclusively forty times, to forty different papers including the *Garment Daily Worker.*

I must be calm, I told myself. Then I realized that Madison, of course, had not had time to stop the story. It takes a few hours to set a newspaper into type and he probably had not been able to stop it.

The viewer was sitting there. How was Heller taking this? Sometimes he stopped by his office before leaving for the speedway.

Yes, there he was. He had newspapers spread all over his desk. Shortly, he picked up his gloves, ready to leave. Izzy was coming in the door. Heller went back to his desk.

"Where is all this coming from?" demanded Heller.

Izzy looked very sad. "A publicist would say you have caught the public fancy."

"But I didn't make any such statement!"

Izzy shrugged and then made a circular motion with his finger around his temple. "That's newspapers."

"What do I do about it?"

"Leave for South America," said Izzy with sudden interest. "I can get you a ticket on the first flight out."

"Oh, this isn't that bad. It's what I'm trying to do, really. But it's strange. No reporters have come near me and here I am making statements."

"Air tickets are cheap," said Izzy, "compared to what this can cost in the long run."

Heller was going to leave again and Izzy said, "Just don't connect any corporations with racing. Or your name!"

I was confident that Madison would have stamped on the campaign by now. I idled away the morning and after lunch, went out for a walk in Central Park. The air was chilly.

Coming back, I chanced to see an advertising sign on top of a building, a big one. Workmen were busy spreading a new display on it.

A corner of what they were pasting up in sections made a chill go through me. It was a *WH*.

I steadied myself against a litter basket.

In horror, I saw it go together piece by piece.

It had a huge caption:

WHIZ KID TAKES
ON SEVEN BROTHERS!

And there was a caricature of the Whiz Kid with glasses, pugnacious jaw and teeth. He was wearing boxing gloves. He had just knocked down one of them. The other six were cowering to escape him. Puddles of oil splashed about.

A billboard campaign! Gotten out and executed at incredible speed!

Well, wait. That would have taken two or three days. It was part of Madison's original effort.

Back at the hotel, I got on the viewer. Heller was leaving the speedway. He was looking at a billboard. It was the same caricature. But he got out and, being Heller, climbed up to the walkway they have along the bottom for workmen to stand on, and read the tiny type, *financed by the Americans for Cheap Fuel Committee.*

He got down and drove along. Sign after sign after sign! Everywhere he looked on his road back through Brooklyn to Manhattan, he was seeing these signs.

I groaned! What a sickening spectacle! The whole town was being plastered with those (bleeped) signs! Usually they advertised air travel or cigarettes or foreign cars. All that had been swept away. It was only "Whiz Kid!"

I tried to phone Madison. I could not make contact.

I tried to phone Bury. He would not be back until the morrow.

But worse was yet to come. Thinking I ought to watch a movie, something calm like the FBI making America safe by blowing up its buildings, I turned on the TV.

A talk show! There sat the Whiz Kid. I realized it was the set that Madison had erected out at the speedway. The Whiz Kid wasn't heard. His lips were moving. The commentator was dubbing in what he was saying.

All about how he had a cheap fuel and America

would be greatly benefited and could now look forward to prosperity.

The interrogator was shot separately.

Half an hour later, another channel, same patter!

Madison again was not available!

All evening, on whatever channel, even in the news, you could count on the Whiz Kid popping up with an overdubbed set of statements.

I suffered through the night. Nothing could be worse than this. Madison had turned his coat! He had sold us out! I knew how he was getting such coverage. He must be in contact with the Rockecenter-appointed bank directors on every paper and TV channel and he was giving them their orders and they were passing them down the line. Madison was selling Rockecenter out, using Rockecenter's own press-control network! A traitor!

Even worse was to come. In the morning, in addition to more news stories, I chanced to turn the TV to a housewife program.

There stood the Whiz Kid before a group of housewives! In the flesh. In person. And he was telling them what a shame it was they had to empty their teapots to buy gas when a fuel existed that was so cheap they would be able to buy mink coats with the money they saved. They were hysterical with joy!

In person?

I went to the viewer.

Heller was en route to the office! He wasn't talking live to any housewives!

I looked at the TV again. Glasses, buckteeth, pugnacious jaw . . .

I phoned Madison. I got him at his mother's place.

"Madison!" I screamed at him. "I thought I told you to mend your ways!"

"I did!" he said. "I doubled the coverage and added

controversy! I know it is awfully fast but I think we're making it. We are forming fan clubs now, coast to coast."

"Oh, my Gods!" Then, as the TV was still on and the Whiz Kid was still addressing housewives, I cried, "But how are you doing this housewife thing?"

"Oh, the double," he said. "Well, in handling publicity, you never can trust a client. They always say the wrong things and are not handy when you need them. That's why I had to have a double. I could have gotten some actor that looked much more like Wister but in his envelope of instructions Mr. Bury said that if I used a double I could only use this young man. He was very emphatic about it. This double has buckteeth and a heavy jaw and he's blind as a bat without glasses. He wouldn't consent to our pulling his teeth and plastic surgery or contact lenses. And Mr. Bury was so emphatic, I had no choice. I had to make Wister look like the double. Do you have him on? I think he is marvelously convincing! I've got to hang up. Good-bye."

I rang his phone again. Nobody answered.

Not for nothing did his colleagues call him J. Warbler Madman. He was as crazy as a coot! He was going to make Heller a household word as the Whiz Kid!

Heller was in his office at the Empire State Building now. He got hold of Izzy.

Izzy said, "They've got a double for you. I saw him on TV."

"Wait," said Heller. "That's impersonation! I've got to get a lawyer and stop this!"

"We don't have ten million dollars," said Izzy. "That would be the lawyer's fee. And it would take years. I got you a ticket for Brazil. There's an unexplored area up the Amazon. There are only soldier ants in it that eat everything. You'd be much safer there."

"They haven't done anything destructive yet," said Heller.

Izzy looked at him and then gave his own Salvation Army Good Will suit a tug. "I think you will find, Mr. Jet, that it doesn't do to raise your head in this world. It's kind of fatal."

"Then there's nothing I can do?"

"Use this air ticket," said Izzy. "And fast!"

Heller brushed it aside and left for the speedway.

But I had quite another view of it. Madison had sold out. He was making Heller a folk hero even with fan clubs! And he was using the Rockecenter power to do it.

I called Bury. He said instantly, "Don't talk about it on the phone. Meet me at Goldstein's Delicatessen at 50th and Eighth Avenue for lunch, twelve sharp." He hung up.

Oh, I could see he also scented trouble. Secret meeting!

In a deadly, bad humor, at twelve I elbowed my way to a greasy, white-topped table in the back of Goldstein's Delicatessen. Despite the crowd, it was apparently reserved. I sat down. Bury came elbowing through the mob seconds later. He was carrying a huge book. He was looking like he might smile if he ever could.

He put the book on the next chair and ordered kosher hot dogs. "I hate these things," he said. "Don't let me forget to put bicarbonate of soda on them this time."

I was too upset to do much talking. I ate my kosher hot dog moodily. Bury ate three.

He lifted up the book. "Madison sent this over for you. You're lucky he doesn't have your address or right name. He said you sounded cross. Why?"

I gaped at him.

He opened the book. It was full of clippings and TV

summaries, a press book showing all the coverage. He was almost smiling as he leafed through the vast Whiz Kid array.

"He's making a hero of him!" I said. "And he's using the Rockecenter power to get the press!"

"Precisely," said Bury. "Precisely. I just picked this up on the way over." He dropped the just-released copy of *Tripe*. The front page had a photograph of Heller standing by the Caddy—the Heller with glasses, buckteeth and jaw. The caption said *American Youth on the March, page 5*. And page 5 began a photo story of a humble cottage where the Whiz Kid had been born, photos of his early teachers, his mother and father and an early Cooper-Martin racing car he had rebuilt at the age of five.

There was something wrong with Bury's attitude. "I had to see you before you upset Madison," he said. "He's sensitive. A sort of prima donna, really, dedicated to his art. So don't be cross with him, Inkswitch. I think he's doing just wonderful!"

I was so confused I even paid the check.

In the hotel, I lay on the bed looking at the TV. They had a picture of the goofed-up Heller in an insert and a station editorial commentator was giving a spiel, "Is this young man, a pillar of American youth, going to revolutionize our culture? It has always been the opinion of this channel that American youth should be given its head and the wisdom of that policy is manifest today in the emergence upon the world stage of Wister. . . ."

I snapped it off.

I knew it would not get better. It didn't.

The morning paper front-paged the scene of Heller's tire blowing out. The headline said *DID THE 7 BROTHERS PLAN WHIZ KID DEATH?*

Anxiously I looked to see if Heller was dead, as it implied. It didn't really say!

The morning TV news carried the whole scene of the skid, including smoke. And then there was a shot of a Long Island police officer holding a piece of rubber. He was saying, "Forensic medicine has just revealed that this tire did not have enough air in it. Members of the Whiz Kid pit crew are in custody and under question."

Insane! He didn't have any pit crew!

Yes, he did. There they were, creeping out of a police van, holding up their coats so you couldn't see their faces.

Worse. The afternoon news showed a fist-gesticulating mob in front of the Arabian-Manhattan Oil Company, demonstrating against its effort to do away with the Whiz Kid!

Bury liked this?

They all belonged in a psychiatric ward!

I sank into a sodden despair.

Maybe the whole planet ought to be in a psychiatric ward!

Chapter 5

I had been so horror-struck by the contents of the newspapers that I had not noticed the progressing date-line. Reading the latest heroic activities of the Whiz Kid one morning, my eye chanced to pause, while I got my heart going again, on the date.

It was days past the time Heller would have sent in his third report to Captain Tars Roke. He had probably mailed it direct to the base and there they would have placed it on the first outward-bound freighter. I had lost a chance to get the platen code.

I wished Utanc would be around some time. I needed somebody sympathetic. But all I ever saw of her was piles of packages being delivered, wrapped in paper, labelled Lord and Taylor or Saks or Tiffany. I half expected to see a skyscraper arrive, neatly boxed: she was buying out the town. But I must say, when I caught rare glimpses of her, she did look extraordinarily chic in her western clothes. One day I had seen her alight from her chauffeured limousine looking like an animated silver statue in her metal-hued gown and slippers. She didn't say hello: she just handed me a rare painting she had got at an auction and promptly drove off. Maybe she thought I was a bellhop.

I was very alone in a very cruel world. If Lombar caught a whiff of Heller's fame and possible success, I was done for! Of course, it did have the advantage that if Tars Roke heard of it, the Grand Council would be so happy that they would forget all about an emergency invasion and I would not be slaughtered along with everybody else on Earth. It sort of depended on the way you looked at it.

But then something happened which jarred me out of my numbness.

Heller was at the Spreeport Speedway. He had not yet installed the carburetor on the Cadillac. He was still using high-test gasoline. At the track they had put on additional security guards and nobody could get through the gate, not even press, except of course on Saturday nights when they had their races.

Thus it was with interest that I watched somebody walking up toward Pit 13. Usually the place was deserted. The newcomer was pretty plump, rather carelessly dressed, a cigar clamped in yellowed teeth.

Around the track, Heller wore a totally enclosed racing helmet with a dark plastic visor, probably a sort of disguise. One couldn't blame him. He had been inspecting his tires after a few turns around the oval.

"You Wister?" said the newcomer. He didn't get an answer but he put out his plump hand. "I'm Stampi. I own this place."

"Glad to meet you," said Heller, shaking hands.

"I just came over to tell you the track was closed now. The season is over. The circuit moves south."

"Sorry to hear it," said Heller. "I was hoping to use it for a longevity trial. Endurance, I think you call it. Just for my own information."

"Oh, hell no, Wister, it ain't closed to *you*. But that ain't the point. I got a call a while ago from the association president and he said somebody had given him the idea we should hold another event. What were you going to do?"

"I was going to get the hood sealed and locked by AAA inspectors and then I was going to run a hundred hours without refueling. Just round and round."

"Oho! The new fuel!"

"Not really a fuel. It's the carburetor."

"Carburetor, fuel, what's the difference? Endurance race, eh? Well, Wister, you been kicking up quite a fuss in the press and the association president said that if you was agreeable, we could make a sort of an event. You know, tickets, TV coverage. Might gate a million bucks. The networks would pay and the gate would be heavy. Could cook up a prize for you. Quarter of a million, maybe? If you busted any records."

"Well, it wouldn't be very exciting," said Heller. "Just a car going round and round."

"Oh, other manufacturers or owners would say their

cars also could do endurance runs. We'd invite a few in. Some sort of event. My only misgivings is that this track is going to start icing in another couple weeks. And I notice you keep worrying about tires."

"Well, if it didn't disqualify me to stop and change a tire, the ice isn't any real problem. One would just drive carefully."

"So ice don't worry you none?"

"Not especially. Couldn't be much worse than wet."

"Well, all right, then," said Stampi. "I'll call him back and we'll put together an out-of-season special event of some kind. And if you win, you get a cup and a quarter of a million. Okay, Whiz Kid?"

They shook.

And a wave of relief flooded through me! That carburetor! I just remembered! It was sabotaged! It would quit after seven hours! Heller was going to lose!

I leaped up. I was in ecstasy! Brilliant, brilliant Lombar! He had foreseen it all from the first!

I dashed to my phone. After fifteen minutes of busy signals, I got Madison.

"He's agreed to race!" I cried.

"I know," said Madison. "We had to twist an arm or two and tell the association president his track would be dropped from the circuit, but it went just like it was supposed to. It usually does."

"But you don't know the good part!" I told him. "His carburetor is sabotaged! It's going to fail in about seven hours! He'll lose for sure!"

"So?" said Madison.

"He's all set up to fall on his head!" I said. "He can't possibly win that race!"

"Mr. Smith, please forgive my abruptness but I have some very urgent things to do. We just got the governor of Michigan to be president of the International Whiz Kid Fan Clubs and he's on the other wire. But when you have *important* data for me, by all means, phone. But right now, I'm sorry. Good-bye."

I sat there gaping. He was not the least bit interested! If he was really selling us out, he would be interested. If he was not selling us out, he would be interested.

There wasn't any way to make heads or tails of it.

I tried to find a movie on the TV and there was the double as a guest of honor at a kiddie afternoon puppet show. On another channel, there was the double, prerecorded, being compared to Einstein by an eminent psychologist who was examining the bumps on his head.

Restlessly, I went down in the elevator. Anything to get out of here. I was surrounded! The elevator boy was wearing a Whiz Kid Booster button.

On the counter of the news vendor was a huge Whiz Kid doll!

This whole thing was out of control. I didn't have the least notion of what would happen now.

Chapter 6

The publicity for the race began with rumors that it might happen. This progressed into predictions that it would be prevented. The build-up continued until the double, asked point blank on a national talk show—Donny Fartson's "It's Midnight All Day"—coyly announced he was willing to race to show off his new fuel.

Instant headlines!

Two days later, when that had dropped to page three, new, instant headlines appeared. I stared at them gloomily:

WHIZ KID
CHALLENGES
RACING DRIVERS
OF WORLD

With the confidence one could expect from this brilliant epitome of American youth, the Whiz Kid said, "I can lick 'em!"

The modest youth then said, "I am better than any of them bums."

It went on and on, paper after paper.

The following day, the spot ads began to appear on radio and TV. The race would be held in two weeks at the Spreeport Speedway under the auspices of the AAA and the International Racing Association.

In two more days, the sky-writing signs began to appear.

The talk shows began to interview the world's experts on auto racing. Learned predictions abounded in the press.

Two days after that, ticket sales must not have been brisk enough, because by popular demand, the race became a Demolition Derby and Combined Endurance Run.

The term was not familiar to me. What was a Demolition Derby? I found out rapidly enough. Cars banged and rammed each other until only one car was left able to move under its own power.

That made me feel a bit better. But when every sports and news announcer kept saying it would be a true test of the stamina of the new fuel, I again got uneasy. There was nothing wrong with Heller's stamina.

Publicity for the race went on. But so did other publicity.

Dirt Illustrated offered a $100,000 prize to anyone who could guess what the new fuel was.

A new game came out called "Whiz Kid." It was a computer game and was instantly on sale in all drug stores. If you won, you got to wear glasses.

The Whiz Kid—the double—modestly declined an invitation to breakfast at the White House, saying, "I'm too busy for trifling."

Through all this hurricane of publicity, Heller just went on working. He got the two tanks to hold oxygen and hydrogen on either side of the elementary-school toy. He made the adjustable ports that would throttle-feed the gases. He made the lever that would push regulated amounts of the fuel in. Apparently he was going to use a chunk of asphalt. He shaped the collar and mounted it all on the old engine block. He started it up and ran it for an hour. It seemed to work great. So that was one hour less before the sabotaged unit would fail. Then he put it over into the Caddy itself and ran it a half hour. Half an hour less. Maybe five and a half hours now? He was obviously unaware that he was dealing with a faulty unit. That was one hope.

He then took all the glass out of the Caddy and welded in a couple of temporary roll bars.

He seemed so calm, just going along doing his job, that it worried me spitless. Did he know something I didn't know?

Then I thought it over. Maybe Madison knew something I didn't know. I went down to 42 Mess Street. I almost got trampled. Madison was rushing about giving orders to three different people at once and when he sat down he was talking to three different phones at once. Busy! He wouldn't even look my way when I yelled at him.

That same afternoon, I walked into Bury's office. He was in rare good humor. It was so un-Wall-Street-lawyer-like that I thought he must have been drinking. But he said no, he had simply gone two whole nights now with no fight with his wife.

"Aren't you worried about this other thing?" I said.

"Miss Peace? Oh, hell no, Inkswitch. She gets knocked up every time she turns around. The man always thinks he did it and of course that's impossible but he rushes her off to the abortion clinic sometimes when she isn't even pregnant. It was the elevator boy this time. No, I'm not worried about that."

"No, no!" I cried. "This *other* thing!"

"No contest at all, Inkswitch. I told him very firmly to get rid of Miss Agnes once and for all so he bought her a half-a-million-dollar land yacht, a beauty. And who knows, she may up and sell her villa at Hairytown and go travelling and maybe that's the last I'll see of the interfering (bleepch). So I can stop worrying about her. Actually, today I haven't a care in the world. Rare day. It ought to be on the court calendar more frequently."

"How about Madison?" I asked ominously.

He actually laughed. That's right. Probably the first and last time in his life, but he actually laughed. A sort of a dry, hak-hak-heh. "Inkswitch," he said, "when you've had as much experience with Madison as I have, that's the last thing you will worry about. I haven't the slightest notion what he has in mind, but I can guarantee you it's not for nothing he's called 'J. Warbler Madman.' So what can I do for you?"

I thought fast. I was dealing with incompetents, surefire bunglers. What if all this messed up? What if Heller did win? Ouch! He'd be the most famous guy on the planet! Rockecenter and Lombar would be finished whether they knew each other or not!

"You can give me Faustino Narcotici's address," I said.

"Certainly," he said and quickly wrote it and the phone number out. "It's also in the yellow classified phone book under 'Family Counseling—Total Control, Inc.'" He tossed me the card.

I left him to his happy day.

I found myself before a splendid new high-rise in the Bowery. It was all black glass and chrome. I thought I must be in the wrong place and almost didn't get out of the cab.

"Sure, this is the Narcotici mob building," the cabby said, somewhat aggrieved that his knowledge of Manhattan was being questioned. "Cantcha see the U.S. Courthouse and Police Headquarters right over there? And up that street, the Federal Building? This place used to be a slum but now it's got some real tone. That'll be five extra for the guided-tour fee."

The splendid sign, *Total Control, Inc.*, fanned above a splendid arch. The lobby had murals of American flags, depicting its evolution from Betsy Tea—calmly sewing the first flag with a joint in her smiling mouth—and adding star by star the appropriate and applicable drug of the state with charming little frescoes of the events. Obviously, American history was firmly based on drugs. The murals stopped with fifty-four stars, which dated the mural. A group of schoolchildren were on a guided tour but I pushed through them.

At the information desk, I asked for Faustino "The Noose" Narcotici and a charming Sicilian girl came right out from behind the counter and personally led me into what I thought was an elevator, until the sliding door closed. In privacy, then, she pressed what looked like a stop-button panel and my side of the floor suddenly opened.

I went down like a rocket! A chute!

Unsteadily, I came to rest at the bottom and found myself looking into the rather large muzzle of a Bernadelli Model 80 .380 ACP, seven-shot automatic pistol. The face above it was very thin and Sicilian.

Somebody behind me plucked my Colt Python out of my shoulder holster and jammed it into my spine. Another Sicilian came running up and lifted out my wallet and I.D.

"Oh, (bleep)," he said. "It's only a Fed."

"A pretty (bleeped) dumb Fed," said the Sicilian with the Bernadelli. "Walking up to a metal detector with a rod on him!" He waved the others away. "You new or something? You coulda got yourself shot! Didn't you see the cloakroom? You check your God (bleeped) gun there."

They gave me back my I.D. and wallet after removing the $400 that was in it to pay them for their trouble.

"Now whatcha want?" said the Sicilian with the gun. "Scarin' Angelina half to death. Ain't you got no sense of decency? Fed appointment time is over! Two o'clock. You want to see some executive, it's gotta be before two o'clock. Green," he said to the other two.

"I want to see Mr. Narcotici," I said politely. "I'm sure you don't classify him as an 'executive.'"

"(Bleep) no. He's the *capo di tutti capi* and don't you forget it. Whatcha want to see him about?"

"Mr. Bury sent me," I said.

He turned to a computer, pushed it and it came up blank.

"Oh, (bleep)," said the one who had taken my gun.

"And this is a good rod. Brand-new." He gave it back to me.

The man who had taken the $400 gave it back to me.

"Well, excuse me for callin' you green," said the man with the Bernadelli, putting it nervously away.

He went to an internal red phone. He picked it up. He said, "Would you tell Mr. Narcotici we got a Bury messenger here under cover as a Federal agent?"

They took me over to another elevator door and I was shortly rocketing upward.

A young man who looked like an *Executive Magazine* clothing ad was at the elevator to meet me. He escorted me courteously through a huge banquet hall decorated with baskets of money and naked brunettes holding them. So this was the place the officials of New York got paid off every Saturday night! Beyond it was a big door. He gently pushed me in.

It was a huge office with murals of Sicily. Warm, artificial sunlight filled the room. Sitting in a shady cupola was a very fat man whose fingers were solidly metal with rings.

He got up and bowed. It was obviously Faustino. He was so fat you could hardly see his eyes. "And how is my good friend, Mr. Bury?" he said.

"Very fine," I replied. "He's particularly happy today."

"Must be a lot of dead bodies around then," said Faustino. "Me, I'm just small time. Bury, he deals in whole countries! Whole populations. Sit down. Would you like a cigar?"

There wasn't any place to sit but it was nice of him to ask. I cut through all the Italian preliminaries. I shifted to Italian to make him feel more at home. "I just need a couple of snipers. For one day only."

"What date?" he said, shifting easily in language.

I told him.

"Oh, I don't know," he said. "That's a crowded date. But you didn't have to come to see me about it. All you had to do was call in at the Personnel Department on the 50th floor."

"I think Mr. Bury wanted someone to look into your health," I said. "He commented you seemed very care-free lately."

He went sort of white. He hastily scribbled something on a card. He seemed very glad to see me leave.

At the Personnel Department a charming young man heard my request.

"That date," he said in a cultured accent. "It's crowded. Isn't that the date of the Spreeport Demolition Endurance Derby? Yes, it is. Well, I don't see..."

I gave him Faustino's card. He instantly started punching personnel computers like he was trying to put holes in them.

Really upset, he said, "I can't get two hit men for that date!"

"I'm only asking for snipers," I said. "Just plain snipers that are good shots."

He went back at it again. With relief he came up with two. I told him where they were to report and how. For I had all my plans exactly made.

He promised they would be there.

I went back to the lobby. I stopped by the Information Desk. "I am very sorry, Angelina," I said to the girl. "I didn't mean to frighten you." It was unlike me but I wanted good relations here. She was quite pretty.

"Excuse me, sir," she said, "but please get the hell out of the lobby. You've got every gun detector going again!"

I left. Reminded of the gun and being both Apparatus trained and of a cautious nature, I stepped into the facsimile of an old-time Bowery Bar, kept there for tourists, I supposed. In a booth I checked the Colt Python. Sure enough, that (bleepard) behind my back had slipped an explosive plug in the barrel just ahead of the cylinder. I withdrew it gingerly and threw it in a spittoon. Right then I knew you shouldn't trust the Mafia too far, even if it did run a lot of the country. If I had tried to assassinate Faustino, the gun would have blown my hand off. They weren't honest.

But I had accomplished what I had come for.

If Heller won that race, he'd do it on wings!

Even if the carburetor failed, it was no longer a factor. I was going to post two snipers with silenced rifles to blow out his tires one by one until he didn't have a single tire left! Providing he hadn't already wound up in the hospital.

Be certain of the result, my professors used to say.

Madison and Bury might both be crazy. But I still had a grip on my wits.

The very thought of Heller succeeding on top of all this publicity was gall upon my soul.

A plane towing a huge sign above the Battery told everybody to see the Whiz Kid race on Saturday just ten days away.

This riffraff wasn't going to see him win. I was making very certain of that!

Chapter 7

Smugly, I watched the pre-race comings and goings of Heller. He was finished as far as I was concerned. The only small worry was that he might get totally killed, for there would go my platen. However, a nice trip to the hospital, maybe with several broken bones and his handsome face smashed in, would do very well. And the wreckage of his reputation on Earth forever was infinitely acceptable.

As one watches the condemned man in his cell, so I viewed his attendance of Babe Corleone's birthday party the Sunday before the Saturday. I hoped I would pick up more data to compound his ruin.

It irked me that he would go and attend a birthday party when he ought to be gnawing at his fingernails with worry, hunched in a room, thinking about his coming doom. But there he was, the perfect fleet officer, courteous and urbane, attending the modest celebration in Babe's Bayonne condo. She probably held it there so as not to advertise that she was a year older. Just a few intimate family members and friends.

He had accompanied them to Mass, probably on the theory that when you are on a primitive planet you include its Gods in your acquaintances. But I noticed that instead of responding to prayers in Latin, he was answering up with Voltarian forms of prayer. I hoped these Earth Gods in their niches didn't speak Voltarian. I didn't want him to get any help at all!

The birthday party itself was quite mild. A little

musical group—a violin, a mandolin and an accordion—played quietly over in the corner of the large living room. Babe sat in a big chair, dressed in white. Staff were handing her presents people had sent—most of them envelopes with money in them.

Heller was over to the side by a big punch bowl, talking with this one or that. He seemed to be wearing a blue suit, made possibly of silk, and he had big cuff links—blue six-pointed stars with a diamond in the center. His fleet rank symbol! Well, (bleep) him! Code break! I made a note of it.

Babe was not busy now. She was just idly chatting with some wives. Heller suddenly made a signal toward the hall. Geovani came in carrying a huge, flat package. Heller went over to Babe.

"Mrs. Corleone," he said with a formal bow. "I would like to celebrate this occasion with a small memento." He indicated the package with a graceful gesture and said, "Happy Birthday to a great lady."

I don't know how he does it. When he talks to people they pay attention and get pleased. Babe beamed and wriggled. She took the package with Geovani's help and began to rip off the paper. Then her eyes got round. She said, "Oooooooo!"

She jumped up and turned the item. "Look! Look, everybody!"

It was a painting taken from that photo of Joe Corleone Heller had found in Connecticut! There was dapper young "Holy Joe"! And Heller had had it framed in a gold frame in the shape of a heart with a lion's head at the top V. I suddenly realized that "Corleone" was not just a town in Sicily, it also meant "Heart of a Lion."

Babe was ecstatic! She was waltzing around showing it to everyone, telling them that even though it was decades before she had met Joe, wasn't it just like him!

Look at that expression! A true empire builder! Even the sub-Thompson looked real! Dear Joe!

The musicians took their cue and began to play "The March of the Lion," the family's anthem, complete with machine-gun bursts in rhythm.

What a stir! That (bleeper) Heller was always creating these stirs! He had gone and made Babe's birthday for her! Well, he'd soon be finished.

It took a long time to quiet down. And then Heller was about to take his leave.

Babe was suddenly very serious. "Jerome, you be very careful in that racing. Drive very slow and safely." She thought for a moment. "There's something I don't understand about all this publicity. You just don't look the same in those photos they are taking of you. Now, it isn't your fault, of course. A lot of stage stars have that trouble. They just aren't photogenic. So I think that must be what is wrong, Jerome. You'll just have to reconcile yourself to not being photogenic. You don't have to wear those awful glasses they show you in. Just turn your head away from the camera. I was a star and I can give you such tips. It's not your eyes. The camera does something extraordinary to your teeth. Maybe they should use a soft-focus lens. And possibly no lights. But even if you're not photogenic, Jerome, the family will be betting on you."

"No, no!" said Heller quickly.

She looked at him very oddly. "But Jerome, we control almost all the gambling in New York and New Jersey except for those slobs in Atlantic City. We have been making book on the race ever since it was announced."

"Make book if you like," said Heller, "but don't let any family member place any bets on me to win."

She looked at him very strangely.

"You know something," she said.

"Mrs. Corleone, please promise."

She just went on looking at him oddly. And shortly he took his leave.

I was troubled. Heller suspected something. Had my hiring of snipers leaked? Oh, I better double-check everything to make sure he didn't somehow turn the tables on me. The man just couldn't be trusted!

Chapter 8

Heller spent Monday morning calling tire stores and distributors, asking questions I couldn't make heads nor tails of. He was using engineering terms that several times must have been very close to a Code break. Slippage and friction coefficients and something he called "residual resistance to side thrust."

About eleven, Bang-Bang, apparently having ROTCed enough for that day, picked him up in the old cab and they went whizzing out to Spreeport.

The garages and shops Heller had been using were quite isolated. They were beyond Spreeport and stood on a rise closer to the beach. Beyond it was all recreation area and public beaches. Of course, at this late season, the whole sector was deserted. Even other racing teams were gone—moved south to warmer circuits. Loose sand and dead leaves were spinning about. It must be quite cold, particularly in the wind from the sea.

The doors of the garages and shops were metal, the kind you lift up on counterbalances. Only one tiny window was in each door.

The trailer truck was stored in two halves: the cab,

a big diesel, was in one garage all by itself. In the next one to it was its trailer. The Caddy was sitting on the trailer.

Heller unlocked and pulled up the counterbalanced door to the larger garage that held the trailer. He went in and punched with his fist at a tire.

"They just don't make tires, Bang-Bang."

Bang-Bang had the collar of a military greatcoat up around his ears. "Sure they do. You ain't had any real trouble."

"I have so. I skidded her one day and bang, there went a tire. If every time I put her in a real skid, I lose a tire, I couldn't win a race against a cat with its feet tied."

"Is that what makes you so (bleeped) pessimistic about winning?" said Bang-Bang.

"It certainly is," said Heller, and he punched another tire. "They buckle on lateral stresses. That's the only way I can figure it."

Suddenly, in a flash, I understood. That (bleeped) Madison! That first day he had had a sniper posted somewhere so he could get a shot of Heller having a near accident! I knew it, just like that.

I verified it. I got the strip of it. I turned the sound volume way, way up. I played it through. What a roar! Screaming rubber. Aha! A distant bang! It was a second after the blowout itself. Must mean that sniper had been three hundred yards or so away!

That (bleeped) Madison might use snipers in the race itself. If so, how many snipers would Heller have on him in addition to my two? Or was that Madison's plan? One couldn't tell.

In a way, it was a relief. Heller didn't suspect that was what was wrong. But in another way, it might make

Heller dream up something to prevent blowouts. The whole thing made me quite nervous.

Heller was out now, standing in the wind. He was looking to the northeast, up the beach. "There's a cold front," he said.

"I know I'm cold, front *and* behind," said Bang-Bang.

"I think it's going to snow," said Heller. He was looking at some high, thin clouds. "Yes, in a couple of days. And then it will be followed by another cold front right out of the Arctic. Bang-Bang, that race is going to be run in frozen slush. Now, I tell you what you do, Bang-Bang. You grab a plane this afternoon. . . ."

"Yes," said Bang-Bang, very alert.

"And you fly up to Hudson's Bay in Canada and you buy the very best dog team you can find and we'll just tow the car around. . . ."

"Oh, (bleeps), Jet. You had me taken in for a minute." He began to laugh.

"I think it's a great idea!" said Heller, dead serious. "We hitch the dog team to the car. You could stand on the two rear fenders with a whip and yell 'gee' and 'haw' at the dogs to steer and I could run along in front on snowshoes to break trail. And we'll put an igloo where the pit is. . . . But no. I don't think NASCAR rules include pemmican."

"What's 'pemercam'?" said Bang-Bang.

"That's the fuel you feed the dogs."

"Jet, you'd find something funny if you were a corpse."

"Sometimes, things are so bad that all you can do is laugh," said Heller. "We're in trouble. All this (bleeped) storm of publicity that's roaring around. I can't back out. If I go on with it, I'm sunk."

"Izzy bought you a ticket for South America," said Bang-Bang.

"I have a feeling," said Heller, "that there will come a day, not too distant, when I'll be asking you to kick me for not using it. But it's against my creed."

I was intent at once. Another Code break? For I remembered clearly that day in the Personnel Office at fleet, the creed of the combat engineers, "Whatever the odds, the Hells with it. Get the job done."

But Heller said, "Come on. Let's go in the shop and get the heat on before you freeze to death. I've got to think of something."

And that was exactly what I was afraid of. Now I had two unknowns. What was Madison really going to do? And what was Heller going to do?

I only knew what I was going to do—stop the Hells out of him!

Chapter 9

On Wednesday it started snowing.

There was a battle of forecasters played up heavily on TV. Was it going to be snowing at race time or was it going to be bright sunlight?

The flood of publicity carried on. Snow or sun, it was never even mentioned that somebody might call the race off.

It didn't matter what the weather was. I had solved all that. I had rented a little van with an independent heater in the back. It had lug tires, being designed for the suburban trade. So let it snow! I also bought a pai of the highest-powered binoculars I could find in a hock shop. I had to acquire them because my efforts with a hacksaw to cut off a tourist telescope from the observation platform of Fort Tryon got interrupted by some schoolkids who couldn't read my Federal identification.

With the snow came new information about the race. The spot ads and talk shows began to talk about "bombers."

I had no idea what a "bomber" was. The hotel TV had a teletext system cable and after rejecting several definitions I found one that fitted. A "bomber" was an ordinary car with no added armor except roll bars. It had all its glass removed. Its object was to ram other vehicles to make them unable to move. They backed, mainly, to protect their own radiator and engine. They were used in demolition derbies. A winner of one of these was defined as a vehicle that could still move under its own power.

Now the controversy made sense. Would only bombers be allowed or also standard stock cars? The racing commission solved it by including both. It said that as this was a demolition derby that would test laps and hours of endurance, both bombers and stock cars could participate. It was a wise decision. The public would have lynched them if they had arrived at any decision that tended to exclude the Whiz Kid's car. It, strictly speaking, was not a bomber but a hopped-up stock car.

The bogus Whiz Kid, Heller's "double," was muchly seen on talk shows and in the news. He was being very pugnacious about the oil companies, bragging about his cheap fuel and generally making an ass of himself.

Then, that very Wednesday afternoon—following th[illegible]h all day Thursday—the *other* drivers began to be [illegible]ced. They were the toughest, meanest bomber drivers that existed on any circuit! There would be eighteen starting cars and the list of names sounded like a horror movie. "Slammer," "Mayhem," "Killer," "Morgue," followed by some last name, seemed to be the order of the day.

Amongst this crowd of wanted murderers, the name "Hammer" Malone seemed to be the star. His car bore a gravestone silhouette for every driver he had killed.

On the national talk show, "America Alive or Almost Anyway," the bogus Whiz Kid and Hammer Malone met head on. They began yelling at each other and then they were at each other's throats and then the cameras fell over and you couldn't see the end of it. Special appearances of the bogus Whiz Kid in his red racing suit were featured the following morning to assure his millions of fans he was all right and that he would get Malone *and* the oil companies in that race!

Heller, through all this, just went on working. He seemed to be using his suite as an office for I couldn't tell what he was up to. The interference was on continually as the UN was in session. He had stopped appearing in the lobby. I sort of got the impression he was lying low.

Snow and more snow. Friday another battle of forecasters. Would it be clear or snowing ten o'clock Saturday morning when the race was scheduled to start? Bets were being laid on that. But bets were being made on everything you could think of. It was difficult to get an idea of what would constitute a win, and as so many people had beaten each other up over trying to decide this, the racing commission announced, in a stop-program bulletin, that the winning car would have to be able to move under its own power and to do one thousand laps. No car could do a thousand laps without refueling four or five times. So if the Whiz Kid did that without refueling, then that was how he would win the race, but other cars could refuel as much as they wanted.

There was an outcry on this but the bogus Whiz Kid stuck out his jaw, opened his buckteeth and said that was fine with him. He knew the oil companies would bias the race. But he was still taking them on.

A presidential statement that Friday night informed the world that America could not lose as long as it had sterling youth of the stamp of the Whiz Kid.

On that note, knowing the roads would be jammed at dawn Saturday, I slid out in my van. I had my viewer. I had my binoculars, I had warm clothes and I had my rear heater.

The spot had already been picked. It was a knoll that overlooked the speedway three-quarters of a mile away, much higher, providing a clear view of the track. It was in the front yard of a house and a hundred dollars had secured the spot.

My snipers, with white cloaks, were posted much closer to the track on building tops, armed with silenced and telescopically equipped Weatherby rifles firing .30-06 "Accelerator" bullets, 4,080 feet per second.

In complete comfort, smug and confident, I lay down on the van's bunk, the viewer buzzer set to alert me if Heller stirred.

What a beautiful victory this would be—for me.

Can Heller escape
17 bomber drivers
and two hidden snipers?
Does he die? Lose? Win?

Read
MISSION EARTH
Volume 4
AN ALIEN AFFAIR

About the Author
L. Ron Hubbard

L. Ron Hubbard's remarkable writing career spanned more than half-a-century of intense literary achievement and creative influence.

And though he was first and foremost a writer, his life experiences and travels in all corners of the globe were wide and diverse. His insatiable curiosity and personal belief that one should live life as a professional led to a lifetime of extraordinary accomplishment. He was also an explorer, ethnologist, mariner and pilot, filmmaker and photographer, philosopher and educator, composer and musician.

Growing up in the still-rugged frontier country of Montana, he broke his first bronc and became the blood brother of a Blackfeet Indian medicine man by age six. In 1927, when he was 16, he traveled to a still remote Asia. The following year, to further satisfy his thirst for adventure and augment his growing knowledge of other cultures, he left school and returned to the Orient. On this trip, he worked as a supercargo and helmsman aboard a coastal trader which plied the seas between Japan and Java. He came to know old Shanghai, Beijing and the Western Hills at a time when few Westerners could enter China. He traveled more than a quarter of a million miles by sea and land while still a teenager and before the advent of commercial aviation as we know it.

He returned to the United States in the autumn of 1929 to complete his formal education. He entered George Washington University in Washington, D.C., where he studied engineering and took one of the earliest courses in atomic and molecular physics. In addition to his studies, he was the president of the Engineering Society and Flying Club, and wrote articles, stories and plays for the university newspaper. During the same period he also barnstormed across the American mid-West and was a national correspondent and photographer for the *Sportsman Pilot* magazine, the most distinguished aviation publication of its day.

Returning to his classroom of the world in 1932, he led two separate expeditions, the Caribbean Motion Picture Expedition; sailing on one of the last of America's four-masted commercial ships, and the second, a mineralogical survey of Puerto Rico. His exploits earned him membership in the renowned Explorers Club and he subsequently carried their coveted flag on two more voyages of exploration and discovery. As a master mariner licensed to operate ships in any ocean, his lifelong love of the sea was reflected in the many ships he captained and the skill of the crews he trained. He also served with distinction as a U.S. naval officer during the Second World War.

All of this—and much more—found its way, into his writing and gave his stories a compelling sense of authenticity that has appealed to readers throughout the world. It started in 1934 with the publication of "The Green God" in *Thrilling Adventure* magazine, a story about an American naval intelligence officer caught up in the mystery and intrigues of pre-communist China. With his extensive knowledge of the world and its people and his ability to write in any style and genre, he rapidly achieved prominence as a writer of action adventure, western, mystery and suspense. Such was the respect of his fellow writers that he was only 25 when elected president of the New York Chapter of the American Fiction Guild.

In addition to his career as a leading writer of fiction, he worked as a successful screenwriter in Hollywood where he wrote the original story and script for Columbia's 1937 hit serial, "The Secret of Treasure Island." His work on numerous films for Columbia, Universal and other major studios involved writing, providing story lines and serving as a script consultant.

In 1938, he was approached by the venerable New York publishing house of Street and Smith, the publishers of *Astounding Science Fiction.* Wanting to capitalize on the proven reader appeal of the L. Ron Hubbard byline to capture more readers for this emerging genre, they essentially offered to buy all the science fiction he wrote. When he protested that he did not write about machines and machinery but that he wrote about people, they told him that was exactly what was wanted. The rest is history.

The impact and influence that his novels and stories had on the fields of science fiction, fantasy and horror virtually amounted to the changing of a genre. It is the compelling human element that he originally brought to this new genre that remains today the basis of its growing international popularity.

L. Ron Hubbard consistently enabled readers to peer into the minds and emotions of characters in a way that sharply heightened the reading experience without slowing the pace of the story, a level of writing rarely achieved.

Among the most celebrated examples of this are three stories he published in a single, phenomenally creative year (1940)—FINAL BLACKOUT and its grimly possible future world of unremitting war and ultimate courage which Robert Heinlein called "as perfect a piece of science fiction as has ever been written"; the ingenious fantasy-adventure, TYPEWRITER IN THE SKY described by Clive Cussler as "written in the great style adventure should be written in"; and the prototype novel of clutching psychological suspense and horror in the midst of ordinary, everyday life, FEAR, studied by writers from Stephen King to Ray Bradbury.

It was Mr. Hubbard's trendsetting work in the speculative fiction field from 1938 to 1950, particularly, that not only helped to expand the scope and imaginative boundaries of science fiction and fantasy but indelibly established him as one of the founders of what continues to be regarded as the genre's Golden Age.

Widely honored—recipient of Italy's Tetradramma D'Oro Award and a special Gutenberg Award, among other significant literary honors—BATTLEFIELD EARTH has sold more than 6,000,000 copies in 23 languages and is the biggest single-volume science fiction novel in the history of the genre at 1050 pages. It was ranked number three out of the 100 best English language novels of the twentieth century in the Random House Modern Library

Reader's Poll. Additionally, this *New York Times* and international bestseller was voted the #1 science fiction novel of the twentieth century by the American Book Readers Association. BATTLEFIELD EARTH is now a major motion picture.

The *MISSION EARTH®* dekalogy has been equally acclaimed, winning the Cosmos 2000 Award from French readers and the coveted Nova-Science Fiction Award from Italy's National Committee for Science Fiction and Fantasy. The dekalogy has sold more than seven million copies in 6 languages, and each of its 10 volumes became *New York Times* and international bestsellers as they were released.

The first of L. Ron Hubbard's original screenplays AI! PEDRITO! WHEN INTELLIGENCE GOES WRONG, novelized by author Kevin J. Anderson, was released in 1998 and immediately appeared as a *New York Times* bestseller. This was followed in 1999 with the publication of A VERY STRANGE TRIP, an original L. Ron Hubbard story of time-traveling adventure, novelized by Dave Wolverton, that also became a *New York Times* bestseller directly following its release.

His literary output ultimately encompassed more than 250 published novels, novelettes, short stories and screenplays in every major genre.

For more information on L. Ron Hubbard and his many acclaimed works of fiction visit the L. Ron Hubbard literary Internet sites at: www.galaxy-press.com, www.authorservicesinc.com and www.battlefieldearth.com.

FOR MORE EXCITING ENTERTAINMENT FROM L. RON HUBBARD SEE THE FOLLOWING PAGES . . . . .

Enter the Compelling and Imaginative Universe of WWW.BATTLEFIELDEARTH.COM

Discover the exciting and expansive universe of *Battlefield Earth*, which has an arsenal of features, plenty of content and free downloads. Here are a few highlights of what's in store for you:

• Universe—Find out about the different characters, places, races, crafts, weapons and artifacts that make up the universe of *Battlefield Earth*. Also discover the major events that led up to the discovery of Earth by the Psychlos, and the technology that they have used for hundreds of thousands of years to terrorize the galaxies and crush their enemies.

• Community—As a member of the *Battlefield Earth*® community you have access to free downloads, including screensavers and desktop wallpaper.

• Trivia—Do you know:
How the Psychlos discovered Earth?
What element is lethal to Psychlos?
Where the Brigantes originate from?

**NEXT TIME YOU'RE ON-LINE
ENTER THE BATTLEFIELD EARTH SITE—
WHERE L. RON HUBBARD'S MASTERPIECE
OF FICTION COMES ALIVE!**

Mission Earth

BY

L. RON HUBBARD

The ten-volume action-packed intergalactic spy adventure

"A superbly imaginative, intricately plotted invasion of Earth."

—Chicago Tribune

An entertaining narrative told from the eyes of alien invaders, *Mission Earth* is packed with captivating suspense and adventure.

Heller, a Royal Combat Engineer, has been sent on a desperate mission to halt the self-destruction of Earth—wholly unaware that a secret branch of his own government (the Coordinated Information Apparatus) has dispatched its own agent, whose sole purpose is to sabotage him at all costs, as part of its clandestine operation.

With a cast of dynamic characters, biting satire and plenty of twists, action and emotion, Heller is pitted against incredible odds in this intergalactic game where the future of Earth hangs in the balance.

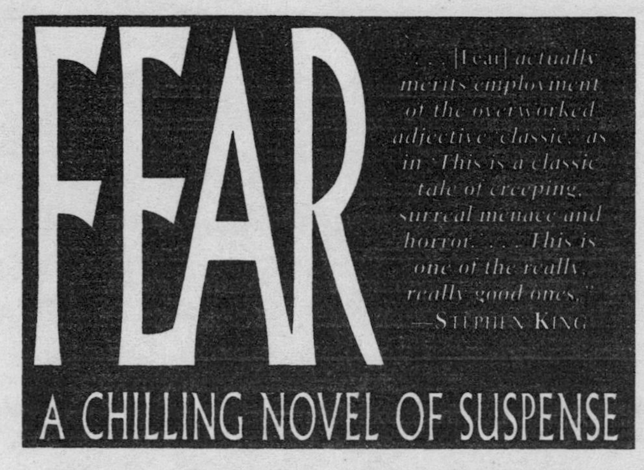

Professor James Lowry doesn't believe in spirits, or witches, or demons. Not until one gentle spring evening when his hat disappears, along with four hours of his life. Now the quiet university town of Atworthy is changing—just slightly at first, then faster and more frighteningly each time he tries to remember. Lowry is pursued by a dark, secret evil that is turning his whole world against him while it whispers a warning from the shadows:

If you find your hat you'll find your four hours. If you find your four hours then you will die. . . .

L. Ron Hubbard has carved out a masterful tale filled with biting twists and chilling turns that will make your heart beat faster as the tension mounts through each line of the story—while he takes a very ordinary man, in a very ordinary circumstance and descends him into a completely plausible and terrifyingly real hell.

Why is *Fear* so powerful? Because it really could happen.

Paperback: U. S. $6.99, CAN $9.99
Audio: U. S. $15.95, CAN $18.95 (2 cassettes, 3 hours)
Narrated by Roddy McDowall
Call toll free: 1-877-8GALAXY or visit www.galaxy-press.com

Mail your order to:

Galaxy Press, L.L.C.
7051 Hollywood Blvd., Suite 200, Hollywood, CA 90028